LAND OF LAST LIFE

PALACE NURSING HOME

JAMES F. WALSH

LAND OF LAST LIFE IS A WORK OF FICTION. NAMES, CHARACTERS, PLACES AND INCIDENTS ARE THE PRODUCT OF THE AUTHOR'S IMAGINATION. ANY RESEMBLANCE TO ACTUAL PERSONS LIVING OR DEAD, EVENTS OR LOCALITIES ARE ENTIRELY COINCIDENTAL.

To Jo Ann, my loving and loved wife of 58 years

LAND OF LAST LIFE

KEY CHARACTERS

NURSING HOME RESIDENTS- Many with vastly different wants and needs.

NURSING HOME STAFF- Nurses, Aides, Social Workers and Housekeepers, the wounded hearts of care.

NURSING HOME FACILITIES- Cloisters of the ill aged.

NURSING HOME RESIDENT FERGUS ORR- An ancient scribe writing his confession, instead decided to confess face to face to the new ombudsman, but at Orr's leisure.

CHESTER ZIGMONT, 'Ziggie'- A source fed him disturbing allegations effecting the elderly in care: counterfeit drugs.

MIKE BRANNAGH- A contentious career in Criminal Corrections was left to work as an advocate for aged residents in nursing homes; and as Ziggie's private investigator.

BELINDA FORDICE RN- A State Health Surveyor who felt it a conflict of interest to be a three day Convention guest of the Nursing Home Association.

REVEREND COPPIN YARD- Minister at Holiness and the 'Saint" of the projects; the publisher of the INNER CITY NEWS.

SUPPORTING CHARACTERS

RESIDENT MARION KAP- A retired Police Officer in nursing home care.

RESIDENT SHANGO GOLAH- Hostility diminished when an Aide would testified on his behalf.

LOU COOPER- An ex-con hired to protect the Project's elderly.

BIG DOUGH BENNY- Getting 'Mama's Bible' from his father who was dying in a nursing home, turned the drug dealer's attention to nursing home medicines.

1

Going to work clear of politicians determined to destroy conceived foes was his for the taking. At age 64, a supervisor of parole officers wanting to change jobs wasn't unusual, but being called for employment with an agency not completely under State auspices, was.

When the arrow on the sign, FIVE COUNTIES AGENCY ON AGING, pointed down a flight of stairs to basement offices, Mike Brannagh hesitated. Was it an off-shoot of the war-on-poverty with penury as pay? Mike figured he was paid poorly enough working for the State. He gave a whisper of thought to skipping the meeting, except the offices were under a bakery. Visions of munching donuts and sipping hot coffee stayed departure!

Down at the bottom of the sixteen steps stood a guy in a blue suit who opened the entry door, and held out a small hand to shake. "Right on time, Big Mike. I'm Chester Zigmont, Director of the agency."

"Nice to meet you Mr. Zigmont. 'Big Mike!' I haven't been called that since 1954," Mike smiled while shaking hands with the chubby fellow, hair graying, eyes brown as leather.

"Call me Ziggie, all here do. Back in '54, I was one of your boxing fans. A few years behind you at Albertus Magnus University, 'Big Al U.'. I saw all your fights. Beating that football player, an All American yet, in the finals was the best boxing match I ever saw, not to mention the money I won."

"A fan, at last!"

"More than a fan, Mike. As I said on the phone, I want to be your employer. Come into my office and we can talk it over."

Mike was a good six foot four carrying 235 pounds in good physical shape from walking the back roads or playing 9 holes of golf every chance he had. If only he could break boggie. Ziggie, on the other hand was an inch or two short of six foot, and not far removed from 190 pounds. He dressed well. Mike dressed as if to walk up the agency's steps to the first tee.

Both sitting, Ziggie explained the open position was that of an Ombudsman for residents in nursing homes in five counties. "The Agency's ombudsman position pays a salary two percent above your present salary with similar benefits, You would be seen by administrators of nursing facilities as this agency's advocate for the rights of elders in nursing homes."

In a deflated tone, Mike said, "Ziggie, don't you read the Oldtown news?"

"I do, but I supplement its bias by reading The Inner-city News, published by Reverend Yard. He told the truth about the Parole Board Scam."

Nodding agreement, Mike replied, "No matter the truth, I'm seen as a whistle blower in the eyes of political types."

Ziggie's eyes glowed. "That's why I offered you the job. The Parole Board's Kickback scam brought back recollection of the 1973 drug smuggling into the County Jail you were running. Back then, I was riding along with stories in the Oldtown News, wondering what had happened to you to sink so low, when Reverend Yard and the Inner-city News published the truth. When Reverend Yard broke the parole scam in the Inner-city News that keyed my focus."

Mike's eyes didn't glow. His tone was low."What's going on?"

Ziggie paused for effect. "There's more to the job than advocacy for the elderly. Before I tell you, I need your promise to keep confidential what I'm about to say if you decline the offer."

Mike agreed, curiosity high.

"I need someone with your integrity to help me and my source chase down street talk that prescribed medicines sold on corners comes from nursing homes' medicines."

Mike blinked. "Damn!"

"Worse," said Ziggie. "My source tells me some medicines prescribed for residents deep into dementia are being replaced by counterfeit medicines. Their FDA meds are being removed for sale on the street."

"Counterfeit?" Mike groaned, shock on his face. "Isn't there an on call Medical Doctor and a full time RN and LPNs in every nursing home? They'd know the difference."

"Would they?" Ziggie said. "It's why I offer you the job. You're a social worker, which is the required degree for the job,   and you know street people."

Mike regained composure. "I do know cons and ex-cons, but I'm a Social Worker with the tag of whistle blower. Using me may get you a lot of attention when it gets to the ear of the Attorney General."

"The hell with him, all politicians. Five Counties' nursing home residents need protection from chemical contamination." Ziggie's head shook from side to side.. "If there's questions about credentials, I've documented your combat record in Korea, grade point and Degrees from Albertus Magnus University, 'Big Al U" as we fondly call it., your years working in Juvenile, Jail and Adult Corrections. As far as Charley Donavan, the State Ombudsman, is concerned, his reaction to your hiring will be 'it's Five Counties call.' He'll need to certify you as an Ombudsman, but you'll work for the Area Agency. Legislators take little notice of this Agency on Aging and those of us who work here." Ziggie winked. "They're fearful cutting their minimal funding would raise considerable negative publicity our congressmen and women, not to mention   State's voters like sons, daughters and relatives of parents and grandparents in nursing homes or those getting home health care. As the Ombudsman, you'd devote full time to the aged in nursing homes, while quietly looking for evidence supporting my source's information. We'll meet and talk.."

Mike's expression was one of disdain as he spoke, "Counterfeit medicines? No one should be subjected to the wrong chemicals in supposedly medically approved drugs. Count me in, Ziggie."

"You're in. Next, you'll need to get through Ombudsman training. It's conducted by Lawyer Jim Jackson at Capitol County Elder Law Center. When you finish, Charley Donavan's certification will get you access to all State licensed Nursing Home." Ziggie paused for effect. "You'll be working in the land of last life."

Mike's frown changed his rugged looks to crinkled cheeks.

"I know it sounds horrible," Ziggie said, "Many spend months, even years in residence. Whatever the length of stay, all should be treated with dignity."

* * *

Mike trained under Lawyer Jim Jackson in Court Opinions, Federal Regulations, State Health Statutes and the Department of Health Nursing Homes Administrative Rules. At graduation, Donavan presented a laminated card that identified Michael Brannagh as a certified advocate within the State licensed cloisters of the aged ill. He looked forward to visiting debilitated elders before he himself was numbered therein. It would be similar to visiting libraries, not of leather bound books, but of skin-covered ancient documents filled with a roguish power of remembrance. Heeding the rights of residents on the global deterioration scale while checking out Ziggie's worries presaged more meaningful benefit than contentious discussions with political power brokers.

* * *

Mike's first visit was to a facility in a small town,

but entrance to Grass Lake nursing home was barred at the gate. Standing in front of the glass door was a short great-grandma, her face sea wave wrinkled, wig bright red, and a round body captured in a tight green dress. She looked a stuffed green pepper. Hands on the bar, she held the door's handle as if it were the last lifeboat in the Atlantic and shook the thin mop of a reddish wig negatively to ward off the barbarian at the gate.

"Excuse me, Ma'am?"   Mike smiled enough to turn the crocodile from her meal, enough to convince stuffed green pepper to let loose the door handle even if she were visibly upset. She did. He carefully approached the pike waiting prey.

"I told my daughter not to see you anymore," stuffed green pepper said, her screech echoing down the narrow hall. Her finger turned a dagger at his throat.

Who ever was the paramour she was repudiating and who on earth her daughter might be or had been, he hadn't an iota of awareness. He rolled with the jab and verbal right cross. Physical imperturbability belied his mental incredulity at this dose of unexpected geriatric incivility. Was she getting counterfeit meds? Still, meeting his first resident in a long term care facility was an upgrade from twenty years back when he'd turned Jail Director and was baptized with urine by a locked down inmate.

"Your daughter dumped me," he said, his imagination percolating, face mournful as a funeral director's, "like you wanted her to do. Your daughter is just too good for me." His worn expression confirmed he'd given her up.

"She's a good girl. She is!" stuffed green pepper said. "She's too good for the likes of a scoundrel like you leaving her that way." Nods of her red wig confirmed her feelings before she retracted her dagger and her wig settled.

"Indeed, she is a good girl," he said, sighing.
Scoundrel?

"Ugliest baby ever I saw, shithead!" she said with an overly exaggerated emphasis on the 'shit' She clasped her tired thin hands as if to pray away illegitimacy.

For this appellation he'd given up work with paroled armed robbers? "Sorry, Ma'am, but I have to leave now. I hear my name being called." It wasn't. He moved aside the tiny person with tongue as sharp as her finger.

"Shithead," she said, the echo of 'e-a-d' rumbling down the hall.

Where in the place was somebody this side of reality? Checking his directory, a Doris Drave was administrator. Numbered high in the residents' council membership as president, was resident Fergus Orr. Where was Drave's office? Mike located the office of the Director of Admissions. A knock and in response to 'come in', he opened the door. Within sat a gathering of well dressed ladies. A mahogany desk and executive's chair was occupied by a personage with chairwoman attributes, the other chairs by lesser executives. He addressed the chairwoman, "Excuse me, Ma'am. Is Doris Drave here?" A guffaw exploded. He persisted. "I'm Mike Brannagh, the new ombudsman." He handed the chairwoman an OMBUDSMAN brochure.

"I'm Belinda Fordice, State Health Department Surveyor team supervisor," she said. Her auburn face and sable hair shaded a wool black sweater dress. "I heard you dancing a two step out there. Come in. This is my team of registered nurses, Emma Tee, Gerri Knit and Inez Mars. We're just concluding our survey."

The other team members were as attractively dressed as Fordice, but pallid-faced, Tee and Knit in their late thirties, Mars in her fifties. She wore a clay and black twill suit, the youngsters marino or black t-neck sweaters and gray herringbone trousers.

"Pleased to meet you, Ms. Fordice. Surveyors? This is my first time in any nursing home. I never expected to run into a survey team."

"Then you seem to be the only one around who didn't expect us to be here," Fordice said, her emphasis the steam of molten steel. "Please have a seat." She waited as he did so. "Time and place of a survey, as you know, is confidential, and a violation of Law to tell of it beforehand. Yet Grass Lake knew when my team would arrive. I find it hard to believe they guessed our visit to the day, hour and minute. I don't feel free to say more than that in this room. Now that we've met, here's my card. Please phone me. If I'm not in my home office, I'll be doing a survey. Call State Health. Right now, I have a conference to conduct. Please excuse us, Mr. Brannagh."

"Call me Mike, if you will."

"Belinda," she said.

They both stood up, his blue eyes to her brown. She was nearly as tall. Hands shaken, he couldn't help but contrast her athletic physique to the increasing misdirection of flesh poorly camouflaged under his baggy clothes. She followed and closed the door behind him.

A puzzled Knit said, "What's all that about 'not saying more in this room'."

"Who knows that it isn't wire-tapped?" Fordice said. "If it is, Doris Drave and Nursing Home Management's Dale Unge should hear this! Do they or you know who that ombudsman is? He's the one who started the fight over kickbacks to the Parole Board. He said 'it wasn't Attorney General Puts' investigation that was set in concrete, it was his head.' Can you imagine someone 'dissing' the Attorney General? Thank the Good Lord my minister, Reverend Coppin Yard joined the fight on Brannagh's side or he'd be doing jail time. He hasn't a political skill in his body, but everything I read about him fighting the Governor's Parole Board said he's concerned about humane social programs. His problem is he expects them to operate honestly. He comes along at just the right

17

time for nursing homes' residents!"

"Why's that?" said Tee.

Fordice looked hard at her, eyes questioning her awareness of time and place. "When's the last time we did a survey on a nursing home operated by Nursing Home Management that our survey findings weren't more r less rewritten back at State Health?"

Said Mars rather credulously, "Brannagh has that kind of influence?"

Fordice answered with feeling. "He comes ready to fight, I hope as much for the elderly   as he did for families of prisoners expecting parole without payoffs."

Mars said quizzically, "I remember Mike Brannagh. He's the one who ran the Jail years back when a Grand Jury was after it."

"A Grand Jury! What about?" Fordice said, her admiration blunted.

"It was on TV news. Something about drugs being smuggled into the jail. It's his red hair I remember," Mars said. "He had a lot more hair then and was thinner. He still has freckles, though. Back then, TV news reports kept hinting Brannagh was the one who did it until your minister, the Reverend Yard got the truth out. It wasn't Brannagh at all, though the media inferred it. It was some druggist."

Fordice freed an audible sigh of relief. If Reverend Yard, her Minister, goes that far back with Brannagh, then there was a star over the stable. "Ladies, lets wrap it up here. We'll meet at my home office to go over our findings."

* * *

Brannagh was pleased the head of the survey team wanted him to phone her, but from where ever privacy was assured. He placed Belinda's card in his wallet. She was worth knowing.

On guard, but uncertain of what he was guarding

18

against walking though the facility, he   knocked on the door of the president of the resident council.

"Mr. Orr? I'm the new ombudsman, Mike Brannagh. May I come in?"

"Yes you may. I'd heard there was to be a new ombudsman," he said, or rather sang in a bass voice. "Nice to meet him in the flesh. Only talked on the phone to the prior fellow." The seated man looked a mummy with wide shoulders in a horizontally striped green shirt, a face with more wrinkles than the Mississippi River had tributaries and a head of white hair thinner than the ombudsman's red overhang. Orr flashed an axe cut smile above a protruding chin and a twig of a neck. Long legs were entrapped by golfer's red trousers; his every inch of backbone upright in a hardback chair. He looked to be a technicolor ancient scribe in a scriptorium illuminating holy script with a quill and blue eyes that singed flesh.

Orr put down his ink pen and threw out his right arm, swinging it to and fro to encompass the reams of paper he'd spread on his desk. The weight of age in his voice, he said "sit down in my lounge chair, Mike. I stole it from the porch at Puella Junior College."

"Thank you," Mike said. The antique chair swallowed him. He had to look up from what seemed a place on the floor.

"Your name," Orr said, "is Irish?"

"It is. Born in American, a son of Irish immigrants, themselves naturalized citizens." "I'm delighted," Orr said, "to have another Irishman in this room.. The forefather of the American Orrs, my great grandfather Blaine, was from Ballymoney, Country Antrim.

"I'll be!" Mike said. "My father was from County Antrim, the town of Loughguile, maybe twenty miles from Ballymoney.."

"Loughguile was papist, Ballymoney Loyalist," Orr said, disdain his tone. His eyebrows crawled his

19

forehead, extra-ocular muscles momentarily misaligned.

Mike sighed. One moment he was sailing on a sweet sea, now? Whatever was kicking snuff up Orr's geriatric nose? Religion? Perhaps he was as advanced in dementia as

stuffed green pepper, recollections of the past acute, of the present minimal.

"Yet they fought side by side in 1798."

"That's right!" Orr said, impressed. In his room he saw a man in a tweed coat who might well have been descendant from the best man in Ireland behind a weapon. Was he? The man certainly oozed a magnetic power that revived the stale air and tingled nerves. "Where have I heard your name before? Are you from Grass Lake?"

"Nearby, out in Blue township. I was born and raised in Oldtown. My wife, Jane, wanted to move out to a rural county, but near a small town. We weren't here long when she passed away."

"I'm sorry," he said, then moved on. "I'm a former Oldtowner, too. Taught American History at Oldtown High until retirement in 1973. Puella Junior College took me on its faculty. Taught History there. Stroke put me in this place in '88. They call me 'Professor'. What did you do in Oldtown?"

"Worked in the Criminal Justice System, last month for the Board of Parole as a parole supervisor."

"Blew the whistle on parole kickbacks a few months ago, didn't you?" Another long look at the visitor. "I remember where I heard the name even before that! Saw your picture in the news papers, on TV! You ran the Francois County jail in Oldtown! Let's see? It was back in 1973, when two of my more miserable high school scholars were lodged behind its steel bars pending trials for rape. Wasn't that when you were alleged to have smuggled prescription drugs to inmates?"

Smuggling! Brannagh reconsidered his initial

thoughts on the old man."You have a hell of a good memory." No global deterioration, for sure.

"I recall you beat the rap," Orr said.

"No rap to beat, Professor, though the Grand Jury beat the hell out of me in the process. You see, I wouldn't agree to take a polygraph, and told my correctional officers that polygraphs were no more reliable than voodoo superstition. That ticked off Tony Taker, the prosecutor, to say nothing of a ridiculous oaf of a Grand Juror. They got back at me by publicizing I'd been subpoenaed, which to the general public, was tantamount to an arrest, if not a conviction. But for the articles in Inner-city News that revealed the prosecutor had reliable evidence on the probable perpetrator, a local druggist, I'd have shared a jail tank with your former scholars."

"The jail and the parole board," Orr said, "twice fifteen minutes of fame."

"More like a half hour of infamy."

There came Orr's nod of affirmation along with the sounds of distant beings. Two female screamers in rooms down the hall wounded the air, one in a pitch of an opera's soprano the other a military drill instructor with cuss words to spare. Echoes mocked their calamity calling but Orr paid it no attention. He'd adapted. It was adaptation or stress! He sighed. "Right now I'm so tired."

"I'm sorry I stayed so long."

"No. Not that. Just that I've been writing a great deal. Hard to write." Then the thought hit him like the iceberg the Titanic. Why write his confession when he might tell it to the former jailor and confess to him before the Grim Reaper's harvest? With a passion nearly a cry, Orr wished to magnetize interest. "I need to confess before the undertaker makes me look good. What better confessor than an Irishman, and an ombudsman to boot!" Orr's words were spoken as if   burning brands. He groaned as he got up. His right leg worked, but his left dragged at a pace that

21

might carry him a mile a century. He turned and sat on his bed, then twisted over onto his right side, face to the window. Silent.

Brannagh went to the bed and removed Orr's shoes. A blanket was pulled up over him, from yellow socks to green striped shirt. "Hear your confession?"

"Yes! Return to hear my confession, Mike," Orr said with whispered urgency. "When you're eighty-four and a victim of strokes, you must repent!"

"Why confess to someone not in the clergy? A confession to an ombudsman wouldn't forgive sins." He wished it were so, his own particularly.

"Ombudsmen can't charge for salvation."

"Lousy joke, Professor."

"No joke," he said, before the reforming backslider fell asleep.

Were the bed rails down one too many times, and the aged man slipped and hit his head? This council president hadn't a court appointed guardian. He was competent, his own agent who didn't want the sun to set on his earthly iniquities; but at eighty-four, he must have a long chain of hourly sins stacked high in a vast storehouse of an uproarious conscience. Perhaps the professor sensed his death and didn't want to be surprised by it without a confession. He'd be surprised at St. Peter's roll call when told an ombudsman had no authority to bind on earth's nursing homes' residents, much less heaven's.

* * *

Back in the nursing home's halls, Brannagh spent time just looking while walking. Nursing homes were new to him, but not institutions.. He saw a half dozen women with limbs as twisted as grape vines who sat on two couches looking at TV. The sounds from the TV were magnified by the sounds of other TV sets, or radios, or tape players in rooms, or discordant with the broadcasts of other channels and radio stations. The similarity of sounds: some residents cursing, others screaming or moaning or talking; plus the blaring of radios, tape players and TV sets dismayed him. He'd anticipated controlled quiescence among the elderly in nursing homes; 'rest homes' as once not facetiously called. How could good sense survive with three residents in a room, each with electronically magnified modern sound machines compounded by strained moans of roommates in the wing of ill humans? The noise was mindful of Francois County jail absent the clanging of tooled steel doors. Subtracting fifty years from nursing home elderly clustered on couches or laying on beds, Mike visualized jail inmates doing the usual nothing but watching TV.

A quarter-moon counter painted brown, a nurse station, with a built-in desk behind it as long as the counter, filled a corner. Open charts of recorded resident care notes were spaced at random over the desk's length. By the station's swinging gate to the left, medicines in small paper cups sat atop a stainless steel cart. A nurse, her slender neck whiter than snow under a cap pinned to golden cirrocumulus hair, was in a white uniform, unable to hide her super-natural feminine characteristics. She sat on a chair the left end of the desk, fingers holding a pen writing on a resident's chart. Nurse looked up. Her face porcelain, hyacinth her blue eyes, golden her eyebrows. A shower of matched pearls smiled brighter than an arc's light. "Yes?" she said looking up.

"I'm the new ombudsman, Mike Brannagh."

"Please to meet you," she said. "I'm Lotta Norse, Director of Nursing. Can I be of help?"

At that moment he realized what concupiscence meant. "Thank you, but no," Brannagh said. "No complaints."

"That's good," she said sounding discontented.

He noted it. "Feeling a bit blue?"

"I didn't mean too. Suppose I am if you picked it up

so easily. Working in a nursing home is exhausting even with a full nursing staff."

"You're short staffed?"

She caught her self. This big guy was the ombudsman. He could ask State Health's Fordice to do a surprise follow-up. Even Nursing Home Management's Dale Unge hadn't advance news of surprise surveyor visits. Lotta smiled. "Not really. Six girls complete their training as Aides this week. Counting them the PPD, the number of nursing hours per patient per day is 2.25; without them it's 2.0 nursing hours per patient per day, the State's minimum standard."

"A PPD of 2.0 in my humble opinion," he said, "isn't enough for therapeutic intermediate care. It must be as difficult for your staff if the administrator limits the number to 2.0. It would exhaust them, and you as the DON, and lead to turnover."

She was impressed with his concern for nursing staff.

2

Close to home, Mike pulled his pickup into his driveway to go in and make phone calls. In the middle of a white plaster ceiling, a turn-of-the-century gaslight converted to one hundred watt modernity illuminated the dining room. The ten by fifteen room was light white from floor to ceiling, except at the double windows. The dining room was his office, an antique dining table his desk. He called Five Counties. A secretary there was to take ombudsman messages that came in on the 800 number.

A soft voice answered, "Five Counties. Lizzy Loam here."

"This is Mike Brannagh, Ombudsman, Ms. Loam. I need to talk with Ziggie."

"I'll connect you as soon as I give you this message. I have on my desk a copy of a Notice of Discharge. It's about Shango Golah, a resident at Palace Nursing Home. He has only ten days to ask for a hearing? Six have passed."

"Thanks. I didn't receive a copy. Obviously, Palace and Golah are next to visit!"

He was transferred. "Good morning Ziggie, Mike here."

"What can I do for you?"

"Tell me about a State Surveyor by the name of Belinda Fordice. While I was at Grass Lake Nursing Home she was finishing a survey and in effect, said, 'not only did Grass Lake anticipate her survey to the day and hour, but to not talk shop while in the home's board room, apparently because she felt the room was bugged. She asked me to phone her at her home office."

"Do it," he said. " She's from Oldtown and is one of very few State Health surveyors who felt it was a conflict of interest to be a three day guest of the Nursing Home

25

Association at its Labor Day convention up in North Woods Resort. The Association's paying the tab, of course, is intended to have an influencing effect on how surveyors cite for violations. It doesn't hurt them to make surveyors a part of their program. Not Belinda! Worked her way out of the Projects pulling the night shift at Palace as a CNA, Certified Nursing Aide, then a year at Oldtown Technical to get an LPN. She followed up and got her RN. While she worked ICU at Oldtown Hospital, she obtained her BSN, then a MSN while working for State Health. She's a top pro! More letters after her name than in a bowl of alphabet soup."

* * *

There were forty miles between Blue township and the City of Oldtown, but the old Ford pickup chugged amiably along a highway sided by farms and pastured cattle. Parking a half block away from Palace Nursing Home, Mike marveled he not remembered seeing this flaring facade! How many times over the years had he driven this very street? Inside, he took note Palace's main lounge's interior decorations were done in prison industry's blue chip furniture with conversation corners of large stuffed chairs fit for a parole board. A china coffee pot was breathing steam. China cups and saucers, not Styrofoam cups, were waiting for someone.

Executive offices in the east and west wings were closed to public view. A glass partition separated wings. Within this glass room the wonders of flashing electronics encircled a bosomy lady in a yellow dress with a rooster tail of long black hair.

"Excuse me, Ma'am, I'm Mike Brannagh, Ombudsman," he said, dropping a smile on brown eyeballs arching their blue eyelids. She was mystified at the hearing of a funny word. He handed her a brochure to see the word 'OMBUDSMAN' in print next to the Governor Study's ubiquitous signature and the State's seal vividly reproduced as if to confer authority. "I'm the person who comes from time to time to help residents work out problems they may have not being in their own homes. Would you please let the administrator know I'm in the facility?"

"I'll page her, 'Mary Lancaster call 200.'" Time ticked but the telephone didn't. "Mary Lancaster doesn't answer her page."

"Please let her know the ombudsman is here." He put his eyes on the listing of residents by room numbers and took off to see his client. Knocking on the door, he said, "Mr. Golah? I'm Mike Brannagh, the new ombudsman, an advocate for residents. May I come in."

"Who you say, man?" said a voice street-wise and threateningly powerful. Golah questioned if he'd heard right. Did the guy say 'Brannagh'? Years back there was a Brannagh who helped him out of a jam in Juvenile! Brannagh had to be a hundred by now. Who was it out there? How did he know Shango was in an old folks home?

"I'm the guy who works for residents in nursing homes," Brannagh said, shouting to be heard over a TV, one of many disturbing the hall's urine laced oxygen. "The nursing home mailed me a copy of the Notice they gave you last week to discharge you. I'm here to help you fight the discharge, if that's your leaning. You can fight it if you fill in the blanks on the form that reads 'Request For Hearing' and mail it to the address listed. You only have four days left of the ten allowed from the day the nursing home gave it to you. May I come in?"

"Yea man," Golah said from behind a curtain that separated his bed from an empty one in the room, "they messing with me. Why I got to do that shit?"

What had happened to Brannagh's idealized version of a nursing home elder? The fellow in the room sounded a jail inmate walking the rails of a cell. A similar reply was permitted. "They'll kick your ass out if you don't."

It was Juvenile Court's Brannagh! He talked

27

straight on like that. "The hell you say."

"Tell you what, Mr. Golah," he said, sensing attention, "if you want to fight being kicked out, fill out the form and I'll mail it for you."

Golah played with him. "Don't care if you do, man. Lancaster be messing with me." There was a pause. He had to see if it were Juvenile's Brannagh. "You want to come in here, man? Come on," he said like a coach to a third string player after the team's star was carried off the gridiron. He turned off the TV and kept his back to the visitor. "You know Lancaster be messing with me, man. All them old nurses Lancaster hire," his left hand rose slowly, its thumb pointing backwards, "be talking shit on me."

The ombudsman walked into the room and beyond the resident and his wheel chair to the room's windows where a hard back chair was cornered, and sat to face a man who wore ship-sharp facial features garbled with stroke's rage. If it represented systolic pressure, blood vessels in his brain were about to whale-blow. His right arm's hand featured fingers twisted like fish hooks while its arm dangled like a butcher's sausage. Yet the man in the gray sweatshirt had a muscular upper body, broad shoulders spreading like hawk wings beyond his wheel chair. His neck was thick as a football lineman's. A wooly head of black hair wasn't completely captured by as wooly a blue winter cap.

"Maybe she is dumping on you," Mike said, "but by law Ms. Lancaster had to send me a copy of the Notice. So I'm here to let you know you can fight her, but you have only four days left of the ten allowed from the date of Notice to mail in the request for hearing."

Damned, Golah thought, if the big, old man sitting down like a boxer in his corner wasn't old Juvenile Court Probation Officer Brannagh, the dude who tangled with the Judge, who kicked shit out of 'Schizo.' And Brannagh didn't reconize the cripple to his front! Golah would ride it.

"What you mean, man, by law?" The words hissed with steam.

Self-righteous anger like Golah's had been a personality characteristic of offenders Mike had handled throughout his work-life. Rarely was it diminished after the court's denial of the accused's version of the facts. It was banked when the reality of doing time inside razor sharp barbed wire stockades among other hostile inmates became clear.

Mike told Golah the Code of Federal and State Regulations required the administrator give written notice to the resident, a copy to his next-of-kin, a copy to State Health and a copy to the ombudsman, even though there were no requirements to detail in the notice how, where, when, what or against whom the resident had offended. Required was listing a section of the rule alleged to have been violated, but with no facts. After reception of the notice, the resident or someone else had to file a request within ten days to get a hearing within twenty four days of the notice. Removal of the resident from the facility was thus postponed, if a hearing was requested, for thirty-four days. At the hearing itself, before a Hearing Officer, usually the only records introduced as evidence were written by the administrator's staff, mostly about incidents they'd been told of. Hearsay on hearsay, in essence. Most residents or their families, beforehand, rarely read the charts, yet it was up to them to refute the allegations and/or find witnesses to refute them. At best, it was necessary for the resident to get everything positive he could into the record if the Hearing Officer's decision was for the facility, because an appeal could be made to an Administrative Law Judge. "She, the Hearing Officer, may decide in your favor," Mike concluded

"Another bitch?" Golah said, emphasizing his disgust with more intense facial rage. "Ain't they got no studs working in these hell holes?"

This client wouldn't pass any gender equality test in a facility where women occupied most all jobs. Mike's face flushed as he said, "How many studs have come in your room and helped you get up out of bed, or up from the wheelchair onto the crapper, or on with your clothes, or given you range of motion? The women on the nursing staff who aren't sick of the kind of crap you're putting out and do come into your room, do so to help restore a human being to his highest level at a pay rate less than an apprentice to a morning shift dishwasher at a downtown greasy spoon. The women running these halls and working these rooms are dedicated nursing staff, the infantry on the front line against resident debilitation and apathy. Only rear echelon nursing home CEOs see the nursing staffs as crap, and pay them in toilet paper."

"Why you shoot me down, man?" Golah said, his eyes beading, but fury lessened.

There was a silence. He didn't pull his eyes from the visitor, but a smile percolated. Old Brannagh hadn't changed. "You a decent stud, man. Call me Shango."

"Shango," he said, nodding, calming down, "I'll need your written consent to show the charge nurse that you're allowing me to look into your chart. It's those writings that Lancaster will submit to the Hearing Officer as evidence against you. We'll need to know their details."

"Lancaster ain't no nice little old lady like some of them young Aides around here. She a bitch, man. Talk mean to them colored Eastside Aides. Gets rid of them quick."

Mike's forehead curled. "Let's get back to your signature on this request-for-hearing." He handed over a pen and placed the form on his note book. Golah struggled with his left hand, signed and dated it. "I'll copy it and mail it today. We'll get a hearing date in a couple of weeks. Now let's discuss why Lancaster wants to kick you out. Who is it that you allegedly endangered? How, what, when and where?"

"My roommate was the one, man." There was bounce in the words. "They moved him away. Name's Loren. One day don't he shit all over. He be calling sweet little brown skin girl, the pretty little Aide who talk with a drawl, 'come on in there'. She come in. Don't know no better being from the south. He a white man. Tells her clean him. She do. I pay no mind. Little brown skin and me ain't no cousins taking up for each other. I hear Loren say she got his shit on her. Must have got him all worked up being off dope! He come out the crapper his pants down on his ankles, pulling her to his bed. He pull down her pants, push her over on the bed, bayonet high, pull her panties down, hop on. Sweet little brown skin girl saying stop, he don't, so I hit old dope head up aside his thick skull with my radio. He be bleeding like a shot rat. Busted my radio. Sweet little brown skin get up, pull up her panties, her pants, run out. Damn if she don't come back with nurse and one of them geri-chairs. They puts Loren on it and runs him out the room to the hospital."

"Is he dead?"

"If he be dead, man, Lancaster have my old crippled ass over in the Francois County jail."

"What's that Aide's name?"

"She's gone, man. Eastside! Not here no more. Never knew her name."

"We'll have to find her to tell the hearing officer she was assaulted, maybe raped and you came to her defense. With her we've the defense of a third person."

"Ain't seen sweet little brown skin since I busted up Loren's head. If that girl ain't here no more, you can bet Lancaster fired her. Tell you what. I'll check around where she be with some of them Aides and old colored womens that be fussing over me for clubbing Loren. I be getting Reverend Coppin Yard on the phone. He be over to the Church of Holiness on the East side across from the

Projects. I be talking about finding that girl, get him to call you."

"Reverend Coppin Yard?" At the mention of Reverend Yard, 'Saint of the Projects', Mike sensed there was much more to Golah than street talk. Something about him. A jail prisoner? On parole? No. Who would have forgotten a name like Shango Golah. "I'll take that written consent I need to look into your chart."

Golah's left hand struggled again but he signed. He put his head down, lowered his wool cap to his black eyebrows, pleased Brannagh hadn't detected the boy in the man.

Mike walked softly from the room. Quiet was superfluous in the hallway. The mouths of talk show hosts' guests and the cries of victims suffering soapy killings were the headwaters of the overflowing auditory riparian bombast. Every one of the rooms' TV sets had to be turned on, yet noise in the nursing home seemed not a hindrance to anyone's sleep in other rooms, either because residents had grown used to the incessant clamoring, or were deaf, or they rode chemistry's sleeping pills.

Several residents in geri-chairs or wheel chairs lining the walls of the halls, sat outside their rooms' doors saying nothing, staring at nothing. Others in their doorways popped in and out like spiders after flies caught in a web. Walkers, scooted along by shuffling elderly, passed other walker-pushers on the right, save two who faced off for the same square of tile. They froze to their spots. Mike redirected snarled traffic. The silence of the encounter was in stark contrast to the noise flowing through the hall, reminiscent of storm sewage roaring to a treatment plant, coupled with similar odors.

The hall, and six others, emptied into a circular area, mindful of a drain pool. Along the Circle's rounded west wall in matching blue bathrobes and pink bunny slippers, four ladies in wheelchairs sang 'mares-e-doats' along with a 78 RPM record playing the tune from the wartime '40-ties. A round nurse station was smack in the center of the Circle. Percolating within were snowdrops, one in a very full white dress and expansive sail of a white cap with a sergeant's black stripe. This Director of Nursing, a Queen Bee, had as rugged a face as a top kick, but with bigger and grimmer lips. She wrote in a chart while giving instructions to four white uniformed and tender years capped registered nurses. Instructions received, the nurses adjourned. Three walked to smaller nurse stations situated between the meeting of two halls, each with twenty rooms and forty beds, and placed bottoms on chairs behind counters. They commenced, as if impelled to imitate Queen Bee, to write in charts while issuing instructions to uncapped Certified Nursing Aides in blue slacks, smocks and shoes, who had clustered around each nurse station. At the wave of a hand beneath a cap, the Aides buzzed into honeycombed wings where brown uniformed housekeepers scrubbed and rubbed everything that wasn't mobile, much that was. Aides entered rooms staying several minutes before returning to the hive.

The fourth capped nurse walked to a hall with locked doors, the Alzheimer's wing. A numerical code was written on a sign above the door. She looked up, then entered the code. An electronic lock clicked. She pushed a door-bar, the door slowly opening inwardly swinging back as she disappeared. It crunched closed and clicked locked.

Mike was intrigued. He'd not walked the floor of a locked unit for the aged ill, nor met a victim of Alzheimer's. He crossed the circle to the door and entered the code, slowly pushing open the door as its sign's handwriting warned. Inside the doorway, a half dozen gray sweat suits filled with a half dozen skinny pedestrians crowded the tiled aisle. An aerobics' center in a suburban mall? There was no order to their movements. Eight blue sweat suited residents walked from yellow ceramic block sidewall to sidewall in the hallway. Three in black sweats were opening and closing doors to rooms as if running bed checks. Several in emerald green sweat suits, geriatric leprechauns, walked up or down the length of the other end of a hall, a longer one. Two of the greens looped over and around the slower yellows expressing ill will in the bluntest fashion. At an intersection, a hall that crossed the T, red sweat suits wandered as aimlessly as the gray, blue and green. A cluster of cardinals were gathered around a piano player, an outsider, judging by the fashionable cut of her clothes. What had Palace's dementia and Alzheimer populace done to be left so unattended and color coded like so many file folders in a clerk's cabinet? Brain disease coupled with personal penury? Mike had seen young men walk as purposelessly in jail tanks where rails, floor to ceiling tooled steel bars, lined short hallways, but the young were there for alleged crimes against persons or property while suffering society's retribution, pointless as absolute jail idleness was. It came as no surprise that public dependency, whether county jail's or Medicaid's, had financial cheapness as its basic premise. Incarceration appeared as negative for the aged as for the young. But why a locked unit for dementia sufferers? For Alzheimer victims? Locked units, a jail's or nursing home's, had to mean minimal staff, a monetary, not a treatment contrivance.

A nurse station cut out of a corner at the crossing had a dutifully charting nurse on guard duty. "Nurse? I'm Mike Brannagh, Ombudsman. Is there a purpose to the sweat suit colors?"

Her Afro wore a cap that might momentarily take to sail. She stopped writing and said, "And I'm Gloria." Her smile was a caring smile on a pleasant inky face. "There supposedly is, despite my objections. I've lived a life of being coded by my color, so it wasn't mere emotion saying colors just for new hires to be oriented as to where residents roomed wasn't done for resident dignity. It was done because we were trying to train too many stupid new hires."

"I imagine that went over well," he said consolingly.

"Not well at all," she said, her smile returning alabaster teeth to her winsome face.

"Where are those new hires you mentioned?" He skipped the use of the word 'stupid.'

"Most gone within a week of certification. Four stayed. We'll soon start with a new class of twenty. By certification test time only three or four more will be left to take it. Even then, the average length of stay of an Aide on the job after certification is only three months." There was knife sharpness in her voice. "That's all," she said, with repeated acuity, "and it gives catchpenny Mary, our administrator, cause to justify the use of colors on residents instead of increasing nursing Aides' pay scale. My son makes ten dollars an hour delivering pizza, four dollars more than the starting wage for nursing Aides. He can't as much put his dirty clothes in the laundry hamper, much less change an incontinent's diaper."

This was one hell of a nurse. "As much as I admire your advocacy for your patients," he said, "when one's position doesn't bring with it the authority to hire or to fire, one's job is an ice cube likely to melt under the boss's heat."

"Maybe. Catchpenny Mary is like that. If I'm relieved for speaking up at staff meetings, or to State Health's surveyors, or to the ombudsman, so be it! There's no shortage of nursing positions in Francois County. I'll get work, loud mouthed or not! Please feel free to look around."

Mike would, but he was hesitant, given that he'd just met Nurse Gloria, to inquire if any of her residents were reacting more strangely than usual, giving the fact many of them were on psychotropics. Down the hall, close to the piano a grizzly-bear of an unshaven time worn resident in a sleeveless t-shirt, red sweat pants and work boots lingered under a ceiling light. His right arm featured tattooed female pulchritude. His back was against a side wall, right leg bent at the knee, foot firmly against the wall fifteen inches off the floor, right hand's fingers snapping a beat to a mental tune. All he needed was a black leather jacket. He wasn't a conversationalist. Perhaps the pianist was. Her face, a pale bloom with cheeks of roses, was taking pleasure in her playing. A resident with a face and hair white as limestone sat on the piano bench taking joy in stroking the player's beautiful chestnut hair.

She looked up. "Hello," she said, "I'm Dorothy Naumann. This is my mother, Betty Hewel." Dorothy's voice was sweet as her music.

"Pleased to meet you Mrs. Hewel, Mrs. Naumann. I'm Mike Brannagh, the ombudsman, an advocate for residents. That tune you were playing, 'Lucky Old Sun', I know it. It might not have been a prayer for Frankie Layne, but it is for me."

"Sing it now," she said with supplication.

"I will if you play as loudly as you can."

Song sung a gathering of roses applauded the tenor. Heading to the exit, the thought came that he'd found a tool, ephemeral as was a song, to communicate with Alzheimer and dementia residents. Nurses like Gloria, and senses of sight, sound and smell could tell him much about the unit's quality of care, and, perhaps, dramatic changes in behavior.

Inside Wing Four's nurse station, a young, pretty nurse in a chalky outfit that fit her upper body nicely, sat at the desk listening to a wide-body woman leaning on the counter.

"I'm the ombudsman, Nurse," Mike said as he showed his ID. "I'd like to see Shango Golah's file. I have his written consent right here."

The unit nurse turned from the desk to pull the chart

from a circular file round and big as half of a fifty-five gallon drum. She handed over a thick spiral notebook.

Mike spotted an empty among the chairs that lined the circular walls, went over, sat, then opened the chart to nursing notes. Line after line, an unholy litany of scrawling notes, paraphrased sexual epithets that gave convoluted connotations to anatomical parts, not to ignore descriptions of nursing home food. On the matter of cracking Loren up against his head with a radio, the writing was succinct: 'Shango attacked with a radio and severely injured Loren this date.' That was it? No statement from the roommate? No statement from Golah? No mention of the Aide? Her story? If she weren't found to testified and Golah's chart put into evidence, any Hearing Officer would tell him to look for a pervert colony to exercise his foul mouth for the rest of his long term care existence. What a case! The man in wing four, room nine was such a case! Where would he go when the Hearing Officer ruled against him? Copies of pertinent parts were made, initialed and dated   by the nurse as verification of the originals.

* * *

Back in his home office, Fordice's number was dialed. "Hello, Belinda. Mike calling."

"Appreciate your call," she said, never for a moment thinking it wouldn't come, "for it's not wise to talk issues within the rooms of any Nursing Home Management facility. Nothing is confidential there. For that matter nothing State Health does seems to escape the attention of Nursing Home Management. Do you mind if I call it NHM? I believe they have penetrated State Health, at least they know when my surveys are coming down, and the report my team is about to submit listing Grass Lake's deficiencies will, no doubt, be returned as revised as Webster's last dictionary. Be on your guard when you visit their facilities. Write them down," she said, expecting he was doing so. "Besides Grass Lake, they include Lobelia,

37

Willow, Anemone, Mint, Daffodil, Palace, Honeysuckle, Orchid, Coralroot and Garland."

"Are you suggesting NHM is playing politics with State Health?"

"Hello?" she said with sarcasm. "You just come out of the womb? Or didn't I read somewhere you took on Attorney General Puts and Governor Story's State Parole Board over kickbacks? I do read the Inner-city News! Quite an article in there by Reverend Yard. He turned the investigation on its ear, exposing the path of payoffs made to Parole Board members wasn't through you but through field parole officers bought off by inner city women to doctor release plans."

"The Reverend did set me free," Mike said. "Getting back to NHM's influence on State Health, I'd like to think politics hadn't a playground in the day to day care of the elderly other than lobbyists finagling for higher per-diems of Medicaid dollars. A rewrite of your findings? I'd like to have thought there weren't political paddles batting ping pong balls over the care of the incapacitated elderly." He sighed, then told Belinda of the visit to Palace. "Might you help me?" She would. "A Palace resident was served with a Notice of Discharge. We've filed for a hearing. The Aide who could be of help as a witness was fired in early September. I don't know her name."

"I'll be at State soon," she said. "I'll look up the names of Palace Aides terminated."

3

Next morning, Mike perused mailed copies of State Health surveys given him during training at Capital County Elder Law Center. Nothing major. He readied federal and state rules to prepare for the day's questions. Preparations finished, he dialed Five Counties answering service. "Ms. Loam? Mike Brannagh, ombudsman, calling for messages.

"Please call me Lizzy, if you will."

"And I'm Mike." He sensed animation in her voice.

"Mike it is. Sorry Mike, but no messages."

Parking his pickup, and with Fordice's list of Nursing Home Management's facilities in mind, Mike opened the directory to read a bit about Willow. At capacity, it housed one hundred and twenty-five intermediate care residents and twenty-five skilled care residents. Looking at the place, an entomologist turned architect had to have designed the murky colored building. It had a long and slender hind body with a robust fore-body with wings. Front windows appeared as enormous eyes. The entry was as if the mouth of a dragon fly, noise from an orifice a swallowing sound. He entered and saw a woman behind a desk making sure it was between her and an elderly man.

"Porter," she said, "it's not up to me about Katie. Mrs. Mallow says she has to move to room 407."

The old guy the other side of the desk was a short fat man with red chin wattles below a grim face. He held a gyrating cane in a chubby hand as red as an uncooked meat ball. "Katie doesn't want to change rooms, Cheri," he said with emphasis, "and Ida Mallow can't make her. If I have to call State Health, I will."

"Please don't get so worked up, Porter," Cheri said

pleadingly.

"It's not right Katie has to move after four years in the same room. Let me in to see Ida."

"I'm sorry I can't Porter. She's in a meeting. I'll let you know when she's free."

He slammed his cane across the desk. It resounded like a clap of lightening.

"Hello there," Mike said, stepping in. Compared to the others, his height and size were the like of Mount Rushmore. "I'm Mike Brannagh, Ombudsman. I visit nursing home for Five Counties Agency on Aging and work only for residents' rights." He showed his identification to Porter, and handed a brochure to Cheri. "I couldn't help but overhear your conversation about Katie being told to transfer rooms. There are some state rules that apply. May I be of help?"

"You sure can, Mike. I'm Porter Litt, President of our resident council."

"Nice to meet you, Mr. Litt. Let's go see Katie and talk about it."

"Sure enough, but call me Porter. Katie's waiting in the activity room."

It was but twenty-seven clicks of Porter's cane on the hall's tile floor. They entered the room. Tables held playing cards, bingo cards, checkers. Straight back and lounge chairs were all about, no organization apparent. Sitting on a lounge chair was an aged woman, hair, face, hands, muslin bathrobe, ankles and slippers ghostly white. She looked a sheep.

"Katie, this here is the ombudsman, Mike Brannagh. Mike, this is Katie Arch.'

"Pleased to meet you, Ms. Arch."

"Mike arrived when I was up to the office," Porter said. "I didn't get to see Ida. Cheri said she was in a meeting. So Mike suggested we meet with you and talk."

"Do you think I can stay in my room?" she said, her

40

voice childlike.

"There are rules that apply to just that purpose," Mike said.

"Then let's go to my room,"Katie said. "I haven't a roommate at the moment."

Porter went to her side and offered a hand up. A tremor shook her like a robin shaking a worm, but she steadied herself. The couple walked with dignity and grace another twelve clicks of Porter's cane. Within room 240 were the things of a lifetime carefully placed on a dresser, on shelves, framed and on the walls. She sat in a stuffed chair next to her bed and waved Mike and Porter to sit down on folding chairs. On her bed were oblong pieces of printed paper. "I look at these ever day. They're streetcar transfers. This one," she lifted it up to show off, "was from Detroit's Grand River street car. I traveled often during my younger years, I'm 95 now. The only way to really see the sights on my budget back then was riding streetcars through the neighborhoods. Then they were gone almost overnight after the second world war. I miss them so. They would be worth all the gold in Fort Knox as tourist attractions today."

"Tell Mike about the room change, Katie, " Porter said.

She said, "my great-granddaughter Jessica brought me from Detroit to live with her in Chickton. Three years later she was diagnosed with cancer and a brain tumor, too late to reverse it. She died, poor child. Jason, her husband, not being family, was going to send me back to Detroit, but there wasn't anything there for me so I just came to Willow. Been in this room since the very first day with many a roommate come and gone. Now Ida wants me to transfer to wing four and room with the new lady, Rebecca. She's a fine woman, but this room is my home, with so many memories. No matter I suggested Rebecca come here, Ida said no."

"What was on the written notice Ms. Mallow give you?" Brannagh said.

"Nothing in writing. She said she needs my room for two men on the waiting list because it's more roomy."

"That's not right," Porter said. "Katie has the right over new folks, doesn't she!"

Before Mike's answer was forthcoming a graveled voice said, "No she doesn't." The scowling mouth was preceded into the room by a needle of a nose. Blackberry eyes glanced at the brute of a man sitting near Porter, Katie's mouse. "I'm Ida Willow, administrator." Her indignant hot glance focused on Litt. "Porter, you may be excused."

"You need not leave," Katie quickly said, her hand taking his. "Porter is my guest."

"He'll help you pack your things then," Mallow said, hectic cheeks flushing.

Mike was awed by Mallow's irascibility. It was obvious Cheri, from the front office, had told her of Porter's cracking cane. Not about the ombudsman?

"I'll not pack," said a unruffled Katie, "so I need no help!"

"You will, or I'll have maintenance do it for you," Mallow said with lips of steel.

Now ruffled, Katie quivered. "Can she make me, Mike?"

Rising to his feet to face the gray hair woman in depression era fashions, vexation controlled, Mike said, "Enough bullying, Ms. Mallow. Back off!"

"Bullying! How dare you!"

"I do dare, ma'am. I've seen more gentleness in a top sergeant's verbiage to recruits in basic training than yours to the lady here. To the point, I assume you are familiar with the rules about intra-facility transfers when there is a proposed change of rooms?"

"Your going to tell me?" she said, indignation like

frosting on her syllables.

What a guard dog she'd make, Mike thought. "I am.
Mrs Litt, would you hand me the written notice of intra
facility transfer you received? It's on a State Health form."

"I didn't receive one."

"You didn't? You should have, two days back. On
it a reason for transfer was to have been set down. For
instance; the safety of others in the facility was endangered
without the transfer; or your health had so improved you
could transfer to assisted living, or a group home; or a
medical doctor wrote an immediate transfer is required
because of an urgent medical need; or your attending
physician wrote transfer is necessary for medical reasons;
or a writing stated the transfer is necessary for your
welfare, or the welfare of others. Nothing given in writing
equals nothing. In summary, if no writing, no notice, no
transfer. If Mrs. Mallow hereafter elects to give you written
notice, you have my phone number on the ombudsman's
brochure. Call it. I'll return right away, day or night and on
the way inform State Health's surveyor and the Lawyers at
Capitol County Elder Law Center."

Disdain rode Mallow's face like a cowboy on a
bucking bronco.

Katie's face was as bright as 100 watt bulb. She
said, "Ida, I'll talk to Rebecca. If she wishes to transfer, it's
her decision, I'd welcome her."

Momentarily silent, but obviously boiling, Mallow
looked down at Katie and Porter, up at Brannagh. "For
twelve years," she said to him, "I've worked these rooms
and cared for old folks. Now you, a new ombudsman, strut
in and cite rules. How easy it is for you to ignore the
facility's financial position. New admissions are necessary
if I'm to budget for nurses and Aides." She turned her back
on him and walked out the door. Its closing eclipsed a view
of watermelons.

"My Lord," said Porter, "she scared the hell out of

43

me."

"You were brave, Porter," Katie said. "Thanks, Mike, for visiting today. But is it over?"

"Should be, but keep in close touch with my answering service at Five Counties."

* * *

Down the steps of Five Counties Agency On Aging, Mike opened the door and entered its brooding reception area furnished with reclaimed folding metal chairs. A gray head of tonsured male hair preceded a walnut face approached. "You work for Five Counties?" said a guy with gale force in his words. Its tenant, an elderly man with a broom, last fitted his coveralls many pounds ago.

"Yea. I'm the new ombudsman. Name's Mike" he said. "I'm here to get messages from Mrs Loam."

"Come on in." He aimed a finger at the comely woman sitting behind a desk half the size of a first grade teacher's.

"Thank you." Mike, though he'd met Ziggie here, hadn't paid attention to staff and decor. Now he took note of Loam's lovely face, a looker four or five years younger than he, thin, attractive and appealingly dressed in a wheat silk skirt, ivory jacket over a blue silk shirt and a big smile under bigger brown eyes set in a very intelligent face. Her IQ might be more than a match for the money she'd spent on clothes. On her desk was a phone with five incoming lines and a typewriter, a prize in any antique shop. Fortunately, a computer was at hand. She got up from her desk, her back turned, to tend to a coffee pots on a table behind her.

Cubicles were small with hanging desks. Very young women with very pretty faces and well coifed hair occupied them. Slim arms and trim long legs were outlined by stylish blouses or slacks. He was a toad among princesses. Dangling from brown partition walls were their

white sheepskins with tall black lettering neatly enclosed
by glass and black wooden frames. The diplomas
confirmed the caseworkers for the elderly were college
grads.

When the coffee woman turned around, he said,
"I'm Mike Brannagh."

"Pleased to meet you in person, Mike," she said
while sitting down to answer the phone. She transcribed a
message. Another ring. Another message. Again and again.
A quiet fell. It was then she looked up, but, as luck had it,
the phone rang again. She answered and transcribed a
message. She finally looked up. "I'm Lizzy Loam." Her
smile was radiant, her voice winsome.

"Are you always this busy?" There was admiration
in his voice.

"Today, especially. I'm sorry I couldn't reach you.
Luckily, you stopped by. Mr.Zigmont left   a couple of
boxes for you to look over. There," she pointed. Her phone
rang again.

"I'll take them with me. Just wanted to put faces to
the phone calls."

* * *

He pushed his pickup to make the resident council
meeting on time. Mrs. Hope Bedico, president of Lobelia
nursing home's residents' council had written her desire the
ombudsman attend. Parking, entering and locating the
room, he saw chairs, except five scattered around the
tables, piled in several stacks in three of the corners of the
large activity room. The day's date, a schedule of events, a
map of the vicinity and imitation Grandma-Moses paintings
hung on the walls from trembling sticky-tape. Ten residents
were in attendance, none having done less than nine
decades in the 20th century except Mrs. Bedico herself, who
appeared to dip into the 19th. Her ancient clothing
simulated a regal appearance, the wry smile Queen
Victoria's in her dotage. Bedico's arthritic hands were fists,

her head slow to turn sideways. She occupied the wide padded seat of a motorized chariot, its hanging knitted pockets stuffed with magazines, titles undetectable. Mike sat on a metal chair with a malleable leg which opened his view to an orchard of faces. A couple of the residents were the color of peaches, one of an orange, three red delicious apples, two bananas, and two grapes. Six wheelchairs with fashionably clothed riders pulled closely to the long table. Two walkers with carry baskets full of the residue of prized personal possessions parked behind two residents sitting in chairs, while two without walkers, a man and a woman, sat side by side holding hands they rested on the table. The couple were intent on publicly squeezing fingers, signing cohabitation with or without benefit of clergy. Shock was the reaction of families that an ancient mother and an aged father retained concupiscence.

Discussion turned from poorly cooked food to a bothersome resident. Bedico's face was as red as her tongue, her accent Eastern. "You should know of 'shark'," she said with heated sighs. "The ombudsman before you knew all about her, and he did nothing."

She looked and sounded like Mike's huge, tyrannical, maroon faced eight grade teacher who threw a right hook to the chops if he dared to act the peasant she'd vowed to subdue. He didn't comment on the doing of nothing by his predecessor. "Shark? Why do you call this lady 'shark'"

"She's no lady," Bedico said, retaining her vividness. "We call her that because she roams the halls like a shark the ocean, never to sleep. She walks right into our rooms, day or night, looking for food, stuffing her mouth with whatever she finds."

"She just spits it out," said a twig of a woman from her wheelchair. She was the orange and wore a long honey brown sweater that crumpled on her lap like a robe. Her gray pony tail was tied by a green bow, pulling the skin of her forehead taut and eyes to slits.

"Nursing staff does nothing about her," the only male resident present said, never missing a squeeze of his love's hand. He sat in one of the two chairs that hadn't a walker parked behind it. He was tall and thin with a banana colored hand and a salesman's dignity that the lady in the chair next to him, a slim woman pink as a peach, seemed deeply to admire. She held his yellow hand reverently.

"Look," a red delicious resident said in a shout, "there goes Shark now."

"We'll excuse you, Mr Brannagh," said Bedico. "Do something about her."

What could he do then, if ever, about a wanderer deeply into dementia? He saw twenty eyes trying to focus on him that expected he'd get up and do something. Perhaps there were only nineteen eyes, as one of the grapes had a droopy eyelid. "I'll certainly look into the lady's situation," he said, "but I can do it after this meeting, if you will." He spoke the words while his mind contemplated the conflict between Shark's rights and the rights of the rest of the residents. Obviously there had to be a balancing. How could an ombudsman talk to a wanderer that didn't talk, who stuffed her mouth with others' personal property only to spit it on their floors? What was the wanderer's care plan? Who was her surrogate? Would the surrogate agree to his review of the wanderer's chart?

"We do not will it," Bedico said in Queenly first person plural. "There is nothing more important than chaining Shark, or sending her elsewhere. See to it."

A summary command and dismissal. He'd encountered more than a few in his lifetime. This ombudsman wasn't much registering on any council attendees positive sides. He'd leave, but a word needed saying. "As important as is the well being of all of you to me," he said in a steely voice, "the well being of the wanderer isn't any less important. There will be no

47

chaining. I don't know at this moment what her care plan is, or should be. This resident council should know right up front, and you Mrs. Bedico, I'll work no less for this wanderer than I would for you if every other resident not at the council meeting wanted you out."

Bedico's sharp nose grunted an un-queenly snort.

Out in the hall, a score of wheelchair residents lined a glass wall to watch the grass bend under the breath of a cool wind. He saw the wanderer at a nurse station, but the nurse there, an obese blond writing in a chart, ignored her, a very short woman dressed in black pants and too large and long a green sweat shirt. As he approached the nurse station, three of the facility's wings came into view. He saw the white of a uniform covering a toothpick of an Aide with a song on his lips darting in and out of rooms. To the right was a pretty Hispanic woman carrying towels and busily talking to residents sitting in room doorways. To the left was a pale faced pudgy male Aide with facial pock marks and long hair tied in a pony-tail. Only three Aides? There were twenty-four elderly in residence in each wing. The unit was staffed four too few.

The nurse station was an elongated but slow curved piece of carpentry that looked like a booze bar on the out side. On the other side was a shelf, desk high, with chairs pulled up to the desk for nurses to sit and chart their residents' ups and downs. Shark stood at the nurse's station.

"Excuse me nurse," he said, "would you please tell me this lady's name?"

The nurse raised her round head as slowly as did a Palm Beach bridge tender her draw bridge for a sail boat. She wore on her white blouse, bosom high, an encased card printed with name and rank: Sharon, Charge Nurse. "Most call her Shark. The social worker would know her personal name. She knows all the black women. Her office is in the front of the building next to the beauty parlor and close to the bookkeeper's office." She turned her large head and flopped her blond locks around her neck, dark eyes as large as an owl's, and pointed her right arm and its bulky index finger down the long corridor.

"Thank you," he said, taking a good look at Shark. She was stringy. Green sleeves were rolled up and revealed brown arms and rose veins. Her feet were attired for a track meet with well worn white running shoes. Barely over five feet, she was as scrawny as a famine elder. Gaudy eyes were lit like lanterns on a river barge, but without a fog horn. She spoke not a word but when she smiled she drooled red. Raw gums? He took a clean towel from an Aide's stack on the counter. "I'm here to help you," he said slowly and softly as he approached her. May I use this towel to wipe your lips?" She didn't disagree. He moved slowly, freed a slight smile and touched her hand in peace, raising the towel to her mouth and wiped it clear of moisture. It was blood!

Down the hall he saw an open door lettered 'SOCIAL WORKER,' There was visible the bent back and shapely stern of a well assembled woman with hair trimmed short and neat. She stood at her desk furiously writing on a yellow legal pad with a pencil until its lead tip snapped off. "Damn."

"Irritating, isn't it," he said.

Her head jerked up. She rotated to face the door. Her coffee-cream face showed the high cheek bones of a fashion model, the rest of her not at all less beautiful. Large brown eyes glistened. Wiping a tear from an eye, her symmetry burning brightly in an ivory linen suit, she calmly walked to the door, and said, "I should keep it closed."

If he went out looking for beauty pageant contestants working in nursing homes he'd found another one to compete with Grass Lake's nurse Lotta Norse. Nursing homes were where women worked, whether nurses, Aides, social workers, housekeepers, cooks or activities directors. Few administrators were women because men clung tenaciously to the majority of those well paid positions. "I'm the ombudsman, Mike Brannagh. Am I here at the wrong time?"

"Maybe," she said as she wiped a tear from the other eye. "No," she said with some force. "No, it's not the wrong time. Just feeling sorry for myself. Personal problems do come at the wrong time, don't they? Come in."

"I've come to talk about the resident they call Shark."

"Alta? Is Hope Bedico off on Alta Ridd again?" The emphasis was on 'again.'

"Mrs. Bedico does seem to have a commanding presence."

"She sicced you after Alta?"

"In a manner of speaking. I went to find her. Have you time to talk?"

"I do," she said. "Please sit down. There's a chair next to my desk." She sat down at her desk. "I'm Mrs. Millie Grain, for a little while yet."

Mike twisted his jaw and puckered his lips musing the husband had to be a queer to leave this beautiful woman. On second musing, there was more to marriage than an investment in gorgeously assembled physical attributes. "I apologize for being so insensitive. That's the reason for your tears?"

"Partly," she said, "and partly because residents like Alta suffer the snideness of a Hope Bedico. We're so short staffed and the residents have so many problems, I'm kept here to all hours of the day and night." She paused to hook her entrancing brown eyes into his washed out blue, and said, "My husband uses that as his excuse, but Javier never has been faithful."

Mike's mind confirmed the man was nuts, but marriage counseling nursing home staff wasn't in an ombudsman's job description. He regretted not having made an appointment when her tears made it obvious the pretty lady had severe personal problems herself. Like most social workers, he comforted her with, "it must be very difficult for you."

"It is," she said, "but I went into the marriage thinking, unlike Javier's first wife, I could solve that particular problem. Oh, never mind me,   you're here to talk about Alta."

"Yes, I am." He told the social worker of Ridd's bleeding, that her mouth might be sore from bad teeth or poorly fitting false ones. Perhaps eating at meals was difficult for her, leaving her hungry and wandering into rooms where there were snacks.

"Alta does have false teeth. I'll check on them. She was a cleaning lady all her life, going in and out of white folks homes. Got paid next to nothing. No social security, no savings, nothing. Outlived two husbands and a child. Got too old, too slow. White folks wouldn't use her any more. She got a place in the Projects. Her welfare check was stolen so many times, FBI should have guarded her mail box. Crack heads broke in and cleaned her out, TV, radio, even irons she used to do clothes for a little cash now and then. Hoodlums scared her out of the Projects into a Medicaid nursing home bed, a sick and silent woman. Her grandniece could care less about her. That's it! That's Alta's life, life of any old black woman who cleaned white folks' homes and lived in the Projects." Millie's brown eyes turned the hue of sunlit wheat. "When Alta came to Lobelia," she said, "she wandered about the units since her first week, because in my opinion she sees white women in their rooms and thinks she needs to clean up after them."

He said with some insight, "That may be the reason behind the wandering! You've got it diagnosed, Mrs. Grain. Alta wanders with a subconscious purpose." He chose the next words with care. "Why not use Alta's life work to her advantage. I don't mean to suggest that she clean white

51

women's rooms, but why not your office when you're in it where she will have company and feel like somebody? If Alta's life calling was housekeeping, why not resume it? Within limits of course. Under your supervision. Might restore Alta's self esteem."

"White folks like you, Mr.. Brannagh, just don't get it," she said forcibly. "There isn't self esteem in a black lady doing cleaning for another black woman, much less white."

A bit defensively, he said, "There's more to self esteem than that Mrs. Grain. There's self respect in a job done right, like a black social worker working all kinds of hours in a nursing home with mostly white residents." He was dismayed she'd gotten to him. "You're upset because you have so many residents, white and black, to help and not enough time to do it." An example came to mind. "Have you heard of Mother Theresa, a Roman Catholic nun in India? She took care of people discarded as refuse to die on India's streets. She's a white woman from Albania working for dark skinned people of India so low on that country's social scale, they were called 'untouchable'. Mother Theresa touched them, and her followers are doing wonderful things for those not even their own countrymen would help." He paused for effect. "Alta's calling is housekeeping. Working for someone who cares about her may restore her dignity. New teeth, bliss."

"Perhaps," she said, her flashing eyes smiling. "I'll see."

He left her office sensing something different about her. Not just beauty, quality.

4

Parking the pickup, Mike walked to the double door of Larkspur Nursing Home and opened it. Entering, he saw by the reception desk stacked high with old newspapers and a bag lady in a wheel-chair. She looked it, wrapped as she was in a mortician black winter overcoat with a sailor's navy blue wool cap covering foggy hair. Child-pink galoshes lazed like docked tugboats on her feet. Heaped over her outdoor clothing was a brown wool blanket, snatched, no doubt, from an Army barrack's bed. A red scarf around her head emphasized a drained face. It fought to elicit a friendly grimace on which a crow had left foot prints.

"Who the hell are you?" she said with a sentry's challenge. "You look funny."

"It's the best I can do." Yet his mind did a double take at his brown check sport coat, light brown shirt, browner tie and tan pants. Perhaps it was the tasseled brown loafers? "I'm the ombudsman, here to talk to you and other residents about rights in Larkspur Nursing Home."

"Rights? Can you get me more money than thirty dollars a month. I need to buy clothes and toss out these rags." She got right to the point.

He'd skip a critique on her clothing. "Thirty dollars is the State's Medicaid rule," he said, pulling a receptionist's chair out from the desk to sit at wool cap's eye level. Why she was so insulated wasn't apparent. It was a sixty-three degrees outside. "The State rule sets the amount that limits the personal allowance to thirty dollars." He took off his sport coat. The heat in the entry was higher than a boiling chicken's breast. "When the State and you talked about coming into this nursing home, there was an agreement you would pay all your monthly income to the nursing home except thirty dollars for personal needs. The State pays the rest."

"That's crap," she said, her drained face refilling with plasma. "The little girl I talked to down at the county never said nothing about cutting me down to a buck a day. It ain't enough to buy underwear, or a birthday card, or a magazine about them sinning actors. And she said nothing about me not getting cost of living increases social security doles out each year to them living outside. Why outsiders get cost of living and I don't, makes no sense!"

"It doesn't. It's our State's Legislators and Governor Study. He appoints Medicaid planners. Together they limit you to the thirty and keep the cost of living dollars paid by social security due to nursing home residents."

"How can a crippled old lady who's freezing in this unheated hovel change it?"

Unheated? A handkerchief was resurrected to wipe his brow. "Write the Governor."

"Didn't you hear me? I'm a crippled lady. I can't use my hands to write. You write," she said tauntingly.

"Tell you what. You do the telling and I'll do the writing. You tell me what you want said to the Governor and I'll type it in a letter for your signature." A pencil went to paper. "Now tell the Governor why you need another twenty a month."

"I need clothes. Costs have gone higher than a ten story building but my thirty ain't changed in years. It was thirty when I came in here years ago. It's thirty now. Even a cup of hot water strained through dung they call machine coffee has gone up another nickel this week. It's gone from twenty-five to thirty cents. I remember when java was a nickel a cup and free refills. Thirty cents is a halt on gossiping over the cow pee that drools from our metal monster."

Some avaricious corporate financial officer was aware residents' came out of a coffee-sipping culture and installed coin operated coffee dispensing machines to take a cut of the thirty dollars otherwise prohibited to state and or company coffers. "I asked you to tell me, and you told me. I have enough to write the letter, but for whom?"

"For me, Blanche Kessner."

"Pleased to meet you, Ms. Kessner. I'll type the letter, but there's more to it than one letter. The letter asking the Governor to increase the personal allowance won't get to the Governor. Someone in the Governor's office will sent it to the Medicaid Department to draft an answer. Medicaid will return it to the Governor's staff who'll review it for the Governor's automated signature. When and if we get a signed reply it'll probably say 'thank you for writing' and 'I have delegated the Medicaid Department Director to look into the matter. Governor Study reads contributors' checks and political polls, not constituents' letters."

"Turd," she said.

Mike did a double take. He hadn't expected such an outspoken great-gram in a nursing home. "I'm guessing," he said, "that there are fifty thousand residents in nursing homes in the state who get the thirty dollars a month. Let me calculate the cost of a two hundred and forty dollar annual increase in the personal allowance." He brought out his pocket calculator and worked the numbers. "The cost will be around 12 million dollars annually. Once the Medicaid Director sees that, it'll take him the remaining months of the Governor's term to look into it before he gets back to you."

"Pig fart," she said with energy.

He rolled his eyes at her fixation on feces' various nominal forms and elements. It crossed his mind there might be some truth in the psychoanalytic dictum that touched on difficult childhood potty training. "We'll need to write to a few State Representatives and State Senators after we hear, or don't hear from the Governor's office. Then if the State Reps and Senators ignore us, which is very likely unless we contribute money to their reelection campaigns ....," She interrupted, and said, "Ain't it nothing but a cess pool in the Capitol?"

"...., we'll have to think of holding a news conference featuring you. It'll be wise to go on TV and call in radio, but outhouse phrases will bleep out sympathy for sweet grannies going flat broke in nursing homes."

"Pay it no mind, sonny. I just speak that way to shake men folk up. Maybe because I'm a tough old broad. Hustled many a plate of chow over in the Chickton Cafe near the fair grounds close to Misty Lake. Each day I beat off more than a score of hands grouping my shapely butt back when my backside looked like smoked hams. Boys had rough hands back then. Farm boys, factory boys, construction boys, WPA boys. My," her tone turned soft and romantic, "WPA boys knew how to make a woman feel good-d-d-d. Oh yes-s-s-s." Her face was lit by the moonlight of that feeling. Not a myth, a legend in her own time. "Wish cold blooded maintenance Sam would kick up the heat in this hovel. Keeps his job if gas bills go down each year." She spun her chair around toward the dining room. "Time for a cup. Care for some cow urine?"

"Can't pass that."

"Lousy pun." The back of her wool cap was a 'period'. She entered the dining room crossing to the third table. "Livinia?" Kessner said to one of Pharaoh's ex-wives seated in a sedan-chair, "as long as you and me been struggling on thirty dollars a month, here's big bull who says he's going write a letter for me to the Governor to get twenty bucks more monthly."

"You been back at Unita's brew?" Livinia said in a voice squeaky as a rusted brake. Her blackened eyebrows crested on a Cambodian goddess face. Eyes rounded to encompass a brown cloud. Hands smaller than an infant's wrapped a cup of coffee. She preferred pouring the coffee out of the Styrofoam cup into her favorite china cup, chipped with love over eighty three years. "If you get us twenty more, Bull, coffee's like to go up to fifty cents!"

Kessner said, "them shits wouldn't dare."

"Wouldn't they?" Livinia's tiny lips were pouting. "Cut back on the hours of the Activities lady, haven't they? Hardly have anything to do as it is. A body gets sick of listening to TV. Can't see much of it, no ways."

"Know what you mean," Kessner said. "If maintenance Sam just got up off his butt and fixed the Van maybe we could go over to Chickton Cafe for coffee."

"Fix the Van!" Livinia said. "You been on him to fix the furnace and see where that got you!" Blackened eyebrows semaphored a rebuke. "She won't see Chickton Cafe, Bull, if it's maintenance Sam she's waiting on."

"Maybe," Kessner said, "but if the Chickton Chorus comes back to sing, I can get one of them sweethearts to give an old lady a ride someday."

"You have been gulping Unita's brew, haven't you, Blanche? Chickton Chorus won't come back,   not when most everybody falls asleep during the singing and Unita threw up on the Chorus leader. Hey Bull, you going to come back?"

"I am," he said. "But please excuse me now." He nodded a goodbye.

Later he'd call State Health's Fordice. She had the authority to check out the hours of the Activities lady, the records of repairs on the furnace and the Van.

Mike felt infected by Kessner's toilet term germs. The narrow hall walls of the old facility looked cow urine yellow; floor tiles dung brown. Two beds crowded the initial resident room he viewed. An air conditioner below the only window peeked from out between the beds. An easy chair between a narrow dresser and a wardrobe rested at the foot of one bed, a narrower dresser with a TV on top, a wheel chair and a wardrobe at the other bed's foot. There was no real privacy in a room. The initial adjustment to a

57

roommate was equivalent to an absolute loss of privacy. Adjusting to a stranger and even-stranger staff had to be monumental.

An old black man was asleep in the bed north of a wheel chair. Was he? There wasn't a sign of visible breathing. His mouth was as open as a hooked fish's. Expired? A cold breeze rustled the hairs on Brannagh's neck. Death of a very old man in a nursing home bed, the land of last life, looked not at all like death on Korea's battlefield. There screams pierced the thunder of incoming shells, heads rolled back as if disengaging from bodies as an orgy of blood re-colored fatigues. Here, this elder was silent, there was an absence of reddish fluid, the head laid on a pillow as if mounted. The pulse was checked. Had he a pulse? "Lord have mercy on your soul, old fellow."

A wide hand opened suddenly. It grasped Mike's wrist. Brown wintry eyes glowed. "I needs all the mercy the Lord can give," the hand's owner said.

Mike fought making noise, but a soft whinny sneaked out of his mouth. "Thought you'd gone to heaven," he said composing himself, the cold bony hand holding tightly.

"Needs to make amends first," wintery eyes' said. "You new?"

"Not as an employee," he said, disguising choking up. "I'm the new ombudsman. I visit residents, see to residents' rights. I thought you weren't doing well. Came in to check. Seeing that you're doing a lot better than I thought, I'll let you go back to sleep."

"Don't needs no more sleep, 'budsman. If you see to rights, get Big-dough Benny to call before I pass. Used to live in Oldtown. Be now in Aquaville."

"Where does he work?" he said, giving thought to a Damon Runyan character.

"Work? Big-dough ain't took to work. This black man worked life a laborer. It be hard work, hard money.

Raised Benny Mack in the right. He don't want hard work. Want big dough. Big-dough's on the corner. He do dope. Dope-heads name him Big-dough, 'budsman."

"Benny Mack's your son?"

He let loose the wrist he squeezed. "Ain't no more Benny Mack." Tears puddled in the basins of his eyes. "Get Big-dough Benny to visit before I pass. I be giving him Mama's bible."

"I'll do everything I can, Mr. Mack."

Fascinated by the moribund appeal for a visit, reality questioned whether it could be brought off. Any hope of a former parole officer getting to dope dealer Big-dough Benny in Aquaville presented a lesser chance for success than an Israeli getting a Hezbolah to visit a synagogue. But then again, Ziggie's source said bad drugs had gotten inside, good drugs on the street. Could Big Dough be of help? For his father? Unlikely!

The boxes picked up at Five Counties were opened at home. Within were copies of the State's Certificate of Incorporation for Nursing Home Management, Inc., it's Articles of Incorporation and Annual reports. Mike wondered why Ziggie left these. A page was flipped. The Board of Directors were a Dale Unge, Chairman, Jose Ramirez and Jesus Garcia, Members. There were two classes of stock, and restrictions on their selling. Common stock had control and voting rights; preferred stock had preference in the assets and earnings. The purpose of Nursing Home Management was to operate nursing homes. Had Ziggie some problem with that company and its facilities that he collected this? Had Fordice of State Health warned Ziggie of NHM like she had the ombudsman. What problem other than inside information on State Health's surveys? Nothing in the package about it. If a problem, why hadn't he told of it, rather than passing the stuff on? Mike thumbed through other documents. There were similar materials for each of eleven nursing homes: Anemone, Coralroot, Daffodil, Garland, Grass Lake, Honeysuckle, Lobelia, Mint, Orchid, Palace and Willow. Each corporation had the same classes of stock, restriction on sale, and preferences of the operating company.

A yellow sheet separated another batch of documents. He perused them. A Certificate of Incorporation, Articles of Incorporation and the Annual reports of Quality Care, Inc. On its Board of Directors were Javier Grain, Chairman, Manuel Mendoza and Doel Espinosa. Grain? Mike recalled the social worker named Millie Grain. Related? Whatever, Quality Care also had two classes of stock, and restrictions on their selling. Common stock had control and voting rights; preferred stock had preference in the assets and earnings. The purpose of Quality Care was to hold corporations that owned a nursing home building. Similar documents for other corporations were found, companies with letters for names: ANF, CNF, DNF, GNF, GLNF, HNF, LNF, MNF, ONF, PNF and WNF." The purpose of each of these was to provide a nursing home building for rent or lease by a nursing home operating company. Was ANF Anemone? CNF Coralroot? And so on? It appeared so. Why did Ziggie leave him this stuff?   It was a matter needing address.

If he had Ziggie's home phone, he'd called him, but Fordice would do. "Hello, Belinda. Mike here. Sorry to bother you so late, but left for me to look at was a stack of corporate documents. I'm calling for enlightenment. One stack pertains to Nursing Home Management and its nursing homes, the other to a corporation named Quality Care that owns eleven companies, each of which owns a nursing home building. If I've surmised correctly, it seems Nursing Home Management operates the facilities it leases from Quality Care."

"That's right," she said. "It's perfectly legal. Arms length and all that legal stuff."

"I wonder why Ziggie would have taken the time to copy their records?"

"He did? Maybe because your predecessor ran into a lot of trouble with NHM's administrators. Quality Care, as far as I know, just owns buildings and leases them."

"What about Dale Unge? Quality Care's Javier Grain?"

"Unge is the political manipulator I've warned you about. All I know about Javier Grain is he's a rich Oldtowner, as black as me, but I don't own any property. By the way, I made a phone check with the people who maintain the Certified Nursing Aide register. Nothing on it about a firing of an Aide from Palace the last few weeks."

"Thanks for help with the register. On another tact, Belinda, besides NHM, I'm in need of advise on other homes."

"You are? Isn't that nice? I mean it! We should always work closely together since you go in and out of the homes more often than I."

"I visited Willow and fought with its administrator, Mrs. Mallow, over an intra facility transfer. Mallow hadn't issue a written notice. She had, however, commanded resident Katie Arch to leave the room she'd occupied for four years because it was 'roomy.' Mallow wanted it for new male admissions."

"'C' for 'coercive' has to be Mallow's middle initial," Belinda said. "I've noted it."

"I also need to know what can be done to check into the hours of Larkspur's Activities Director. I was told they've been cut to the bone, and to top that, the furnace is said to be running poorly, the Van not at all. Residents are bored stiff not getting out. Do you have authority to check out the hours of Activities and repairs on the Van?"

"We do. I'll take the complaint," she said. "State Office could too, but a week would pass before I'd get it. I'll detach one of the team tomorrow. And Mike, be careful out there among all those women."

5

In no other position had he a better way to start off a work day than with a phone call to Five Counties, particularly since he'd met the winsome woman who answered the calls. "Good morning, Lizzy. Any messages."

"Three, Mike. There's one from Fergus Orr at Grass Nursing Home. He wants to meet you at Puella Junior College at 2:00 PM today. He has a ride there, so call him only if you can't keep the appointment. The other messages are from social worker Shelia Clan at Tulip and from a Reverend Yard in Oldtown. He asks that you drop in and visit him at the Church of Holiness tomorrow morning."

"Reverend Yard!" Had Golah made contact? "I'll be there."

"Isn't he the one who took your side against State Attorney General and the Governor?"

"You've read about my tribulations?"

"It's coffee conversation here among our social workers."

He dialed Tulip Nursing Home. "Is social worker Sheila Clan in, please? This is Mike Brannagh, Ombudsman, returning her call."

"Mr. Brannagh? Sheila here," she said stoically. "We have a Ted Kemt in residency who has gotten well, but his wife wants to transfer him to another nursing home rather than let him return home. Ted is doing nothing about it because he's afraid of her. She verbally abuses him every time she shows up to visit, usually with her boyfriend. Ted's willing to go to another home. He knows her boyfriend is living with her at their house."

"The Kemt's must have a lot of money to pay the private pay rate."

"Ted's on Medicaid," Sheila said.

"On Medicaid?" his disbelief ringing on the telephone line. "If he's well enough to leave Tulip, a Medicaid review will reclassify him out of twenty-four care. He'll be lucky to find a room, board and assistance facility that'll take him in for his social security income. Assuming she's not got a lock on it herself."

"I know," Sheila said, the gloom in her words growing.

"It's crossing my mind Mrs Clan".... "Please call me Sheila".... "crossing my mind, Sheila, that Mrs. Kemt has more going than a boyfriend. She wants the house free of Ted and his tenancy by the entirety. If he comes home, Medicaid may attempt to put a lien on the house to pay for his stay at Tulip. Do you know if Ted deeded the Kemt's house to his Mrs?"

"Under Medicaid's communal spouse rule," Sheila said, "it was exempt. I don't know if he deeded it to her."

"Fascinating situation. To expedite looking into it, would you please contact Wendy Connors at Adult Protective Services? It may take legal action to protect Ted."

* * *

Aquaville's residences might have been pretty and its downtown bustling before and during World War II. Proximity to deep water was an invitation to industry, bloated with war contract dollars, to purchase lake front real estate and build rows of factories. Smoke from their chimneys repainted city hall, shops and business buildings funeral black. Post war conversion still wasn't complete. Though the bones of many of the factories were buried, excretions of bladders and bowels remained below the surface of the ground. Junk yards dared rent the toxic soil, but not buy it. Someday, Superfund would clean it up if the city's voters ever voted right. Those who would have done, moved to clean air in walled suburbs and worked in secured sculptured buildings on broad parklands far from

Aquaville's human residue residing near the downtown morgue.

There was Under's Home to visit on the east side, a block from downtown. Years ago Sloan Under's three story, thirty room 'Under's Hotel' catered to Military on shore leave, and post-war, renting rooms. hourly. Sloan's grandson, Mike, a born-again Christian fundamentalist, developed a disgust for the hotel's low-down scummy clientele and converted its rooms to meet the needs of downtown's elderly men, his grandpa first among them. Mike Under obtained a license from State Health as a RBA, room, board and assistance facility. Resident's paid their own way. Those not so flush could be assisted with supplemental State funds. The mortality rate of elderly men versus that of elderly women being what it was, there weren't enough old male codgers available to fill the rooms and meet expenses, so women were recruited. That worked out well. There were three subsequent remarriages, none at the point of a shotgun.

To the west of Under's, beyond a closed store and a shuttered house, a street deal was going down, dealer and buyer oblivious to a parking pickup. An old guy getting out to go up the two steps to Under's was worthy of no more than a glance. He stopped on the first step and looked again. The dealer was Cooper, an ex-parolee from Oldtown.

"Hey Cooper," Mike said, shouting. "What's going down?"

Cooper's arms. and hands snowed in all directions. He stomped feet on fallen merchandise faster than an Irish step-dancer's feet touched a stage. The buyer, quicker than a crow with a burning tail, fled across the street, cut through a yard and leapt a fence with a champion hurdler's form.

"Oh man. You working parole in Aquaville?" Cooper thought of running.

"No. I've left Parole," Mike said. "I see you've left Oldtown too, but not the street."

They faced each other. Cooper was six-six, candle thin and so light skinned he nearly passed. There was no shortage of brown leather on him though, from shoes, pants, belt to jacket. His shirt was silk. "Quit the job you got me, man. Needed cash. Ain't using, man, just hustling good stuff. Takes a doper's mind out the ghetto, quiets the nut. Here, try them."

Mike held two pills in hand. "Prescription stuff? From drugstore burglaries?"

"No, man. Hustling for the man what knows where to get the stuff the Feds say be good."

Mike was astounded. Cooper, without knowing it, had confirmed Ziggie's source. There was FDA approved drugs being sold on the street! But where obtained? Hopefully not from Nursing Homes? How to handle Cooper? An approach came to mind. Mike said, "I assume you mean the Federal Drug Agency. The narks are all over the place, and they'll get you as hard for hustling FDA stuff without a license or doctor's prescription, as they would crack. It's hard time either way, Cooper. Quit before a nark finds you."

Relief flooded his face. "You a fair dude, Brannagh. If'en I pull out, where I get a job. Need money. Got me a woman. She's had my kid. A boy. Me a daddy?"

Mike thought Ziggie would want to get to Cooper. "Just happens I'm in touch with an outfit and it has a few openings. Where can I reach you?"

Cooper wrote down his address and phone number. "I be sick of pushing, man. You scared shit out of me. Going over to Charlene's in Oldtown Projects. This be her phone number." He gave Mike a piece of paper with her number. Both nodded agreement. They departed.

The lobby of Under's Home was spacious. Clustered couches and stuffed chairs created   conversation corners. Lighting was by lamps. They cast pale seductive glows. On an easy chair a snoring elder in a double breasted blue serge suit was dreaming of a historic encounter. A quartet of ladies wearing white wooly sweaters, cream colored blouses and light tan pants conversed to be heard the next county over. They looked at the newcomer.

"Ladies?" Mike said. "I'm the fellow they call the ombudsman in the Older Americans Act, part of Federal Law. The Law helps protect your rights while in Under's. The Ombudsman is the person under the law who visits residents to let you know there is somebody who's available to help out. There's no cost for it. This brochure explains." He gave each one.

"What's he's saying, Enid," first wooly sweater said. She sat on the right side of the couch and appeared to have talked to the fourth lady, the one on the far left side of the couch, not the two in the middle.

"You talking to me, Thelma?" third wooly said, not the fourth.

"Verda? What does the big man want?" second wooly said.

"Speak up, Edna," the fourth commanded.

Not a word heard. He elected not to put names to ladies, but smiled a lot while pointing to his own name on the brochure. If they read it they would understand. In the meantime, on with the visit. He excused himself. There wasn't a receptionist in sight but noise out of a room to the west of the lobby gave evidence of activity. He entered a dining room. Residents were taking a coffee break. Three smiling women sipped coffee at a table with a dirigible of a middle-aged man, bald and tan on top as a basketball. The square oak table was exceptionally large, even with a semi-circular stomach half devouring it.

"I'm the ombudsman, Mike Brannagh."

"And I'm a Mike named Under," dirigible said,

introducing himself. No move was made to get up but he extended his hand. They shook hands. "Welcome. Have a coffee?"

"Yes. Thank you, Mike." He pulled a chair from another table, sitting on a corner between Under and a resident. "Hello ladies," he said, smiling and pointing to his name on the brochure as he passed them out. If auditory senses were as scarce at the table as in the lobby, he was saving time. A cup, saucer and napkin appeared as he distributed brochures. To his right, coffee poured from a pot that barely cleared the cup. In kids' clothing, a napkin for an apron, a yellow man so small a field of dandelions would hide him, waited table. "Thank you," Mike Brannagh said acting nonchalant.

"That's Charley," Under said, looking at a waiter no wider than a strand of spaghetti. "Let me introduce my table guests. This is Maybelle," her red face below a red wig smiled with even redder lips, "Frances and Margaret." Frances wore a brown wig and eyes browner than winter grass. Margaret's plentiful and well coifed gray hair was her own. There were dimples deep as the Grand Canyon on an attractive face. She'd win any grandma beauty contest entered. Nods were exchanged. "Margaret was Star of Aquaville's stage in the good old days. Sings for us when she's a mind. Beautiful voice."

"I sing," Maybelle said in a huff.

"Like a semi's horn," Frances said.

Margaret and Under worked hard to contain facial movements, Mike too, sipping coffee to stay out of it. Maybelle, to disprove the criticism, launched into "Rock of Ages.' Frances was correct. A semi was running through the RBA until Margaret saved the moment. She sang along, the beauty of her voice joining the other in a not too discordant duet.

"Wonderful," Under said, applauding. Thank you Maybelle, Margaret.

"They were wonderful." Mike said looking to Under. "Do you mind if I look around?"

"Go right ahead."

Meeting so many energetic elderly was encouraging. They needed it to climb stairs. What a different health model. A tour of the floors of the three story building found hallways carpeted and vacuumed. There were common bathrooms, men on the west, women to the east. In the mens' were four shower stalls, two toilet stalls, and two urinals. Tile floors and ceramic showers were spotlessly clean. A door to one room was open. Ten by ten, the room had a window with frilly curtains that opened to the Lake. There were many personal decorations about, a bed neatly made, an easy chair, end table, lamps, a TV, dresser, carpeting and a closet. A resident could have her privacy. This room's resident, if not forgetful, apparently didn't worry about entrants.

* * *

A heavy overcast sky darkened the sun. Puella Junior College's parking lot was sparsely populated, students delaying arrival at the source of wisdom for refreshments at the town of Grass lake's Jellybelly's Cafe. The '83 Ford pickup was parked close to the sidewalk by the main building, Mike slipping off the seat, the door crunching behind him. Flakes of fender rust broke free. The temperature was fifty.

Orr, wrapped in a parka and in his wheelchair, waited outside the main building.. "Get me out of the air, Brannagh!" he said, hollering.

"You need the air, Professor, being cooped up inside day after day."

"Speaking of hot air," Orr said, "you're going to be deflated if you don't get me inside. I've reserved the President's Room next to the faculty lounge. Take a good look, Brannagh. This is the College's main building, 'Main' is recreated history. It was built in the style of the Early

English Period, a style that evolved from 1180 to 1300 AD. Henry II and his sons' Richard and John may have walked under similar acutely pointed arches, their soffits richly molded with series of rolls and hollows and edges simply chamfered. Its architecture is exceedingly beautiful and chaste, simple, yet elegant in design. Note the drip stones over doors and single windows follow the form of the arch, but where windows consist of several separate lights, that is, where each window is made up of several others placed closely together, the drip stone formed a sort of gathering arch over all. This led to tracery. It's magnificent don't you think? Let's go in!" His pious whisperings became those of an Abbot leading a newly tonsured monk into a noble abbey with a splendid chapel. "The President's Room is to the right. I need a cup of coffee."

The room had clusters of easy chairs of various hues. Four padded walnut benches were fitted into the corners. A long walnut table, with bookends squeezing books in its middle, divided the space. Embers glowed within the marble fireplace. A mantle clock chimed. Sea green draperies were tied back to reveal two Gothic leaded windows that opened to the lake where the waves rose and fell with the wind's every breath. A despairing wind whined around the window.

Orr pushed himself up and out of the wheelchair to sit on a red easy chair nestled close to the fireplace. He wrung his hands. His eyes traversed the entirety of the room. "How I loved this room. Many the hours faculty committees discussed changes needed to help our graduates succeed. We believed more than one of our ladies would attain the pinnacle of leadership." He sighed. "Past regrets! Ah, how long it's taken to get around to confessing!"

"Like I said back in your room, Professor, I'm no confessor." Intrigued, he sat down on a green stuffed chair.

"Absolution for the soul is more than bending knees in a dark cubicle, a tonsured cleric the other side of the curtain. Confessing to one who can act to change what may be unchanged, can be a reprieve from future fears. Let me update you, Brannagh. It was the death of resident Harry Cutan that kicked off my remembrance of past evil. A nitroglycerine patch sat on Harry's chest, a medicine that was prescribed for his roommate, Eddie Tar. It crossed my mind Harry's sudden demise was an adverse reaction to the patch. Then there was Chloe, a tough old bird, gone from self-ambulation to walker, to wheelchair, to Geri-chair, to bedfast, to a coma before her death. Physical deterioration or adverse reactions to prescribed medicines?"

Mike couldn't believe it. Fergus Orr confirming counterfeit medicines were inside Grass lake Nursing Home?

"Lyle, over in room 28 hadn't done as well as Chloe or lasted as long," Orr continued.. "Vivacious Winifred wilted within a few months. Flabby Vernon took little interest in food and detested the feeding tube. Ava's stupor was endless. Once again, I pondered was it because of progressive diseases or negative chemical reactions? The thought that residents I knew had adverse reactions to a physician's prescribed medicines activated the need to purge pieces of my sour soul." He patted the green chair. "You're the right one to hear my confession." His brown eyes turned dark. He coughed consumptively, spitting into a red and white handkerchief returned to pocket. He took glasses out of his shirt pocket and put them on noting Brannagh's widen eyes and creased face that flashed astonishment.

Orr was intimating residents' deaths were caused by 'bad' medicines. Cooper came to mind. Were his drugs from a nursing home, and counterfeit accountable for the failing elderly? "Now I need coffee, Professor. I'll refill yours." It was refilled and set on an end table. Mike returned to the chair, balancing cup and saucer on a knee. "Please continue."

71

A sip taken, Orr did. "Why did I take the assistant professorship at Puella in 1976?" he said, as if putting forward a syllogistic premise. He thrust forth a chin high as FDR's. "In retirement I realized time back I did wrongs that affected people. I want now to expunge those crimes!"

"Crimes?"

"Yes! There are crimes I need to tell you of," he said, his face appearing to mummify, his voice lowering. "In the seventies, starting in 1973, while Narks were chasing hippies and beatniks and hard dope smugglers, an Oldtown druggist married to a Mexican National wanted to buy Mexican prescription drugs at extremely discounted prices. At his request, and for considerable remuneration, I organized a travel program called 'Elder Trippers'. A flock of us retired old folks went to Mexico on discounted trips for discounted medicines. A Medical Doctor there, a member of the druggist's family rewrote prescriptions in Spanish that were filled at certain pharmacies. Each Elder Tripper got what each came for, and I, far more. My medicines were returned stateside in bottles labeled in Trippers' names, although none were in the know. No problems with customs. They weren't concerned about legally prescribed   drugs, but about heroin, cocaine, hard stuff. On return to Oldtown, the bus that carried the luggage, also carried my Mexican goods. The stuff was removed, luggage returned. A Druggist handled the stuff from there. Perhaps he sold them over the counter, or on the street. That was his role, not mine. My role was simple, get there and bring it back. Profitable!"

Mike blinked. 1973? That was the time of the smuggling of prescriptions drugs into the Francois County Jail! Was that why the professor recalled the name of the Director of the Jail?

"Professor, were these Brand name drugs, generic equivalents, or what?"

"Generic equivalents," Orr said," and in late 1975,

counterfeit generics."

"Counterfeit? My Lord!" His sound was soaked with incredulity. Then he realized that was nearly twenty yeas back. Now tied to Cooper's man? Doubtful. Stay calm. "No wonder back in the seventies there were so many inner-city hoodlums bombed out of their minds! I had a lot of jail adjustment problems because of it. Are you telling me this continues to operate?"

"I left Elder Trippers in the summer of 1976 to come to Puella, not so much because of guilt or a desire to teach again, but because the druggist passed away. His son disbanded the Elder Trippers and sold off the drugstores. Instead, he went into prescription drug wholesaling."

"Thank goodness!" Mike said, as if he'd no further interest. "And this is the confession you wanted to make, Professor?" He nodded. "Then you want God's forgiveness, not mine. God's is a theological construct beyond the comprehension of this earthly ombudsman. I can't be more than your therapeutic confessor. Having said that, I think any criminal Statue of Limitations has run."

"I didn't come here worried about a trial or prison, it would take longer to try me in court than the time I have left to live, but to let you know of the past, that it not be repeated."

"Repeated?" He was intimating it was. "You said Elder Trippers was disbanded, that the son sold off the drugstores!"

"I have no facts anything is wrong now. Just worries."

"No facts? But worried? About yourself? Because of Harry, Eddie, Chloe and Lyle? Professor, you called this confession. Tell me all."

The door flew open, crashing with a bang. Big Aide Holly entered. "Time to go back, Fergus. Van's waiting," she said, helping him to his wheelchair and out the President's room.

He went with her, no objection made.

Watching the back of them, Mike's opportunity to get names was posponed.. What did Orr say? A Oldtown druggist was behind the Elder Trippers who returned Mexican prescription drugs stateside? A druggist married to a Mexican National with connections to prescription writers and pharmacies in Mexico? A druggist who died in 1976, his drugstore sold by his son who became a licensed drug wholesaler. Was that 'who' in Orr's confession? Was that what he wanted not repeated? The son dealing Mexican stuff? Who? To whom? Hopefully not to old folks in care.

Out the window, the lake flexed muscles against the shore. The weather was easier to understand than the professor, a drug runner in his time. Driving the pickup from Puella to home in the township, the '83's window down, the dreary door to evening opened, its cool wind cutting through clothes as if cheese cloth. It was a revitalizing slash. Comprehending the terrible trespass of counterfeit generics was unimaginable. What if the they had gotten counterfeits? How could anyone in the business of peddling prescriptions sink so low? Counterfeits could only happen where a government hated its people; North Korea for instance.

6

The formation of the terrain of Oldtown required the passage of countless millennia. Raging storms carved river valleys through bedrock surfaces. Advancing and retreating glaciers filled the old valleys, cut new channels and created new waterways. A great river that had run southeast was blocked. Floods over thousands of years reversed its flow and cut a bend to the north west in a mound of post-glacial gravel. Above and around this bend in the river, Indians lived the good life for thousands of years until challenged by white explorers who spread diseases and built forts to keep the Indians out. White settlers followed, decimating more Indians by sickness than gunshot. Tribes faded away none too amicably.

Oldtown took root. Industry followed, flourished but faded. Wars of white men followed the defeat of the Indians. The Civil, Spanish American, World Wars I and II were fought with Army ranks full of Oldtowners who'd left their factory jobs. Blacks came north to fill them. Returning World War II GIs expected re-employment as a matter of right and employed blacks unemployment as a matter of discrimination. Uneasy the relationship between West side Whites and East side Blacks. The Nation's infantry wars in Korea, Vietnam and Kuwait saw Oldtown Blacks and Whites dependent upon one another in combat. Veterans returning to the city in the howling winds of job scarcity left behind war time memories of racial harmony. The flight of factories to the South's and Mexico's warm weather ruptured the heart of everyone's employment. West side Protectors and east side Wolves clashed over the factory and service jobs yet remaining. Never dismayed, hosannas were raised the years of the late nineteen-seventies and eighties by Oldtown politicians and clergy at the opening of each new Convenience Store on busy streets. Most closed post haste pursuant to a Wolf's' pistol whipping. Yet, Oldtown was rediscovered in the nineties to function as a transportation hub with abundant cheap labor and low cost land, lower taxes, location on railroad right-of-ways, proximity to East-West Interstate and St. Albertus Magnus University, Big Al's, as it was best known. Cost of shipping to large urban centers was now less! It was a go! Oldtown's suburbs welcomed distribution centers, warehouses for the Midwest. Raw materials flowed back. Out of the raw, finished goods were formed. There was hope for work for the 'hard working honest people if Personnel Officers avoided the lowering of profits by hiring more than necessary of 'those people.'

A sane citizen didn't walk at night on Oldtown's east side. For that matter, the partly sane didn't walk any Oldtown street at night unless a masochist who enjoyed being trod upon. That was if the muggers were civilized. If the muggers weren't, weaponry cared little for a victim's longevity. Victimology wasn't a matter of intense study. They willingly, but stupidly, were in the wrong place at the right time for muggers.

Mike Brannagh's inclination wasn't masochism though he preferred fists to weapons, although a career of boat rocking might belie the avoidance of psychological pain. He acquired a little wisdom, some called it experience, when going to east side streets near the Projects. He went when muggers, rapists, robbers, dope fiends and prostitutes slept away a hard night's work perpetrating felonies, turning tricks and bragging over wine on the corner. East side felons crashed before dawn and slept away a lot of daylight. Mornings were the safest time to park on the street of Reverend Coppin Yard's Church of Holiness.

Reverend Yard and his Westside congregation were, for most of a post war decade, spectators of Eastside life. Satisfaction over the building of Eastside high rise housing for poor folk turned to indifference over embarrassment at lapses of morals in the Projects. Reverend Yard didn't castigate his congregation's impassiveness, for his head, too, had turned from those hovels of hell. He changed his outlook and way of life to an ascetic's life, and became a minister to the people of the Projects. He moved to the Inner-city and led a life bleaker than the poor people imprisoned in high rise dungeons. His savings were sufficient to purchase a closed church across the street from the Projects. Life would be lived in the belfry with naught but a wardrobe, bed, chair, a table, stove, refrigerator, sundry pots and pans, no bell, and a bathroom in the basement. A poor man, he dressed in donated hand-me-down shoes and clothes from his congregation's deceased faithful. He ate casseroles and leftovers sent by pious and worried church ladies who had their own to worry about feeding. Sunday collections kept the church's furnace on low, its light bulbs at forty watts and water flowing for drinking, bathing and flushing. He preached the 'Word' on street corners, on balconies and in the apartments of the people of the Projects. Through the practices of poverty, abstemiousness and abstinence, he was free to speak of the glory of God, help the poor and crusade against drugs. He was free to encourage children to attend school, teenagers to abstain from unmarried sex, adults to discover the joy of sex only in marriage, the satisfaction of work, of love of children returned by Welfare to attentive parents, of a father's pride in family and self.

For the bodies of Project people, he raged a two front battle: a crusade for freedom from dope and volunteer service on the Board of Directors of Inner-City Community Reorganization Inc., 'Inner-com', its focus, jobs to free Project people from State indenture. But Inner-com's programs set up during President Lyndon Johnson's war on poverty ran low on money when President Nixon pulled the plug on Inner-com, the inner-city and Oldtown's interstitial rings clear to the suburbs. It isolated Blacks of the Projects within a wall of abandoned factories. Poor Whites were frozen to their unsaleable real estate. Jobs left were low paying, as if serfs under medieval Lords, but street dope dealers hadn't a recession.

Mike steered his pickup to the side parking lot of the Church of Holiness, an ancient yellow brick structure twenty-five feet wide and forty feet long. Stained glass windows featured illuminated Irish Saints: St. Patrick, St. Brigit, St. Columbanus and St. Brendan. All still glimmered in the glass of former All Saints Church. When last did an un-saintly or saintly Irishman attend Mass here or live in the neighborhood? A thirty foot turret fronted the edifice topped by a fifteen foot steeple with a lightning rod beside a Celtic cross. Double oak doors, richly carved with angelic creatures surrounding the relief of a sword swinging St. Michael, opened at the ground floor of the turret. St. Michael was so formidable, the ecclesiastical edifice hadn't gang graffiti.

Recalling what jailed junkies had told him about their competition with juvenile dealers, Mike checked in all directions as he parked. If it were day light, mugging wouldn't likely be by a grown crook, but by a pistol packing boy whose Mama rousted him from bed to go to a school he rarely attended. If mugged by brats with weapons, he was advised to give up and satisfy the kids with a wad of folding cash. Fifteen or twenty dollars, singles, with a fiver on the top. Give no lip.   Kiddy-punks would desert the scene for wine and crack and hairy pussy.

He'd given the advice credence and, back home, emptied his wallet of credit cards, car insurance proofs, extra car keys, photographs and anything of value, except protective cash and a driver's license with the ugliest of all his photos sealed in plastic for the license's five year life. Looking out the rear view mirror, girls wiggling against red bricks and plywood windows were visible. Two were so short they'd need to stand on different steps of a kitchen step-ladder to reach the wash basin. The third was a taller girl. The three of them looked at his pickup. Though it wasn't anything to see they left the bricks to cross the street, not stopping at the curb to look both ways for traffic. Three little lion cubs, and him their prey? No! But intuition said yes. Watching the girls in the rear view mirror, he considered starting the pickup and easing away, just as if he'd not noticed them in nylon jackets with hoods pulled over their heads. As one, they hopped the near curb and came into the parking lot. He watched them separate. Lion cubs circling? Little girl lions? It couldn't be! Two came to the driver's side, the littlest to the passenger side. A glance confirmed the passenger side door was locked. The girl out the door window looked about eight with shining eyes and facial skin the color of a cantaloupe. Were they carrying guns? They were too young. Girls didn't fit the description of gun packing hoodlums, at least not little girls wearing blue jeans, white tennis shoes and black nylon jackets with hoods up just like any kid going to school on a windy day. But they weren't going to school. It wasn't windy. He chastised himself for thinking little people could be targeting him, a man who worked years with the toughest criminals in the county. In the left side-view mirror, black hoods framed two pretty cocoa faces. The littler girl looked ten, the taller girl twelve? Sisters? What difference did that make? He could lift both of them, all three for that matter, and squeeze them like lemons. A cold chill surged through his tense body, the same kind of coldness he felt in Korea when his position was probed by the enemy. There, he cut them to shreds with machine gun fire. There, both sides were armed. Who in hell so psychologically brutalized inner-city girls that they might be armed robbers? Were they raised in the hell of the projects? He'd cut short their incipient criminal careers. Left hand on the door handle, he waited to swing it into the twelve year old to knock her off balance before she drew down her weapon, then leap out and seize the ten year old, hoping that sudden speed would neutralize her. He'd subdue both before the question of a concealed weapon arose. Seizure of two should frighten the tiny one away. She couldn't have a gun! It would out weigh her. Girls didn't carry guns in his time with the Juvenile Court.

The taller girl was five feet from the door, hand in her jacket's right pocket. It bugled. Brown eyes flashed the glint of steel on the face of a smooth skinned six grader. Her physical biology needed only a spurt of growth chemicals to finish a frame nature had already lavished with femininity. He gently pushed the door handle down, shoulder ready to slam the door into her. He hesitated. Perhaps he misread the scene. He worked his youthful years with kids from the inner-city, even if that was thirty-five years back. Few boys, much less girls, carried a gun. Most delinquent boys were unarmed robbers, purse snatchers, or strong arm robbers, taking nickels from smaller children at school or on the street. Girls were shoplifters, truants. Could the kids from today's Projects have changed that much that they were into robbery with a weapon?

He believed she wouldn't have a gun so he would social work her like he had her maw and grandma before her. He eased the pickup's door open and slipped off the seat to the ground, closing and locking the door behind him, car keys in hand. He faced the taller girl, prettier than any toy store's best selling doll. If only she were playing with dolls. A small hand gun slid out of her jacket pocket. It looked real. A second or two looking at it, it became a 155 howitzer.

"I don't believe you mean to do this," he said, his voice firm.

"Yea girl," she said sweetly, "I do believe I do." The

other girl kept her hands in her jacket's pockets as if she had two revolvers backing up the play.

"No you don't believe it," he gently said, "not to one who's here to get help from Reverend Yard for an old cripple man in a nursing home."

"Piss on cripple's head," she said with a hiss. Her pretty face contorted. "You ain't no retard, big shit. Give me money or I blow your dick off. You can believe that."

As her weapon was pointed at the surgical angle necessary for a quick castration, Mike said, "I believe," his eyebrows waving like surrender flags. So much for social work. "I have to reach into my pocket to get my wallet. Okay?" When he handed it over, he'd attack.

"I be a squeeze from shooting your balls off, you get in my face."

Then sounded a deep bass voice from behind. It said in a roar, "Put it down, bitch!"

Her concentration disappeared. She looked away from Mike. He grabbed the weapon from her, but missed his hold on her. She took off full speed, little shadows chasing after her. He thanked God for the miraculous appearance of a policeman in the inner-city, a rare event, and said, "How glad I am you appeared, Officer." He turned to see not a cop, but a civilian! A man in a dark suit, a woman in tan and red.

"Mr. Brannagh? Is that you?" said the woman.

"Yea," he said, the words carrying surprise at being recognized in the inner-city. How could he forget her? "Millie Grain of Lobelia?" Who else could so fill out a tight red wool sweater protruding from a tan rain coat? Next to her was a huge muscular man, six foot six and two-hundred and twenty pounds of well proportioned muscel. His face was broad, cheeks sunken and his features those of a conditioned athlete with skin as brown as a deer's winter coat. He was dressed in fashionably tailored suit that gave him the look of a panther with eyes burning terribly bright

81

enough to burn the lion cubs.

"Who's this, Millie?" the big man asked. "You shacking with him?"

"Don't be ridiculous, Javier," she said, disgust coating her words. "That's Mr. Brannagh, the old man who works for old folks in old folks' home."

Mike thought she included one too many 'old.' He hid his feelings. He thought a second about the big man's intended insult. Millie could do worse. He took the measure of Grain and conceded so far she hadn't.

"Mr. Grain, my thanks for scaring those kids."

"You're lucky," Grain said. "Kids around the Projects don't usually scare." He turned and walked away without Millie.

She and Mike watched him walk to a Cadillac, get in, start up, and drive away.

"What you doing here, Mr. Brannagh?"

"Come to see Reverend Yard."

"Not," she said, teasingly, "for marriage counseling?"

"No," he said with a mock, "even if your husband thinks I'm your man. I've got to admire his judgement. I'm here on behalf of a resident in a nursing home. He's likely to be kicked out if I can't find his witness."

She smiled the smile of a halo sun. "Can I help?"

"Well yes. Come in and re-introduce me to Reverend Yard. He may have forgotten me."

They walked to the church's front door. He held it open and followed her up the single flight of stairs. The legs he saw Betty Gable would have negotiated for, legs that ran up to a behind formed by a sculptor infinitely more gifted than Leonardo. What the hell was Grain's trouble? Mike felt like a lustful crud. She hadn't done a thing sensual except exist in beauty of body, kindness of spirit. Yet his phantasy life soared. He shook his head to shake off lust.

"Reverend Yard's office is behind the altar. Isn't it beautiful," she said, stopping in mid aisle, "with its white marble and gold leaf tabernacle."

"I remember it as All Saints," he said. "It's the same altar, one with numerous spires. My mother said they pointed the way to heaven. This was my dad's original parish, mostly Irish parishioners, poor to a family, pushed to contribute to the building fund when the Parish Priest proclaimed the church's holy altar would be an everlasting tribute to God on which the sacrifice of the Mass would be forever offered. Then Vatican II dumped traditional altars, and our good Bishop, not to be out done by the Pope, dumped the church when the neighborhood became more black than white. Religious practices may have changed but not this prayer to God sculpted in stone, no matter the faith of worshipers."

"I'll introduce you to Reverend Yard, then wait for you in the back pew," she said, as if setting out an agenda, "until you can get back in your pickup and leave the area. If I'm with you, children won't rob you." There was a touch of mockery in her tone.

He knew she could shield him, a man infinitely bigger and stronger than she. The whole way of life of the inner-city had changed. He'd worked here with kids when the building of the high rise Projects first stacked poor blacks on top of other poor blacks. Project children were isolated from homes and schools in white neighborhoods. Drugs became more assessable than candy. Street gangs even forced the once feared Irish organized crime out of the area. "Sad commentary on our times, Mrs. Grain."

"Call me Millie, please."

"And I'm Mike."

The minister, in a blue serge suit   from out of the past, walked from behind the altar. He stood lean and tall, another six footer. He featured high cheek bones and large eyes set off by plentiful hair, cloud white. Eyes flashed the power of lasers.

"Reverend Yard! It's me again," Millie said.

"Millie?" His voice had a magnetic resonance that revived the stale air of the church. "Did Grain leave you?"

"In a matter of speaking. The man with me is Mike Brannagh." Her left hand settled on his right shoulder. "He visits my Lobelia nursing home residents. Advocates for them. We know each other from work. I'm waiting on him to take me out to barbeque for lunch like he promised."

A promise of barbeque? He'd take her anywhere she wanted to go.

"He's a good man then?" Reverend Yard said.

"Mike is," she said. A ray brightened her butterscotch skin. She removed her reassuring hand from his shoulder and sat down in the pew, hands folded on her lap.

He, smiling rakishly, nodded to her. She was on his mind, not a resident's witness.

"Come into my office, Mike, and we'll talk about my friend, Shango Golah." The office was All Saints' sacristy, still painted Blessed Virgin blue and furnished with six early twentieth century county court house oak chairs and a roll top desk. Oak filing cabinets were selling in the antique shops north of Oldtown for two hundred dollars a drawer. Round top oak desks weren't within the price range of the middle class. "Have a seat."

"Thank you." he said, and sat down. "I take it you've heard from Shango about the need to find his witness? He needs her or he's going to find himself looking for another nursing home."

"Shango, in his prime, was quite a man," Reverend Yard said, emphasizing 'was.' "He's a Vietnam war hero who overcame his wounds and the army to build a construction business with his own hands in the inner-city. He was numbered highly by the older members of the Board of Inner Community Reorganization. After his

84

illness struck, a multiplication of parasites devoured his construction company. They ate, drank and fornicated in luxury. Shango entered darkness. Anger gnawed his soul. Tamar," he said, huffing her name as if evoking it, "Shango's ex-wife, fed it. She as much as cut his spinal cord. She turned her opossum eyes and luscious body loose on a slick dude built like a sprinter. She deserted Shango for the dude's Chicago and took Shanette, their daughter, out of his life. The hardest of all living is living without the returned love of a beloved child. Shango's blood ran cold. Anger filled his arteries. His heart pumped hostility to his head. Hence his second stroke."

"Where's this daughter now, Reverend Yard?"

"I don't know. I've tried many times to locate her, to no avail. Tamar would tell me nothing. She and the dude apparently dipped Shanette backward from salvation."

"Too bad," Mike said. "Shango needs someone in his life."

"He does. It's unfortunate Javier Grain, and not Shango, didn't marry Tamar. She would have run Javier into poverty instead. They were all close friends once. Javier and Shango served on the Board of Inner Community, but Shango won Tamar to his everlasting injury. Why Millie Hopk succumbed to Javier's courting, ignoring his womanizing reputation, I'll never really understand. I expect she thought she could change him. She comes from a fine, Christian family. I..." He stopped, eyes downcast, embarrassed he'd said so much.

Mike, to lessen the frustration, returned to his purpose. "Was Shango able to find the name of the nursing home Aide who was assaulted?"

"Yes!" His eyes came up. "Fanny Brown is her name."

"Really?" A little ironic Mike thought, considering what had happened to her. "Do you have her address?"

"I have, but she'll not meet with a white man. I can

quote her: 'White folks all of a kind. If I talk on Shango, be sicced on by the sheriff's dogs when the white man tells the old folks' white boss lady."

"Darn!" he said with disgust, "what's the matter with her?"

"She's afraid of the nursing home boss, a white woman. Fanny Brown comes from a place where the white sheriff still says whites are right and blacks wrong."

"I assume," he said, "Lancaster, the nursing home administrator, told Fanny Brown something about the sheriff. Hell of a world, isn't it Reverend Yard? Whites afraid of blacks, blacks afraid of whites."

"And here in the Projects," he said, "blacks afraid of blacks. Any vulnerable person, anyone of any age without a weapon or a police escort, white or black, who ventures out on the streets at night, not necessarily near the Projects, is a volunteer victim of crime. It isn't an accident that white criminals committed ninety percent of their crimes against white victims, or black criminals committed eighty percent of their crimes against black victims. It's because segregated whites with criminal inclinations can't find enough black victims in white neighborhoods, or black criminals can't find enough whites near the Projects to victimize. Whether a white or a black with a criminal inclination, pigmentation translates to visibility in the others' neighborhoods. Whites with criminal inclinations have a virtual monopoly on the segregated wealth of the milky ocean in which they swim. Blacks with criminal inclinations keep in mind the ease of swimming in a swarthy sea. Criminals are prone to swim where they won't drown."

"Well said, Reverend Yard," he said, presenting him a brochure, "Shango and I appreciate you effort."

"Here's Fanny Brown's address," he said, taking the brochure and handing over a piece of note paper. "She has no phone. Write her a letter and include a brochure like

86

this, maybe that will help convince her. If you go into her neighborhood, folks there may turn on you."

"Thinking of folks turning on me, I again want to thank you and Inner-city News for coming to my rescue when Attorney General Puts started investigating me about the parole kickback scandal."

"Oh yes," he said, his face darkening. "I thought I recognized you. That was a time of turmoil! Mothers from the Projects recruited to hustle drugs to get a dealer to buy paroles for their men. Black parole officers took bribes for favorable reports. Certain parole board members got kickbacks for favorable votes. Ties right up to Governor Study. I presented the facts to Attorney General Puts with no success. So I published the story to Inner-city News. True, the Attorney General dropped the investigation of you but the outcomes I sought were indictments of men on the parole board." Reverend Yard took out a handkerchief. "The white parole board members weren't indicted." He wiped his brow. "Black parole officers were as they should have been. That's not unusual in this state's Criminal Justice System. It's over now." He got to his feet and offered his hand to shake. They shook hands.

"Good day, Reverend Yard, and thank you." He nodded a goodbye, turned and exited the blue walled sacristy into the sanctuary, past the altar and down the center aisle of All 'Irish' Saints, still operating, but now under the name Church of Holiness of the Lord and Savior.

Millie looked up. "Success, Mike?"

"Of a sort," he said, his face reflecting discouragement. Time for barbeque, Millie. I know just where, 'Jocko's Place'. It's near Big Al's."

The street was a major north south thoroughfare, heavily patrolled by city and campus police, a street on which blacks with whites and whites with blacks could drive, park, walk and shop as nearly free of muggers as was a police station. Jocko's was Oldtown's only acknowledged cross racial bar and restaurant. It was a place where College's liberals went. White and black women met black and white men there and devoured the city's best barbeque and fries drowned in Jocko's homemade sauce, a closely guarded secret. It was the place black men with jobs, men who'd escaped the Projects but not all the ghetto, came to socialize and to see what was happening. A man could bring his lady. Jocko Lee, a body builder who won a world's weight lifting title, heavy weight division, while on a furlough from state prison, kept the hoodlums out. Jocko discovered a hoodlum's count down on whiskey ignited rage like NASA ignited rockets.

"Jocko's fine, Mike," she said. She arose and pulled on her coat. "I'll walk you to your pickup. I'm parked the other side of the church. I'll follow you to Jocko's."

He shrugged his shoulders a lot recently, what with a girl putting a weapon on his privates, Reverend Yard telling him his lot in the kickback scandal was mere trivia, Fanny Brown's fear of him and Millie protecting him. It made him feel like a soft turd in a new baby's diaper. There was no sign of hoodlums coming on from the Projects. He unlocked his driver's side door, got in, closed and locked the door; started the motor and backed up, then forward in first, gearing up, following Millie, eyeballs glued to her back. Tan raincoat or not, her movements within its folds were a lyrical ballet. At curb side the other side of the church, she unlocked the door of a Buick and slid within like a movie star framed by a plush blue front seat.

* * *

Jocko's large front window in a square building loomed on Big Al's Street. Mike pulled in, parked, got out and waited by his pickup as Millie parked. He walked around to her door, opened it, his eyes again on legs that led the skirt by a yard. He held out his hand. She grasped it for a hand up. Side by side, a woman fit for a model's runway and an old man in need of more work in a physical fitness gym, entered.

"Mike Brannagh!" said a goat's voice, a bray. "Where you been, man? I heard you quit parole and left town. What you been doing?"

"Jocko!" he said, his tenor an octave higher. "I've been away visiting the sick and infirm in nursing homes. Work for the old folks now. Good to be back. Excuse me for impoliteness, Millie. This guy with the enormous chest in a gray polo shirt with the barbell logo is no ordinary muscle man. He's my good friend Jocko Lee. Jocko this is Millie Grain, social worker at Lobelia nursing home. Millie this is Jocko, restaurateur extraordinary, son of Willie Lee. We did combat together in Korea."

"Willie's son did his own time down state, Millie," Lee said, "but damned if Mike didn't come to visit and do the right thing by me. Got me out to compete in weight lifting, got me out on new evidence, got me a new trial, got me acquitted. I got a life long debt."

Millie's dark eyebrows arched. If preconceived attitudes were negative to the old ombudsman, she reconsidered with Lee's testimony. She was leaning to an attitudinal change anyhow, since the discussion on Alta Ridd and the trip to Reverend Yard's by the Projects to help a black man. "Pleased to meet you," she said to Lee, the smile of spring's sun on her lips.

"Name's Jocko," he said, his gold tooth gleaming as much as his winking left eye.

"Millie," she said, the radiance of her white teeth exposed.

"Take my table," Lee said. He escorted them to the southwest corner of the dining area. Two could sit back to wall on a cushioned bench. It was Lee's private table. He could watch humanity driving by on Big Al street. He saw who walked passed. He checked out who came in. He'd hidden an alarm button to push for the cops. These days hoodlums carried guns, not knives. Fists were useless. "Sit in my seat, Millie." He helped her to the bench. "There's room for you Mike next to Millie. Need menus?"

"Not I," Millie said. "Beef and fries with orange soda."

"Same," Mike said.

"Still need to fetch the sandwiches from the counterman, Mike," Lee said. "Come on." He gave Mike's arm a Clydesdale pull. At the sandwich counter, Lee ordered for three. "You're inviting me to join you and Millie, right man?" Before the answer came, he leaned over. "Millie is Javier Grain's woman. He's rich, man. Runs a big company that sells stuff to drugstores. Owns a lot of buildings. Don't know why Javier cats around like he do, looking at Millie."

Mike glanced back at Millie who was looking out the window "She's one beautiful woman. I ran into her at Reverend Yard's church. Invited her to lunch."

"What you doing at Reverend Yard's?"

"He's helping me find a witness for a nursing home resident."

"Why some old shit in an old folks' home be needing a witness?"

"The old shit isn't even fifty yet. Stroke. Palace nursing home wants to kick him out."

"Orders up!" said the beef-stick of a counterman.

Jocko pulled a chair over from another table. They sat down to eat. There might not be a meal served in any of the world's fine restaurants with the delicious taste of Jocko's stacked barbeque beef on sourdough bread, crowned by pickles and Jocko's special barbeque sauce.

"Mike?" Lee said. "Why does Palace want to kick the dude out?'

"Let me explain. The dude in the nursing home told me he busted his white roommate's head to free an Aide from rape. Reverend Yard gave me her name and address, but warned me not to go to her neighborhood. I need to talk to her. She's the resident's only witness."

"I'll go with you," Millie said.

"I appreciate it, but there's a little matter of confidentiality."

"Bull," Lee said. "You get trouble if you go. Me and Millie going with you."

"Yes," she said, eyes on Lee. "We'll all go together."

7

At his home office, Mike entered notations on residents. Larkspur's Livinia's reference to lack of Activities, the broken down Van, and Mr. Mack who wanted son Big-dough Benny to come fetch his Mama's bible. There was work to do on Blanche Kessner's letter to Governor Study, the epitome of ah elephant's dropping, on raising the personal needs allowance. Medicaid nursing home residents weren't a lobbyist power, but if a letter or two to the Oldtown editor were published, who knew. The writing took a while, what with steam out of Mike's ears slowing composing over politicians sinking his ship, while ignoring reality.

Governor Luke Study
Office of the Governor
State Capitol

Larkspur Nursing Home
Rooster County

Dear Governor Study,
I am a resident of Larkspur and represent other residents who have expressed sentiments similar to those I write about. All of us have found that a long life may not only have had severe health problems but also devastating financial consequences which placed us in the position of spending down resources to not only pay for ongoing community living expenses but medical, dental, hospital, home health care and now nursing home bills.
This spend down reduced us to our monthly income, mostly social security benefits which by Law we now apply to the cost of our long term care. We are very grateful that years ago our elected representatives at our urging passed Federal and State Laws to set up the Long Term Care

92

Medicaid program. Over decades of hard work we helped fund it by paying our taxes. We continue to help fund our care through our social security benefits.

Will you consider a change in the state Medicaid rule that takes all of a nursing home resident's monthly social security benefits except $30.00 called the personal needs allowance? Out of the personal needs allowance we can't afford to pay the ever increasing prices for new underwear, clothing or other items of personal need. Why? Because the cost of those items have continued to go up but the monthly personal needs allowance has stayed at $30.00 for the last several years, despite cost of living increases which have been granted every one of those years to every recipient of social security benefits.

We are asking that the State not take, every single year, all of our annual social security benefits cost of living increases. We are asking that the personal needs allowance be increased annually a sum not less than the percentage of each annual cost of living increase. If this was in effect years ago, my personal needs allowance would be over $40.00 a month and I'd have nothing to complain about.

Gratefully Yours,
Blanche Kessner, Resident

Mike ran off three copies of the letter, keeping one, writing DRAFT in red ink on the pages of a copy and a notation to Kessner to return the draft in the stamped envelope with his return address after she made changes. If she declined to use the letter, she was to rip it up and throw it into the trash. If she elected not to make changes and mail it, she would need to sign and mail in the enclosed addressed, stamped envelope.

Letter written, he'd update other notes. Under the file heading 'Golah, Shango', in the folder Palace Nursing Home, he wrote of the allegations, Golah's denial and his story as to what had transpired.   No cousin of his? Now it was he who needed a cousin in Fanny Brown, former Aide. Perhaps Reverend Yard's information on Golah's youthful prominence, business success, stroke, wife desertion and bankruptcy explained his miserable attitude.

Then came to mind, Palace's Nurse Gloria's positive outlook for her residents deep into dementia. Maybe, as he gets to know her, he could pursue questions as to unexpected physical or mental deterioration among her patients.

What could he write about the encounter with Willow's Ida Mallow over Katie Arch's intra facility room transfer? He'd write there was a meeting over the applicable rules with the parties involved, and thought Mallow disagreed with the Ombudsman's discourse on the law, Katie Arch declined to transfer rooms, offering instead, to talk with another resident about her moving into Arch's room. He wrote positively about the efforts of council president Porter Litt to work out the matter. Hopefully, after Mallow reread the Rules, she'd accept the outcome.

Under the file heading 'Ridd, Alta', in the folder Lobelia Nursing Home, was summarized the imperial Bedico's dominance of the resident council. He also summarized the discussion with social worker Millie Grain to help Alta recover her dignity by doing meaningful work. The write-up included no mention of Millie's domestic trouble with Javier Grain, his chasing away the girl armed robbers, or, at Jocko's BBQ the apparent interest of Jocko Lee in Millie Grain, and vice versa!   They'd help with Fanny Brown.

The entry on Under's RBA remarked on its operator's enthusiastic interest in his clientele. Mike didn't associate Under's with street hustler Cooper. There remained the need to connect Cooper with a job through Five Counties, if Ziggie will go along after he's told of

Cooper's record and sale of prescription drugs.

Under the file heading 'Orr, Fergus', in the folder 'Grass Lake Nursing Home', were summarized the date of the meeting with the council president, Orr's teaching background. Not a word entered about the Elder Trippers. It ceased to exist sixteen years ago. A shudder worked the spine to the shoulders. Mike remembered the Francois County Grand Jury of years back that subpoenaed every scrap of paper, but toilet, his administration had used to keep information on prisoners, visitors and staff, unaware a Grand Juror sought indictments for someone on the correctional staff allegedly running prescription drugs into the jail. Mike hadn't, and wasn't indicted, but only because an Inner-city News' article quoted documents clandestinely obtained from the Prosecutor's office which had implicated the true culprit and exonerated the Jail Director. All political hell had followed the Prosecutor's suppression of those exculpatory details. Were the drugs that ended up in the jail back then ferried to Oldtown by Orr's Elder Trippers? Why now was he atoning for those well seasoned sins? Mike's mind pirouetted like a ballet dancer with thoughts of who was the Oldtown druggist behind Elder Trippers, a druggist who'd died, whose son sold off the drugstore and opened a drug wholesale business. It had been druggist Guido Nozlo who'd been exposed by the Inner-city News' article as the smuggler of prescription drugs into the jail. He'd beaten the allegation by producing a Medical Doctor's prescriptions. Mike doubted Nozlo was the head of Elder Trippers. His drugstore was operating a decade later when he passed away. Elder Trippers' druggist was married to a Mexican National with connections to Mexican prescription writers and pharmacies. An arabesque! There were Mexican surnames in the list of directors of Nursing Home Management. The son of the Elder Trippers' druggist would be of half-Mexican blood! Was Chairman of the NH Management Board Dale Unge half-blood? If Orr were correct, the son who closed Elder Trippers had opened the drug wholesale company, not a nursing home management company. Could Unge have sold the wholesale outfit and organized the management company? Another review of the corporate papers reflected a date in 1976 as the initiation of the management company. A look at the organizational date of Quality Care with Javier Grain as Chairman of the Board, revealed a month in 1976. Javier Grain? Millie's Javier? The big guy who stopped the Projects' armed robbery? He sure didn't look to be of half Mexican blood, and yet, his own corporation, Quality Care, had Board members with Mexican surnames. Why not? It was very American to have minorities on a Board, and on reflection, businessmen would be likely to plan the initiation of their reciprocal businesses at the same time. One that owned and leased nursing home buildings, the other that rented and operated them.

The head shaking offered visible validation Mike's current line of thinking was as paranoid as were his musings on the source of smuggling prescription drugs into the jail. Asking Millie about Javier Grain's ethnic makeup would do nothing to resolve their marital difficulties. Staring at Dale Unge to determine if he were half-blood was as inane.

8

"Good morning, Lizzy."

"Hello Mike. Mr Zigmont left an envelope on my desk addressed to you. He won't be in until late afternoon. Should I mail it to you?"

"No, please don't. I'll come by for it today. Maybe catch Ziggie."

* * *

There was a giddy group of tender and mellow folks singing in Iris Nursing Home's dining room. A young man dressed in a blue business suit pounded piano keys. Rows of wheelchairs and hard back wooden chairs next to residents' walkers marked mellow residents from tender visitors. Age and clothing were as distinctive. There were fashionably attired young women milling about, waiting on the overly ripened, serving coffee, tea or milk shakes.

"What's going on?" Mike said to an Aide, a teenager in blue clothes.

"Grandmother-Granddaughter Day. Mary Held's idea. She's the pretty woman with the metal splints down her legs. Polio. Glad polio isn't around any more." Held's flowered dress was pinned with a corsage in honor of the day. She sat next to the piano player, a fellow whose name tagged had 'Herbie, Mary's grandson'. "Mary hasn't a granddaughter," the Aide said, "so she has Herbie dance his nimble fingers on the ivories. She has a lot of other good ideas since she took over as president of the resident council. Kids from kindergarten, Granddaughters, Grandsons, ministers, teachers from the colleges, politicians, businessmen. Even a stockbroker visited, though funds for investment from residents' thirty dollars a month isn't much. Family Council meets two times a month. Ralph Pott, administrator, never misses."

"All Mary Held's doing?"

"Mostly," she said, "but Greg Stam, the last president, was a great help until he went to skilled care. Talk to him about her."

"I will," he said, and went the way directed. The northeast side of the home, the skilled care unit, was near as lively as northwest. Nursing staff were entering and leaving residents' rooms. Doors were closed or opened according to request.

Not all in rooms were serene. Chipper as a sparrow, a young woman's voice said, "Ain't no order, Miss Johnnie. You don't go, no telling how doctor going to get it out of you. You don't get it out yourself, doctor do." With a squeak, Johnnie said, "Help me to the potty."

Down the hall there was a different tune. Said a tired throat, "Get out my best dress, Julie. Your great uncle Ian's coming to visit. Haven't seen him in years. Helen was a good wife to him. She was a war bride from England. Passed away last month. Ian's doing none too well himself. One last earthly meeting, brother and sister, then eternal togetherness with mother and father and Ian back again with Helen." A vibrant woman with a chiding tone, answered, saying, "You have years ahead, Great-Grandma." There was momentary silence. "You're young and beautiful, Julie. You'll enjoy the years clear through the next century. I enjoyed my life in this century. When you reach your eighty-eight year, and I pray you do so without impairments, but if you don't, you too will look forward to leaving them. I wish to see God in the face."

Where the wing was expected to end, it didn't, but erupted into a half star burst. Stubby wings of four rooms either side of a hall ran north, west and east. A half moon nurse station faced the half star burst. Aides entered residents' room and turned the bedfast gently, like rotating hot dogs on a grill. Among the residents recumbent in geri-chairs, two Aides helped a lady to her feet and walked her a few steps. Sitting behind the nurse station, a short woman in nurse's whites, hair black as charcoal, furiously scribbled in a chart. There was no shortage of nursing staff in the skilled care unit.

A knock on Gregory Stam's door. "Mike Brannagh, ombudsman, Mr. Stam."

"Ombudsman? Come in, come in," said a raspy voice feeble as a newly hatched bluebird. The double bed room was dark, quiet and very warm. Window shades were drawn. A burning bathroom light let in some illumination. The occupant was covered from toe to mouth with white blankets. Dark eyes peeked from behind half closed lids. The face that lodged those eyes and a bald head were robin breast orange. Ears were yellow. Whatever sickness invaded his system carried with it vivid manifestations. He coughed, wracking his belly and chest with wave-like spasms. He wiped his eyes with tissue, looked, and said, "I heard the last ombudsman quit. Did he tell you what he was trying to do here?"

"No."

"Well, maybe you can do it instead. There's a woman here who could buy and sell out of her business' petty cash the insurance company my casualty agency represented. She built up a mechanical engineering company from scratch. When she retired she sold her shares for enough cash to buy a majority position in the chain that owns this nursing home. She's spend a lot of her fortune on the residents here and the staff who run this nursing home. Her one regret, due to polio, was she never attended a day of college. She talks about opportunities missed by not going, the difficulties caused by it though she's the smartest person I know or ever knew. She's generous as Santa. Even paid college costs for every one in her family, her grandson, several of the staff."

Puzzled, Mike said, "What was the prior ombudsman going to do for her?"

"Get Mary Held an honorary college degree."

"An honorary degree?" Mike's tone was subdued. "Mr. Stam, someone might have such influence with a college, not me. My time at St. Albertus Magnus University was an every semester battle over paying tuition on time, GI Bill or not. I haven't influence at Big Al's, or with any college President."

Tears bloomed in Stam's eyes, necessitating his handkerchief wiping the moisture. "That's all right," he said, "Just a pipe dream. Goodbye!"

Feeling downright mortified, Mike hastened his walk out of the room and down the hallway. The songfest was really bubbling, grandson massaging the piano keyboard, grand mothers enthralled with their grand daughters. Back in the pickup, peeling an orange, Mike marveled over all that polio victim Mary Held had accomplished and done for others. It was worthy of an Honorary Degree, but beyond him. Professors from his time at Big Al's would be dead. They were dying back then. Professors? Fergus Orr? He was a blade of cut grass on a Junior College lawn. Why not?

* * *

Carnation Nursing Home's activities room was full of residents of various ages, sizes, pigments and shapes playing bingo. A few uninterested in putting poker chips on bingo card numbers wandered the room, stopping from time to time at various tables, nodding approval or disapproval. Not all present paid attention to the heavy lady with the big voice and dimes for the winners. Some residents dozed in wheel chairs, or if restrained in geri-chairs, tugged at unyielding straps. A lady, mouth agape, slumped across a couch. No one paid her any mind. But for slight movement of a finger she'd gone to heaven. Women at the games varied in bodily proportions, some with dumplings of flesh giving away to gravity, others with bony arms and legs thin and sharp as razor blades. A train engineer, a man wearing a railroader's bib overalls and cap, slept in his chair at his table, smiling, his jaw slack and limbs limp, perhaps driving a steam engine through a dreamy tunnel far away from voluntary confinement in twenty-four hour nursing home care. Clothing worn was as colorful as yard sale specials. Residents dressed in wine-reds, yellows, rose and blue dresses or plaid shirts and blue bib overalls as if imitating the haze they saw painted in the trees outside the homes' streaked windows. Noise of strife between elderly ladies reverberated down the long hall the ombudsman walked, observing, listening, smelling, touching. Bitter cries came from rooms where bedfast residents couldn't recall anything but not being in their own beds back home. By a nurse station, a lady in a mechanized wheelchair smiled as if seeing the beatific vision. She glowed with a facial look visitors to Lourdes attributed to Virgin Mary. The lady wore a light blue sweater opened at her waist that revealed a pink dress underneath. The sweater spread over a blue wool blanket covering her braced legs and built up shoes. Her left arm hung like a loose rope, the right hand a hilly road. Her quiet spirit shone beyond her frailties.

"You have the nicest smile," he said by way of introduction. "I'm Mike Brannagh, Ombudsman." He handed her a brochure.

"It's too late in life to buy Omni insurance now," she said, her glow brighter than a search light.

A soft bottom chair next to her wheelchair was pulled over to sit on. Mike gave her the best smile he had, spreading freckles to all sides of wrinkles. "I'm dealing in goodness, not insurance. Never too late to deal goodness. By goodness, I mean I'll be coming here and to other nursing homes to work for residents that may need my help. I'm not employed by any nursing home. Being an Ombudsman means I'm a part of a program carrying out the Older Americans Act, a federal law on behalf of folks in nursing homes. I like to let residents and their families know there is someone who can listen and do something if there is a problem and it seems none of the staff is doing anything about it. I'm here to help residents avoid problems. So I deal in goodness, right?"

"You deal in long wind, for sure," she said, still smiling. "I'm Ethel Lewes."

"Delighted to meet you, Mrs. Lewes."

"It's Miss, but call me Ethel."

"If I did my saintly mother will come back from the grave to hit me across the head with her halo. She taught me to be respectful."

"I like your mother," she said. "At Carnation, nursing staff and nursing Aides as young as high school sophomores, call me Ethel. They talk baby talk to me. They scold me like a child when I drop a spoon or fork." Her head gave a negation. "I don't know where the home can find such poor quality tableware. I thought Asia quit exporting it." Her glow diminished behind a cloud. "But the nursing Aides are all right," she said, her smile rising then setting like the sun, "if they would stay long enough to get to know us. Turnover is high. This very morning a new Aide, a young woman of nineteen or twenty, came into my room to answer my call light. 'I need help to dress,' I said. She said 'dress yourself, being you not a baby.'" Lewes faded to anger. "I told her, 'I'm ninety-one and confined to a wheelchair with non-responsive arms and legs, but if I could dress and bathe myself, I sure wouldn't be in Carnation, young woman'." A twinkle came to her eyes. "This young girl huffed and puffed like a mating frog. She walked right out. I've heard she quit then and there. Can't blame her," she said, now more sorrowful than angry. "I shouldn't have told her off. What young girl wants to change an old wreck like me, or help me dress. Can't blame her at all." Lewes eyes sought out his, and said, "Carnation is typical, all the ladies say."

"How's that?"

"Managers pay nursing Aides poorly. Aides do ninety percent of the things we old people need help with every day, activities of daily living, like getting up out of bed, combing hair, getting dressed, feeding. Little things, but little things are all we have left in this boarding house they call a nursing home, and we need help to do them. Aides are our eyes, arms, legs, ears, fingers. They're paid minimum wages and minimum benefits, if any. A grocery boy told me he gets seven dollars an hour, two and a half more than an Aide gets. Does society value the help Aides give only two-thirds as much as a boy sacking soft goods below cans in paper bags?"

"My Lord, Miss Lewes," Mike said with awe, "were you a labor organizer?"

"I should have been. I was a school teacher whose stubborn pride kept her at it for forty years despite the school board paying less annually than Moose County's sheriff paid his jail guards for keeping the bad boys locked up." Her lips pursed. "I had the notion the community would see to taking care of me for educating their children. They let me down. I spent my last penny trying to stay out of here, but now I'm in a Medicaid nursing home. When management pays Aides the minimum wage, it's an executive decision just as onerous as the school boards' for underpaying teachers. It's based on the fact that the long lived elderly who go broke trying to live alone on an under funded pension and social security have no where else to go but to a Medicaid nursing home. Managers take no pride in keeping nursing Aides. We and Aides are as undervalued as a basement sale." There was no winding down. She'd been ignored too long. "We need to convince government an adequate wage and benefits for nursing Aides frees them from food stamps. If turnover went down from a hundred percent annually to a fifty percent, quasi-stability of nursing staff will do more good for residents than any fancy medicine."

She sighed heavily before her hilly hand hit a lever and her mechanized wheel chair spun slowly. It rolled with a hum on the tiles lining the floor of the long hall with numerous doors.

"Just a minute, Miss Lewes!" He chased after her. She stopped. He went to a knee beside her chair and saw a kindly, but worn out face. "You can write your congressman about the poor pay of Aides."

"How?" she said, lifting her rounded hands.

"From what you've said I'll draft a letter for you. If you agree with the draft, sign it and mail it. If not, rip it up and thrown it away."

She gave him a pat on the head, teacher to pupil. "Never could resist freckled red heads."

"Not much red hair up there, but the freckles linger. I'll get on the letter."

Watching her move away, he wracked his mind to recall if Elder Law Center's Director Jackson ever spoke on lobbying to increase Aide wage rates and benefits to reduce turnover and improve the quality of care. The Center trained him to receive, investigate and attempt to resolve residents problems or complaints, not lobby. Was his mission Elder Law Center's or Lewes? Both. He'd develop approaches to resolve residents' immediate problems as best he could, but what touched residents more negatively than staff shortages? There was more to being an ombudsman than the Center instructed. Carrying out residents' needs included writing letters.

"Who are you?" she said, surging out the doorway of her room like an eel its underwater lair. Her lips kept puckering. "Look! I"m getting fat. Are you that nice druggist who put me on milkshakes?."

"No Ma'am," he said, stopping. He handed her a brochure. "I'm the ombudsman, an advocate for residents." She was hardly fat, a tall five foot ten, mindful of a bamboo stem in an evergreen dress wearing a blond wig. A flattened chest imitated depressed balloons. "A milkshake sounds good though."

She took a moment to look at the brochure. "Neat!" she said. "I'm Arba Sand. I wasn't doing well when I got here. I lost forty-six pounds so my doctor ordered a liberal diet with all kinds of supplements and vitamins. It tasted terrible even when the nurse and dietitian poured in flavor packets. So I refused any more, until they called the druggist. He looked over my medicines and switched me to milk shakes, can you imagine? I"ve gained back twenty pounds. Nurse tells me each milk shake cost about twenty cents compared to a dollar for each supplement, a savings of five to six thousand dollars a year."

"That's wonderful. Quicker than a wink, you'll be back dancing in West Side Story."

* * *

He hustled to get the '83 pickup over to Five Counties offices. The doors weren't yet locked. Within, Lizzy Loam was putting on a burgundy shawl-collar yoke sweater over an oatmeal colored button front polo shirt. "Caught you in time," he said.

"Yes," she said with a smile wide as San Francisco Bay. "Just in time." She moved papers on her desk, found the envelope, and handed it over. "I'm sorry I can't talk, my ride is waiting. Mr Zigmont is in his office."

"Thank you and goodnight." He passed by all the social workers' empty cubicles, down the hall to Ziggie's office in what had been a storeroom. The door was open, light on, the one window up high letting in the last of the day's sunshine. Ziggie didn't look up "Hello, Ziggie."

"Mike! Come in. Did you get my envelope?"

"I have it here, but first let me confirm that I believe FDA quality drugs are being sold on the street, at lest on one corner. I recognized the seller. We talked. He said he had FDA and gave me a couple, but said nothing about his source. I'll get to him again when I find him a job. In the

105

meantime we need to have these pills tested."

"I'll get them tested," Ziggie said, then looked up. "What did you say about a job?"

"A job for an ex-con promising me he'll quit selling dope in exchange for a decent job. If I can get him work, he'll be inclined to lean in my ear. We get along."

"In that case, maybe I have a job for him. I need a man as a Projects escort, to walk the elderly to and from drugstores, groceries, etc. I need a man not intimidated by Project toughs.'

"That's Cooper, for sure," Mike answered, pleased.

"Send him to see me. I'll work out employment details."

"Will do," Mike said as he sat down and opened the envelope, removing a piece of paper to read. He said, "Psychotropics drugs. What?"

Ziggie near as stared. "My source won't give the medical names, fearful they may be incorrect, but on the street they're called 'uppers' and 'downers' In nursing homes, they're administered to some dementia residents. They are also believed to be the drugs being counterfeited."

"Uppers? Downers?" Mike shook his head as if to rid it of an ache. "Once my seller's drugs are tested, maybe they'll confirm your source. At least confirm the street side of your source's info. But I have heard nothing about counterfeit in nursing homes. Nothing about who, where and how, if your source is correct in that regard."

Ziggie answered, "I believe you may find answers by focusing, without creating awareness, on those who run the corporations in those documents I've given you."

"I certainly can look around in those nursing homes but I'll need help. Do you mind if I bring in State Health's surveyor, Fordice. You apparently think very highly of her."

"I do," Ziggie said. .

"Good!" He dialed her. "Mike Brannagh, Belinda.

I'm with Mr Zigmont. He's picked up an extension. "What we are about to tell you is confidential, something we're looking into."

"Told of FDA psychotropics on the street, she said, "Uppers and downers are the street names for anti-psychotic drugs, hypnotics, antidepressants."

Ziggy said, "My source has reason to suspect some of those FDA drugs are being removed from nursing homes and residents are getting counterfeit." He heard her gasp.

"I'm shocked," she said, her breathing slightly labored. "Psychotropic drugs are the most misused for the geriatric population in general, worse if counterfeit. Studies indicate upwards of fifty percent of residents in nursing homes, especially those in dementia, are prescribed at least one psychotropic. Although there's no accepted model for drug related problems in nursing homes, studies indicate upwards of two-thirds of drug regimen reviews find significant problems that are drug related. There are medication errors, contraindications to drug usage, drug reactions, duplications, efficacy, forgetting to administer or over administration. On and on. Yet, all the while drug therapy is the most frequently administered treatment modality. So the likelihood of a drug causing problems is greater than other treatment methods like nutrition, psychosocial or physical activities. The problem should be of concern for doctors and consulting pharmacists. Maybe your source is telling you to look at the drugs doctors prescribe, or what the consulting pharmacists are doing if there are indications of adverse drug reactions. Whatever the source intended, I'm glad you called this to my attention. Drugs are within the scope of surveyors, so I'll have my team spend extra time reviewing charts where the psychotropics have been prescribed, and each resident's reaction to it. None-the-less, if you do hear or see something more, please make me immediately aware. And I you. Thanks for the call."

There were now three looking into counterfeit medicines in the land of last life.

9

"Good morning, Lizzy. Mike here."

"Morning, Mike." There was glee in her tone. "Did you hear about old Horace getting married just three weeks after his wife was buried? Well, as he tells it, he never was much of a body to hold spite!"

"Oh-h-h," he said, a wail.

She ignored the auditory rejoinder. "No messages."

* * *

Next on the day's work agenda was a visit to Candytuft. Entering he saw stuffed animals cuddled residents in quiescent conversations in comfortable lounges and decorative dining alcoves. Rooms with double windows and two beds were on either side of halls' numbers two, three and four, all areas quite tidy with beds neatly made. Inside rooms looked out upon a grassy court yard's white gazebo and green benches etched with dust. The home was a square donut, its parlor a part of hall one. Hall four was an Alzheimer unit. Its door wasn't locked. In a unit housing wanderers, an unlocked door was symptomatic of a staff opposed to restrains. Mobile residents were clothed in current styles clean and neat. A few were dressed as if going to dinner at a fine restaurant. Nursing staff and housekeepers were in abundance, one serving coffee in an alcove to a Hispanic lady caressing a black-baby doll. In the game room, a freckle faced red head recreational therapist was busy guiding her semi-circle of residents through a soft beach ball kicking game. Peals of laughter resounded at a kick well made or a ball surely caught. Recorded music was playing. A pinkish face lady in a green dress stood up tall in the semi-circle of seated residents, her arms outstretched. With full vocal frenzy, her worn out soprano threw random notes at Rogers' and Hammerstein's *'You'll Never Walk Alone.'*

Mike didn't resist walking into the room to join in. They dueted. Perhaps they weren't on high opera's stage, but a rec-room's audience was in awe at the beauty and clarity of the high notes sung to the closing line, softer and softer until the end.

Applause poured like wine in Italy. The soprano's eyes were brilliant. She put her arms around his neck to plant a kiss. Falling considerable short of her facial target on a startled ombudsman, she bussed his Adam's apple instead. Her hug tightened. He thanked her, and to his surprise, needed more than minimal effort to loosen arms.

"Who are you?" said the soprano.

"The ombudsman, Mike Brannagh. I've come to Candytuft to sing with its top soprano."

"Name's Minnie Horn," she said, delighted this stranger praised her in front of her peers. "Call me Minnie," she said sitting down. "What's an ombudnic?"

It was an impossible word! "Beside the pleasure of singing with you, Minnie, an ombudsman is an advocate for residents." He handed her and each resident a brochure, then faced the semi-circle. "The word 'OMBUDSMAN' is spelled out in big letters on the brochure right there." He pointed it out and explained its purpose.

"Thank you. Don't need to call you on any problem here at Candytuft." She smiled coyly. "Might call to sing."

A sickly looking man with eyes that didn't blink, but in clothes ready for a New Year's Ball, came over and tugged on Mike's sport coat. "I'm Alex," he said. "Come with me." He took the advocate's hand with a grasp that matched Minnie the hugger's, and led him to a room in the Alzheimer hall, motioning him to sit in the chair next to the bed. He did, looking into Alex's faded blue eyes in a wrinkled pale face. His pointed chin was covered by a silvery goatee. Sitting on his bed, he said, "Since Mary passed away, it's been sad here."

"I'm sorry." One of the more difficult times in

nursing home residency had to be experiencing the passing of a spouse.

"It wasn't as bad when Dolores or June passed away because I had Mary. Now no one."

Outliving wife and daughters, Mike reflected, was an agony beyond understanding. "Your memory must be full of the great times with your family members."

"Not family," Alex said soulfully. "I roomed in another unit with Dolores, then June, and last Mary."

"You shared a room with them?" Mike said, hoping to avoid obtuseness.

"Not all at one time," Alex said. "First Delores, then June, then Mary. Since then, I moved to area four and George Derfer, the administrator here, won't let Agnes move in with me. He told me Agnes' mind just wasn't up to consenting to sharing a room. That violates my rights, doesn't it?"

Mike felt as if his eye lids were made of cast iron. "You see, Alex," he finally said, sweet talking as best he could, "consent means both parties agree. If Agnes' mind isn't up to agreeing it means she can't consent." The quiet that followed was encouraging. He'd found the right words. Alex appeared to understand.

"Could you," Alex said with feeling, "get me the names of women whose minds are up to agreeing? It's my right to know!" Alex eyes were wider than his glasses.

Mike questioned the diagnosis that placed clever Alex in an Alzheimer's unit. Wishing the man up there might illuminate him, Mike grasped at a response but said with deliberation, "Some where within the law on resident rights," an inspiration was coming on, "is the matter of confidentiality and the right to privacy. Every resident has a right to privacy. If you tell me about yourself, I must by law keep it confidential without your written consent to reveal it to a third party. It's the same for other residents. I don't know if there are ladies up to agreeing to move in

111

with you, but if I did know," he said with emphasis to duck future pursuit of the topic, "without their written consent, I'm legally bound by confidentiality from telling any third party."

Alex was puzzled, his eyes black as beetles.' "What does that mean?"

"It means you're on your own, Alex."

How fried must a mind be before the sexual instinct was extinguished? Would there be others in nursing home care as hot as Alex?

* * *

The little home out the pickup's front window looked quiescent. Were its inhabitants? The three residents visible through Gentian's window were asleep in their wheelchairs just inside the locked double glass door. No staff was visible. A sign on the door advised visitors to enter from the side parking lot, the door opposite his parked pickup. Another sign directed he ring the doorbell. He did. Its clamorous jangle awakened ghosts. One appeared. Through a tiny square of a window it stared hard enough to break him down to confess. The door finally opened.

The nurse beneath a blue wig inside an immense white uniform, legs tree trunks in tennis shoes, stepped outside, and said, "Yes?"

"I'm the new ombudsman, Mike Brannagh," brochure handed over, "here to introduce myself to the council president, and to the administrator."

"Fine," she said. "The council president is Mrs. Goeths. I'm Angie. Go on in." She moved out of his way. The door opened inside to a small hall which crossed a wider hall making a 'T'. A nurse station occupied its corner. Another nurse occupied the desk behind the counter. She was a counterweight to the door opener. "That's Marjorie, the DON," Angie said. "This is the ombudsman, Marj!" They stood the opposite side of the counter from Marj.

"Suppose you're wondering why the doors are locked?" she said, moving right into the story. "A burglar broke in here the day before yesterday. Angie was on night duty working on charts just where I am when she felt a cold breeze and followed it to Clarence's room. She thought he must have opened his window." There was a half grin. "Clarence was a farmer, outside in the fields and barn most of his life. He's ninety-two. It wasn't him. Then Angie saw this middle aged man going through Clarence's dresser drawers."

"I screamed," Angie said, picking up the tale, "and yelled to Tina to call 911. The man came out of Clarence's room and down the hall after me, just when Tina came out of Greta's room. Tina tripped him and he fell down. I hurried back here quick, yelling for Tina to come on because I figured if the burglar didn't get the drugs in the medicine cart, he'd get her. She came running. She pushed me and the med cart into the business office, the room just behind the nurse station, hit the crook with a stapler, rushed in and locked the door. He pounded on it while I called 911. Tina was yelling as loud as she could and got so mad she grabbed scissors and wanted at him. I wouldn't let her go. As long as he was pounding on the door, he wasn't hurting any patient. He took off when the cops' siren cut through the night. I gave them his description. They went after him, but didn't catch him."

The thought the burglar was involved in obtaining street drugs for sale crossed Mike's mind, but the incompetency of the burglar quashed it.

"I moved Angie and Tina to the day shift for a while," Marjorie said, "until the police find the burglar. Angie's description was so good, they'll make an arrest. They figured the burglar is a known drug user. Here's Tina now. Tina, this is the ombudsman. He works for residents' rights."

She could have played center for a basketball team,

or modeled tall Aides' clothing. Fine boned and slender, her face porcelain paleness, black eyebrows arched and night dark hair gave her the look of a model. "Please to make your acquaintance," she said with the drawl of a Kentuckian. The gap of a missing front tooth matched her hair coloring. It didn't distract from her good looks. "Scared me near to slivers," she said, "then fired me up, his pounding on the door like to wake everybody and me just after getting them settled for the night."

"Glad the cops got here first," Marjorie said, "or the burglar would have sued us for Tina's cutting off something. Mr. Quinn, our administrator, has been coming in nights since the burglary, staying all night. He's got his video camera ready; won't bring a gun, but he's got alarm buttons rigged to the police. He's brought a hammer too. Silas, he's our maintenance man, put temporary stops on every window. Can't open them more than four inches up. Fire Marshall okayed it. Police hang around now like we were a downtown donut shop. So Cook whips up a batch three times a day." Marjorie patted her stomach. "Better donuts than downtown."

Mike was escorted to the council president's room. He knocked on the open door. It raised bright raisin size eyes from her knitting. Her hands were time worn, wrinkled. A white dress had a prune on its shoulders. The prune had roses for lips, a nose the color of a pine cone. "May I come in, Mrs. Goeths?" There was an approving nod. He walked in, pulled over her roommate's chair and sat beside her. A ball of orange yarn, bright enough for a hunter's cap, was on the desk beside her. A glove, a work in progress, was stuck with a small harpoon as long as a new pencil.

She studied the big form that knew her name. Her small eyes sparkled. Her mouth worked up a smirk as he made himself right to home. His red thatch and a face with an expanse of snow broken up by two blue ponds above a

114

children's ski slope suggested he was a kindly soul, though big enough to wrestle a garbage truck.

"I'm Mike Brannagh, ombudsman. I visit and work for residents in nursing homes."

"You a preacher? Never saw a preacher so pale all over as you!"

"Probably never saw any one so wide, either!"

"A funny man?" she said. "Heard this one? Preacher said to me and Goeths, 'forgive and forget!' I came back next prayer meeting and said, 'Preacher, it don't work, this forgiving and forgetting'. Preacher said, 'why not?' I said. 'I'm always forgiving and Goeths is always forgetting.'"

Mike let out a joyous hoot. Composed, he said, "Reminds me of the time at a church picnic and dance when I said to the guy sitting at the next table, 'Is that fat high school girl, the one wearing a dress made of a yellow shower curtain, making eyes at you or me?' He said, 'I'll ask her. She's my daughter.'"

Goeths let out a yelp like to be heard clear up to the dining room. "You're mouth wanders into deep holes, I reckon, but you're all right. Going start knitting you a pair of gloves soon as I come back from eating. I want to see you glow in the dark." She lifted herself to her feet, displacing a minimum of horizontal and vertical space. "Still can walk with the best of them. Walk with me." She looked up at him.

"Alright, but together we'll look like a mouse with a moose." They laughed all the way down the hall to the dining area. Ten tables, each with places set for four, were decoratively set, a vase with fresh flowers on each, cloth napkins and china, like dining at a fine restaurant. Soft church music provided background atmosphere. Aides and nurses served with the finesse of trained waiters. It was an experience, not a meal. "What's the occasion, Mrs. Goeths?"

115

"Occasion? Oh! You mean the place settings and flowers? Mr. Quinn won't have it no other way," she said, beaming.

Mike helped her to her seat.

He left Gentian, an oasis in a desert.

10

Sad and partly naked, bushes at roadside rustled as the pickup's tail wind stimulated them before dawn broke. Winds whirled falling leaves against the windshield. Weird tunes out of the north gave notice winter's sword wasn't far behind Fall. Darker and darker, clouds shadowed the highway to Jocko's Place in Oldtown. Mike parked the '83 on Big Al Street and crossed the road. Jocko and Millie awaited. Millie was prettier under the street light than in the dim light of the BBQ. A navy-blue coat was unbuttoned, opened, revealing a side-buttoning blue skirt and a blazer with Native blanket designs. Her white blouse's french cuffs were closed with silver concha. Black boots were pull-ons. She was as smooth looking as a calm sea. "Good morning, Millie; Jocko."

"Good morning, Mike,' Jocko said. "It's so early, not another car in sight."

"Wise to go early." He went into the back seat of Jocko's car, Millie in the front. "Ready to talk to Fanny Brown?"

"Ready," Millie said.

Head lights cut cones over inner-city streets through the darkness under shattered street lights. Nothing roamed the sullen streets of the East Side, not a bus, a delivery truck or a cop's car. Winos and hoodlums, like blood sucking bats, had crashed before the club of day light.

Jocko's eyes looked into the rear view mirror, as he said, "what we going to say, seeing Reverend Yard told you Fanny was afraid?"

Mike had an approach worked out. "Millie will go up to the door and tell Fanny who you are, why you're with her, then tell of me. I'll wait in the car."

"Maybe she's not home," Jocko said

"I doubt she's working a night shift," Mike said, "at

least in a nursing home because she was fired as a Certified Nursing Aide. Lancaster probably wrote dirt in her personnel file."

"You know what?" Millie said. "That's just what nursing home administrators do to cover themselves. Fire the Aide, the social worker, the housekeeper, a nurse. Dump on them."

"Fanny's getting her fanny kicked, ain't she?" Jocko said "Think she'll listen?"

"Don't know," Mike said. "We'll find out soon enough."

Morning's light revealed a single story house, quite worn. Front porch wood and clapboards needed white paint A screen-door was where a storm door should have been, but someone was caring for the little place like caring for a feisty great-grandma on her last crutch not yet ready for a Gospel-choir's farewell. Lee pulled over to the curb to park. He got out and hustled around the car to open the passenger side door. "Let me help you, Millie."

"Don't recollect when last a man held open a door for me."

"Then you've never met a real man," he said. "Ain't no less a man doing for others."

Mike rolled his eyes. "Hey Jocko, do for others by letting Millie go on up to knock on the front door."

Millie smiled, took Jocko by a hand, and lead him up the porch steps. She rapped twice.

A kitchen light turned on. "Who that?" a frightened voice said. Its head peeked from out behind an opening kitchen door.

"Miss Fanny? It's Millie, social worker from Lobelia Nursing Home come to visit. I have a man with me."

"Miss Mary send you?" she said, standing in the light of the open kitchen door.

"No! Shango Golah sent us."

"Why he done that?" she said, her voice softening. She came forward from the kitchen, its door swinging back and forth in shorter half-circles, fanning the electric light. She stopped by the front door and peeked through its glass. She was wrapped like a Taco in an Army blanket.

"Mr. Golah asked me to bring a man, the one out in the car, to come talk to you."

"What the man want to talk on?"

"On what Mr. Golah did to his room mate, Miss Fanny," Millie said.

"Don't know," she said, opening the front door, peering cautiously through the screen. "My," she said, seeing Lee, "that man bigger than a power plant coal pile! Who he be?"

"He's Mr. Lee. Works down to Jocko's Place."

"He do?" Fanny said, sudden irritation evident. "Mr. Lee, why don't folks down to Jocko's tell a body they ain't a hiring stead of doing nothing with her application?"

"Well Jocko?" Millie said, amused.

"Miss Fanny, I don't know what to say, except I'm Jocko."

"You be Jocko? My, my, come about a job?"

"Come about the man in the car talking with you on Shango Golah," he said.

"That right?" Disappointment flooded her words. "Don't know what going to happen to me." She pushed the screen door open and backed out of their way for entry. "Tell the man out there, come on in. All of you." Lee waved to Mike. He hopped out of the car and joined them inside the house. Fanny closed the door after them. Inside might have had ten thermal degrees more than outside. "Gas company upped and cut off the gas. I sleep in the kitchen. Heat on the electric stove. Leastwise, till the Electric Company cut it off tomorrow. Come on to the kitchen. Got me some chairs in the kitchen." There was an absence of furnishings on the living room floor but on its

119

walls were hung pen and pencil sketches of black field hands, tired, sad and troubled tenant farmers, their children around the cabins, draft animals straining, folks picking cotton under a blazing sun, a home place.

"Miss Fanny," Millie said, "where's your furniture?"

"Here and there. Here at the pawn shop be my lamps, there at the salvage store be my couch. Since Miss Mary fired me and no work, sold them. Kept my place till now. Ain't never lived so fine."

"Are these sketches your work, Miss Fanny?" Lee asked.

"Yes sir! I be away from home, bring home here. That be my Momma," she said, pointing to woman in a rocking chair on a cabin's porch. Momma looked an antique woman. Bare headed, her thin body wore a long black dress. She had screened her eyes against the light of a dying evening. Her face was incomparably sweet. "That be Momma's cabin."

"Your sketches are art, Miss Fanny!" Lee said. "You should hold an exhibition."

"What be that?"

"Have a showing to the public at Jocko's Place," he said. "Sell some. There's good money to be made."

Fanny stepped away as if struck. "Won't sell my Momma, my people." Little water falls fell from each eye.

"Didn't mean nothing wrong, Miss Fanny," he said.

Fanny fled from the living room to her kitchen, its solid wood door swinging, thrown open, it hit a cabinet and ricocheted. They followed after her. There were metal folding chairs, an electric stove with one red burner, a half size refrigerator, cabinets with a few plates, saucers and cups; a place setting for one and other kitchen utensils on the counter. The white enameled kitchen sink had two sides. Floor to ceiling, wall to wall, counter tops and sink, were spotlessly clean. Fanny sat herself down on an Army cot and pulled a khaki blanket around her.

"You must miss your Momma a great deal, Miss Fanny. Jocko doesn't want you to sell Momma's drawing," Millie said softly, giving Lee a bold wink to let him know this talk was restricted, woman to woman. "What Jocko means to say is your sketches are so good, they remind him, me, of our people, our ancestors who came from the deep South to seek their fortunes in the North. We should never forget our History. Your sketches bring our History to life. Jocko and I, many others would love to look at your sketches every day of our lives."

"You would?" Fanny's shoulders uncurled from the khaki blanket. She was young with a cranium mindful of a child's elongated and oval head, its widest portion just below the ears. Her forehead was full, flattening to the eyebrows. The bones of her face, small. Skin carried the color of a black olive, hair blacker still, eyes brown as rust maple leaves. She was quite pretty, an innocent's glamour, the glow of spring on her face, suns in her eyes.

"They are wonderful, Miss Fanny," Mike said. He saw a child with eyes bigger than caves. Fanny Brown? Golah's sweet little brown skin girl! Would a Hearing Officer believe her testimony? Within the legal presumption of competence, a child witness under seven was presumed incompetent to testify in court. From seven through the thirteenth year the presumption faded with the child's alertness, and was lost, barring mental retardation or mental illness, at age fourteen. Brown looked no more than twelve, and as appealing as a poster-child.

"You be the man what wants to talk on Mr. Shango?"

"I am. May I sit down?"

"Yes Sir, you may." Lizzy and Jocko sat down alongside him.

"I'm going to turn on this tape recorder, Miss Fanny. Tell me about Loren, about what happened that day between you and him, and between Loren and Shango," he said softly.

Fanny puckered, looking more the child than ever. She looked at him, then to the others. Satisfied she was safe with Jocko and Millie near by, she said, "I be in the hall by Mr. Loren's room, who be in his bathroom. I be hearing him call, 'Fanny, come help'. I do. Mr. Shango, he be by his bed, don't so much as say, 'how do, Fanny'. Mr. Loren be on the toilet saying, 'Fanny, help me off the potty'. Tears formed in her eyes. "Mr. Loren be grabbing on me where decent man shouldn't. He be rubbing warm poo-poo from his hands on me. I be saying 'please stop Mr. Loren', but he won't. He be getting up by himself; strong, pull on me. He say 'come on girl, gonna get me some'. He be pulling off my pants. I be hollering 'let me go', he be pushing me down on his bed. He climbs on pulling his thing, putting it ...." She didn't say. "He be moaning." She looked at Brannagh. "Then Mr. Shango whopped Mr. Loren's a'gin his head. I be hearing Mr. Loren cough like to die. I be getting free. I see Mr. Shango be holding a busted radio. Mr. Loren, he be bleeding on the head. I get on my pants, run, get the nurse." Fanny reached for Millie's hand.

"Did you tell the nurse and Administrator Mary Lancaster what you've just told me?" Mike asked.

"I be telling Miss Mary. She say I be doing wrong to Mr. Loren. She sent me on home saying I better hush my mouth or she be telling the white man's sheriff I be touching Mr. Loren's thing. I ain't never done nothing wrong she say I do."

"I believe you," Mike said, consoling her. "Were there any other residents or nursing staff who saw Loren grab you, or heard him say, 'come on girl, gonna get me some?"

"There be folks in the hall but don't rightly know who. The nurse be knowing what hurt Mr. Loren."

122

"Fanny, since you've been gone from Palace, have you seen or heard from any of the other Aides?" There was a negative nod. "Okay," he said. "At Mr. Shango's hearing, I'll ask you to tell it all over again to the Hearing officer. Will you do it?"

Before she could answer, Jocko broke in. "I'll pick you up and stay with you, Fanny."

"Then I do it," she said to smiling faces.

Millie said, "What's this about cutting off your electricity?"

"Ain't got no more money, Miss Millie."

"Well, I have," she said. "Would you like a roomie? Me? Please let me move in with you. I need a place. I'll pay all the bills, past and present. I have furnishing and things to spare."

"It be true, Miss Millie?"

"It be true, Fanny. I'll gather my things and move in here before the day's out."

Fanny leapt off her cot like leaping for joy. She was thin as a tomato pole and dressed in Salvation Army finery. "Ain't got no clothes but these, Miss Millie. Hocked what I had."

"I got enough to open a clothing store," she said. "We'll share mine. I'll need to take in a stitch or three for some one so tiny. Let's get to it, Jocko."

* * *

Mike moved on to Garland Nursing Home, another of Nursing Home Management's facilities. It lolled on top of a knoll in sight of the town of Rock's sewage treatment plant on one side, affording the home's owners no drainage problems, and a fertilizer plant the other side, its smokestack residue assuring perpetual green grass late into the Fall. No secretary at the front office, but a brochure was left, as if a salesman's calling card. The lounge's TV was blaring. Eight middle-age visitors encapsulated in jackets attended to a program's jabbering idiot while elders dozed at their sides. One of the somnolent was as hairless as a fish in bib overalls. A woman's puffy eyebrows matched her pink sweat suit. A woman was awake and dressed in her Sunday best red dress but days late for church. For her, movements of a gray squirrel outside the room's plate glass window was infinitely more interesting than talk show performers.

A nurse station, a sweeping desk below a right angled wooden bar, strategically bisected the northwest corner of the residential wings. Five nursing staff in white frocks, pants and shoes circled a RN in a white dress wearing a cap sporting a wide blue 'M.' She was as rigidly fixed to her chair as a screw, but studiously writing into a clinical record. The circle of onlookers' eyes were on the scrivener. Wheel chair residents, a few pushed by visitors, rolled up and down the hallways.

A slim hipped man with big shoulders stood at the window in a residents' room. He was counting, "one, two, three."

"Hello. May I come in?" Mike waited for the invitation.

"Come in," said someone else from behind a drawn bed curtain.

The counter was up to, "eight, nine," as Mike walked toward him. In the third bed, the one behind the curtain next to the window, was what appeared to be an emaciated escapee from a prisoner of war camp, blankets piled thick and stuffed right up to his neck. "I'm the ombudsman, Mike Brannagh." He handed a brochure to the pinched face man in the bed.

"It's a waste giving one to Vito," pinched face said. "He just counts trees, cars, leaves, snow drops, streaks of lightning. He talks only to count all day and half the night. Used to work in a maximum security prison. Must have taken the count every two minutes. Drove him nuts. Driving me nuts." He paused to look at the brochure and again at the visitor. "Brannagh? I remember you from somewhere! Everything about me is going down hill except my memory. It was the best on the Force. I remember! Brannagh! The Francois County Jail Director!"

"Yea," he said, caught off guard. Who was this? The names on the room door were Vito, Stan and Marion. Not a clue there. "You know me from the jail?"

"I remember you from the prescription drug fiasco. What was it? Eighteen, nineteen years ago! Once, back then, I was Detective Sergeant Marion Kap of the Oldtown Police. When I retired I went to work doing investigations for Francois County's Prosecutor. The next prosecutor had no place for me, so I moved out to Bovine County to read crime stories to my grandkids until cancer forced me into this place. What a bore that drug investigation was."

"A bore? Not while I was waiting to go before the Grand Jury."

"No, you wouldn't be bored," he said, sincerity in his sound, "but it turned out boring as hell for me. You see, I wanted you as much for drugs as the Governor wanted blame cast on you and the Attorney General for parole kickbacks! I figured you for another political appointee taking a cut. I took an oath to keep investigative confidences but the Prosecutor should have told you the outcome before you read about it in Inner-city News. I should have told you, oath or not. I thought of it again when I saw your name in the newspapers about the parole kickback."

"Told me what?" he said, intrigued beyond belief.

"Every single statement I took from a jail correctional officer said, 'if anyone was clean from bringing prescription drugs in, you were.'"

"Faint praise if any of them were dirty."

"They weren't dirty, that's the point. Don't be cynical. There's more to it," he said. "Subpoenaed by the Grand Jury, fear of contempt or no, Inner-city News nor

Reverend Coppin Yard would reveal their source about how it learned a pharmacist brought drugs into the jail. Well, you know now, and I'm glad for my part in getting the truth out. I just hope the long departed prosecutor, Tony Taker, as deeply as he must have descended, doesn't have enough influence with the devil to cause an earth quake to swallow me live."

Mike blinked. "Your part?" Was Kap the guy behind the court house?

"Yea, my part. How glad I am," Kap said, "that you come in from out of the past. I needed to tell you this. Not my wife, nor Reverend Yard had the vaguest idea I was the one who set it up. You see, there was remodeling going on in the Prosecutor's wing, and the construction foreman and I were buddies. He had night access. So we worked it out so he could get copies of the pertinent files and get them to Reverend Yard. As they say, 'the rest is history.'"

"You set it up?"

"We did. Over the years I thought of getting in touch with you, but this illness got to me first and took me down hard. It isn't about to let up. Time left isn't long."

"Your cancer is that progressive?"

"I can't get up anymore. One of those little girls who works here has to come in and change me. Embarrassing. I came into life bed bound and diapered by my mother. I'm going out bed bound and diapered by women younger than Mom was."

"Your mind isn't diapered."

"Maybe, but my body is. It survived the depression, fought the Second World War, used the GI Bill, graduated from College, spent twenty-five years on the Police Department and eight years working investigations in the Prosecutor's office. I retired expecting to live to see at least one grand kid get as old as the little girls who work here."

"They'll hear how you earned the respect and

admiration of citizens for fighting the war, serving them on the Police force and will know the God that created your temple and gave it breath and spirit will welcome you home. Not a bad admiration society that." Mike was deeply moved. He'd anticipated sorrowful moments while with resident's whose life's flame was flickering in the land of last life, but not with one who did a good deed for him. It was joy he sensed.

* * *

On the road to Mint Nursing Home, another of Nursing Home Management's operations, the thought it might be as marginal as Garland, Palace, Grass Lake, Willow and Lobelia bothered him. How much power had Dale Unge that the surveys written by impartial and dedicated state surveyors could be rewritten to minimize deficiencies?

Entering the facility, just inside, there was an astigmatic jockey with a rummy nose, but dressed up, who wore an oxford white buttoned down shirt, a hand made imported tie with geometric print and light olive designer slacks. His cardigan was two tone brown. He appeared to be lying in wait or on perpetual guard duty in a sentry box standing at attention at the castle's drawbridge. "Welcome to Mint. I'm Elmer Salol. Administrator. May I help you?" His voice was as cool as the draft of outside air from the opened door. A scent of marshmallows wafted.

"Mike Brannagh, ombudsman," he said, putting out his hand to shake the hand of another of Nursing Home Management's administrators.

"Here on a complaint?" Salol didn't wait for an answer. "Do you need to see me or any of my nursing staff?" He sounded cooperative, if the manner of biting his words and contorting his lips were discounted. His teeth grated like Arctic ice flows against the Titanic.

"No, but thank you. Just an introductory visit." Partially true. He was to investigate a mail referral from

127

Betty Zeel who'd written she was the granddaughter and guardian of Babo Zeel, an eighty-two year old resident in the Alzheimer unit. For reasons unknown, Babo was demolishing her room's curtains and other artifacts of decoration within her reach. Betty offered to replace the destroyed items but when Salol declined, Betty feared he would ultimately put Babo out.

"Feel free to go anywhere," Salol said.

Mike pushed the Alzheimer Unit's electronic door lock. It opened one side of the heavy green steel double fire doors. He walked into a hall with the feel of a tunnel. Every other overhead light in the white acoustical tile ceilings was turned off. The effect was stripes across the floor like those across Belty cattle. Healthy looking men and women, bodies cloaked in worn-out clothes, eyes with thousand yard stares reminiscent of GI combat infantrymen coming off of Korea's front line, walked in files up and down the north and south corridor going somewhere, but not getting there. At the meeting spot of three short halls, a chicken appeared to have pooped a nurse station. Within the white circular station were checkers, black and white faces of nursing staff whose elbows hung on to their desks for dear life. There were residents on all sides of the nurse station, fifteen in wheelchairs, four restrained to geri-chairs. Clothing worn was the color of unwashed gravel. Faces carried sunken cheeks. Eyes bore the frost of psychopathology. Chatter was incessant, whether to relatives, friends, wives, husbands, sons or daughters playing on movie screens in their minds. They were in a unit where faded yellow walls and pale yellow wax build up on floor tiles of bright colors. A woman, with a very thin high-rise gentleman, held his hand while wandering around, the slightly limping lady in a fashionable red dress and blue bootie house slippers. His left arm curled upward to his chin. He wore a blue plaid shirt with a red and white checker handkerchief in its left pocket. His pants and slippers were brand new. The limping lady sang, 'merrily we roll along.'

"Can I help you? I'm Mrs. Jay, charge nurse," she said to Mike. She was a huge woman, round as a farm silo, short as a barrel. Her dark brown face was as large as the Presidential seal on a national convention's podium.

"Yes you can. I'm the ombudsman, Mike Brannagh. I'd like to visit Babo Zeel."

Jay raised her right arm and pointed a ballpoint pen, her short white sleeve retreating. An upper arm's flesh waved a salute. "That's Babo in the geri-chair. She's the one in the black sweatshirt." Pulling the chart, Jay read out loud an entry 'about ripping down curtains and destroying personal items: a stuffed teddy bear and a family picture.' "I'll remove her restraint for you." Jay grunted while her legs sought leverage to elevate her massive remainder from the chair. A matched pair of schooners on high seas, fleshy cheeks bobbed each step she took the short distance. She unbuckled belts that had lashed the resident down. The chair was pushed to its forward position. Her feet touched floor tiles and Jay assisted her to two feet, walking her until steady, then sat her on a black plastic chair. Having done, Jay returned to her desk chair. Her head ducked out of sight.

Mike sat in the chair next to Babo, a bent woman with stringy gray hair clusters twisted into tornado funnels. Her head pressed into her chest. A black sweat suit paraded laundry name-tags sewn around the back of the neck-line and pants top as if laundry workers wouldn't accept less than five per clothing item.

"I just got loose," she said not lifting her head. "Have you come to tie me up again?"

"I haven't, Mrs. Zeel. I've come to find out why you were tied up."

She raised her head. Front line trenches dug during a life of care for husband, children and grandchildren ran an expressive face. Eyes as gray as confederate uniforms were glazed. Over medicated? "They did it," she said in a voice calling out of the depths, "because Andrew peed on the curtains. Smelled worse than a diaper pail. I pulled them down." A tear fell. "Betty's the one who dumped me here to be locked up." Babo's fist doubled. "Keep my grand daughter away." She arose and walked over to and sat again on the geri-chair, then leaned way-back to kick her spidery legs at a ceiling too high to strike. Her head bobbed like a woodpecker's on a tree trunk. Soon she wore out, apparently groggy from a psychotropic drug, quieted and napped.

Mike wondered if her agitation was an adverse reaction to a counterfeit medicine? He couldn' tell. Perhaps Fordice's Survey team might find something indicative in residents' records. Babo's clothing was clean, hair combed, tennis shoes new. Staff were tending well to her care. Or was it grand daughter Betty? Since she was in a geri-chair nothing else had happened, nor could it, restrained as she was. Absent a medical doctor's order, a restraint wasn't necessary for her medical treatment.

Mike returned to Nurse Jay. "I have Babo's guardian's written consent to see her record." Jay handed it over. There wasn't an order in the record though a Doctor Chevey's clinical diagnosis indicated probable Alzheimer's. Dementia had been established by a clinical examination, documented by a mini-mental test and confirmed by neuropsychological tests. He found deficits in a couple of her areas of cognition, a progressive worsening of memory but no disturbance of her consciousness. There was an absence of systematic disorders or other brain diseases that in and of themselves could have accounted for her deficits in memory and cognition. The diagnosis was supported by deterioration of functions like perception, impaired activities of daily living, altered patterns of behavior. Laboratory results from lumbar punctures and an electroencephalogram, EEG, of brain wave patterns further supported the diagnosis. Dr. Chevey was also Babo's protector from polypharmacy, too many drugs, but nothing in the record except the recent order for the psychotropic drug indicated he'd seen the living chemistry experiment within the last sixty days.

Mike felt a greater degree of comfort reading the minimum data set, MDS, for nursing home resident assessment and care screening, primarily because the form was completed by a nurse, not an esoteric medical practitioner who specialized in aboriginal penmanship. A nurse, shortly after admission, had summarized a number of facets about Babo's functional levels, cognitive and behavioral problems, special care needs, skin condition, nutritional status and psychosocial well-being. Identified problems triggered more detailed documentation called resident assessment protocols, RAPS. MDS and RAPS were the bases for nursing staff care plans. These he could read and understand. If the goals determined achievable were charted as the law required, there would be a flow sheet. Progress, or lack of it, could be seen at a glance. With the staffs' own data, an ombudsman could argue for an improved care plan, but where were the quarterly updates? None in the chart! Deficiencies loomed where a home's care plan wasn't updated. The present care plan seemed no more than putting a resident under restraint in a geri-chair, plus her physician, from a distance, prescribing a psychoactive drug.

He turned to Social Worker Notes, hoping she might have gotten to know more about Babo, but found little. After the curtain incident, instead of a restraint, the social worker might have involved Babo in more activities out of the unit instead of unending residency with those of similar diagnoses. Babo's plight was gist for State Health, but Nurse Jay and the social worker, not Dr. Chevey or Salol would be the sacrificial lambs. It raised a twinge.

Mike would relieve it.

"Mrs. Jay," he said, "there are no care plans, or MDS updates in Babo's chart and I can't find the MD's order for the restraint.' He handed her the chart.

Her head popped up, eyes wider and redder than rising suns. After quick contemplation, she said, "Must in the DON's office. She told me of the restraint."

"If you say so, but all of them are supposed to be written and in the chart. If State Health takes a peek at this chart as it's now constituted, the charge nurse, not the DON, would be doing a ballet out the front door. It would be helpful if the charge nurse discovered the absence of any MD's order for a restraint, and charted such, freeing the resident from punishment in the form of a restraint just because she pulled down curtains soaked in some male resident's urine."

"I'll talk to the DON," Jay said, acknowledging the protective hint. Yet she opened the chart to 'Nurse Notes' and charted she'd found no MD order for the restrain, thus removing Babo from the geri-chair.

There was a phone call to make. Mike found a public phone. He inserted a quarter and dialed. Three rings. "Hello. This is Mike Brannagh calling for Betty Zeel." He informed her he found no medical order for a restraint, that he believed Babo was restrained for disciplinary reasons, contra to law. He suggested she find the services of a different MD, another consulting pharmacist; and that she come to the home this day to copy Babo's entire chart; that State Health see it, particularly because of the absence of an updated MDS or care plan. By copying the chart, Mint's DON and Administrator would know she was deeply involved after the ombudsman's visit, with the probable result a sharp improvement in Babo's quality of care.

"I'll do it," Betty Zeel said.

11

"Hello Lizzy, Mike here."

"Good morning, Mike. I heard you sung to Alzheimer's residents at Palace."

"I imagined there would be a lot of complaints!"

"No, but as Artemus Ward said, and I paraphrase, 'When you're sad, sing, and then others are sad with you.'"

"Oh my. Any messages?"

"A Marti Nelsen wants you to call her about fund raising in a nursing home. And, Mr Zigmont wants to talk to you, but he's late this morning. Will you call back shortly?"

"I will." He wrote down Nelsen's name and number. "Ms. Marti Nelsen please, Mike Brannagh, Ombudsman calling."

"Thank you for returning my call, Mr. Brannagh. My mother, Olivia Haughy, is a resident at Buttercup. I'm vice-president of the Family Council there. Let me tell you our problem. Mr. Rode, the administrator, wants to have a fund raiser and use the money for Christmas gifts for staff. It struck me if mother or I didn't give, staff wouldn't pay mother much attention, not that they do now. Besides, isn't it wrong to collect money for staff from residents on Medicaid? They're only allowed to keep thirty dollars a month as it is. But I sat there like a button on a blouse and said nothing."

"There is a regulation that covers it, Ms. Nelsen," he said, opening the book. "Get a pencil ready to copy it, it's long and Rode should know it. It's section 483.12 (7) (d) (3) (ii) of the Federal rules.. This regulation says: 'the home must not charge, solicit, accept or receive any gift, money, donation or other consideration as a precondition of a continued stay; but, the home may solicit, accept or receive a charitable, religious or philanthropic contribution from an organization or a person unrelated to a Medicaid eligible resident, but only to the extent it is not a condition of a continued stay in the home.' The way I read it, it means Rode shouldn't have a fund raiser involving Medicaid residents or the relatives of Medicaid residents. He'll probably claim the fund raiser is unrelated to a precondition of a continued stay, and may be sincere in his claim. Then again, you were there and didn't hear it that way."

"Oh, I'm so glad there's a rule on that," she said, but sounding quite anxious. "He has posters all around the halls and this is such a delicate matter. If there is a resident or family member who doesn't feel she's walking on banana peels every time he does something like this, it's someone with dementia. Thank you for the information on the rule. I've written it down. Somehow, I'm going to find my courage and bring it up to the Family Council. Goodbye."

Mike was impressed over her courage. She didn't ask him to do it.

* * *

Time to call Ziggie. He dialed Five Counties Organization on Aging.

"How may I help you?"

"Mike here, Lizzy. Ziggie get in?"

"Mr Zigmont is in. I'll connect you."

"Hello. Mike. You asked me about a job for an ex-con?"

"I did, for one in particular"

"There's a need for someone, maybe an ex-convict, who isn't afraid to go into the Oldtown Projects to pick up old folks and take them to and from the Free Clinic, grocery and so on. There have been muggings for prescription drugs, food stamps. Folks are even afraid to come back alone to their apartments."

"The one I have in mind meets that qualification.

134

He grew up in the Projects. Did time for dealing drugs there. Told me he's out of dealing, but it would be wise your sources check his rap sheet. His name is Lou Cooper." Mike filled in all know details on Cooper.

"Hold on a minute." Ziggie spent a few minutes on the phone with his Police contact. "Not wanted or suspected."

"Copper has a lady and a baby now, seems pleased over it. Wants to support them. He probably knows many of the folks afraid to come and go from their apartments. I'll ask him to call you for an appointment. I'll call him. Be back soon." He dialed.

"Hello," a soft voice said.

"Is Lou Cooper in?"

"He be asleep."

"Please wake him, Ma'am. Tell him it's Mike Brannagh. He'll want to talk to me."

"You with Big-dough Benny?"

Big-dough Benny? Oh Lord, Mike realized, he forgot about Mr. Mack, the resident he thought died at Larkspur. Mack asked to see his son Benny, disowned son that was, one last time. "No I'm not, Ma'am. Cooper knows me from the parole office."

"He's done did his parole!" she said, fright in her sound.

"I know. He's a good man. That's why I'm calling. He asked me to help him find a job."

"A job?" she said, her tone rapidly changing, "I go get him."

"This you, Mr. Brannagh?" Cooper said.

"Yea. I got a job lead for you to follow up. Five Counties Agency on Aging is looking for someone to go in and out of the Projects taking old folks to the clinic, the grocery, and back."

"Oh, man!" From the tone, Cooper thought little of it. "That ain't no man's job."

135

"You think not? I was across the street from the Projects the other day and a little girl with a big pistol was about to neuter me for my money, very little at that, when along came somebody to chase her off. Old folks in the Projects are being mugged for their prescriptions and food stamps, cash if they have any, when they leave their apartments. Mugging the elderly is easy. Five Counties needs someone who isn't afraid of muggers, winos, druggies. I figured the job needed a man. Guess I made a mistake calling."

"Hold on, Mr. Brannagh. Me and my big mouth. What I do?"

"Got pencil and paper? Good! Write this down. Mr. Zigmont, Z-i-g-m-o-n-t, the Director. Five Counties main office wants to meet you to look you over. Can't guarantee you'll get the job. If you get it, it's on the straight." He gave the phone number and address.

"Got it, Mr. Brannagh. Thanks man."

"How about a favor in return?"

"Name it, man."

"Where can I find Big-dough Benny?"

"Man, how you find he's the dealer?"

"Nothing to do with dealing. I need to visit with Big-dough about a family matter."

"Big-dough got family? Don't tell him where you got this. I done quit him and he ain't took nice to it. He hangs over to Calvin's on the corner of West and Washington in Aquaville. Them Aquaville studs don't dig me, man. They be talking all that heavy shit on my woman's baby. Follow my drift? Wineheads. Watch you white ass, Mr. Brannagh. And thanks, man. I be after this job like a toilet flushing piss."

Mike gave Ziggie the relevant details.

12

What was the time? Time enough to visit Fergus Orr before going home. The question of a Puella Honorary Degree for Iris' Mary Held could be raised as a cover to slide into any connection the Elder Trippers might have had with today's prescription drug street dealing and his past smuggling. The pickup hustled to a place in Grass Lake's parking lot where a tall evergreen broke the wind. He entered the narrow front hall, crossed the rounded units and knocked on a half-opened door. "Professor?"

"Come in, Mike, and sit on the lawn chair. Why have you come so late? Never mind." He was pleased for the company.

Orr didn't look too scholarly wearing a worn out woolen green sweater over a red-striped dress shirt and purple tie. Tired black trousers were once a part of a suit. White sweat socks and woolen slippers offered warmth.

"By the way, Professor, is Puella's library opened to non students?"

"Not in my time. I doubt if its changed. Why do you ask?"

"I need access to the library's microfilm newspapers to check out the story I was told about a resident in an Aquaville nursing home. Despite polio in her youth, she, without so much as a high school diploma, was quite successful building and running a mechanical engineering business. She made a lot of money. When she had to go into twenty-four hour care, she bought a large interest in the stock of the chain that owns her nursing home. That's been tremendously beneficial for her fellow residents and the staff. Another resident asked me to help him honor her. Her one great grief is the void of a college diploma. He suggested an honorary degree and asked if I could get St. Albertus Magnus to grant her one. I told him I hadn't any influence at Big Al's. Then you came to mind as one who has profound influence at Puella."

"Maybe I do have a little influence," he said with a touch of modesty. "What do you want me to do?"

"First, if I can't use the library, if you would go for me and check out Aquaville and Door County newspapers for articles on Mary Held, I would be very grateful."

"I will," he said. "Puella is in the inter-library exchange system. I expect if Mary Held has been written up, I'll find out."

"Next, dear Professor, once there's impartial and written evidence to support her accomplishments, might you put it to Puella's President that honoring a woman a success like Mary Held would be an inspiration to the ladies in attendance at that esteemed Junior College."

"Honorary Degrees are difficult to come by, Mike."

"If you think there's no chance at Puella, Professor, maybe I should try Big Al's. Its four criteria for student selection are wealth, wealth, wealth, and a large contribution to the college. I have no idea of Mary Held's current financial position, other than stock which she votes to benefit others in the nursing home. Maybe Big Al's will consider an assignment of her stock holdings in nursing homes sufficient to honor her?"

"You mock the process. It's not that way at all!" he said, annoyed.

"I hope so. Will you take a shot at it?"

"I will," he said, simulating acquiescence. "I'll get the home's van to take me over to Puella. How soon?"

"Soon. If you're as influential as I think you are, maybe Puella will confer the Honorary Degree at the end of the winter semester." Mike changed his mind asking for the name of Elder Tripper's Oldtown druggist. Caution told him not to put too much on the back of the old codger. One thing at a time.

"Rest assured I'll get over to Puella and research the

doings of marvelous Mary Held. Good night, Mike," he said lowly.

"Good night, Professor." He struggled out of the lawn chair, then across the lounge toward the front door hoping stuffed green pepper wasn't guarding it.

13

Mike's appointment at Five Counties to meet with Ziggie wasn't until 10 AM, time enough for the ombudsman to compose the letter for Carnation's Miss Lewes. Her spirited remonstrance gave resident credence that minimal staffing standards and pitiful wages paid to certified nursing Aides were the causes of the critical problem of nursing staff turnover and shortages:

Congressman Richard Rial
Office of the Congressman
Washington D. C.

Carnation Nursing Home
Moose County

Dear Congressman Rial,
Numerous times and over my many months of residency in Carnation Nursing Home, I've had discussions with Ms. Tillie Versal, our administrator. I've said, 'where are all the certified nursing Aides gone to'? She said, 'unemployment's so low in the county, and Medicaid won't let me pay much, so we get very few new applications'. Then she says, 'we're staffed at state standards'. She doesn't mention the State's nurse staffing standard is a minimum standard. I've argued with her that the main reason Carnation's owners should be in the nursing home business is for quality care which depends on a sufficient number of certified nursing Aides, reasonably well paid. Why? They do ninety percent of the work we residents need. She wouldn't let me check the payroll to see the number of certified nursing Aides actually on the job each shift. She said it was Corporate policy. I would need to see the company's officers but Carnation's Corporate officers are as accessible to me as North Korea is to nuclear bomb

inspectors.

Why the problem over sufficiency of certified nursing Aides? Rules! I read the Federal and State rules the library got for me. Carnation's owners aren't dumb. They take note of the vagueness in Federal rules and refuge in State rules. Federal rules say Carnation must have sufficient nursing staff to provide nursing care to all residents in accordance with resident care plans. What's sufficient? Federal rules don't say. Who writes residents' care plans? Under the direction of Carnation owner's, the Director of Nursing and her staff does! I do love the nurses and Aides who stay on the job, for some months, but not more than a few. God bless those who stay for they are few in number. They are caring people in the writing of our care plans but often the Director of Nursing is limited by Tillie to no more Aides than the state's minimum standard, and that rule is a mathematical calculation. If a resident is at the intermediate care level, she is to have two hours of nursing care daily. Nursing care means all of our care by registered nurses, licensed practical nurses and certified nursing Aides. Aides, as I said, do ninety percent of nursing care. Carnation has one hundred residents in intermediate care. Multiply one hundred by two and the result is two hundred nursing hours. If each member of the nursing staff works an eight hour shift, divide the two hundred hours by eight and you get twenty-five nursing staff, ninety percent Aides, needed over three shifts every twenty-four hours, seven days a week. As most residents are awake during morning shift, Tillie might employ twelve nursing staff at that time; eight in the afternoon; and five during the midnight shift. If there are no call-offs for sickness, the number of nursing staff on each shift are only the number necessary to meet the minimum standard, not the number sufficient to provide quality nursing care in accordance with individual care plans.

Any resident or Aide will tell you the minimum

nurse staffing standard is insufficient, if for no other reason than home health care agencies are keeping out of nursing homes some of the less acutely ill. On the other hand, Doctors and Hospitals, rather than keep the ill in hospitals beyond the time period private insurance and Medicare payments run out, send them to nursing homes. Yet the Federal and State minimum nurse staffing standards for those who need either skilled or intermediate care remain unchanged.

How can we avoid insufficient nurse staffing? Easily! If individual care plans and daily staffing payroll detail are reviewed bimonthly by State Health, and the home fails to meet the number of nursing hours required by the minimum standards, then Medicaid and Medicare should have legal authorization to recapture that part of the per diem paid to Carnation that wasn't used to meet the state's minimum nurse staffing standard. If there were a recapture of that part of the reimbursement not paid because of staff shortages, Carnation's owners will profit less. They may take notice that the reason for being in the nursing home business, (they agreed to the minimum standards when they entered the Medicare- Medicaid contract), is quality care.

If Federal nurse staffing standards continue to adhere to vagueness as if it were an infallible health doctrine, and if the State does not rewrite the minimum nurse staffing standard, or if there is not a recapture, Carnation's owners will never exceed the minimum. They will continue to profit to the maximum.

Misery will be residents' last companion.
Yours Truly,
Ethel Lewes, Carnation Resident.

* * *

Invited in and offered a seat, Mike sat opposite Ziggie, the director pulling out of a desk drawer a large manila envelope, and from it, a pile of newspaper clippings.

142

He said, "I've been wondering why there's so much political interest in funding nursing homes, so I hired a clipping service. These are about the payments of Federal and State tax dollars, not to Welfare Queens but Medicaid Kings! Reporters found private for-profit nursing homes more lucrative than owning stock in the nation's publicly traded health care providers. Most privately held homes had but a few owners, who not only were salaried but received their stocks' annual dividends."

Mike immediately saw similarity to the ideas Miss Lewes had expressed and he wrote in her letter to her Senator, who won't see the letter, a staff member will. A prepared thank you will come back in the mail. That will end it.

"For instance, Mike, the Borrs were a family that owned and operated three nursing homes with a total of 540 beds. Medicaid paid the daily cost of care for fifty percent of the residents. The husband was the medical director, his wife office manager and administrative assistant, and sonny boy an administrative assistant. Sonny earned but $93,000, Mom $338,000 and Pop $342,000, not including a rent return of $308,000. Salaries to owner-operators were in addition to operating profits. Together, the Borrs earned $1.2 Million last year, though their nursing homes were often cited for deficiencies for under staffing, improper care of bed sores, poor food services, failure to properly care for the incontinent or to turn bed fast residents as often as medically required.

"The Moon family operated five nursing homes. They earned $347,000 the year before and $386,000 last year. Sixty percent of their residents had daily costs paid by Medicaid, a sum of $6.38 million a year ago. Two of the Moon's homes were cited for failure to properly test Aides, the deliverers of ninety percent of resident care. A utility bill of $14,000 went unpaid for months despite the fact Medicaid automatically reimbursed such payments.

"The Letha family which operated three homes in an urban area was reimbursed from Medicaid funds to the tune of $1.8 million a year ago. Despite the claim of the Nursing Home Industry that it was losing money on Medicaid residents, the Lethas' made an average annual profit of seven percent.

"The Poena family's income a year back was $2 Million. They operated five nursing homes with 750 beds, sixty percent of which held Medicaid residents. Medicaid paid the five homes $13.8 Million. Abel Poena earned a salary of $445,000, Cain Poena earned $500,000 and the oldest brother, Shiloh, earned $512,00 out of deference to his age. The rest of the family had to divide $500,000 in dividends."

Ziggie's cheeks were flushed, but he continued.

"Olgt and Soth, two owners of a nursing home company pocketed $1.02 million in dividends and $213, 000 in salaries last year. Sam Stev, owner, made $300,000 in dividends and $504,000 in salary that year. Not to be discounted was the annual increase to the cost of living paid to the homes of Olgt and Soth and Stev.

"Cecil Horney was out doing all of the other small operators. He was principal stockholder of a chain of twenty-eight homes in one state and another nineteen in surrounding states. They were five-thousand seven hundred elderly in residence. Horney also owned a company that built nursing homes, a pharmacy chain, a medical supply company and a therapy company. His Central Management Company rented and operated all the nursing homes. One of the chain's homes showed a loss on its books of $150,000 but paid Central Management $190,000 for overhead. Last year Central Management and its subsidiaries, excluding most of the nursing homes, earned $1.26 Million on $21 Million in revenues, a six percent profit."

Ziggie handed Mike a hand written note scribbled

on the Horney clipping. It read 'Local Nursing Home Management methods are similar to Central Management's operation of a chain of nursing homes.'

"I wrote that," Ziggie said, "Central had a cash flow from a steady daily average population of residents and a steady income from Medicaid. But how were the owner's construction, pharmacies, medical supplies and therapy companies like Nursing Home Management? How could either avoid the issue of arms-length contracts if one was feeding the others and vice-versa? Can you believe as for Central, it was held to be arms length the State Auditor told the news reporter. Why? I suspect there may well have been campaign contributions, but the reason given to the public was those companies did substantial business with other companies unrelated to Horney's. Consequently, his companies were allowed to charge the nursing homes enough for their services to allow for a profit. Otherwise the charges had to have been at costs. It was evident that there was considerable room for discussion about the meaning of the term 'substantial business'. Enough room for the manipulation of Medicaid's reimbursements?"

Ziggie handed over a second scribbled note. Mike read it out loud, "'a deal between Nursing Home Management and Pharmacopeia?'" Looking up. he asked, "Who is Pharmacopeia?"

"It's a locally owned company," Ziggie said, "a whole seller of prescribed medicines."

Bother by his lack of background on many of the elements involved in delivering elderly care, Mike said, "Fordice should be here."

"Indeed!" Ziggie confirmed. "Work closely with her because I now have confirmation the street drugs you obtained are FDA quality. But we don't know if street dealers got them from drug store burglaries or elsewhere, just that they are sold on the street. What we really need is their source and some evidence drugs like those might have

145

been counterfeited and are actually getting to nursing home residents. If so, how did they get into the pipeline, and if they are, why haven't any nurses spotted it. I can't believe they would knowingly dispense them." As if shaking the horrible thoughts out of mind, Ziggie read more, "Medicaid paid Horney's nursing homes $84 a day per resident in intermediate care, $17 of which per day per resident went to pay administrative costs like salaries and utilities. If the $17 wasn't spent, it was kept as profit." My hand computer calculates the $17 a day multiplied by five thousand seven hundred residents equals a daily income of $96,900 and annually $35,368,500 for administrative costs." He shook his head in awe contemplating the sum." Thirty-five million annually for administrative costs?" The hand calculator went back to work. "$67 of the $84 per day per resident was for medical care. If the $67 for medical care wasn't spent, it had to be given back. Multiplying the $67 by the number of residents, equals $139,393,500. Annually, over one hundred and seventy-four million Medicaid dollars went to Horney's operations! Not included in Medicaid's reimbursements to the nursing homes was income from Horney's construction company, pharmacies, medical supplies, therapy companies, income from private-pay residents and the Medicaid residents' liability, their social security checks less $30.00."

Mike sighed. "Why had I gone into social work? If only I'd stayed a brick-layer's laborer and built and rented buildings to an operating company of nursing homes!" The vast sums of tax payer dollars put into the nursing home industry staggered him. To take in that kind of money the industry had to have political clout.

"Here's what the investigative reporters wrote," Ziggie said, "why the industry got a for-profit status with the best features of a non-profit entity, such as guaranteed revenue and minimized risks? Because Medicaid reimburses legal fees, even if nursing home Lawyers are fighting violations of State Health regulations or lobbying for higher reimbursements. Medicaid also reimburses the homes for dues paid for memberships in Associations pertinent to the business of the industry. From these dues, Associations hire Lobbyists who contribute an annual average of $125,000 to the campaigns of selected State Representatives and Senators. How much went into the campaign coffers of a former Governor, now the industry's TV spokesman? Governor Study isn't excluded. In return for political contributions, is it mere happenstance he and his party's elected officials passed Laws that controlled appointments to Boards that review Nursing Home Certificates of Need; the Examiners of Nursing Home Administrators; Medicaid reimbursements and approve nursing home regulations? Not unsuspected, the appointed majority of each such Board works for the nursing home or health care industry. For instance, as the heading of an article seemingly blared, nursing home residents are being betrayed by the State Board of Health Facilities Administrators, a Board created by legislation twenty-five years back. The eleven member Board's appointees include five nursing home administrators, three appointees from health care facilities, two from State Health, an agency obligated by Law to enforce nursing home standards, and one appointee from the public. Charged with establishing and enforcing standards for nursing home administrators, it never established any standards. So there was nothing to enforce. The last seven years when some records were kept, the Board considered only three disciplinary actions with outcomes unrevealed."

Mike shook his head in amazement. "The whole system of regulating and financing nursing homes is a sweet heart contract between elected officials, their selected Board appointees and the for-profit Nursing Home Industry. Federal and State Politicians are aiding and abetting owners and operators of Nursing Homes to use

Medicaid funds to pad out the bottom line at tax payer expense."

Ziggie agreed. "I wonder how ordinary citizens can bring about fiscal restraint in a huge public program that subsidizes a powerful, private sector industry hungering for a profit and politicians lusting for contributions? Clearly, the more the chronically ill elderly and disabled enter Nursing Homes, the more there is to be made."

Mike took over the adding machine. "If all of Palace's three hundred and twenty-seven residents were costed out at $84 dollars a day, it's annual income would be $7,996,785, about $5.9 million of which would come from Medicaid. If Palace took all but $30 from Medicaid residents' monthly social security checks, an average of $400 monthly after deduction of the personal allowance, Palace gets another $1.1 Million annually. Nine million dollars a year is no small fiscal operation! Ninety percent of the ill elderly and disabled had to enter nursing homes. They went broke spending down. Too soon nothing remained to pay rent or the one who came into their homes to look after them, helping to shower, dress and cook, even do dishes. Where would they have gone for care if there weren't a nursing home?" A thought! "Why in the name of governmental fiscal sanity doesn't it have a Law that might appropriate $500 a month for a part time housekeeper and other home bound services for many of the elderly able to stay at their places while paying rent, utilities, food and necessities out of social security or disability checks? Landlords, power companies, grocers and city water systems aren't inclined to ship them out unless they tried to beat them out of their cut. What public policy requires all Americans to pay higher taxes to cover the costs of twenty-four hour nursing home living rather than pay for a few hours a day assistance at home? The difference in dollar costs between the two, one hundred and sixty-eight hours of alleged nursing home services weekly versus ten to twenty hours weekly in ones own place, exceeds in costs a multiple to the one-hundred power." He then felt a sermon coming on. "If one stayed out of a nursing home, Medicaid didn't need to pay twenty-six hundred dollars a month for a twenty-four hour stay when the nursing care didn't amount to any more care than the visiting nurses gave at home. Sure the home's staff cleaned rooms, cooked food, heated and cooled the home, did laundry, but one could see to the same on the outside at far less cost. One could stay near the people and places known on a few hundred dollars more a month. Aren't there visiting housekeepers? Aren't there private or public houses, group homes, where two or three elderly or disabled can stay at a thousand a month and get some assistance? Aren't there fifteen hundred dollars a month assisted living facilities out in the community? Are there as many home care, room and board homes and assisted living facilities as there are nursing homes? Absolutely not!"

Ziggie knew why not. "The Nursing Home Industry and its political supporters see sensible alternatives to twenty-four hour care diminishing financial pots and dipping into political campaigns. Government creates wealth for those who early on captured the field of housing the ill elderly. It can only remain that way if nursing homes haven't any significant competition. The Industry knows it and never for a moment forgets it. There is gold for investors in the golden years!"

"Fascinating." Mike responded. "I had no idea of the vast sums of dollars paid to nursing home owners and operators out of Federal-State tax money. It's in the billions! And what a sweetheart deal! An underwrite of the operation through tax dollars while retaining a for-profit status and strong political influence over the regulators. No wonder there's hesitation among administrators when a loose cannon like me shows up to look out for residents' rights!"

Outside Ziggie's office Mike found a social worker's cubicle empty. He sat in her chair, and dialed her phone. "John Horvas please?"

"This is John."

"I'm Mike Brannagh, Ombudsman, a part of a Federal and State program that works for residents rights in nursing homes. I work only for residents, not the home. I got your message about your Aunt's house. I was told she's a bit perplexed about the sale of her house."

"So am I," he said with resignation, "and I'm in Real Estate. Lord knows why Medicaid wants me to sell it now. The appraised value of the house is less than the rotten wood on the front porch. It's so badly run down, I can't rent it. Too costly to repair. There's a garbage dump next door to top it off. Next year the dump will be made over into a golf course. Then would be the time to sell. Aunt Naomi's land will be worth something. Sell it now for a few hundred dollars or in a year or two for a few thousand. Bureaucrats tell me to sell now. Just can't convince them they are enriching the dump owners instead of the tax payers. Bureaucrats are dumb as tree stumps." A pause. "Sorry fellow. I don't mean to down grade all bureaucrats."

"They sound dumb," he said, by-passing further comments on bureaucrats, one of whom he had been, but a bright one. "The social worker told me she sure would appreciate it if you visited and explained it to your Aunt."

"Explain it? You mean about selling or renting?"

"Right! Few understand the law of Medicaid, particularly those who administer it, much less an aged woman who sees the loss of her home as the end of her reason for living, convinced she'd return one day."

"She thinks that? Not likely."

"That's just what I mean. She needs to hear it from someone she loves."

"Gee. I never gave it a thought. Just assumed she

150

knew."

"Thinking of thoughts, Mr. Horvas. I've got one. I'd like to ask you a few questions about the appraisal on Mrs. Horvas' house. You understand?" He did. There followed a series of affirmatives to: "It's an arms length appraisal? Medicaid has a copy? Medicaid directs you as Mrs. Horvas Power of Attorney to sell it for no less than the appraised price? To Any bona fide purchaser for value? Medicaid has been made fully aware of the potential value of the land within another year or so?" Then Mike paused before he said, "then buy the property, Mr. Horvas, as a bona fide purchaser for the full amount of the appraised value."

"What? Can I do that?"

"Why not? It's legal, honest and ethical. You've gotten an arms length appraisal. You've fully informed them and been more than open and honest with Medicaid. Buy it for the current appraised value and turn that money over to Medicaid! If the future value of the land should appreciate like you think it will, why shouldn't Mrs. Horvas and her nephew use the funds to enhance her quality of life."

"Why didn't I think of that?"

"Takes an ex-bureaucrat."

* * *

From outside Hyacinth, Brannagh saw more wings than a geriatric farm house had additions. The nursing home's original wing was a bright yellow brick with a canvas canopy over a double glass door entry. The view of the facility, post Medicare-Medicaid approval, was two 'U' shape buildings, one upside down. Unsatisfied with the harmony of the 'U' architecture, the owners apparently contracted the local kindergarten for drawings of a headless stick man. The top of both 'U' buildings were extended to the east and west, but the bricks used for the additions hadn't as serious a case of jaundice. Visitors' parking was to either side of the additions, then a long walk around the wing and into the pit of the top 'U'.

He didn't know what gases he'd sniff inside Hyacinth. The air in some facilities, Palace's and Mint's, weren't worth the taking. The double glass door opened into a waiting room of couches, easy chairs and end tables decorated with vases filled with plastic roses. An aged man in bib overalls, gingham shirt and tattered brown sweater was asleep on a plum colored easy chair. His newspaper was a lap blanket. The receptionist sat behind the name plate 'MARTINA' set upon a simulated wood desk. Martina's brown eyes matched her ribbed vest over a herringbone shirt. Her smile danced across a youthful face. Her first job out of high school?

"May I help you?" she said.

Handing her a brochure, he said, "I'm Mike Brannagh, ombudsman, come to introduce myself to residents and the president of the resident council. I'd like to meet the administrator if she is available."

"Eula is with State Health's surveyors."

"A survey?" He got a positive nod. "I thought a Kate Wung was administrator." His listing of administrators indicated such. "Who's Eula?"

"Eula Wellnar. She's the council president. She's with the surveyors. They're holding a residents' meeting in the west lounge." She pointed to the west. "Follow the 'u' turn up to the north end, then turn to the left. The west lounge is at the very end of the wing."

"Thank you." It was an opportunity to meet many residents at once, and to visit with Belinda Fordice. "Please let Mrs. Wung know I'm here and with the surveyors?"

He undertook the trek. It was worth it. If Hyacinth were as clean the remaining fifty-one weeks of the year as it was during the annual but unannounced surveyors' visit, this wasn't a Nursing Home Management facility. Administrator Wung ran an antiseptic home. Room after room was clean enough to serve as medical operating rooms. Were the residents sterilized? Their debilitation and clothing styles, unlike Palace's Alzheimer color coding, weren't uniform. Not one resident in her room's recliner wore Yard-sale specials. Dressers were neat. Bathrooms were shared by the three roommates. The facility was mindful of an assembly line. A look in one room was a look in all.

At the end of the west wing was a door. He knocked. Fordice, every inch the look of the person in charge, opened it. Her hair was combed to the back of her head sleek as a hood ornament. A burgundy Isle crew sweater and midnight long knit skirt on her lean and lengthy ebony form, black stockings and shoes, gave the appearance of a ship prow's maiden. Beyond her, sitting behind a table that faced a score or more of residents in wheelchairs or on lounge couches, were her team: Emma Tee, Gerri Knit and Inez Mars, all as attractively dressed.

"Mike! Welcome to the surveyors' meeting with the residents. Please sit in. I'll introduce you. Say a few words, then take a seat with the residents." She let him in, closed the door, and facing the residents, said, "Folks, this is Mike Brannagh, the new ombudsman, an advocate for residents. I've asked him to say a few words."

He blinked, but verbosity ingrained as it was in all Irish descendants, said, "Ladies and gentlemen, glad to met you. I'm a part of the Federal and State ombudsman program. I visit residents in nursing homes in five counties. Hyacinth is one of them. Ombudsman means advocate. So, I'm your twenty-four hour advocate, if you wish to have me do something for you, or for all, I'll go at it. For instance, at the request of a resident in another nursing home, letters are being written to the Governor and Legislators asking them to take less than all of your social security annual cost of living increase, so the personal needs allowance can be increased from the current $30.00 to hopefully, $50.00 a month." He wasn't surprised there was a vigorous clapping of hands. "It may not happen, but it won't be because of lack of effort." No applause.

He handed out brochures to hands thin as twigs or plump as cabbages. Time and illness might have combined to reduce bodily activity but not gleams in their eyes. They were uplifted thinking of a bit more money to buy clothes or a magazine or a birthday card for a grandchild. No chairs were empty. He went to the back of the room and leaned against the wall.

"I'll continue with the remainder of my questions," Fordice said. She sat on the edge of the front table. "Is there any problem in receiving your mail, or using the telephone in private?"

"No," was the mumbled response.

"After a survey," she said, "a copy of the survey results have been and will be placed at the reception desk or other public place for you and your family to read, if you wish. Is it there, and have you read it?"

"Don't recollect seeing it," a woman said. "It's there," another said. "Kate told me so." Other responses were mixed as to whether or not the survey copy was at the receptionist desk, more saying it was than saying it wasn't. None had read it.

"Does staff ask you in advance to attend care plan?"
"Yes."

"Is there any problem with staff if you want to attend the council meeting, or any activities, or with other residents"

"No."

"Are your bed sheets changed at least once a week? Rooms cleaned daily?"

"Yes."

"Do staff open your dresser's drawers without asking you first?"

"Somebody does," a very little woman in a pink dress said. "Missing my best slip."

154

"Did you notice if the drawer were open when you missed the slip?" Fordice said.

"I don't remember if the drawer was open," the lady in pink said, as if raising a question. "Did you put the slip in the laundry?" Fordice said, searching for a hint.

"I don't remember if I did or not."

"Gerri Knit," Fordice said, "the surveyor at the table sitting in the middle will visit you afterwards to look into your missing slip." Continuing, Fordice said. "Are personal belongings often missing?"

"Not often," was mumbled.

She sensed theft was a problem. "If any one wants to discuss missing items in private, or anything else, just come up after this meeting and give us your name and room number and one of us will visit you in private. Are there enough Aides to help you when you need help?"

"On the day shift and up to about 9 P.M.," a lady in a brown dress said.

"What happens at nine, Eula?"

Mike took note Eula Wellnar was wearing a white sweater over her dress and was in a wheelchair.

"Aides vanish into thin air. For all I know Kate Wung sends them home when we've gone to bed. I can push the call button until my thumb swells, and no Aide. Have to put towels down there in case I can't hold it until the charge nurse answers."

"Do the rest of you have this problem?" Fordice said.

"Yes!" Resounded throughout.

"Inez," Fordice said, "pull all personal records and time cards for the last two months to determine the number of Aides and nurses on duty each shift." A nod of acceptance. "Are there activities you can attend daily if you so wish."

"Nothing but preaching and psalm singing on Sundays, unless my lazy son visits," a slender man with a gray sweater and blue pants said. His wig was redder than a sunset.

"Play cribbage with me, Don," a man said. The eagle on the back of his leather jacket was poised to strike."I never can find anyone to play cards during psalm singing."

"Emma, check out activities," Fordice said. "What about the food?'

If all the football players in the professional leagues had arrived at a sports banquet to find nothing but a sprig of parsley to share among them, their grumbling would have been a light breeze in comparison to the earthquake rumblings of Hyacinth residents. The four surveyors were inundated with complaints of 'rotten', 'stale', 'cold', 'putrid', 'inedible'. Fordice was overawed. She wasn't any longer in charge. Clusters of residents were on all sides of her, Emma Tee, Inez Mars and Gerri Knit, all furiously taking notes

The council president wasn't among them. Mike took the moment to introduce himself. He knelt at the side of her wheelchair. "Quite a meeting, Mrs. Wellnar."

"If something can be done about the food, you're right. They don't know how to cook from scratch, is the problem. Kitchen empties cans and heats to tastelessness."

"Have you considered asking Nurse Fordice to assist you in setting up a Kitchen committee of two or three residents and an interested family member or two who know about food preparation. Perhaps the committee might meet biweekly with the dietitian and head cook, to discuss menus and food preparation? A family member could take notes, write them up and circulate them among the residents and staff, with a copy to Nurse Fordice, perhaps to the local newspaper. I've found administrators of institutions pay attention to things like that."

"You mean right now? Alright, I will." Her face was as glowing as a Christmas candle. "Seeing that you have good ideas, what can be done about theft of personal items? This is a very big place with many residents, some who take things because they don't know any better, other residents, one or two staff and maybe several visitors who do know better, pick off valuable things. Trouble is, too many of us old folks don't know we're missing something until a sister visits and asks after it. Kate Wung says if the resident doesn't know, how can she?"

"There's your answer, Mrs. Wellnar. Let Mrs. Wung know. At admission, some council members acting as 'Welcomers' can appear and request the resident's family write out a complete inventory, with reasonable valuations made of all the resident's property brought to the home. The family member keeps a copy. The inventory should be updated each time something of value is added. It's the law that nursing home operators have a responsibility to protect the persons and property of their residents. A resident has a right to reimbursement or replacement of stolen items. Put the operators of this nursing home and their insurer on notice. An inventory goes a long way in doing so. There will be a lot more attention paid to the protection of resident's personal property. It won't eliminate theft but it may well cut its frequency. One other thought," he said, "really valuable items, like wedding rings, are very likely to disappear when sleeping or under the influence of some medicine. I realize the immense emotional attachment to engagement and wedding rings, but inexpensive duplicates would minimize heartbreak if stolen."

"I follow you," she said. "If Kate Wung says, and I've heard her say it, staff had no awareness of the thing lost, she can't say it if she has a list. You've put a burden on me, young man," her expression bright as sun lit snow.

* * *

Fordice saw Brannagh walking by the door. "Mike," she said loudly, "have you a minute?"

"Sure have." He entered a well appointed room. Fordice was sitting in an executive chair going through file folders. Records were piled high on the table top near her. "What room is this?" He entered and stood by the door.

"Hyacinth's Board Room. We're using it as our base for the survey. What did you think of the residents' meeting?"

"You conducted it quite well," he said, meaning it, "but you must have been as surprised as me at the hubub over food."

"Food selection and preparation are leading complains during most of our surveys," she said nonchalantly, "but I must admit, never to the magnitude of Hyacinth's."

He informed her of the Kitchen Committee suggestion he'd made to Mrs Wellnar. "What about theft?"

She said, "An inventory should be done upon admission. The home is responsible for handing out to families a sheet of paper that informs them of the need to make an inventory to include all possessions, and if something valuable is brought in later, to add it on. I'm going to discuss it with Eula that admissions and the resident's family jointly signed a copy. One goes into the chart, the family keeps the original.."Fordice's expression changed from professional surveyor to curious investigator. Let's take some air."

In the parking lot, standing next to her car, she said, "What's going on since your phone call about those psychotropics? I've been thinking about those medicines ever since you called. I even took some time to go through Hyacinth's pharmacy, looked at several containers, even handled capsules of psychotropics. Nothing out of the ordinary. It has me puzzled."

Mike answered. "Those were the drugs believed to be sold on the street. I got hold of a couple. Ziggie had them tested. Results confirmed they were FDA quality. We don't know the source and we haven't a thing that similar medicines are being counterfeited."

"The puzzle grows," she said, ""I've done some reading of patient charts to determine if there was a sudden, even a mild change in the health of residents prescribed any psychotropics, but, no clear cut suggestion there's anything wrong. Sudden resident illnesses, even deaths aren't out of the ordinary in nursing homes."

Mike recollected Ziggie calling nursing homes 'Land of last Life.' He updated Fordice on Ziggie's news clippings. "He had me come in to take a look at an investigative reporter's findings about nursing homes making fortunes from Medicaid payments. I don't know why that surprised me, but it did. Ziggie noted there was a principal stockholder of a chain of homes that not only operated homes, but also owned a company that built nursing homes, leased them to other operators, ran a pharmacy chain, a medical supply company and a therapy company. Nursing Home Management does lease its buildings from Quality Care, which does do all that. Ziggie wondered where Pharmacopeia fitted. Do you remember we talked on the phone about Quality Care leasing its buildings to Nursing Home Management, but what is Pharmacopeia to Nursing Home Management?"

Fordice's expression gave evidence of fascination. "As we discussed, drug therapy is the most frequently used treatment modality for the elderly. Pharmacopeia is a wholesaler of prescription drugs to licensed pharmacies, not to Nursing Home Management. Doctors write the prescriptions for their patients in nursing homes, and licensed pharmacies fill them, sending the medicines to the nursing homes. There are no pharmacies in any of Nursing Home Management's nursing homes. It does use the services of a consulting pharmacist, but his role isn't to fill prescriptions. He's there to decrease, prevent if possible, the frequency of drug-related problems, to seek ways to resolve them, perhaps by a therapeutic substitution, a different therapeutic alternate with anticipated similar outcomes. At that, he needs to inform the Medical Doctor. I doubt there is anything between Nursing Home Management, an operating company, and Pharmacopeia, a drug wholesaler to licensed pharmacies." She shivered. "It's cooler out than I thought."

"Let's go back in," he said, "If I get it, the functions of Nursing Home Management and Pharmacopeia are worlds apart. Pharmacopeia sells psychotropics only to pharmacies, where they are ordered by an MD to be delivered to a nursing home, and there they are subject to a check by a consulting pharmacist, and nurses on the floor, and from time to time, State Health Surveyors. Quite a chain." He held the door for her. "So far all we know is FDA psychotropics are being sold on the street, and if there is a chain, only Ziggie is calling for an investigation."

Inside, while walking back to the Board room, she said, "Pharmacopeia wholesales psychotropics of course, but there are even more stringent regulations and checks. The industry is electronic, there are automated entries of purchases, sales. The wholesaler is, in essence, the purchasing agent for pharmacists. Computerization has introduced not only cost-effective technology, but accountability."

"Excuse me," surveyor Mars said, "but you should see this Belinda."

She said, "Thank you for being here, Mike."

14

Mike parked his '83 in Hawthorne Nursing Home's parking lot. The pickup shuddered from the long trip. Note book, brochures and Nursing Home Rules in hand, he got out to call on Nan Wooden, administrator, before visiting resident Pearl Nech.

Hawthorne was deep in the bowels of north Moose County seven miles east of Currus City. The 'C' shaped brick building was hidden on a side road behind tall evergreens. Mike followed written directions pasted to the glass of the doors and opened the right side of the first set of double doors, the left side of the second set of double doors. The purpose: to cut down on cold air. There wasn't any cold air beyond the second set of double doors. It was as warm in the hall as in a rain forest. Opposite the doors, a haystack of blond hair over a very broad white brow and wide brown eyes peered from above a semi-circular reception cubicle. Inside the cubicle was a very expansive woman in an ivory brushed tunic, family size. "May I help you?"

"I'm the ombudsman, Mike Brannagh. Here's the State's brochure that explains I'm an advocate for residents' rights. I'm here to visit residents. Is the administrator in?"

The two words of interest to the receptionist were 'state' and 'administrator' and not in that order. She picked up the phone, dialed, then picked up the brochure. "Ms. Wooden, there's a man from the State here to see you." Haystack hair hadn't put the phone back on the receiver before an office door behind her opened.

A young woman came out. She was five foot eight, hair blacker than West Virginia coal, facial skin whiter than an Angel's halo. She wore an unbuttoned at the collar blue broad cloth shirt and slim trousers that tapered to her black shoes, but looked as grim as if she'd caught a finger in a pencil sharpener. "You're from the state? Sooner than I expected. The police are back again investigating the rape."

Rape of a resident? Nurse? State Health wouldn't be called if it were the rape of a nurse, just the police. Mike figured Wooden was obviously expecting someone from State Health, not a lowly ombudsman. "I'm the ombudsman, Mike Brannagh, ordinarily here to introduce myself to you, the council president and a few residents. You say rape? A resident?"

"You're not from the state?" she said, her fair complexion muddying. "Why didn't you tell Audrey you were the ombudsman when you came in?" She was seething. "Did he Audrey?"

Audrey quickly picked up the ringing phone to answer. Haystack leaned to the fore, a hairy tower of Pisa. She wasn't about to raise eyes or to hang up no matter the intent of the calling party. Mike intervened. He reached for the brochure Audrey had set on the cubicle's counter, picked it up and handed it to Wooden. "Maybe," he said, "when Audrey called you, she missed the word 'ombudsman' and my name on the State brochure."

"Brannagh," Wooden said, "the matter of the alleged rape of a resident is a matter for State Health and the police, not the ombudsman. Do not interfere." Her words carried disdain.

"Ms. Wooden," he said, marveling over the command given more succinctly than a platoon lieutenant ordering his rifle squads to attack in the face of enemy fire, "You're right, that's usually not an ombudsman's work or area of focus. As ombudsman, my focus is the protection of the rights of residents. Included in those rights are safety of the person from physical and psychological attack. You'll find in the Federal and State Rules considerable legal authority that details the role of an ombudsman in nursing homes licensed to care for Medicare and Medicaid

162

residents." He noticed her expression change from disdain to dismay. "Let's set aside tempers and discuss this calmly some where else than in the hall."

Her chest heaved and nose whistled. "Alright. Come into my office." She wheeled about and hurried in as quickly as she had earlier hurried out. Following, he entered her office and closed the door. She went behind her maple wood desk and sat on a padded maple desk chair motioning him to sit in any one of four wood office chairs situated the other side of the desk. He picked the chair closest to the double window. The office was brightly lighted from inset ceiling fixtures. Decorative cabinets lined the mauve walls. Paintings of old introspective faces were hung at random. Medical and Nursing home books and magazines were arranged in orderly ranks on top of the cabinets. Research papers were stacked high. The desk was crowded with collectibles, two phones, a keyboard, computer terminal and glaring monitor.

"This is what happened," she said. "Emmy, one of our morning Nursing Aides was changing Rea Short. Rea's eyes may follow movements, but she doesn't talk. She isn't ambulatory. Emmy saw bruises. She called in Alexa, the charge nurse who confirmed Rea's bruises couldn't have been self inflicted and Rea was sent to the hospital. She was there when the hospital informed me that, besides bruises, Rea had been raped. The hospital called the police and they are here again investigating. I informed State Health, so when you arrived, I assumed you were from State Health."

"When did Emmy see the bruises?"

"Two days back."

"When did she come on duty?"

"7:00 AM. She saw the bruises about 7:30. Alexa, came in and looked at Rea a few minutes later. Rea was sent to the hospital within a half hour. EMS took her."

"I assume Alexa logged the bruises in Rea's chart

and the incident was called in to State Health the same day."

"Alexa logged the bruises, but no incident report was made to State Health until I was informed of the rape by the hospital."

"Did you call State Health about the bruises as an unusual occurrence?"

"No. What was unusual about bruises?"

"Their placement and apparent infliction by another person." He'd the urge to lecture this self centered administrator. "If Rea didn't do it to herself, someone else did. That's the crime of battery. If Alexa sent Rea to the hospital, she must have felt the infliction of the bruises to be unusual. State Rules require a call the same day of an occurrence that directly threatened the safety of a resident. A written report is mandated within twenty-four hours."

Wooden appeared closer to anger than angst. She resented this snide old man more than her employer, who at her promotion saw more a shapely female than a well trained professional. "I reported the unusual incident when the hospital informed me of the rape."

He had a pang of remorse over his heavy handedness, but felt this woman would check the rules hereafter. "We differ Ms. Wooden as to when an incident report was to have been made. Battery should have been reported before the rape was confirmed, but that's a matter for you and State Health to reconcile. My interest, as ombudsman, is in your steps hereafter to assure the safety of all residents. Safety isn't low on the list of residents' rights."

"Safety?" she said with exasperation, "I always look out for residents' safety."

"I'm sure you do. For certain during the sixty to seventy hours you're here working," he said, returning to his lecture, "but there's one hundred and sixty-eight hours a week in a nursing home, fifty-two weeks a year. Safety during the hours you're not here has a lot to do with staffing patterns, the number and competence of nursing staff, the frequency of nursing staff involvement with residents on all shifts. A rape doesn't always occur in the dark, but it's more likely. Check your evening and midnight staffing patterns."

"Are you saying the rapist works evening or nights and is one of our male staff?"

"Unlikely, but I'm sure the police will focus on staff. That's a police tendency. It's always deviant staff that do the evil deed." Remembrances of accusations that Jail staff, not outsiders, had smuggled drugs to inmates resounded in his mind. "I'm talking about the number and competence of nursing staff on duty evenings and midnights. There's a tendency in the homes I've visited to cut way back on staffing after bed hours. That provides opportunities for those who might know staffing is minimal and to know who isn't able to resist a sexual assault."

"A resident?"

"Sexually acting out isn't unheard of as a stage in dementia or Alzheimer's disease."

"Most likely a visitor," she said."

"Perhaps, but what are the odds a visitor is so sexually deviant that he would take the time to know what particular resident is non-mobile and speechless? But, if true, it supports more nursing staff on duty during prime visiting times."

"You just want me to hire more nursing staff."

"Do you want a safe facility? Do the residents and their families? Safety is synonymous with sufficient and competent nursing staff on duty one hundred and sixty-eight hours a week. There's the key to the welfare, safety and health of Hawthorne's residents."

"I have a budget to follow! Have you ever been subject to an institutional budget?"

"I have, but an institutional budget must have as its

165

basic premise sufficient staffing for a human service program. Included in the basics are top flight shift supervisors who supervise on their feet. An administrator can be no better than her supervisors. She looks good if her top supervisors have as much on the ball as she has."

A knock on her office door. She was glad of it. "Come in," she said. She was pleased to see Brannagh get up to leave.

"Nan," said Detective Schrim as he walked in, "Jackie here says I need your okay to get a list of all male staff and the days last week they were on duty. Going to run polygraphs on every last one of them."

"Every male on the staff?" she said, her embarrassment vying with her astonishment. "All are suspects?" She looked at the all knowing ombudsman. "Most of the men work days. What makes you think it's male staff?"

"Hey Nan," Schrim said, "it was a male that penetrated. Why would any kind of a normal man work in a nursing home? It's women's work. Perverts go for very old gals; need access to weak gals, easy to overpower. I want that list, Nan."

Her nerves froze, and she walked up to the receptionist. "Jackie," she said. "get Detective Schrim the personnel files on all male staff."

"But Nan, my Tony is on days in maintenance!" Jackie said.

When Brannagh walked out of the office, Wooden's imagination heard a rooster crow. "It was a male who raped Rea," Wooden said with a bite. "Get the files for the detective, Jackie."

"Oh Nan!" Jackie said with disgust.

Wooden heard another crow of the rooster.
* * *

Down the hall was an occupied nurse station.
Charge nurse Alexa? The way the lumpish, middle aged red

166

face woman in nurse's whites was watching his approach, it was clear she was sizing the stranger up and comparing him to other visiting men's images she retained in her memory bank. A negative shake of her head released him from suspicion, her's at least.

The thought crossed his mind, though he'd never been to Hawthorne before, if Alexa cried out to the detective, an arrest of the ombudsman would cut short working for anyone.

"Ma'am," he said over the counter of the nurse station, "I'm the ombudsman here to visit the council president. Could you tell me who, and where the president's room is?"

"The ombudsman?" Alexa was surprised. She too had been looking for an investigator from State Health. "Nice to meet you," she glanced at the name on the brochure, "Mike. You want to see the council president, not me?"

"Right. Ms. Wooden already told me of your involvement with Rea Short. I won't be asking you about it. The police and State Health will."

"The police already have," she said, clearly relieved there would be one less. "Causby Pring is the president of the resident council. He's in room 218 down the hall. He's having a lot of visitors today. The police, Nan, now you." Alexa shifted her eyes from him to a delivery man carrying a package to a front office.

Why had Nan Wooden dropped in on Pring just a moment ago? Why not! She had the right to visit any resident in the home.

The hallways of nursing homes were all beginning to look the same, brown with matching tile floors. Some had brown carpeting, but stains, like bacteria, grew. Each room had its door open, a resident laying on a made bed or sitting asleep in a wheel chair. The rooms were all painted in some light shade of brown. Dresser drawers were closed, closet doors shut, bathroom doors open, occupied or not. Windows needed washing from the outside. He stopped at the opened door of room 218. A gray haired man in a blue sweat suit was sitting in a wheelchair.

"Mr. Pring?"

"What?" he said. If hostility could be converted to a solid, Pring's face effected it.

"I'm the ombudsman, advocate for residents' rights. Here's a brochure that tells about the ombudsman's program. May I give it to you?"

"No! I'm not interested in any piece of paper."

A cranky old goat! "Are you interested in talking about the resident council?"

"Council business isn't any of your business." His defiant look was challenging. His tone cross, nasty.

Mike persisted. "I take it Hawthorne's staff and programs meet residents' needs?'

Pring gritted his false teeth. "Nan told me about you. I don't need to tell you anything."

"No, you don't." Pring raised a butt cheek and proudly farted. As if that weren't sufficient, he said, "I don't want you to bother any residents, understand?"

Mike turned to face the old gasser despite the odoriferous halo. "Mr. Pring," he said with a touch of submission rolled in steel, "before you needed the care of this twenty-four hour nursing home, I'm sure you ran your business as you saw fit. Seeing residents in nursing homes is my business. Your command to the contrary, if any resident in Hawthorne elects to talk with me, we'll talk."

Down the hall was the dining area. Five females were sitting around a table sipping coffee. All but one wore sweaters over their dresses. "Hello ladies, I'm Mike Brannagh, ombudsman. This is my first visit to Hawthorne." Brochures were spread around.

"Are you a policeman, sonny?" said the grand motherly image of 'Rosie the Riveter' of World War Two fame, dressed as she was in pants, a blouse and a red and black bandana wrapped around her gray head. Her question went right to the heart of his interest. How were residents reacting to the rape? He pulled a chair over, sat down and joined the quintet. "I understand there is a police detective here, but I'm the ombudsman, not a policeman. That means I work only for residents' rights in nursing homes. I work as their advocate with the staff or with outsiders, if that's what a resident wants me to do."

Rosie said, "Sure do want the police to talk to us about what's going on. Have the police arrested anyone yet?"

"Have you asked the detective?" he said.

"No, but he's been talking to all the men, residents or staff," Rosie said. "Hasn't talked to us yet, has he girls?" Four gray heads nodded agreement.

The thought crossed his mind a male resident into dementia might not be capable of consenting to an interview. "How many residents are male?"

"Lets see," Rosie said, "there's Daniel, Gerald, Russell, Eugene, Luther and Raymond."

"Don't forget Tony and Jess," the lady in a blue sweater and pink dress said.

"And Conn and Roger,"said the lady in a yellow sweater and matching dress.

"Mark is the worst of them all," the lady in brown said. "It's him." The color of her face matched walnut bark.

"Why do you say that, Jenny?" Rosie said.

"Well," Jenny said, "I don't like talking behind anyone's back, but Mark's been seen wandering at night."

"I seen him myself," Rosie said. "That doesn't mean it's Mark. He has prostate cancer. Can hardly tinkle. I doubt it can do what was done to Rea."

"No one thinks it's Mark?" Jenny asked. She received four negative bobs of gray heads.

Mike changed the subject. "Are there enough staff

on the evening and night shifts?"

"I counted," Jenny said. "There's no more staff than usual after midnight."

"I don't think anything changed," Rosie said. She looked at the name on the ombudsman brochure. "Mike, would you ask the detective to meet with us to discuss what can be done to protect us?"

"I will." He left the ladies to look for the detective, most likely up front with Wooden. Reaching the administrator's office, its open door revealed an empty office. "Ma'am?" he asked the receptionist. "Could you tell me where the police detective is?"

"Gone," she said, "but Nan Wooden is here looking over police photos. She's in the DON's office. Third door to your left."

"Thank you." Police photos? Possible those of known sex offenders. She'd look them over to see if she recognized any as recent visitors. He knocked on the office door.

"Come in." She was behind the DON's desk, alone in the room. Looking up, her face grimaced. "You?"

"Yea me." he said, ignoring her irritation. "There's a group of ladies in the dining room who told me of the rape and are worried about their personal security. They asked me to fetch the detective to talk to them. He's gone. It might be wise, in his absence, for you to bring the residents up to date, to offer assurances. While on the topic, rumors are flying that this male resident or that male resident is the perpetrator. I suppose it's possible, but as these men are here for nursing care and under medication that may affect their mental alertness, or are into dementia, being interviewed by the police without a family member present may impinged upon their rights. If families are unaware of police interviews, one or more may see their way to challenging Hawthorne in court over an invasion of privacy."

170

"If I call the surrogates of each man here, it'll frightened everyone," she said, unreceptive.

"It might," he said. "Depends how you and the operating company handle it, but it's your call. I'll let the ladies in the dining room know the detective is gone."

He'd walked into a buzz saw, was seen as deceitful, and tagged negatively during the rest of Wooden's administrative life. Winning over administrators was obviously not his forte. Advocating for residents with administrators wasn't running so hot either. He returned to the dining room. There were his five ladies. Three men had pulled up a table and joined the women.

"Ladies," he said, "and gentlemen. For the benefit of the men, I'm Mike Brannagh, ombudsman, an advocate for nursing home residents' rights. Let me give you a brochure." He gave each one. "Sorry folks, but the detective is gone. Consequently I couldn't ask him to meet with you like you wanted. I suggest you ask Nan Wooden to invite him back. Besides, he may want to talk privately with some residents to gather information. If you get nervous about talking to the police, or your medication makes you nervous and forgetful, schedule the detective when you can have a family member with you."

"No one here did anything to Rea, pal," said large male lips from a gruff whiskered face.

"Don't need my daughter when I talk to cops."

"Perhaps no one here needs a family member present. Perhaps, however, there's two or three residents in Hawthorne who can't remember what day of the week it is, or that the visitor in his room is his wife. I've met more than one resident who agreed with everything said, like they set the fire in the barn, but there was no barn. That's the purpose of the presence of family."

"Oh yea," said whiskered face as if awakening, "like when you're drunk."

"Not really," Mike said, "because you're

171

responsible for getting yourself drunk, but not for being ill or for the effects of medication on your memory."

"I get it," whiskers said. "You may be under meds and not know what you're saying."

"That's it. A family member can tell the police about the mental state of their loved one and have the police check it out with their doctor."

"The DON can do it too," Rosie said.

"She can if she's here," Mike said. "So can the charge nurse. But family is blood, not employed by Hawthorne. Family can stop an interview."

"Sounds like a warning," whiskers said.

"Not so much a warning," he said, "but a statement of one of the rights of all American citizens, especially those ill and under medication. I'm an advocate for those rights."

"Makes sense," Rosie said. "Thanks for telling us."

"You're welcomed. So please pass the word to other residents and their families."

* * *

Would Big-dough Benny Mack be around? Cooper indicated he'd be found at Calvin's in a tough area where other than a girl-child robber might lurk. Yet, day time was the only quasi-wise time for a man of Mike's pigmentation to show up on West and Washington Streets. What would justify a trip to try to locate Benny Mack? Justify? It was a trip to help a resident carry out a last wish! Even if the only thing done was leaving a note with the bar-keep for Big-dough Benny to visit his terminally ill father in Larkspur, it was justified. Why justification? Years of work for Public Agencies acclimated Mike to be prepared for unjustified accusatory scrutiny from self righteous elected officials.

A tough looking quartet of men dominated the corner by Calvin's. A wine-head staggered out, saw the toughs, turned and staggered the other direction down the block. An old man came from across the street and stopped. He pushed his face up against the tavern's window, but said nothing when a big muscled dude came out, took him by an arm, and escorted him to a cardboard box in the alley. A few vacant lots to Calvin's east was a Laundromat. Women in its front window sat as if in Holland, not selling themselves, eye balling the passing parade. Children at play, some in coats, ran the vacant lots tagging one another, getting home free. Cars' with white folks gawked from behind locked doors and rolled up windows. Mike parked by the lot next to Calvin's. Children stopped play to watch him.

"Got a quarter, man?" a boy, not five, said. Big, brown eyes begged.

"Broke,' he said. He'd again repeated the removable of valuables from his person. It left him feeling he was unfairly indicting a tough neighborhood. Then again, he'd be unfair, but quiet about it. He walked with purpose toward the corner guys. They turned to face him. He nodded, their scowling mouths mindful of a platoon of mortar tubes. He turned abruptly and entered Calvin's. There was a minimal moon inside. Eyes adjusting, he saw tall to small men perched on top of rotating stools. He felt a spotlighted leading man. The look of a small guy at a table revealed another possibility: A spotlighted leading lady.

"You the parole man," said a brooding voice from near the bar. "You be parole. You busted my dealer." Brooding voice's owner stepped forward. He was big across the shoulders, hips narrow as his head.

The silence was intimidating. Busted his dealer? Was this the guy who ran off the day Mike called Cooper's name from near Under's Room and Board? What were the odds of meeting narrow-head face to face? What were the odds of ever going to Calvin's and getting out a non-eunuch? "I don't work parole these days. I work for old folks in nursing homes. That's why I'm here."

173

A sinister smile crossed narrow head's face. "Old folks? Shit! Whitey want these studs believe that shit, Calvin? I be checking outside." He exited.

Mike attempted a smile, more a shrug, standing there like a lone Elm surrounded by lumberjacks. As his eyes focused, the men at the bar didn't look too threatening. Some turned around, getting back to booze and chatter. The guys at the tables got back to their cards. He wasn't of much interest. His hands conveyed a 'that's the way it goes' gesture to the man wiping the bar. Narrow-head returned.

"Guys on the corner say he come in a junk pickup, Calvin."

"I'm Calvin," the barkeep said. "This my place, man. Ain't no old folks home. Wish it was sometimes." There was laughter. "Come on over here, man. Tell me what you be doing in Calvin's?" His tone was civil. His long upper body was within a cement colored solid twill shirt, no fat anywhere, with shoulders that must have excelled at football.

Mike felt comfortable enough to walk to the bar. "I work for old folks in nursing homes. I'm here hoping to get a message to the son of a very ill gentleman in Larkspur Nursing Home over in Chickton. I was told his son hangs out here."

Calvin's eyebrows lifted when he said, "How a black man get over in Chickton?"

"I don't know, but I know his son's name is Benny Mack. Would you know him?"

"Mack? Don't know nobody named Mack."

"He might be better known as Big-dough Benny."

Before Calvin could answer, a chair crashed. Mike turned and caught a little guy's burning stare. He looked ready to sail some where, dressed as he was in a sand colored Bivi over a white tee shirt, tan pants and half sneakers. He had his right hand in his pocket. Mike gulped.

174

He'd seen too many Western shoot-outs. He raised his arms slowly. Bar stool sitters dispersed.

"Don't do no bad in my place Big-dough," Calvin said forcefully. "Out to the lot!'

Oh Lord, Mike thought, Calvin's fastidiousness wasn't at all satisfying.

"Undercover!" Big-dough Benny said, hissing. The nervous little guy's pocket jumped.

"No!" Mike said with vigor. "I'm not undercover. I'm not a cop." He thought it unlikely a white cop could be stupid enough to go undercover within a ghetto tavern. He wasn't about to taunt Big-dough Benny on that point. Instead, he raised his hands higher. "Believe it or not, I'm here at the request of your father, Herman Mack in Larkspur Nursing Home. He's not doing well. He wants to see you. Wants to make amends. Asked me to look you up to tell you."

"You a dumb shit, you think I believe that."

"I am a dumb shit for coming to tell you your father wants to make amends. He said he also wants to give you your Mama's bible."

"Mama's bible?" Big-dough Benny's mouth twisted in surprise. He looked to Calvin, who nodded positively, then, taking the hand from the bulgy pocket, Benny looked to the caller.

Was Big-dough Benny grimacing? Smiling? It was difficult to tell with the light reflecting off his gold front teeth.

"Mama's bible?' he said,. "Old Pop say he be giving me Mama's bible? She put me down in her bible, man. Mama's bible!" There was joy in his sound. "You for real, man!"

"Not for much longer at this pace," he said, his hands cupping his heart. "Larkspur Nursing Home's visiting hours are from 8:00 AM to 8:00 PM every day. Here's a brochure with my name and 800 number. It's an answering service. If you need me to work out details, just leave a message. I'll get back to you. Nice to have met you, Big-dough, and you too Calvin."

"You don't mean it," Calvin said.

Mike tilted his head and twisted his lips with a skewed smile. He got his butt out and into the '83. It was up and running, in gear and moving out more swiftly than an eagle swooping to claw a fish out of a lake.

15

He dialed Five Counties. "Lizzy? This is Mike. Any messages?"

"So many, they've gone in one ear and out the other."

"Nothing to stop it?" His receiver vibrated with her guffawing.

"Very good," she said, composing herself. 'There's a call from social worker Tervana of Amaranth in Moose County about a husband wearing his wife's underwear. They are roommates there, a Mr. and Mrs Malts."

"Not well blended, I see." He phoned Amaranth. "Hello. This is Mike Brannagh, ombudsman, returning social worker's Tervana's call."

"Mr. Brannagh,' she said. "I called about Casimir Malts. He and Janet, his wife, share a room, but lately, Casimir has been wearing her underclothing. She's terribly embarrassed but Casimir doesn't care what she thinks."

Mike was taken back. "Was there a prior history?"

"None that Janet knows about. At least she said she hadn't noticed it back home, only since he joined her in the nursing home."

"I wonder if her absence from home started it and he brought it with him when he followed her? If that were the case, it shows an attachment to her, by underwear at least." He felt foolish about that comment. "Anyway, other than Mrs. Malts' embarrassment, is her husband causing other problems?"

"No, but Janet is riled. She wants to move to another room and take her underwear."

"A long-term marriage breaking up over underwear? "You might want to spend a little time with them before any move, to see if there's more behind it. Maybe a marriage counselor will come to see them. There may be a resolution other than separation!"

"Like what?"

He was hoping she'd not ask. "Like convincing her his wearing her garments show his attachment to her. If she doubts, and he persists, get him to buy his own."

"Marriage counseling sounds preferable. I'll ask the Malts to look into it. Goodbye."

Was there no end to old age oddities?

* * *

Daffodil was a gerrymandered facility. Its one story turned more directions than the combined speeches of political candidates on stumps. The home's original and main wing paralleled old highway 22, starting from Road 1000 East and running west. Off the west end, an equal-sized wing rose to the northwest, another from there to the north-north-east, then another east-north-east; and the last and newest, southeast. A six-foot fence, running from the southeast wing to the original east building, enclosed a grassy area. In an overflight, Daffodil looked a baseball stadium with a short right field fence, a left handed hitter's home-run park. Fall's first frosty bites had apparently postponed the game.

The '83 pickup found a snug parking spot between newer vehicles. Mike turned off the ignition and walked. A small portico covered the home's main entry. Its sidewalk was swept of farm plowed grit. Slips and falls were to be confined to residents within, not visitors outside. He entered. A receptionist sat in a fish bowl. "Good afternoon, Ma'am. I'm Mike Brannagh, ombudsman. Is Mrs. Vict in?"

"You're the ombudsman?" There was trepidation in her sound that quickly changed to puzzlement. "Why would you want Mrs. Vict to know you're here?"

"I let all administrators know when I'm visiting residents."

"Very well." A number was dialed, her lips moved, and features scrunched again when, from down the hall, a

178

snorting water buffalo crashed out of a door.

It snorted, "Where's the ombudsman?"

If the six-foot female in a brown tent dress to her ankles was Vict, she was a super-heavyweight. Her face was scarier than Richard Nixon's at resignation, fists bigger than the world's boxing champ. She glared at Brannagh but a nanosecond. Her eyes scalded the vestibule, the hallways. "Where in the hell is that traitor of an ombudsman? Where are you hiding?" No one would have answered even if he were protected by an armored division. She turned seething orbs on the visitor. "Who are you?" The inflection put on 'you' had a alligator's bite to it.

"Mike Brannagh," he said, and unhesitatingly added, "the new ombudsman."

"New? The old one ran out on me, did he? I could kill him for what he did."

Mike wasn't going to tempt the woman's temper further by asking what his predecessor did. Back in the old days of youth, he'd taken to the boxing ring against the toughest kids on the East side and again in college. He'd beaten every opponent. Age and the formidable feline too near him raised doubts he'd last the first half-minute of a two minute round against her.

"I'll tell you what he did," she said, cracking a verbal whip. "He said it was my fault, not the nursing staffs' because Stella had pressure sores. He had Stella's daughter visit. When she woke up from her faint, she pulled a cellular phone out of her purse and called her lawyer. Not the doctor, mind, but a lawyer! He called the prosecutor." There was a sorrowful shaking of Vict's head, a deadly seriousness in her tone. "I'm going to get that guy if it the last thing I do before I lose my license." She glared. "What was your name?"

"Mike Brannagh. I'm here to introduce myself to you and the President of the Resident Council." Why hadn't the State Ombudsman informed him on Daffodil?

On Stella? About the prosecutor? Something more appeared burning behind Vict's orbital embers over loss of license. "Come on in my office a moment?" she said, her bellow mellowing.

He felt a fly entering a web. The office was spacious, its wallpaper and wall to wall carpeting brown as her dress. A blue metal desk's top was neat as a scoured knife. Four filing cabinets, one in each corner, had opened drawers dangling like participles. Inset ceiling lights spotlighted four chairs around the desk.

"Take a chair," she said, sitting down behind the desk. She pointed to the chair under the brightest light-beam, readying for a grilling. "What happened to the other guy?"

"He left the ombudsman program."

"Where is he now?"

"Don't know. I suggest you direct your inquiries to Charley Donavan at State."

"You won't tell me?" She knew he wouldn't. There was more to say. "If Stella had but a superficial skin opening, would you have called her daughter?"

He long ago learned not to answer an adverse question with the specific reply desired, but to redefine the loaded words. By redefining the maliciously intended word or phrase, a saving response might be made. "If you mean by using the phrases "superficial skin opening' and 'calling her daughter' that there was in the resident's chart awareness of initiating pressure sores and the daughter is Stella's next-of-kin," he watched her eyes grow hot as red peppers, "then she should have been informed from day one that the skin opening was being treated. If I walked in and discovered Stella with pressure sores that were acute, I'd not only alert the charge nurse, your DON, you and the daughter, plus also Adult Protective Services and State Health."

"You assumed an awful lot,' she said curtly.

"Tell me your facts then."

"I'll tell you this," she said. "There are four stages to pressure sores. The first is a superficial ulceration over a bony prominence; the second, an acute inflammation with the appearance of a blister or abrasion; the third, a full thickness skin ulcer through fat, infected and often foul smelling; the fourth, an ulcer clear through to a visible bone. My nursing staff know what to do. Daily and frequent irrigations are called for on stages three and four with cleansing by saline or peroxide solutions and wound dressing, but Stella's was but a stage two."

"If so, and your nursing staff were treating it, then why all this about my predecessor?"

"Ask him!" she said, shouting. "You're as one sided as he and the prosecutor. Bye!"

It was as one sided a good riddance as apparently was the predecessor's. Mike got up and out, her flame throwing eyes burning a hole in his neck. There was admiration as to the action in doing something about pressure sores. But a prosecutor at stage two? A criminal charge might have substance if Stella's sores had reached stage three or four, the nursing staff knowing pressure sores were preventable and treatable. But a prosecutor? What crime? If a coal mine company's executives and owners could get away with a civil action in negligence and monetary damages after ignoring mine safety standards for years and the coal mine collapsed killing miners, what difference where Vict and her nursing staff ignored treating Stella's sores? Neglect was a tort, a civil law wrong. Why was Vict subject to criminal sanctions with its deprivation of liberty? Why didn't Donavan, the State Ombudsman, during ombudsman training mentioned the case?

"Ma'am," Mike said to the receptionist, "which room is the council president's?"

Wide opened eyes expressed surprise the ombudsman had emerged from Vict's hell hole with his scalp. "Room 550. Mrs. Chrissy Schal."

Residents were smiling, rolling or walking up or down the halls in wheel chairs, with walkers or canes. An eyeball check of clothing detected not the first trace of a food stain, or pants' moisture with subsequent odor. On the contrary, clothing was clean, even if old fashion. Daffodil's outside rooms held three beds. Inside rooms overlooking the courtyard, two beds. Beds were made. Floors in the bathrooms shined. A maintenance man was striping a ten-foot patch of hallway flooring. Mike skipped past orange cones warning of wet floors. Nursing staff, in excess of minimal staffing standards, circulated from resident to resident room. Daffodil was as active. Nursing Home Management's Corporate reaction to Stella's case? The endless corridors came to a close in the five-hundred wing. He knocked.

"Mrs. Schal? I'm the new ombudsman, Mike Brannagh."

"New? Oh my goodness! Fran finally killed the other one over Stella?"

Stella's case had to be a humdinger. "Not that I know of Mrs. Schal." He was talking to her from the opened door. She looked in her eighties sitting in a rocking chair next to her bed. A barn red wig emphasized a pillow white face. She wore an emerald sweater over a lemon dress.

"Last I heard, he's alive and enjoying retirement."

"I'm so glad he retired. Then he's out of the witness protection program?"

Witness protection program? Why was he mentally repeating every surprise sentence? "May I come in?"

"Yes, please do. There's my roommate's chair. Pull it over and sit a spell."

He pulled the chair to the other side of her bed. "Let me show you my Ombudsman Identification Card so you know I'm so authorized." He handed her the laminated card. She held it very close to her eyes. Satisfied, she handed it back. He sat down.

"Mrs Vict is upset because of Stella's daughter, Bobbie Genn, was called to come and look at Stella's bed sores. Bobbie came later, she wasn't one for visiting much. Stella smelled skunk bad. Bobbie goes to change her when she. . . .," a pause, "... saw them ...,"   a gulp, "...maggots!" Schal's face contorted. "Maggots like on roadside kill. Bobbie Genn passed out." A fly buzzed. Schal cringed from the descendant of the infestation, a hand going to the mouth to keep in whatever wanted out.

"That's terrible," he said. In Korea but a month, he'd seen maggots on bodies of enemy soldiers killed in fire fights during the heat of September, the duration of battle preventing removal of corpses. As Schal had, he too, at the sight of maggots crawling on faces or limbs of GIs killed in action, hadn't avoided vomiting. Why maggots in a nursing home? Flies must have deposited eggs in Stella's pressure sores. The eggs, through the process of metamorphosis, developed into larvae, pupa and adult flies. Larvae, called maggots, consumed living tissue. Stella's sores would have enlarged as more female flies were attracted to her sores for egg deposits. The cornerstone of Nursing Home Management's professional staffs' care of Stella's skin should have been prevention. Sanitation was the best method for fly control.

She said, "Things are changing since Bobbie came and Stella went to the hospital. Bobbie Genn's lawyer has sued Daffodil. Fran has put on all kinds of nurses and housekeepers ever since. Food's great, even hot. Place is cleaner than a dairy. All kinds of activities. Aides fall all over themselves getting residents on and off the toilet. That isn't the whole of it. Fran is going to court before the County's old rooster, Judge Shear."

"Bobbie Genn must have sued Mrs. Vict, too."

"Don't rightly know about that. Heard Judge Shear

threw out what the Grand Jury said about Fran, but a bigger court said Judge Shear was wrong. She goes on trial no matter what, excepting she cops a plea, like they say on TV."

Grand Jury? Criminal charges? Enough of this merry-go-round. What was the story?

"Mrs. Schal, from what you're saying, Mrs. Genn brought a lawsuit against Daffodil's operators, and, apparently, the County prosecutor obtained a Grand Jury indictment against Mrs. Vict, but in court, Judge Shear threw out whatever the criminal charge was. However, the Appellate Court reversed Judge Shear. So Vict, apparently, is going to trial for a crime."

"That's it!" A big smile crossed her lips.

"A criminal charge is a public record. I'll phone APS to find out just what the charge is. I need to find a public phone."

"Use mine."

"Thank you." He dialed Adult Protective Services. "Wendy? Mike Brannagh calling from Daffodil Nursing home about . . ."

". . . about Fran Vict," Conner said, interrupting. "It's alleged she 'neglected a dependent'. It's a class four felony. Vict's lawyer argued to Judge Shear, and he agreed to their argument that the Juvenile Statutes applied only to parents or guardians of children. He dismissed the Grand Jury indictment because its language was found in the Juvenile Statutes. He held it applied only to neglect of a child dependent. The Appellate Court reversed. It held one who has the care, custody or control of a dependent may be liable for criminal acts that constitute neglect. A dependent is a person of any age, not just a child, who is mentally or physically disabled. The Jury decides Stella's dependency, the Appellate Court said, and the State Supreme Court let that ruling stand. Even though the administrator wasn't responsible for the direct delivery of medical services to residents, she was in a position to have obtained necessary medical services. Fran Vict didn't, that's what the Grand Jury indictment stated, and the Prosecutor has to prove."

"Thanks, Wendy." He hung up and said to Schal, "A higher Court said Judge Shear's dismissal of Vict's criminal charge was a mistake. The Appellate Court said a dependent is a person of any age who is mentally or physically disabled, and the administrator is in the position to see to it that necessary medical services are given. It's alleged Vict didn't do that. She's charged with class four crime!"

"What does that mean?"

"It means our State's Criminal Law has provisions for punishments that are most severe for the worst crimes. For class one crimes, murder, rape, it's imprisonment from twenty years to life; for class two crimes like burglary in an occupied home, from ten to twenty years; for class three, auto theft, from two to ten years; and class four, up to two years."

"Fran is worried she'll go to jail."

"If she's found guilty of a class four felony, she more likely will get probation, not jail. Chances are she'll cop that plea you mentioned, but a plea to a misdemeanor plus resignation from administering Daffodil or any nursing facility."

"Oh my goodness. Fran's still running Daffodil."

"Innocent until proven otherwise," he said. "In any event, while Vict's and the operators' cases are waiting trial, Daffodil should be the safest and best run home in the area."

* * *

On his way out of Daffodil, the thought crossed Mike's mind that his predecessor's resignation was closely associated with Fran Vict's and Nursing Home Management's pending legal problems. He must have felt threatened. Having met Vict, there was support for that

185

assumption. However, quitting the ombudsman's job, plus obscurity, was an over-reaction. Ombudsmen had legal immunity when acting in good faith on behalf of a resident. Reporting Stella's maggots underscored good faith.

He wondered if Ziggie's interest in Nursing Home Management, Quality Care, psychotropics on the street and his source's belief counterfeits were reaching residents in nursing homes was motivated by Stella's plight? After the resignation of the prior ombudsman, there quickly followed the hiring of the new, and for him to do more than advocate, to look into street drugs and counterfeits in nursing facilities. But no mention was made of maggots or corporate wrongdoings. And later, didn't Ziggie bring up an alleged tie of Nursing Home Management with Pharmacopeia Wholesalers? Mike questioned his taking the job. Looking out for the well being of residents, plus taking note of drug dealing, FDA quality or otherwise, had been his missions. Now, additionally, he was to look at alleged Corporate malfeasance? If his predecessor had been asked to do so, no wonder he'd quit and disappeared. Tough enough to take on a well funded corporation, but drug dealing? Fordice, as much in the know about Five Counties' nursing facilities as any health professional had told him, she knew of the connection between the Nursing Home Management and Quality Care's buildings for lease, but saw none between Pharmacopeia and Nursing Home Management. She did state Nursing Home Management had clout with State Health's HQ staff. That was politics, not per se wrong, just highly unethical. Campaign contributions are powerful speech, but recipients thereof are hardly free.

* * *

Escape from mental rumblings found Mike and his worn down pickup parking in another nursing home lot. Except for the six foot fence enclosing Astea's front yard there was the look of a four lawyer office building on a corner across the street from court house square. Parking was in the rear. The '83 found a resting place under a bald maple shielding a little of the home's parking lot from the fury of a sudden sprinkling. A review of the directory of nursing homes revealed Astea's administrator was Ken Flow, the home's capacity fifty intermediate care beds. Mike walked the parking lot to the sidewalk along side of the building. Twelve windows up high were bright with light, casting shimmers into late day's creeping dusk. A gate was double chained. He unhooked a clasp fastening a waist high chain to a fence pole. Up high, he lifted the circular length of chain up from the pole. Next, he raised a metal stirrup on its hinge. He pushed the gate open and entered the front yard, closing the gate, replacing chains and gadgets to their locked positions. Why did management enclose the only yard space with a tall fence? And place security devices on the only gate? Protection against crimes? This side of the town hadn't a high rate. What then? The front door of the nursing home was locked. Unusual! A small sign gave notice to enter the numbers: six, three, seven, four, in that order, then pull the door's knob at the sound of a buzz. A hell of a security feature! He entered the required   numbers. The door buzzed. He pulled it open. Upon entry a very little woman in a quite rumpled orange dress came forward, face round and luminous, a toothless mouth drooling. One arm was uplifted to hug, the other outstretched to shake hands. She hugged while shaking. Other residents, whether mobile males or wheelchair females, all of whom looked more physically debilitated with limbs more contorted than the hugging woman's, but alerted by her squealing, turned from the TV. Legs and arms went in all directions but the direction desired. Faces, long as mourners' had angles and turns not studied in geometry. Eyes, ears and noses varied in facial placements far from the norm. Speech was unintelligible. Were they forming for turns at hugging and hand shaking?

They were! Communication was a hug and hand shake with moisture to boot. He gave each his want in a nursing home for the chronically ill mentally retarded.

"Hello," said an old timer coming out of a receptionist's glass bowl. He wore brown jeans, a white shirt and brown tie, with bodily parts located as expected. "I'm Ken Flow, administrator."

"Mike Brannagh, ombudsman. Quite a welcoming."

"It'll take you a while to dry," Flow said. "Let me help get you loose. Now Gertie, Joel, George, let the nice man come in and talk to Uncle Ken. That's nice, that's nice. Thank you Teddy. Yes, the nice man's coming back, Bonnie."

Freed from the affectionate dousing, he followed Flow into the glass wall office. Sitting down in an executive chair behind an oak desk, he directed Brannagh to a wooden, hard back chair.

"Sorry we haven't a softer one. Too expensive to keep that type clean. What brings you?"

"No complaint. I'm stopping at all nursing homes in the Five Counties Area to introduce myself to administrators and council presidents. Astea is on my list, but not a word about its clientele. I had no idea."

"You weren't put off by them," he said with an admiring smile. "Most visitors cringe. It's pathetic to see them react."

"Your calling to work with the developmentally disabled isn't heard by many."

"I accept that.."

"Have you a council president?"

"No."

"Do you mind me looking around?"

"Please do."

Mike exited the glass wall office, turned left, and left again. A nurse station opened on the hall immediately behind the back wall of Flow's office. A door connected the two places. Down the hall resident rooms ran the window side of the building. The doors of the rooms were open. A young person under a wool blanket laid on a bed in the room across from the nurse station. Upright rails turned the bed into a crib. The back of a woman in nurse's whites was visible. She sat on a chair at bedside. Other residents' grunts, screams and noises failed to turn her from her charge. Exclusion of residents' and electronic media noises were auditory inventions of nurses to preserve sanity. If the resident's blond curly hair and face fair as a white campion flower were indicative, she was eight or nine. A child in a nursing home? Then, most of the hugging residents up front were child-like, though in their twenties, thirties or forties. He noted the child's eyes wander, her hand come out from under the blanket through crib bars to catch a beam. The nurse touched the girl's finger with the gentleness of a mother. The child drooled, nurse quickly producing a towel to wipe the moisture. Curly haired was a child with newborn movements. What terrible illness devastated the little goddess?

The nurse turned to look. She wasn't much older than the girl in the crib, golden hair as lustrous as the child's, eyes as blue, face as pretty.

"What A beautiful child. What happened?"

"She's Debbie! A swimming accident. She hit her head on the bottom of the boat. Her father finally found her under the pier. There was considerable brain damage."

16

"Hello, Mike," Lizzy said. "It's a madhouse here this morning. Accountants are in and checking our books, bossing us around."

"I supposed they're just asking staff for receipts to back up expenditures, Lizzy."

"That's funny. That's what my tax accountant used to ask me to keep."

"Time to flee, Lizzy."

"You're little help. Two messages. Call Mrs Brick at Poppy and a Millie Hopk." She gave him the phone numbers.

He dialed, wondering who the Millie named Hopk was. He knew the Millie named Grain. "Mike Brannagh, returning Millie Hopk's phone call."

"This is Millie, Mike. I'm living with Fanny now. That's where you're calling. You no doubt noticed I've taken back my maiden name. Javier and I have agreed to a divorce."

"If it has to be a divorce, I'm pleased for your sake it's agreeable."

"Has to be. We signed prenuptial agreements. The reason I called you is Fanny told me Ms Lancaster, the administrator, runs the Aides like they're in a boot camp. Fanny says Lancaster is particularly cross with black Aides. One perceived strike, you're out, like Fanny. I was hired by CEO Dale Unge to come to Lobelia, so I'm going to call him and ask him to look into it."

"Does Javier Grain own the nursing home building?"

"His company Quality Care does. It leases them to Nursing Home Management. That's how Javier and I met at Lobelia. Unge introduced Javier and I."

"As your ex-husband's company leases buildings to

Nursing Home Management, and when the word of your divorce gets back to Unge,   the guy may see your call in a wrong light. If Fanny's correct, letting the guy know could undermine the true facts you hope to uncover at Palace. Sour grapes and all that rot. If we can show at the Golah hearing that's what happened to Fanny, she may well have a cause of action for wrongful discharge. Hold off, OK?"

There was a grudging 'yes'.

Poppy Nursing Home was dialed." This is Mike Brannagh, ombudsman, returning Louise Brick's call."

"About what?" The inquirer wasn't too well versed on phone etiquette. Poppy's clientele were similar to those from Brannagh's days at the Parole office, working on regaining stability from alcohol and street drug abuses. Etiquette wasn't numbered highly among virtues sought. Still, he admired their effort. They'd lost the way but were trying to walk the path of sobriety at a site more than a way station to redemption, at a residence until income could rent a place.

"She'll know. Just tell her it's the ombudsman." He hadn't an overload of etiquette himself. In the background, the phone answerer yelled, "Louise! Phone from the 'omnibus'."

She heard. "Just a minute. I'll take it in my office." The phone clunked against a hard object. A half minute later, she said, "Hello Mr. Brannagh. Just a minute." There was another pause. "Tom," she said politely, "hang up." She returned to the line. "I can talk now. Sorry about the delay. I called about Sylvester Merba. He's presenting a lot of problems, like pinching a couple of our women. Says he'll toss their good clothes out the window if they tell. I'd like to issue him an involuntary transfer notice but not send it to State Health, just to you. When I issue him the Notice, I'll scare the wrong behavior right out of him for a while, but I'll need you to drop in and reinforce good behavior. Syl isn't a bad sort. He's come a long way. No family.

191

Works nights in a bakery. He's saving money. I can really shake him up by telling him you're coming, that you use to run the parole office. He'll be on good behavior for a long time."

"Mrs. Brick," he said with a touch of drama, "the ombudsman's job means I'm Merba's advocate." He changed tones. "Having said that, I understand. If my reinforcing your scare will help keep him sober, working, and at Poppy while not pinching gals, it's a technique as good as any. I'll do it as soon as I can visit. Just mail the Notice to me." He sensed Brick could be trusted.

* * *

Nursing Home Management's Coralroot's one story building stretched its brick facade and asphalt parking lots over four acres of formerly low yield corn fields. Forty front windows marked rooms with views of the setting sun, if September's clouds didn't clothed it. Three back wings of the home poked into the east like pitchfork prongs, the northern and southern wings for residents, the middle for dining, laundry and staff lounge. Administrative offices occupied the vantage point of the middle wing's front entry.

After opening the front door and causing a light to flash at the desk of the administrator's secretary, visitors to Coralroot were observed through a one way glass wall window by Pamela Hushed, secretary. Her all encompassing eye quickly refocused after the flash of the entry strobe. She couldn't miss a big old man carrying a notebook. There were hints of vague importance, a brown tie and white shirt, but not brown jeans. A salesman? Watching him come in, a double take was made of the long white wool sweater he wore that covered from his shoulders to his waist. "May I help you, sir?"

The woman's closely cut brown hair, pinched face, carbernet sweater and relaxed-fit elastic-waist jeans gave her the appearance of a basketball forward, a young woman

192

with scarce beauty but with a frame ideal for drives on the hoop.

"I'm Mike Brannagh, ombudsman, here to introduce myself to the council president and the administrator."

"Mrs. Hann is holding a meeting in her office but I'll let her know you're here." She left her desk to open a door at the back of her office, entered and closed the door behind her.

He scanned the immediate premises. There were staff offices on all four corners of the cross formed by the west building and the middle prong. Next to each of the four offices appeared another. There was no nurse station in the middle of the building. A wide aisle ran to the east down the middle wing. The hallway floors appeared to be scrubbed and waxed. Ivory was the paint color of choice. It covered every wall. Finger print smudges weren't discernible to the distant eye. There wasn't the odor of urine so prevalent at Palace, nor were Coralroot's residents wearing fourth-hand clothes. As colorful and clean as was their apparel, it was only a decade dated. Railings, like monorails, ran the walls along well traveled routes. Trains of wheelchair riders pulled themselves along the rails to their rooms. Wide doorway spaces presented hindrances necessitating a jerk and glide to the other side. Sporadically, a trailer bumped a lead wheelchair the distance across a door opening. Either side of the east aisle were large rooms. In the next to last room on the right, a dining room, a woman in a rose colored dress exited, her toothpick exuberantly stabbing teeth for a late snack. Failing to harpoon the morsel, she stopped, removed her teeth, and proceeded to successfully reclaim it.

Attention returned to the office when Hushed reemerged. She was noisily followed by a ghostly face and hands as if detached. As the face loomed into view, it was on a heavy set woman in a long sleeve black wool sweater dress. Her hair, stockings and shoes matched the dress. Many, many black sheep relinquished wool to provide the dressmaker her materials.

"I'm Zelda Hann," she said. "Pamela tells me you are the ombudsman. You're late for Quinta's hearing. The Hearing Officer started without you."

A hearing? He'd known nothing of a hearing. He wasn't at Coralroot for a hearing, but what the hell, he was now. "After you." Quinta who? Why?

He was led through a waiting room into an office. At the head of a table to the side of the administrator's desk sat a young woman with an intelligent face and, in a tailored blue business suit, as sharply dressed as a new lawyer swearing in before a State Supreme Court Justice. Her blond hair glorified the handiwork of a very skilled hairdresser. She frowned. Behind and to her right side sat a lady two times as old, hair gray, face wrinkled, but casually dressed in a camel colored blazer and blue jeans. At the other end of the table, in a wheelchair, sat a sleeping, pitiful specimen of a very old lady in a pine colored housecoat and green slippers, face and hands as white and thin as toilet tissue.

Hann said, "This is the ombudsman, Mr. aw-aw."

"Mike Brannagh."

Hann sat down to the hearing officer's left and guided Brannagh to sit on the wheelchair's right. Instead, he stood there looking at his putative client. She appeared immobile, abstracted from time, place and alertness. What could she have done? How could she testify?

"Mr. Brannagh," Hann said by way of introduction, "this is Miss Mary Barr, the Hearing Officer, and Mrs. June Scott, court reporter."

"Pleased to have met you Miss Barr, Mrs. Scott." He smiled, nodded, and sat down.

"Why are you late Mr. Brannagh," Barr said, a touch of petulance in the sound.

"Are we on the record?" he said. Scott wasn't transcribing. She started up. "I received no Notice of the Involuntary Discharge as State Rules require, Ma'am." State Rules required the notice be transmitted to a family member, the legal representative and legal guardian, if known, State Health and the ombudsman, if an involuntary relocation or discharge. He'd tell what he knew, but not that he knew nothing else, like Quinta's's last name. After all, this was the age of elderly rights and Barr might fear reversal by an Administrative Law Judge if she proceeded without the ombudsman being notified and the case appealed.

"My secretary Pamela mailed Notices to the ombudsman, State Health and Quinta's daughter, Peggy Ding," Hann said with bluster.

Where was daughter Peggy Ding? Snoozing Quinta wasn't up to presenting any kind of a defense. Nor for that matter was he! He'd bluff. "When, to whom and at what address?"

"To the other ombudsman. His address."

"My appointment was effective September first. It was announced by State Ombudsman Charles Donavan by mail to all nursing facilities in the Five Counties Area. He told me he even sent a Fax to State Health." Mention of State Health was an afterthought. Miss Barr was retained by State Health. "Might I look at Quinta's chart?" The huge file was pushed across the Board Room table. He opened it. What the hell should he look for? The date of the Notice, of course! He attempted to look intelligent thumbing through page after page. Barr was quieter than Hann. Scott's fingers rested. There it was, a copy of the Notice. Quinta Ray was his client and the form indicated she was a danger to others. A danger? She'd not twitched a hair. "This Notice is dated September 5, Miss Barr," he said, presenting his argument to the Hearing Officer and Scott's nimble digits. "It was mailed after the announcement of my appointment was made to this facility. So Coralroot was on notice of both my name and address. Coralroot was required to mail the Notice to me. They didn't! Consequently, it's defective." He shut up not wanting any inquiry as to whom it was that mailed in the form requesting a hearing.

"Be that as it may," Barr said with irritation, "I'm not continuing this hearing to another day. We'll proceed."

"Proceed to do what?" he said, disappointed his first shot across the table missed. He'd fire another. "Mrs. Ray is obviously not up to testifying, judging by her sleeping as we talk and it's a hearing on discharge," he said, exerting a touch of his past executive tone. "With only Mrs. Hann presenting her data, it would be tantamount to a kangaroo court."

The red flush on Barr's cheeks told of her deep irritation over his words.

Hann sensed a kill. "Peggy Ding," she said piously, "is her mother's legal guardian. She was properly notified."

"Show me," he said, "where in the record it indicates Ding is her mother's legal guardian?"

"Right here," Hann said, handing over a couple of stapled pages.

"This is a copy of a Power of Attorney," he said. "It gives the daughter certain powers to act under certain circumstances, but it doesn't make her a legal guardian. A court does that. I'd like it in the record that Mrs. Ray isn't alert at the moment, whether or not that's her normal state or a reaction to medicine. She can't assert or waive her rights much less tell her side of the story. Under such circumstances, this hearing should not proceed at this time."

Had he missed again? Was she not going to back off no matter the cogency, or lack, of his points. A delay was in order. Perhaps the daughter was on her way? "Will you grant us a recess, that I might review Mrs. Ray's clinical chart?"

"Fifteen minutes," she said, standing up abruptly, then hurrying out of the room. Scott exercised her fingers, then legs in pursuit of Barr.

"Mrs. Hann?" he said. "Where might I have some privacy?"

"Here," she said. She pushed up from her chair and exited, closing the door.

"Well, Mrs. Ray," he said to the immobile face, "it's you and me against Coralroot." He opened the chart to Nurse's notes. There was entry after entry about daughter Ding's behavior complaining over her mother's care, or lack of it. Ding had even hidden behind curtains one night to check if nurses gave Ray her treatments and managed to scare the be-jabbers out of one. Ding had also entered the kitchen and threaten to force feed cook the cold, tasteless food cook had prepared for Ray. To protest the lack of attention given her mother's bowel movements, Ding placed a brightly wrapped package, turd within, on Hann's chair. Mike took an instant liking to Peggy Ding. Where were the notations as to Mrs. Ray's danger to other residents? None in the Nurse notes. He skipped to Social Worker notes. It was Ding, not Ray, who again was recorded time after time protesting Coralroot's quality of care. Teaching housekeepers how to make beds the way Ding learned in the Military wasn't of itself a grievance with Social Worker Emtra, but making the bed so tightly with house keeper Sandra pinned down under its blankets was a grievance made by the housekeeping supervisor. There wasn't a bad word about Ray in her chart, but a book of controversy with Peggy Ding. Was Mrs. Ray's alleged danger to others actually her daughter's challenges to Coralroot staff? Hann was trying to discharge Quinta Ray to get rid of Peggy Ding!

The trio of woman reentered the hearing room and returned to their places. Administrator Zelda Hann wiggled a sizable behind into her chair. Court Reporter Scott sat down and readied her fingers for transcription. Hearing Officer Barr took her seat and lifted some papers. She read: "All matters involving the Involuntary Discharge will be heard at this time, the nursing facility first to present the substance of its case, then the resident's representative, in this case, Ombudsman Mike Brannagh. Thereafter, communications with me by hearing participants is ex-parte and precluded. My finding will be mailed to all participants before the expiration of thirty-four days from the date Quinta Ray first received notice. Have you some procedural objections to present Mr. Brannagh?"

"I do. Procedural Rule 6 requires a copy of the involuntary transfer notice be transmitted to the ombudsman. The Notice dated September 5 wasn't sent to Mike Brannagh who was publically   appointed Ombudsman on September 1.   Rule 18 requires a planning conference. There is nothing in the record to indicate there was one. Rule 19 requires Mrs. Ray's medical, psychosocial and social needs be considered and a plan devised to meet those needs.   There is no such plan in the record. Rule 22 requires a relocation plan. If done, it's not in the record. Rule 23 requires a written report of the discussion of the relocation meeting for review and comments. No review or comments were found in the record. Rule 24 requires this written report, if disputed, be placed in the record. It's not in the record. For these reasons, and for the reason the Notice of Involuntary Discharge of Quinta Ray is defective, this matter should be dismissed."

"Mrs. Hann," Barr said, "have you a response to claims as to procedural errors."

"Yes I do," she said. "His claims are ridiculous. How could I conduct a conference or hold a relocation meeting. Quinta isn't alert. It is impossible to discuss anything with her."

"If she's not alert," he said, jumping in with all

teeth bared, "how is she dangerous to others."

"Her daughter Peggy scares my staff to death." she said, shifting from right cheek to left.

"Miss Barr," he said with the sweetness of a pound of sugar, "as you just heard from the party moving to involuntarily discharge Quinta Ray for being dangerous to others, she isn't. That admission totally refutes the allegation that she was, or is, or will be dangerous to others. Due to this admission and the procedural errors I cited, I ask the nursing home's involuntary discharge request not be allowed."

Barr's expression of irritation changed to chagrin. "Mrs. Hann? If Quinta Ray isn't dangerous to others, on what is your allegation based?"

"On her daughter's attacking my staff. Peggy Ding is frightening. If Quinta is transferred, I and my staff will be safe from Ding's taunts and vulgar escapades."

"Oh my!" Barr said. "That concludes this hearing. Thank you all. You'll have my decision quite soon."

"But Miss Barr," Hann said, pleading, "there's so much I need to tell you about Ding."

"Ex-parte Mrs. Hann, ex-parte," Barr said. "Mrs. Scott are you ready to leave?" She was. Together, they left the room.

"She's going to rule against me!" said Hann in a chiding tone, eyes cutting Brannagh to little pieces. "Look what you've done!"

He felt the urge to blast back, but was, momentarily, meek. At the rate he was making friends with Nursing Home Management's administrators, he'd not be remembered at Christmas. "Done?" he said. "The burden of proof that Mrs. Ray was dangerous is on the nursing home. What I did was to see that you met that burden. I believe you didn't. Perhaps Miss Barr will agree." What else was he to say? Hann and her nursing home had a lawyer on retainer. Danged if Brannagh would suggest if there were a case against Ding that Hann should have taken her to court for a restraining order. "Mrs. Ray," he said, "I'll take you back to your room."

Hann didn't protest his pushing the wheelchair out of her office. She was glad to be shuck of him. The secretary wasn't at her desk to ask where Ray's room was. A tall woman behind a walker was in the corridor. She would have been noticeable a mile away in her orange turtleneck shirt and a pumpkin and jolly jack-o-lantern sweater. "You look wonderfully," he said to her, "and in the spirit of the approaching season."

"Thank you," she said, her tooth missing smile matching that of her sweater's jolly jack-o-lantern. "Are you Quinta's boy?"

"I'm not. I'm Mike Brannagh, ombudsman." He handed her a brochure. "Your name, Ma'am?"

"Mazie Fac," she said. "Is Zelda going to kick Quinta out?" she said fearfully.

"Zelda? Is Zelda Mrs. Hann, the administrator?"

"Yes. Zelda was fed up with Peggy's interference with staff. Thank goodness for Peggy," Fac said. "I don't know what we're going to do without her. She was our good right arm. You didn't answer me about Zelda putting Quinta out."

"I can't," he said, surprised by the use of the past tense regarding Peggy Ding. She must have passed on. The daughter before the mother? "I'm bound by the law to respect Mrs. Ray's privacy but I can tell you this. A part of an ombudsman's job is to fight tooth and nail for the resident should an administrator want to put any resident out. The final decision is up to a Hearing Officer."

"I saw her, a fashionable young woman, isn't she?" Fac said. "She stormed out of Zelda's office and I just happened to overhear her complain to the other woman about the senselessness and waste of money for calling them in for such a charade."

"Mrs. Fac," he said, his smile as wide as hers, "you know more than I do. I have to wait for the written finding of facts and conclusions of law."

"So you were in there for Quinta?"

"I was."

"Peggy will appreciate it."

Fac switched to the present tense on Ding. "She will? Why wasn't she here?"

"Peggy's in the hospital. A car accident."

"Oh, my! How is she doing?"

"Well enough. Thank God she doesn't have to come to Coralroot to recuperate!"

"I'm glad for her," he said, his stomach twisting thinking Hann took advantage.

"Quinta will never know," Fac said.

"No, I guess not," he said, wondering the opposite. Wouldn't Ray's senses, if not deep intellect, miss Peggy Ding's touch, caress, sound, smell? He concluded Ray would know her spirit's spark wasn't present. She'd suffer from her absence. "Could you tell me which room is Quinta's?"

"Down the hall that way," she said, pointing to the north. "I'm going the other way, pity, or I'd show you. It's Room 42. Used to be decorated so beautifully. Zelda ordered housekeeping take all of Peggy's stuff off her walls. Will you be coming back?"

"I will, Mrs. Fac. Nice meeting you." He nodded his goodbye, turned and pushed Ray's wheelchair to her room. It was a room as plain as the inside of a cardboard box. What a difference to Quinta's quality of life the frequent visits Peggy Ding made. Would that all residents have such a frequent visitor! Visitors could constantly put administrators to the standards set out in Federal and State Rules. If so, nursing homes, under family scrutiny, would operate as owners and administrators agreed to run them when they signed up for Medicare and Medicaid reimbursements. In Ding's absence, and the infrequency of family or friend visitations, the ombudsman was at a loss to head off difficulties before they mushroomed.

There was unfinished business. Brannagh returned to the front offices. "Ma'am," he said to secretary Hushed, "would you tell Mrs. Hann I'd like a moment of her time."

"Just a minute, please." She got up and went through the rear door into Mrs. Hann's office, closing the door. A minute stretched to five, the ombudsman gazing at residents passing by, some heading up the middle corridor to the dining area. Others passing each other as if those on the west side of the main corridor had to go east, and those east, to the west. The door to Hann's office reopened. "Please come in," Hushed said. She waited for him to enter, then stepped to the side of the door jam as if a Secret Service Agent protecting her President. Hann was behind her desk. She didn't ask him to sit.

It didn't matter. "Mrs. Hann," he said, "you might recall some mention being made in State and Federal Rules about resident's rights?"

"Your point?" she said, sick of the sight of him.

"My point is this. Mrs. Ray's property, whether the clock on her dresser, the clothes within or decorations on her wall are personal, and are to be treated with consideration and respect. For some reason, housekeeping removed her decorations. A mistake, no doubt, I pray you'll have it rectified today. Thank you for your time."

She didn't reply.

Nothing remaining to discuss, he about faced, passed the sentinel, and exited the home.

He had the urge to cuss. Instead, he spat on the driveway's asphalt. But for the happenstance of his visit to Coralroot, he'd never have known of Quinta Ray or heard of Peggy Ding. At any given moment in the homes he visited, half the residents were under the spell of medicines, another quarter not alert, the remainder hesitant to discuss troubles out of fear of retaliation, real or imagined. How many like Ray were there? How could one ombudsman ever protect their rights? The question presupposed administrators, many of them, ran their facilities to suit their own interests which might not be those of aggravating residents or their relatives. As a Jail Administrator, he would have been sued at the mere suspicion of violating an inmate's civil rights. Where were the Civil Rights Lawyers for the elderly in nursing homes? A few publicized lawsuits would shape up the money grubbers who controlled the for-profit industry.

* * *

Pine Nursing Home was in a grove of weeping willows a hundred yards from a main tributary to the river that flowed through Oldtown. Currently, it wasn't named for a flower. It had gone by the name 'Fuchsia' until the survey of October 1991, then 'Holly' until the follow-up survey, then to 'Pine'. The recent purchasers of the aged building shaped like an inverted tuning fork, and the out of county operators contracting for a fat fee to run it, eagerly desired to escape the odor of the flower years by name change, not investment. Quincy Yeak was the administrator of the month, the fourth since the follow-up survey. Yeak's predecessors hadn't been given a budget by the operating company sufficient to hire necessary staff, much less pay competitive salaries or hourly rates, even as compared to other Francois County nursing homes. Yeak, however, did tricks with the pay rates. If an hourly employee gave up benefits: health, sick days, vacation days, her hourly rate was raised the amount otherwise paid out. For grass widows and divorcees, most of the nursing staff, it was a here and now living wage if they and their offspring remained healthy. There wasn't money for vacations in any event. Hopefully, current experience as an Aide or nurse meant a better paying job in the future, for the future of Pine was tentative at best. Pine's Admissions Director and social worker, Orvilla Choke, was down to accepting recalcitrant elderly from other nursing home that had convinced relatives the happiness of a loved one lay in voluntarily transferring to the home beneath the willows.

The overgrown beds of flowers between the forks of the tuner were brown, kissed by frost. The red brick building's windows were dark to the west, lighted on the east. The main entry was on the east wing. Mike parked beside that wing. Residents inside sat rigidly immobile on hard wood chairs around tables. Not even a cup of coffee was visible on the bare tables. If they were looking at something specific outside the dining room windows, it wasn't apparent. He entered the top of what appeared to be a long tunnel. To his left was the customary plate glass enclosing the receptionist desk, except there wasn't a receptionist. Around the corner to the left from the enclosure were two closed doors, one with a card inserted in a slot that read 'Quincy Yeak, Administrator', the other with a card taped to the wood, imprinted 'Orvilla Choke, Admissions and Social Worker'. Orvilla's prestige didn't warrant a card slot. Mike knocked first on the door of the administrator, then the social worker. Neither responded. To the right of the front entry, across the tunnel of a hall and ten feet beyond the reception booth was a double door into the dining area. He crossed over and entered. Those residents with eyes transfixed to a point in space were still in place, but not as rigid as they appeared from the outside. Radios were playing quite loudly. Several tuned to different stations and the quality of music ranged from hill-billy to classical. Listening to one, as opposed to another, was impossible. No wonder eyes were transfixed. He went up to each table to detect alertness, but failed to get a single radio turned down. He left a brochure at each occupied table.

A serving window to the kitchen was open. Staff in white dresses and dingy white aprons had gathered around a metal table with a jug of coffee, donuts aplenty. They chatted amiably.

"Hello. I'm the ombudsman." He set a brochure on the table. "Could you tell me where Mr. Yeak is?"

There was mumbling, before a sturdy woman responded. "He's not in the kitchen."

"By the way, when is resident coffee break?"

"Over a hour ago," she said. "They is waiting on supper."

"Well, if you see Mr. Yeak before I do, please let him know the ombudsman is here." The nod she gave was as indifferent as a Roman citizen's thumbs down. He continued down the tunnel. There was a nurse at a nurse station down the hall. A man all bones and knuckles stumped, it wasn't a walk, out of a room across from the nurse station. Like an old dog he dangled his tenderloin. She got up and approached him, whispering into his ear, turned her back and returned to the chair. Old dog quickly hibernated the bear and zippered his fly.

"Thank you, Flory," he said, stumping away toward the dining room.

"All kinds of professional duties befall a nurse," Mike said in commiseration, leaning on the station's counter.

"Most not taught in school," she said with a sigh. She was a thin woman, thirty, her face very slender with hair corn-gold and silky straight.

"I'm Mike Brannagh, Ombudsman, here to introduce myself to you and a few residents."

"Flory Kenmore," she said.

"I noticed many residents already in the dining room, most playing radios. It's an hour or so before meal time. Is that usual?"

"Until we get a new activities director," she said, "which is unlikely. Not enough new residents being admitted. No money, I suspect. We sure need an activities director. The recently admitted aren't as easy to work with

205

as Matthew. He may forget his incidental from time to time, but he handles himself well."

"He sure did handle it well when you whispered to him a moment ago," he said, unable to resist the pun. He got a laugh. "What about the recently admitted?"

"Many behavioral problems."

"That's what your social worker and this ombudsman are all about, resident problems. Hopefully to minimize them before they become acute."

"Mamie's problem was already acute before she transferred here," Kenmore said, "and Orvilla isn't in the building many times to work with her."

"What's with Mamie.... who?"

"Mamie Lutti. She transferred here from Rooster County. It's an impossibility to meet her demands to go to the bathroom. I have her on a bladder control program, but if someone within ten yards so much as pours a glass of water, Mamie screams she has to go, and I mean scream. Listen!" She got up from her chair and walked over to a drinking fountain and ran the water. There was a fifteen second hiatus.

"Flory, come quick before I wet myself! Quick! Quick! Quick!" Lutti called, her sound out the open door next to the drinking fountain an octave higher than owl's hoots.

Kenmore popped her head into the doorway. "There's a man here to see you, Mamie."

"A man? He can't take me to the toilet."

"You can hold it," Kenmore said.

"Maybe you should run her in," he said, "rather than have her wet while I'm in there."

Kenmore went in, but wasn't long at the chore. "False alarm!" she said.

"Just out of curiosity, why do you have Mamie's room next to a drinking fountain, knowing that running water triggers her mental bladder?"

206

"Oh my goodness," she said, astonishment spreading like measles over her face, "why do I? Will you ask her to move?"

"We'll see." He knocked on Lutti's door. "Mrs. Lutti? I work for residents. May I come in?"

"Yes, I'm decent." She was decent in a blue bath robe that wrapped around her like a Turkish towel. She was small as a ten year old girl, bony as a fish, ears big, eyes sleepy. The hair on her head was stacked like a huge white cloud. She sat in a wheelchair with legs jack- knifed.

"I'm the ombudsman, Mike Brannagh, Mrs. Lutti. May I pull that chair over here and sit?"

"It's an uncomfortable chair, but okay."

He sat a few feet from her. "I noticed when Nurse Flory took a drink, the running water turned on your own spigot. Does running water bother you?"

"Yes it does. Sometimes I think they run the water just to make me go."

"With the drinking fountain right out side your door, I can see that would be a pain. Particularly when the heat's up high in the building, like today."

"That's right; that's right! Why don't they move the drinking fountain?"

"Probably attached to pipes in the wall. Say? I noticed several empty rooms as I walked down this way. Maybe you can choose the best of the lot far away from the drinking fountain?"

"Flory would have to come farther to get me off the wheelchair onto the toilet."

"If you tell her you wouldn't have to go so often far away from the drinking fountain, she might agree. Just nice talk her."

"Nice talk her? I will. Flory is really sweet."

"Now remember to talk nice and maybe she'll get you the best room far away from the fountain sooner than you would think."

At the nurse station, he leaned over and whispered, 'she's going to nice talk you into giving her the best empty room farthest away from the fountain."

"She is?" she said, delighted. "I'm sure she will."

He hadn't gone far down the hall when a hiss stopped his progress.

"In here," said hisser, motioning to come into his room. The old gent looked as soldiery as he must have in 1945. His Ike jacket with corporal stripes, olive drab shirt and pants, brown tie and shoes, and an infantryman's peaked cap with blue piping that fit him well were as neat as new issue. "I'm getting it ready for the Halloween party next month. Do you like it?" He didn't wait for more than a nod. "I'm Corporal Luigi Anthony. Did my time in North Africa. Got hit. Disabled. I missed getting to Rome. Papa came from there. I wanted to see relatives if they weren't for Mussolini. Never did find out."

"Sometimes hard working stiffs haven't much of an alternative to a dictator's troops. No money to get out, no country to take them in. They were probably stuck."

"That's right!" he said with an upbeat tone, wanting to believe. "Have you come to work for Pine? That's the new name."

"I'm the ombudsman, part of a federal-state program." A brochure was handed him. "Ombudsmen work only for residents, not for the nursing home. We try to work out problems before they get too big and miserable."

"Too late for Pine. It's fading away like an old soldier. My grandson is working on getting me into Proteas over in Trinton. He lives near there. Were you in the military service?"

"I used to be Staff Sergeant Mike Brannagh, Regular Army, assigned to the Army's Twenty-fifth Infantry Division, Thirty-fifth Infantry Regimental Combat Team, Dog Company Machine-gun Platoon, third Section. I did my combat time in North Korea, at Kumwha and the

Punchbowl, 1951-1952."

"Look me up at Proteas," he said.

* * *

Back home, body fatigued from riding the pickup, he dressed in sweatpants and sweatshirt, cotton socks and walking shoes for a three mile hike around the wetland. A sweat jacket provided a windbreak against variant breezes; the baseball cap sheltered an overhang of hair and gloves minimized a left thumb and little finger from contracting, as was their recent inclination. Just one of life's numerous injuries.

The evening sky was filled with blue-gray bubbles, the water in the swamp sable. Geese known to inhabit weren't visible. September was preparing October for Nature's paint crew's re-coloring. A few maples had set the annual trend by changing green hues to orange, brown, red and purple peacocks' plumage. Elms, withering and thinning, were dropping those leaves turned golden to enrich the soil. Evergreens poked spear points into the horizon. Weeping willows stood droop-limbed. Revolving in flight, coal colored birds crossed the gray clouds, coming and going from limbs high up in the trees. Some on thin branches scolded the foot-free walker.

He didn't much notice their blistering chatter, what with a mind whirling over FDA drugs on the street, vacuum of information on counterfeit drugs being administered in nursing homes, the pyramiding of corporations dealing with Five Counties' nursing homes. Why cause an ambulating ombudsman awakening the back roads of his mind over Nursing Home Management and Pharmacopeia Wholesalers somehow tied? Fordice had poured water on that piece of wood on the fire, in that Pharmacopeia dealt only with licensed retail drug stores. The woman was an incorruptible State Health surveyor who wouldn't jazz the area ombudsman. She was right on warning of Nursing Home Management's administrators.

On the way home, he gave though to what might be going on with Nursing Home Management and Quality Care's cash income from private pay residents, and reimbursements from Medicaid residents' Social Security benefits and Medicare and Medicaid insurance reimbursements for services rendered. Nursing Home Management had cash expenses of rent, salaries, supplies, administration, ancillary expenses, and fees payable. Were rents raised enough by Quality Care that expenses might well offset income? If taxable income were zero, taxes were zero.

Was Quality Care sheltering rental income received from Nursing Home Management, and taking depreciation expense for the cost of buildings, and interest expenses from mortgages provided by loans? Was the cash income received being offset by non-cash depreciation expense and any cash interest expense deductions? If taxable income were zero, taxes were zero. On the face of it, Unge and Grain were enterprising entrepreneurs, unless there was a pyramidal conspiracy to maximize profits at the expense of those who paid nursing home residents' costs. Pyramiding corporations for excess profits from local, county, state and federal governmental tax entities was an art raised to the highest levels by the nation's business corporations. Had the Nursing Home Industry less ingenuity?

No sooner had October's colors become artistic triumphs, than November's paint-strippers would shrivel all to haggard gray thickets, an austerity welcomed by Trappist Monks. Being neither a Trappist, nor inclined to austerity, Mike missed morning walks before work. Coming inside where coffee percolated, grapefruit was lush and egg boiled was a savored moment. Reading the newspaper, plus soothing Celtic music and the comfort of the redwood chair restored body and soul. The athlete cooled, sipped hot coffee, ate vitamin enriched food and read woeful political views.

210

Showered, shaved, deodorized, tooth brushed, and dressed, he was revived for an evening free from nursing homes until he looked at resident Blanche Kessner's postcard. Somehow it had gotten delivered despite a drawing depicting disgusting things shoved up notable parts of the governor's anatomy. Larkspur's cess-pool stirrer wanted a copy of the letter the governor didn't answer sent to her State Representative. Inserting Representative Thomas Tube's name and Statehouse address with a few other minor modifications took care of it. Mike would mail it.

Driving to town, he recalled 'Anesthetized!' Shango Golah used the street version of the word to explain the lack of 'dope' was why Loren raped Fanny Brown. The implication was others of Palace's residents were drugged. Fordice had described psychotropics as the most frequently misused drugs in nursing homes, the same stuff Cooper called uppers and downers. Abuse? Was that Shango's point? Palace's residents abused by psychotropics? If so, with the firing of Fanny Brown plus boot camp, Palace had to be hades for black employees!

.Kessner's letter was mailed in town center, an early prototype of a strip mall if only the town folks at the turn of the twentieth century were aware of it. On Turtle Street, the main north and south street, there remained three blocks of facing store fronts from Flow Avenue on the south to Apple Way on the north. The stores were mostly empty but their varied vintages and architectural styles told there was a lively town in the past. A red clapboard building sported a faded 'Five And Dime' lettering on its side. It housed a dormant antique shop downstairs.

Grass Lake Nursing Home's Aides worked the rooms of the unvisited residents. DON Lotta was out of sight administering medicines. A dish washer rumbled in the kitchen. A clothes-dryer hummed. Lounge couches captured bottoms of family members who had fought the good fight at home as long as they could handle the illnesses of their elder. Visiting gray heads, sons and daughters in their sixties, consoled enfeebled dads or haggard moms in their eighties. The young, grandsons and granddaughters in the flower of their forties, chastised teenagers for fussing so little over great grandma, so much over a soda-pop dispenser.

Resident Fergus Orr sat at his desk, quill scribbling on parchment probably purchased at Pharaoh's tomb.

"Professor?"

"Come in, Mike." Shirt, trousers, socks and shoes were black as gang members' jackets.

"Thank you. A new chair?" Its seat and back, padded thinly, slanted like an outdoor chair. Wooden arm-rests provided some comfort.

"This is great, Professor, thank you."

"Your Mary Held is quite an achiever. She's a business, social and charitable success. Newspaper article after article told how, despite crippling polio and dropping out of high school, she built her company into one of the top Mechanical Engineering Companies in Door County, if not the state. She served on Boards of Social Agencies, moved among the social elite and by her own admission, until her failing health necessitated skilled nursing care, which she could have paid for at home, instead chose a nursing home. Prior, she had lived her life completely detached from the less fortunate she later met in the nursing home. She remedied that shortcoming by purchasing a majority stock ownership position in the building and operating company. Under her guidance, they've turned Iris Nursing Home and all of their other facilities into leaders in the field of geriatric care. She's a woman to honor alright!"

"Successful enough for Puella to award her an honorary degree?"

"It's up to the President," Orr said. "I'll get to work on that, though it's not likely."

"Not unlikely, Professor, to a man of your influence."

"I could have been influential if I gone to teach at Puella out of college, but I wandered off into high school teaching, then Elder Trippers. What lack of funds can make one do who's facing retirement on social security or a teacher's pension is unimaginable to those employed lifetimes in the business world."

"The world of retiring social workers, too. But talking of Elder Trippers, you mentioned your ran prescription drugs for a druggist married to a woman a Mexican National. Who was the druggist?"

"He's dead these sixteen years, Mike. What difference does it make?"

"Strange as it may seem, Professor, in 1973, when you said Elder Trippers first started returning prescription drugs from Mexico, I was operating the Francois County Jail. I and my staff were suspected of smuggling prescription drugs into it. I was subpoenaed before the Grand Jury, and, but for a newspaper article at the time telling of the druggist responsible, I fully expected to be indicted, Lord knows for what. I wonder if that druggist was your druggist?"

Orr looked long and hard before asking, "Who was your druggist?"

"A man named Guido Nozlo."

"Not my druggist. I worked for Maurice Grain."

Though Orr's Elder Trippers brought Mexicans to Brannagh's mind, speculation was declined on the relationship, if any, between Maurice Grain's Mexican wife and the Hispanic names on Nursing Home Management's and Quality Care's board of directors.

17

There was a distance to walk to Shango's room. Mike crossed the circle under non-interested eyes of old bodies sitting in wheelchairs which lined the curving walls like sprockets on a fly-wheel. When would he be able to get back and sing to the sweat suit colored coded residents in the Alzheimer Unit? To get to know just a few more of the old folks huddled here? He was but one ombudsman for thousands in more than a double score of nursing homes in five counties. Forty hours weren't enough, nor was four times forty.

"Shango? Mike Brannagh here. May I come in?" He pushed the door open a few inches. Shango was in his wheelchair, blue wool cap on, his sweat suit black as the dark of his room. Curtains were closed.

"Who?" He hadn't expected company. Then again Reverend Yard must have passed the word to Mike of the whereabouts of the pretty brown skin girl. What was her name? Yea, Fanny Brown! Funny name for what roommate Loren did on her.

"It's Mike! Let's don't go through all the same crap as last time."

"What you mean, man?" He enjoyed putting him on. "Ain't never give you no trouble, man. Come on in, if you keep your mouth clean."

"Sure. May I turn on the lights?"

"No! I'll open the blinds." He pulled a cord in various directions. "Tough to get them up. That's why I leave them down most times." He turned his wheel chair around to face his visitor. "Close the door and sit on my bed. Why you here?"

Mike sat down. "I'm here to tell you I interviewed your witness. She confirmed what you told me. She'll testify."

"How does she get by Lancaster?"

"I expect she'll be in the hearing room with the Hearing Officer, you and me, when the testimony starts. A friend of mine, Jocko Lee, will bring our witness to the hearing room after proceedings start. When it's our turn to testify, I'll call her in."

"Jocko's Barbeque. That Jocko? He your friend?" Shango's body slid to the right, his face opened.

"He is. I couldn't have interviewed our witness without his and Millie Grain's help. 'Hopt', is her new last name. She's a social worker in Lobelia Nursing Home. Believe it or not, now she's sharing Fanny's place. Did you know Fanny's an artist?"

"No! Paid her no mind back then."

"She's really skilled. Came up from the South to find work, got it at Palace, but home sickness got her drawing her folks. I've seen sketches." He wasn't here on her artistic skills. "We need to go over the procedural rules on the informal hearing, whenever it may be."

"This Tuesday, man, 10:00 A.M." he said. "Got notice in the mail on Saturday."

"I didn't!" Had Nursing Home Management that much influence with State Health to not mail a letter with the hearing time? "Anyhow, there's a lot to go over. We better get on it. If I start sounding like a school teacher, stop me. Ask me questions at any time. Firstly, the Notice you were given that Lancaster mailed me is a very unfriendly form. State Health makes the home do next to nothing when it fills in the blanks. Lancaster only has to put your name on it, the date, the place from where you are being discharge, why, the effective date, and to where your are being discharged. The local ombudsman's name, address and telephone number are written in too. That's it. On the rest, State Health tells the resident of his rights. Did you read it?"

"Not really. Saw they were kicking me out because

215

'the safety of an individual is endangered'. Got me mad."

"Would you have asked for a hearing if I didn't tell you about your right to have one?" A nod said 'no.' "Were there, or have there been, any meetings with Lancaster, the DON or social worker about the incident? About alternatives to discharge?" Another negative. "I've had a good look at your clinical chart, the minimum data set, and care plans. Your anger and language pop out like a jack-in-the-box. In light of that if the hearing Officer believes what Lancaster and her staff have written about what you did to your roommate, you're likely out."

"What about the sweet brown skin girl?"

"Hopefully, the Hearing Officer will believed Fanny, though there's no record the police were called about any sexual attack. And, Fanny stated she was fired, but there's no entry on the State Certified Nursing Aide registry about it. After we call her, believe me, her personnel records will be produced and reflect problem after problem. We'll have difficulties with Palace's written records. Lancaster claims your attack was unprovoked and we have nothing in writing to the contrary. So, at first, I'm going to argue procedural errors. Then, after Lancaster tells her lies and I cross examine her, I'll put on Fanny."

"Will it work?"

"Who the hell knows. I've done it but once."

"You an amateur?"

"Better than you not asking for a hearing, in which case you would have packed and moved on. Lord knows who would have admitted you to a nursing home with Lancaster's records on you." Eyes flashed at him but nothing was said. "Lets take a look at the procedural rules. Rule 3 states when discharged is proposed, 'provision for continuity of care must be provided' by Palace to the next home. Where? Nothing in the chart. Rule 9 (c) says the location must be included. Lancaster never wrote the location on the Notice. She wrote 'where he chooses.' So the notice is defective from the beginning. Rule 6 (A) (vi) says your physician must get a copy of the notice. Nothing in your chart indicated a copy was sent to him. Who is he?"

"Palace's old guy. Be named Box. Lives in Oldtown, somewhere."

Mike concluded Box was Palace's medical director. "Does he write your prescriptions?" A positive nod. "Who fills them?"

"Drugstore down the street. Victorio checks them out."

"Who's Victorio?"

"He was the druggist over to the corner way back when. He don't work for drugstore no more. He be a consultant. Gone uppity. Why?"

"Mere curiosity," Mike said thinking of Fordice saying their was no tie she knew of between a drug wholesaler and Nursing Home Management. With Shango getting his medicines from a local drugstore, and consultant Victorio checking them out for adverse reactions, that confirmed Fordice's belief. "Anyhow, Rule 18 requires a planning conference. Lancaster or her staff must prepare a relocation plan, preparing you for relocation. Did they?" Another negative bobbing. "So, Rule 19 requires your medical, psychosocial and social needs be considered and a plan devised to meet those needs. Was it?" Again a 'no' nod. "Rule 21 says Lancaster's staff are to sufficiently prepare and orient you for transfer. Have they?"

"Haven't seen so much as the social worker's big nose," Shango said.

"Rule 22 says if the relocation plan, which hasn't been done, were disputed, a meeting was to be held prior to relocation with Lancaster or staff to discuss possible alternatives."

"No plan, no meeting, no discussion, no alternatives." Shango said in the swing of it.

"Rule 23 says there was to have been a written

report of the discussion of the meeting for review and comments."

"No written report and no comments," he said, smiling, never thinking he'd have a chance to say the second phrase.

"And Rule 24 says this written report of the disputed relocation plan meeting was to have been placed in your record."

"Is it?" Shango said. He realized Lancaster wasn't beyond doing it.

"I'll look after I leave you and pull your clinical record to make a copy. If I find a written report I'll come back and tell you. If I don't, I won't come back. We have a goodly number of procedural errors to get on the record. If the Hearing Officer is deaf to our procedural arguments, and to our witness, we'll still have the right to post hearing procedures, like an appeal for a hearing before an Administrative Law Judge. We'll have to find another home in the interim if we lose the informal hearing."

"Lose!" he said, smiling. He rolled over to the bed and placed a hand on Mike's shoulder. "You ain't gonna' lose. You the man!"

* * *

"Nurse," Mike said to a young woman at wing four's nurse station, "I'm the ombudsman, Mike Brannagh. I have Mr. Golah's written consent to see his records. How much will it cost to copy a page?"

"Just one? Free. The copier's back here," she said, smiling. With all the energy of a young nurses' good training and healing hands, she looked the picture of a skilled professional who somehow had escaped Lancaster's influence.

"No. The whole file, and I'll need you to initial each page under today's date."

"Ten cents a page. Why initial them?"

"So someone from the nursing homes acknowledges

they are copies of the originals in the clinical record."

"Are you a lawyer?"

"A social worker, more's the luck." He copied the entire record and put the day's date on each copy. "Not that you don't have enough writing to do in charts," he said, presenting the numerous pages for initialing.

She dutifully did it, accepted cash and wrote a receipt.

* * *

Services at the Church of Holiness were over, men, woman and children of the congregation departing in cars, church buses, on foot, bicycling. Mike parked out front. Lo and behold, lingering on the church's front steps was the pistol packing pretty little girl, now in a red coat over a blue dress. He prayed her endeavor on this Lord's day was mystical, not diabolical.

"Pretty young lady," he said, nodding respectfully as he passed by going up the steps, "good to see you and the Lord so closely united."

He was through the big front door before she thought to 'present arms.' Reverend Yard was in the midst of a gathering of women, most talking, him listening. He must have been glad to look beyond the circle and see the man in a brown check sport coat, brown tie, pants and shoes under fading maroon hair with a face white as the shirt he had on, for eyes smiled before the infection reached the lips.

"Have you a moment to spare, Reverend Yard?"

"Brother Brannagh. Come on in my office. Excuse us ladies." They parted as if waves of the dead sea to allow the wan visitor his moment with the Man of God who closed the door behind them. "Please have a seat." He sat behind the desk. "How's Brother Shango?"

"I just left him. He's fine, but the informal hearing is the day after tomorrow. If we don't prevail, we'll know either way in a couple of weeks, he'll have to relocate.

Shango has high hopes now that we've found and talked to Fanny Brown." He brought Reverend Yard up to date on her statement, Millie's moving in with Fanny, sorry as he was about her pending divorce. "I'm here, not just for Shango, Reverend Yard, but for the Aides in Palace. I'm afraid black Aides, like Fanny, who displease the administrator, don't get a second chance. In Fanny's case, she was the victim, disbelieved by the administrator, and discharged while being made fearful of the sheriff being called. Now it's Shango's turn. I need help to get something done about it. A mere ombudsman, white to boot, doesn't impress anyone when it comes to discrimination. A Man of the cloth together with notarized documents from Aides could shock Nursing Home Management, the operating company, into doing something about Lancaster's methodology." Mike, hesitating to mention Belinda Fordice until he'd contacted her, went on about Church of Holiness holding a Religious Service some early evening away from Palace for interested black Aides and residents, brought by those Aides. While that was ongoing, in the quiet of your office, he, with a Lawyer and a Notary present, would obtain volunteered statements.

Reverend Yard was more than caught up to find out for himself through the doing of a prayer meeting. He set the Service for a week from Tuesday, to say he'd personally announce it to Palace's Aides and residents, to Lancaster and Nursing Home Management, the whole of Oldtown via Inner-city News, and to obtain the services of his Church Men and Women of Righteousness, to transport the aged and Aides in ambulances and Vans, among them, nurses and paramedics in abundance. If the tenor of the statements were as Mike indicated, he would take a lead to put a stop to unfair and discriminatory employment practices.

Mike prevailed on the good man to walk him to his pickup, and safely passed the pretty little girl in the red coat.

* * *

The microfilm reading machines at Oldtown's library weren't in demand, nor at the moment was the Oldtown Times' microfilm for the year 1976. Maurice Grain died on June 19th of the year, leaving behind his wife, Concetta Ramirez-Grain and son, Javier. Sure as the dark of winter would come to Five Counties, this Javier was Millie Grain's Javier, and, although Orr, the Elder Tripper, hadn't said it, Javier was the son who'd sold Maurice's drugstore and closed down the Elder Trippers. Since, Javier was an entrepreneur, not only in the prescription drug wholesale business as Pharmacopeia Wholesalers, but also as Quality Care, the owner of ten nursing home buildings. To say the least about the father, he must have been financially successful if the sale of his assets, legal and otherwise, under wrote the wholesale and buildings businesses of the son. Or was the money from the mother, Concetta Ramirez Grain? Wasn't there a Ramirez on the Board of Directors of Nursing Home Management? A relative of the owner of Pharmacopeia on the board of directors of Nursing Home Management? So! Fordice had indicated Pharmacopeia's business was with drugstores, not with Nursing Home Management.

* * *

Back home, he dialed. "Belinda,? Mike." He told her of alleged discrimination, of Reverend Yard's agreement to hold Religious Services a week Tuesday next, of his intent to take statements from Aides, employed and terminated from Palace, and obtained her accord to attend, all to be kept secret. "By the way," he said, "what's the name of Palace's consulting pharmacist?"

"Victorio Pulvis," she said. "Are you having trouble with him?"

"No. I've never met him. Just that a resident at Palace told me the consulting pharmacist was named

221

Victorio. No last name."

"So?" Fordice said, deducing there was more to it.

"Years ago I was subpoenaed by a Grand Jury over prescription drugs brought illegally into the jail. It wasn't me, but my name was all over the news in Oldtown as if I were a gang drug lord. Oldtown Times coverage had me rowing a boat for the Columbian drug cartel. Leaks followed, questioning my administrative skills, dedication, competence, good sense, honesty. I felt like a withered wind-blown leaf tossed by a tornado up into a murderous sky. Then, through all those thunder clashes came Reverend Coppin Yard who was on the Board of Inner-city Community Reorganization. He, through Inner-city News, told the world the prosecutor knew the alleged perpetrator was druggist Guido Nozlo, not me. But for Reverend Yard and Inner-city News, I'd still be doing time in my own jail cell. Do you know Pulvis?"

"Not personally. He owns Prescription Consulting, Inc., and has a contract as consulting pharmacist with Nursing Home Management's facilities to review residents' medicines. There's nothing negative I've heard about Victorio. I'll ask around."

* * *

Watching the sun set on a back road was like waiting for a bus in Oldtown, scheduled but late, so Mike set out to walk. Never mind that cloud cover as thick as quilts on grandma's bed were also moving toward the wetland. There was a slip on a wet spot. Contortions of limbs and trunk took routes not calculated by the engineer of the human body. He weighed laying there until deer hunters informed the Sheriff they had found a corpse. He got up and went home.

18

'Hello, Lizzy. I'm here to see Ziggie."

"You look wounded, Mike," Lizzy said. "Are you alright?"

"Not considering the bruises on my legs, backside and shoulders, I'm fine. Just a tumble off the side of the road down into the ditch."

"Anything broken?"

"My self importance. I was so far down slope, grazing cattle ignored me."

"Here's a letter addressed to you."

He opened the letter from State Health. It was the Hearing Officer's notice on the time of Shango's hearing. "It's a notice of tomorrow's   hearing. Why hadn't the hearing officer mailed it to my address?" His thoughts bordered on paranoia. Nursing Home Management? It brought to mind an important need. He borrowed a chair in an empty cubicle and dialed the phone.

"Hello, Mr. Jackson, please? Mike Brannagh calling."

"Mike, old man, how's the new ombudsman coming alone?"

"Seems to be no bottom to residents' problems, most not of their making. Short staffing, for instance. That's not why I'm calling. I need your help. Rather, Aides at Palace Nursing Home in Oldtown need your legal services." He told Jackson of Palace's firing of Fanny Brown, the alleged treatment of black Aides as if in boot camp, of Reverend Yard's religious service at Church of Holiness in the early evening a week from Tuesday for Palace's Aides and residents members of his congregation, during which statements could be taken in private, Fanny's particularly. "It crossed my mind," Mike said, "if the racially based termination of Aides is to be stopped, it would if the well known Elder Law Center's Civil Rights litigator contacted Nursing Home Management about it's Palace administrator's practice."

"Isn't it chancing the health of residents to get them over to the church on a Fall evening?"

"Perhaps, but Aides will be with them at all times. Many of Palace's staff, white or black,   are aware of the administrator's one-sidedness, but jobs are scarce in the heart of Oldtown. As for chancing health of the residents who come, Reverend Yard's nurses and paramedics are going to transport the Aides and old folks in ambulances and Vans."

"Of course I'll be there," Jackson said

Ziggie hollered, "Hey Mike. Come in and close the door." A pause. "My source asserts there is ongoing replacement of FDA generics with Mexican counterfeit generics for   nursing homes residents."

"Mexican? How? Did the source have a sample to test?"

"No."

"Your source is way the hell ahead of me!"

* * *

Back in the '83 pickup, Mike recollected Fergus Orr's stories on running Mexican counterfeit generic medicines for Elder Trippers, last in 1975 for Pharmacist Maurice Grain and his Mexican wife Concetta Ramirez-Grain. Could it now be their son Javier Grain and his board of directors with Hispanic surnames smuggling Mexican drugs and working a switch? Assuming it might be so, why. If Grain did so, where would he make the exchange? He didn't sell to nursing homes, but to drugstores. If an exchange was inside a nursing home, would that involve Unge? Grain owned buildings and one of his companies sold medicines to drugstores, who sold medically ordered prescriptions, to residents like Shango. Grain's buildings were leased by Nursing Home

224

Management. It also had Hispanic surnames on its board. How could either Grain or Unge substitute counterfeit generic medicines for FDA generic medicines in any of those facilities without the Medical Director, Consulting Pharmacist, Directors of Nursing or charge nurses knowing? It made little sense for Grain or Unge to so jeopardize their businesses. Only Ziggie's source said it was so, but no counterfeit to test .

* * *

It was surprising to see Fanny Brown at Jocko's Place, the very reason Mike had driven over to ask Jocko to fetch her for the hearing tomorrow. She and the BBQ entrepreneur were busy hanging Fanny's sketches on the walls.

"Mr. Jocko say for me to test the market," Fanny said, "whatever that be. Did me some drawings of old folks in Palace."

"Ain't they something," Jocko said with unrestrained enthusiasm. "Fanny done agree to sell the drawing so she can buy her mama's house for her. Great, ain't they? Going to hold an exhibition soon. Don't you know I had one of them artist come on over. He said 'grand' when he saw her stuff! Ought to sell!"

"I think so," Mike said. "Let me know the date of the exhibition. In the meantime, Fanny, Jocko, the hearing for Shango is tomorrow at Palace at 10:00 AM. Fanny should be there by fifteen minutes after ten. Lancaster will be in the same room with me at ten, so she'll not know Fanny's waiting in the main lounge until I call her in. Still, you're going to stay with Fanny all the time, right Jocko?"

"Right, man. We be there."

"Good. Mind if I use your office phone, Jocko?" He didn't. Mike went back to the office, closed the door, and dialed. "Belinda, glad to have caught you. Can we meet later today?"

"Where and when?"

225

"I know just the place. May I call you back in a few minutes to see if it's available?" She agreed. He dialed. "Reverend Yard? Mike Brannagh. May I and another person meet you at your church office this evening on a matter as grievous as that we discussed?"

"Why sure. I'll be here. I'll look for you're coming."

Another call. "Belinda, Mike. Can you meet me at the Church of Holiness across from the Projects around seven?"

"Reverend Yard's church? He's my Minister! I'll be there."

Mike thanked her and moved out. "See you at the hearing Fanny, Jocko!"

* * *

Honeysuckle Nursing Home in Door County was southwest of downtown where the hospital, courthouse and jail, doctors', lawyers' and accountants' offices vied for clients, hogged parking spaces and congested traffic. Mike turned the pickup onto a road of potholes nearly large enough to serve as fighting-holes for a squad of infantrymen. Honeysuckle's red brick facade, fortunately, didn't match any of the decrepit white frame houses across the street. The neighborhood gave an impression it was there long before the war, the first of the two world wars, and long run down before the Crash of '29 caved in property values. Low cost land was a nursing home builder's dream. Southwest Doorham inhabitants never recovered from the Great Depression. It was the domain of sociology's lower-lower class of sometime bread earners, even lower in voter turnout and consequent clout. Its people were prime recruits as nursing home Aides, housekeepers, yard, maintenance and kitchen staff. The nursing facility was a half block long, west to east, with two 'Y' wings. From a traffic copter it might have looked a two legged, four footed saw horse. He parked on the street and checked his listings of homes' administrators. Nursing Home Management's administrator Joan Riff presided over one hundred and fifty residents.

Mike entered the door that bisected the building. There were four women, residents by the worn, aged look of their clothes, not faces which weren't as nice looking, sitting in the entry alcove on a former church pew ten feet long. Two of the women took twice the allocated two and a half feet. The other two were mortar between bricks.

"Good morning ladies! I'm the ombudsman, Mike Brannagh." He handed each a brochure accepted in silence. Not so much as a sneer cast. Eyes that peeked didn't spark. Too many years and perhaps too many tears had dimmed their fire. A receptionist was across the hall from the pew. She had a lot of someone else's curly blond hair around an orange face, but she wasn't much younger than the pew sitters, or better dressed, or too far this side of awareness. "Ma'am, I'm the ombudsman, Mike Brannagh, here to introduce myself to a few residents. Would you let the administrator know I'm in the building. And," he emphasized the word to get some attention from her folding letter size paper into triangles, "would you tell me who the resident council president is?"

"Council president?" she said, looking up from her stack of triangles, "It's Plet Band, that's who. One of the few alerts."

Curly was churlish, to think the best of her. He elected to mentally transcribe her resident descriptions and get along to a visit. "Would you tell me Mr. Band's room number, and the room number of Tiana Buss?"

"Plet's in 109. Tiana," Curly said, eyes opening to dump more baggage, "transferred to Orchid. She said the food's cooked there." Her facial disgust was plain.

"How about Keith Wick?"

"Not back from the hospital," she said, returning her concentration to another sheet of paper, folding it into

227

quarters.

Sensing Curly's misgivings about the occupants in her work place, he moved on to the administrator's office. Her door was closed. He knocked. No response. He moved to the 'Y' wing on the east. A young capped nurse infinitely prettier than the warhorse up in reception, sat inside the nurse station. As was usual with RNs working in nursing homes, she was furiously writing in charts.

"Sorry to dis..."She jumped, her ball point pen flying out of hand, hitting the wall behind. "...turb you." He backed off. "Wow! You have the reflexes of a panther. I'm sorry."

Tears flowed from eyes as light brown as desert sand. She raised a handkerchief to dab at them. "It's me," she said, "not you. How may I help you?"

"I'm Mike Brannagh, the ombudsman, looking for Plet Band."

"The ombudsman? Oh, then I can tell you. Plet certainly will. I'm Hanna, East wing charge nurse. I was worrying about this resident I'm charting. She's gone so far into dementia I don't know her anymore. She's become incontinent, aggressive. I believe she's taking on, absorbing is a better word, the characteristics of our other residents."

Mike's curiosity was aroused. An adverse reaction to counterfeit meds? "I'm not sure what you mean about characteristics."

"Honeysuckle seems to have a straight pipeline to State's mental institutions, the few remaining. Most of our new admissions have been in one or more mental health setting. They come here when the years and psychotropics have calmed them. So we're told by admissions. Many are far from calm. Marian, the resident I'm charting, is imitating their behavior."

"Has her doctor reevaluated her? Her medicines?"

"Yes, but just prescribing a psychotropic by fax isn't the answer. I'm staffing her. Family's coming in.

Maybe we can come up with a new care plan. Perhaps a voluntary transfer?" she said, looking at him. "I'm sorry for sounding so disjointed. We have too many mentally ill and dementia residents and so few nursing staff trained to work with them."

Definitely a high usage of psychotropics in Honeysuckle, Mike concluded. How to get one to test? Just new to the nurse and facility, there was no way. He could encourage her to continue verbalizing her dismay. "Too few? It seems turnover and lack of trained staff is epidemic in many of the nursing homes I've visited to date, with more to go." He refrained from specifically mentioning Nursing Home Management's. "Residents are saying the same thing. One resident is even writing letters to governmental authorities saying if three-fourths of the money being paid to nursing homes are from tax dollars then far more of it should go to keep and train nursing staff rather than to reimburse distant shareholders."

"That's exactly it," she said. "Plet will confirm it."

"He sounds like an active council president."

"He is. You'll like him. He's down this wing in room 109."

"Thank you. I'll look him up." He knocked on a closed door. "Mr. Band? This is Mike Brannagh, ombudsman. May I come in?"

"Come in," said a hearty voice.

He opened the door and entered a room with bright lights, one in the ceiling, one by each bed. The Venetian blinds were up. Daylight trickled in no matter the misery outside. The room had two beds, the one close to the entry as ruffled as if a track meet was run over its blankets. Sticking out from under those blankets was a small head. It looked as if liberated from the tower of London a year after a beheading. On the other side of the room sat Sigmund Freud, pointed white beard and whiter hair, but not in a Psychiatric suit. He wore workman's blue shirt and trousers and rubberized boots. Magazines flopped in all directions on his bed's spread, still neat. Beside him in the wheelchair were hardback books, maybe six. Saddle bags dangling from the chair's arms were stuffed with paperbacks. He was holding another open. By its size and his place in the book, he was eight hundred pages in with six hundred to go.

"Mr. Band? I'm Mike Brannagh, ombudsman." He handed him a brochure. "May I sit on the chair?" There was an agreeable nod to do so.

"An advocate for residents," Band said, reading the brochure. "Where have you been?"

"Just started as ombudsman several weeks back. There was a guy before me."

"There was? Can you do something about all the trouble around here? This place is getting dangerous. I've talked to Joan Riff until I'm blue. I said, 'Joan, bring in all the mentally ill you want, but not the hostile disturbed. You're filling the place with dangerous mentals. It's not safe anymore. We haven't any male Aides, and men mentals take up half the beds. Joan,' I said, 'we need male Aides.' She said, 'I'm doing all I can to find male Aides.' I said, 'Joan, it wasn't like this when I came in three years ago before you came. She said, 'times and administrators change. My management company instructed me to bring the occupancy rate up. Mental Health needed space for its patients. We had it. Otherwise Honeysuckle might have closed. Just look out any window at what we have to put up with in this neighborhood. Two of us have to escort every Aide to her car so she's safe. Besides, the mentally ill deserve a decent residence too.' That's not the point, I said to Joan. The mentally ill are as welcomed here as are the physically ill, but not dangerous whackos! If you escort Aides to their car, your residents need escorts down these very halls. 'I've got my orders', she said in a huff, 'I'm going to admit whomever my staff can help.' She walked out on me."

"Your's is a good argument, Mr. Band. About admissions, however, any nursing home's assessment team, after a pre-admission screening okayed the person for nursing home placement, can admit any one they want to admit. The administrator isn't to discriminate, of course, and if she elects to enter a deal with the mental health system, that's her choice; more likely the home's management company's choice, like she told you. Having said that, she and the management company still owe you and every resident safety, a given included in the quality of life standard."

"Can't we do something about safety?"

"I hope so. I'll look around the place to see what's happening. I'll talk with Mrs. Riff about it, if I can find her. I'll get hold of Mr. Zigmont, head of the local Agency for the Aging and asked him to contact the State Ombudsman. Perhaps they can intervene with Mental Health's big shots, get someone from Mental Health to meet with you and the Aides. They may tell them no. In the meantime, why don't you write your State Representative and Senator. Ask them to come visit, or send some one from Mental Health to visit with you and the resident council. Most likely they'll push someone from Mental Health to visit. Let me know, and I'll be there."

"Good idea," Band said, "I'll write. Will I hear from you again?"

"Long before I get on your couch for psychoanalysis," he said, rising from the chair.

"Wondered when you'd bring up Sigmund," Band said with a chuckle. "Every social worker does. Sure would be helpful in here if I was into psychiatry, then maybe I could treat some of the cashews. Use to be a tool maker over to Wippit Tool and Die. Started learning die making on a Navy LST. I was in the Phillippines the day MacArthur landed. After the war I went to Oldtown Tech on the GI Bill. I was a good machinist."

"And a loss to psychiatry. See you later, Mr. Band."

"Plet! Call me Plet, Joan Riff does. By the way, she's a Miss, not Mrs."

"I will, Plet. I'm Mike. Thanks for correcting me."

The 'Y' wings weren't evenly divided between male and female rooms. Plet Band's wing was four-fifths male, the other 'Y' four-fifths female. The rooms in both wings most distant from a nurse station were for males, the men in Band's 'Y' far more mobile and boisterous than their fellows the other side of the building. Joan Riff was attempting some type of classification. Quiet males weren't in Band's wing. Was he on the mental wing because of his pleadings to limit the admissions of those mentally ill he described as dangerous? Mike shook his head to rid it of another paranoid thought. Not every Nursing Home Management administrator had to be strange.

It was the men in activities who gave credence to Band's observation. There was a curse a minute, arguments over the next puff on a cigarette butt, a scream over dealing cards. When an shaggy hair guy in bib overalls stuck out his cane to trip a limping woman, Mike moved quickly to prevent it. He took the cane in hand and sat down opposite Bib's nose.

"You were a bit careless with the cane," he said with firmness. He looked into eyes that blinked in unison, a face than hadn't a normal form. Perhaps if Bib had his teeth in, or his nose was centered and other than orange in color, he'd have minuscule appeal. Bib did no more than return a distorted grin. Was there intelligence? Whether or not, Mike said, "Don't be careless with the cane." The grin got wider when the cane was returned.

"It's my turn," a Tasmanian devil screamed, or so the voice sounded.

Four tables over, two men arm wrestled for a cigarette butt. It evolved to slaps, then swings of fists across the table. They got up to fight. The danger wasn't to the fist fighters, but to other residents sitting at near-by tables grinning in absentia, some quite old and rocking back and forth. The younger residents snorted fearfully through their grins. A thin guy cursed at everybody. Bedlam inside a nursing home! Nary an administrator, Aide, nurse, cook, social worker or housekeeper present. If the activities director had been there, she was now safely snuggled in her equipment room. He moved between the residents to break up the fight, towering over the antagonists, holding them apart from one another. There was minimal resistance. What disease so distorted the looks of these two men no older than the ombudsman? Compared to the symmetry of the Witch of the West's flying monkeys, these were her rejects. Had looks caused their illnesses? Or did illnesses cause the distortions? Counterfeit drugs? Was there a correlation between good looks and sanity, ugliness and mental illness? He'd never read a paper on it, but these residents' features were more than anecdotal evidence. Empathy flowed through his emotions as blood did the veins. He too wasn't a beautiful baby, best looking boy or most handsome man, but was loved by parents. Might that be it? Love! Hadn't the garbled humanity at his side experienced parental love?

"Sit down, fellows," he said, a command. They did. "Rest easy, folks. It's okay now." Plet Band was right. Male Aides might just do the trick. "Everybody enjoy themselves without fussing or fighting. I'll be right back." He wouldn't if he could find Joan Riff.

"Yes." She answered the knock on her door.

He opened it slightly, "I'm Mike Brannagh, ombudsman, Miss Riff. May I visit?"

"Come in," she said. Surveyors were bother enough in the facility, now an ombudsman? The last one was a mere voice. This one looked not too bright. So old? She'd play the sweet grand-daughter rising to introduce herself.

"Joan Riff, Mr. Brannagh. Hanna told me you were here. Pleased to meet you." She held out her hand to shake. His grip was firm."Have a seat, please." She pointed to a chair at her desk. "Coffee?" Her brilliantly blue eyes were fringed by long black lashes, hair black as coal, face prettier than Cinderella's and younger than the famed step-daughter's.

"Yes please. Black." He sat down.

On the cadenza, a pot of coffee steamed. She filled a paper cup and placed it across her desk before him. She sat on her desk chair

"Thank you," he said. He sipped an ounce. It was bitter as bark.

"Hanna said you talked to her?"

"I did, and to the receptionist to let you know I was here. I toured the facility too," he said, avoiding the mention of Plet's name, "and ended up working a fight card. A resident tried to trip another and a fight broke out. I stopped all of them or there would have been injuries, any one of which could be the basis of a lawsuit alleging neglect of dependents." He'd turned on his supervisory tone. "There wasn't a staff member, male or female in sight when the fisticuffs, tripping and slamming one another was taking place. This time I stopped the perpetrators before real harm happened, but I don't work here. Someone who does will have to be in activities full time watching the residents."

"We do the best we can," she said, with a touch of irritation.

"With no staff member in activities?"

"She must have taken a break."

"Then another should have been there in her absence," he said, pouring it on. "This is the day and age of litigation. Do you believe Mental Health will put up funds to pay for your defense in a Civil Action when one of your residents is badly injured by another resident, and a long absent family member with lawyer attached appears and alleges there were no staff around to prevent or limit the attack? More likely Mental Health will join the plaintiff 's cause of action, naming you as their adversary. They will tell the Judge you've failed to meet the terms of your contract. Good luck in court!"

"We've not been sued," she said, bothered by his lecturing.

"So far, but with the aggressive clientele you have in Honeysuckle and the days ahead of you yet to work, don't count on it. Avoid litigation, Miss Riff. Get someone in activities and walking the halls who can command combatants to stop. I did. It worked."

The size of him, no wonder, but there were years of work ahead in the nursing home industry that she didn't want to be haunted with a trail of lawsuits alleging neglect of dependents like Fran Vict over at Daffodil.

"There should have been a staff member in activities," she said, returning to the demeanor of the sweet grand daughter. "I'll get that corrected immediately. I've been in discussions with my management company. There's an advertisement in today's newspaper for male Aides, and female."

Good," he said. "I've a suggestion in the interim. Hire off duty Police, Parole or Probation officers. An officer might well bring around the calm between residents you seek."

"Officers?" Her doubt was thick as her black hair. "No. I'll get it worked out." She stood up, a dismissal. "Thank you for dropping in."

"See you." He left her office.

Litigation? Police officer? She gave it more than a passing thought. Would the management company's lawyer allow Mental Health to cross examine her on the witness stand? Her own management company turn on her? Not Dale Unge. He wouldn't let her fall into a career pit as did

Fran Vict. No! She'd talk to him again. He'd know where to find men to calm this troubled ship and her threatened future.

* * *

The town of Trinton's Proteas Nursing Home was on south 'L' next to Kultuski's Grocery. The town hadn't a State road running through it, just County Road 'L', a tar and rock road that crossed the narrow bridge over Wozni's Creek and snuck in from the north, turned right for three blocks, then slipped south and out of sight a half mile into Rzyjaski's woods. Several of Mike's nursing homes were situated in small towns like Trinton, population two thousand two hundred. Folklore held small town folks with historic ethnic attachments took care of their own. The facility was built of yellow brick. Its original single story rectangular building started fifty feet from 'L' road and ran west. An addition that ran from north to south crossed the original structure at the west end. A third addition was added to the south end of the second. A fourth was added to the west end of the third, while the fifth addition closed the gap between the fourth and the second. It formed the letter 'R' and occupied acres of clipped grass. In summer, grass on all sides of the home's land was just out of reach of Guernsey cows eyeing uncut clumps of lushness a few yards beyond a voltage charged single wire fence. There was the air of pastoral quiescence about the place. He entered a lobby of beautiful furnishings, clustered for conversations, but unoccupied. An interior decorator painted the walls a light green compatible with the color variations of the furniture. To the right of the lobby were offices: the DON's and social worker's. To the left were offices of the administrator and office manager. A sliding glass window between the two administrative offices opened. The young woman behind it was a brunette, a blue ribbon in her hair. Her smile welcomed.

"May I be of help," she said.

"Yes, thank you. I'm Mike Brannagh, ombudsman, here to introduce myself to residents and the administrator, if she's available."

"Mrs. Egan, the administrator, and Pearl, our council president, are at the resident council meeting . Senator Gustaff is speaking. It's a meeting open to all residents and staff. You may go right in. They're meeting in this wing, down the hall, in the room with 'Activities' on the door. Don't go in that door, but the next further down the hall, same side. The speaker is usually standing near the first door. If you find yourself in dining, you've walked to far. Turn around and come back about fifteen feet."

"Thank you," he said, smiling in return for her courtesy.

He headed through the lobby to the rooms she described and passed the pressed wood door marked 'Activities' and opened the next. The room was full of people milling around a tall, well groomed gentleman in a double breasted blue suit. His face was younger than his gray hair. Younger people in white uniforms, older people with walkers or wheel chairs, vied to shake his hand. "How nice," he said repeatedly while pushing his way out of the room. "Remember me when you vote." No sooner was Senator Gustaff out the door marked 'Activities' than white uniforms disappeared and residents scooted walkers or wheel chairs out of the room to the dining area where sugar free snacks awaited. A woman in a floral dress remained. She stood behind a wheelchair, holding its handles, preparing to walk while pushing it for support. Her face was fine boned and slender, expressive. Frost silver plated her hair.

"I got here too late," Mike said.

"You missed a good speech."

"About what?"

"Who cares. What's important is Senator Gus came at my request."

Mike sensed this resident had a story to tell. "Let me introduce myself. I'm the new ombudsman, Mike Brannagh. This is my first visit to Proteas."

"Ombudsman? Are you? I'm Pearl Whiley, council president."

"Delighted to meet you, Mrs. Whiley. If you aren't in a hurry to join the others for a snack, might we talk a few minutes?"

"It's Ms. Whiley," she said. "I never married. We can talk here." She moved around her wheelchair to sit down in a chair at the head table.

He came over and sat on a chair to her right, facing the open door of the activities room. "I'm curious, not so much about you're not caring what the senator said. Most of us feel politicians talk about their own wonders, real or imagined. I'm curious about you saying 'what's important is he came at your request."

"We had a resident council at Poland Nursing Home that attracted residents to its meetings because of the open and happy way we conducted our business. We were like Senator Gustaff, actively pursuing and promoting our own interests. We made it clear to staff that their role is a supportive one."

"You 'had' a resident council? Wasn't the meeting I just missed a council meeting?"

"Yes, but perhaps the last of its kind. The Rzyjaskis sold their interest in the home to Hood Enterprises, a corporation with emphasis on short-term rehabilitation of Medicare residents from rural hospitals, a more lucrative line of business than care for us Medicaid lifers. Hood renamed Poland after a South African flower, Proteas, probably because the corporation operates in a manner that makes apartheid government looked liberal. We now live with a management that wants to get rid of long term care residents, no matter our time left on this earth." She was on the stump herself. "Over the decades of the Twentieth

Century, the Rzyjaski family farm provided plentiful work, housing and food for brothers, sisters, aunts, uncles, offspring, cousins of many degrees and long lived relatives. Agriculture changed. Expenses increased, income decreased and the way of life faltered, but not Rzyjaski family ties. Clem and Stella open and operated Poland Nursing Home in Trinton with the availability of federal and state dollars for care of the chronically ill. Rzyjaski elderly were among the local admissions. Rzyjaski kin were numbered among the employees. Poland Nursing Home was paradise for residents and employees. That's why I came here. My maternal grandmother was a Rzyjaski. But paradise changed when Poland was sold and so many staff were laid off. Down at Adalbert's Donuts and Carwash Cafe in town, the leading topic for conversation is local people losing jobs at the nursing home."

"My goodness," he said, flabbergasted at her forcefulness, "there are laws that sharply curtail non-voluntary transfers or discharges. The key word is 'voluntary.' An ombudsman rarely knows of voluntary transfers. He has to rely on the resident, their family, or perhaps members of the council to let him know the administrator is working to cause an alleged voluntary transfer. You can count on me being here every minute necessary to fight it, if one, anyone lets me know about it. I'll leave several brochures with you to give to other residents. The brochure tells of residents rights pertaining to transfer and discharge."

"Thank you. I'll pass them out," she said, sizing him up."You do look like a fighter with that mashed nose. I do a bit of fighting myself. Senator Gustaff is one of my artillery pieces."

"I thought you said whatever he said wasn't important?"

"I did. What is important is he came to Proteas at my request. Management knows I know a politically powerful State Senator, also a U. S. Representative, several newspapermen, TV News anchors, published writers, actors and actresses. I've invited them, one and all to address our council. Some of us, as a result, have been on TV, or had pictures in the newspapers, testified at hearings at the county court house or the state capitol. That's what is important. Managers of Hood Enterprises know it. "

"I can see that." He thought of Mary Held. "Were you politically active before you entered Proteas, rather Poland, Ms. Whiley?"

"In a manner of speaking. Women weren't recognized on the job in my time. For thirty years, I was Administrative Secretary to the President of Longley Life Insurance Company. Ten of those years I worked with Ceoff Longley after working twenty for Lucas Longley. Ceoff inherited Lucas's stock but never took the time to learn the difference between a life or term policy. No one at corporate headquarters doubted or questioned my management of Longley Insurance, albeit through Ceoff's signature. He loved the spotlight. I arranged his schedule of meetings and invited the guests he would honor. It was a never ending parade of very important people. Health removed me from Longley Insurance, but not from the contacts I made. I still know how to go about honoring notables."

"Judging by the number of come-uppers to see Senator Gustaff, that's apparent."

"You noticed that. I do encourage residents to be come-uppers. Guests love it. Now that I know you, Mr. Ombudsman, I'm inviting you to a council meeting, time and topic your choice."

He wrote it down in his notebook, and said, facetiously, "What's important will not be my oratorical brilliance but that Proteas' management knows I come in response to your invitation and will look into every 'allegedly voluntary' transfer to another nursing home."

240

"You catch on quickly," said the wily Whiley. "Time for my snack." She got up from her chair and into a wheelchair. Hands on its wheels, she rolled out the door and said, "Not too bad for a ninety year old secretary, huh?"

"Not bad at all." He watched her push the wheelchair to the dining room. Any others in Proteas with her dynamic disposition? He heard a piano. It hit him that he should take advantage of their snack time, sing a song, introduce himself as the ombudsman. The dining area was spacious. Tables were white paper covered. Three or four elderly women were gathered around eight of the twenty tables. An Aide, each hand holding a pitcher of liquid, was refilling cups to heart's content. Some sipped coffee, others juice. All were conversing, many at the same time. A lean man in a black sweater, blue shirt and gray pants was translating music in his mind to precise and delicate notes as he tickled the ivories. The piano player's head was in the atmosphere. His very pointed nose jabbed at a ceiling light.

"You play beautifully," Mike said.

"My own composition. I hear it in my dreams. I play by ear."

"Do you know, 'Believe Me, If All Those Endearing Young Charms'?"

"Hum the tune," the piano player said. He listened. "I've got it. Sing along."

Mike began with the second stanza. His clear tenor filled the dining room.

Frazzled faces with eyes open turned to the tenor. Smiles played on ancient landscapes. A veritable garden of cheeks, like flowers, blossomed. Applause was sustained.

"Ladies," he said, and turning to the piano player, "Gentleman, I thank you. Doesn't he play beautifully. He makes even me sound okay." He turned to face his unsuspecting audience. "Folks. I'm Mike Brannagh, the new ombudsman. An ombudsman is a part of a State and

241

Federal program, the one that protects resident rights in nursing homes. I do not work for this nursing home. I work only for residents in nursing homes like this one." He grabbed a handful of brochures and moved from table to table thinking on what to say about transfers. He decided to hit the topic head on. "I'm going to leave at each table a brochure that explains what I do. There's a brief list of some your rights on an inside page." He stopped to show them. "If you or your family are thinking about the rights you have in a nursing home, say for instance, staying in this home and not transferring to another if someone not from your family makes a suggestion about transferring, you do not have to do so. There are State Rules that apply to protect your right to remain here and not transfer. If you like it here, stay here. Feel free to call your singing ombudsman at his free 800 telephone number and I'll get back to you that day if humanly possible. The next for sure. I'll come here any time you feel worried about any of your rights not being met. Just let me know."

There were nods from snow-capped heads. Conversation resumed. The pianist returned to his reveries.

Pearl Whiley pushed her wheel chair over, her smile radiant. "You're a hit. They liked what you said! When you come back, you don't need to speak, just sing!"

"Discovered at last!" he said, reverting to the teasing manner she'd used. "What really matters is not that I sing, but that Hood Enterprises knows I come at your invitation."

"It does really matter," she said with sincerity.

19

The pretty little girl with the gun wasn't on the steps of Holiness Church. Fordice and Reverend Yard were. As Mike walked up the steps, Fordice said, "my mind was more on what you said, rather, didn't say on the phone, than on today's work. What's the mystery?"

"Let's talk in the office," he said. "May we?"

Reverend Yard led the way, closing the door behind him, moving over to sit on his desk chair, the others on office chairs.

"Just yesterday," Mike said in a serious tone, "I told you of a form of employment discrimination effecting Aides at Palace. Now this." Mike told of Ziggie's gathered corporate papers and his newspaper clippings; of Nursing Home Management's business leases with Javier Grain's Quality Care's ten nursing home buildings; and of Pharmacopeia.

Belinda again noted the corporate ties were arms length."I also told Mike that Javier Grain's Pharmacopeia is a wholesaler of prescription drugs to licensed pharmacies. It has no connection to Nursing Home Management, other than medical doctors prescribed medicines filled by licensed pharmacies, which are sent to nursing homes for review by a consulting pharmacist, then to the nurses for residents usage. Nursing Home Management hasn't any licensed pharmacies."

"She did," Mike continued. "It all seemed much ado about making a lot of government money until this morning when I went to Five Counties and Ziggie read me this, 'replacing FDA generics with Mexican counterfeit generics. I felt you needed to know Ziggie's latest info."

Reverend Yard's mouth gaped. "In nursing homes?"

Belinda jolted to life. "Mexican counterfeit

generics? Mike," she said in a tone of incredulity, "didn't you tell me you were subpoenaed before the Grand Jury and feared an indictment over someone illegally running prescription drugs into a jail you ran?" Your recollection of all the pain you suffered is affecting your judgement!"

"I did tell you that, Belinda, and your reaction would be warranted if Ziggie hadn't read the note to me. It's Ziggie's source, not mine. That's why I also called Reverend Yard. Yesterday, I asked him, you, and Lawyer Jim Jackson to help end Palace's employment discrimination, but of all of you, only Reverend Yard was there about the jail in '73 and on the parole scam. If there's anything remotely true about replacing FDA generics with Mexican counterfeit, I sure do want him to be there again."

Reverend Yard's eyes opened widely to reveal brown moons. "You have no idea who is giving Mr. Zigmont this information?"

"Confidential source, he said. But it was Ziggie who got a hold of the corporate papers, and who hired a clipping service to gather financial data on income made by owners of nursing home management companies. Ziggie also got tested the street drug I acquired. It was FDA."

"Belinda," Reverend Yard said with more than a touch of bewilderment, "is it possible to replace real drugs with counterfeit drugs?"

Fordice was hesitatingly shaking 'no' but eyebrows rising, contradicted. "When Mike called me about the note on psychotropics, I spent extra time during the Hyacinth survey, it's a Nursing Home Management facility, to check residents' medicines as prescribed by prescriptions in the resident's charts. I've already told Mike nothing seemed amiss. I must admit, however, thought there was a time nurses could identify prescribed medicines on sight or by looking through the photo section of the Physicians Desk Reference or manufacturers' catalogues to become familiar with the sizes, shapes, markings and colors of generic medicines; now, with the rapid substitution of generics for brand name medications, few nursing home nurses, or nurses working as state surveyors for that matter, can, with any reasonable consistency, tell one little white, red, green or blue pill from another manufacturer's. Generic medications rarely look like their brand-name complements. Many aren't manufactured by the final distributor. The same generic purchased by a drugstore from Pharmacopeia Wholesalers months apart often times look as different as the same generic purchased from a different supplier. Even lists and identification guides for generics published one month are obsolete before they reached pharmacies. New generics come on the market while the guide's in the mail. Even though both the Federal Drug Administration and the United States Pharmacopeia made proposals for imprinting identification codes on all oral solid dosage forms of medications, no such requirements are as yet required. A uniform code on capsules and tablets would have make them easily identifiable. Pharmaceutical manufacturers, however, claim a standardized code won't reduce counterfeiting but would increase costs significantly. I hope the National Association of Pharmaceutical Manufacturers will voluntarily implement a three letter and three number generic code; a hope yet unfulfilled." She looked at Mike, then to her minister. "Yes, Reverend Yard, it's possible to replace a FDA approved generic with a counterfeit without a nurse knowing it. I question whether it could be done on a nursing home basis, perhaps it could on a patient by patient basis."

"Is there a way of knowing?" Reverend Yard said.

"If adverse reactions to drugs were out of line," she said." To know for a certainty, each generic drug would have to be tested for its active ingredients. Generically equivalent means it contains the identical quantity of active ingredients in the identical dosage forms, but not necessarily the same inactive ingredients that meet the identical physical and chemical standards in the U. S. Pharmocopeia. If a test found the active ingredients weren't identical, it's counterfeit. There are a few thousand residents in Nursing Home Management's care; each of whom may be on two or three or four or more prescribed medicines. It's a monumental undertaking on the basis of a source's report."

"And you, Mike," Reverend Yard said, "you believe Mr. Zigmont's revelation is true?"

"I believe in Ziggie, but I have no way of knowing without having a medicine from a resident for testing."

"Then I suggest both of you," Reverend Yard said, "continue close observation of the aged and their medicines. I'm always on call." His tone implied the ombudsman and Mr. Zigmont were being misled as to counterfeit versus FDA quality.

20

In Palace's front lounge, the one with large stuffed chairs fit for a parole board, Mike saw a pale old man big as a mule in a blue work shirt and trousers, white socks and untied black shoes. The poor fellow, inflicted with the loquacity of dementia, mumbled to an oracle. He stared with a look of doom at the frightening china coffee pot breathing steam. Was this Loren?

Within the Director of Admissions' office, behind a mahogany desk and sitting on an executive chair was Miss Mary Barr, Hearing Officer, of recent acquaintance at Coralroot nursing home on the Quinta Ray discharge hearing. Barr was in another tailored business suit, this one gray, a white shirt and red tie. Her blond hair was piled up, not a strand seeking escape. By no means was she manly looking. June Scott, Barr's court reporter, was again casually dressed, blazer and tan jeans. She was sitting to the right of Barr, the machine anticipating massage.

"Miss Barr, Mrs. Scott," Mike said by way of greeting.

"We'll start promptly at ten, Mr. Brannagh," Barr said authoritatively.

"I'll go get my client." He stopped at the nurse station, not recognizing the middle age woman, a bit chubby but with a nice smile. 'Donna RN' was typed on her name card. "I'm Mike Brannagh, ombudsman, working with Mr. Golah." He held out his ID. "Have you his chart?"

She gave the ID a glance. "I was just about to carry it to the front office."

"First, would you please allow me a look?" She handed the chart to him. He compared its pages to those copied. Only Nurse Notes had been updated and inserted. Nothing indicated any new problem. "Thank you." He handed it back. If Lancaster had additional data, not putting

247

it in the chart was grounds for an objection and possible exclusion. A brisk walk.

"Shango?"

"Come in, man." He turned his wheelchair. "You going carry me to death row?"

"I won't have that privilege. Lancaster might."

"Ain't funny, man." The light from the hallway pierced through to Shango. His usual sweat suit had given away to a red sweater, white shirt, black pants, socks and dress shoes, not gym shoes. His hair was recently cut, face shaved. He looked every inch a kindly cousin.

"Don't tell me the man of steel is up tight?" Mike said.

"You don't know the half of it."

"Tell me the half I don't know."

He pushed the wheelchair out into the hall and headed down to the circle. From the doorways of several rooms, Aides smiled at him. Ladies in flowery dresses threw Shango kisses; men, encouragement.

"You the man," they said more often than a fight mob to a boxing champ.

"Is that the half I don't know? What the hell have you done?"

"You gave me shit, man, about Aide Fanny Brown not being my cousin. She do for me. I do for them Aides and old folks."

"Do what?" There wasn't an answer when the Director of Nursing, Queen Bee, was heard ordering Aides and Nurses around. She came into view. Music played. Residents sat along the walls, many of them waving. A Shango fan club? "Tell me what you did that every Aide and resident knows and I don't."

"Reverend Yard told me what you do, man," he said, "about that there Prayer meeting. Told me to get Aides and old folks to come over to Holiness. I be cousins with all the Aides and little old folks in Palace."

They entered the administrative area. No Loren. No Fanny or Jocko in the lounge. Then Jocko's instructions were not to appear until 10:15 AM. Mike wanted Fanny's appearance a surprise. Shango worked his wheelchair and rolled over to the right side of the office where there were two empty chairs and space for the wheelchair. Mike followed. He didn't know the guy in a pin stripe suit sitting in an easy chair by the side window.

"Mr. Brannagh," said the fellow as he got up. A six footer, his muscular body enhanced a very expensive suit. Weekly haircuts stylized a full head of hair as brown as his piercing eyes, a moustache giving a forty-something look the weight of maturity. "I'm Dale Unge of Nursing Home Management. Palace is one of our facilities. This is Ms. Lancaster, administrator." Hands were shaken.

"Pleased to meet you, Mr. Unge. Ms. Lancaster," Mike said. Then turning, he said, "this is resident Shango Golah." Nods were exchanged.

Mike wondered why the CEO of Nursing Home Management would attend an inconspicuous resident's discharge hearing? The conclusion was inescapable. It wasn't the resident that was of much interest. It was the new ombudsman. Lancaster must have told Unge of him, as must have a few of the other Nursing Home Management administrators.   Twice before, at the Jail's Grand Jury and the probe into parole kickbacks, Mike had worried about an onset of paranoia. What with all of Ziggie's suspicions about Nursing Home Management's ties to Quality Care plus counterfeit medicines in nursing homes, wasn't it time to worry about mental stability? He postponed worrying. There was a defense to conduct!

"While I'm at introductions, Shango, I'll introduce you to the Hearing Officer and court reporter." They turned around. "This is Miss Barr and Mrs. Scott. Ladies, Shango Golah."

More nods exchanged. Across from Barr, Lancaster

sat down. Despite a bright blue dress set off by frilly white lace, she appeared angry. The Director of Nursing in her whitest nurse's whites, chart in hand, sat to the right of Lancaster. The DON had walked lounge loquacious Loren into the room. She sat him to her left and signed him to be quiet.

Mike said. "I'm sorry, Ma'am. I've seen you several times, but not met you."

"Belle Ricks," she said, "DON."

"Nice to meet you Nurse Ricks," he said, and sat down.

Eyes turned to Miss Barr. "Shall we begin?" she said, then read: "All matters involving the Involuntary Discharge will be heard at this time, the nursing facility first to present the substance of its case, then the resident and his representative. Thereafter, communications with me by hearing participants is ex-parte and precluded. My finding will be mailed to all participants before the expiration of thirty-four days from the date Shango Golah first got notice." Barr looked to Mike. "Have you some procedural objections to present, Mr. Brannagh?"

"I do." He was pleased she was following the procedure used last time. "Procedural Rule 6 (vii) requires the resident's physician be notified when the discharge alleges 4 (C). He wasn't. There's no copy of such in the clinical record I copied and again checked ten minutes ago. Rule 9 (C) requires the location to which the resident is to be discharged. The Notice set down no such location. Rule (18) requires a written relocation plan to prepare the resident for transfer to provide continuity of care. There is no written relocation plan in the chart nor was there preparation for such. There was no Rule (19) relocation conference. Consequently Mr. Golah had no opportunity to discuss the preparation of a relocation plan, much less dispute it, as Rule (22) requires. So there wasn't a meeting in that regard as set out in Rules (22), (23) and (24). In sum, the liberty interests of Mr. Golah set out in State Law have been systematically denied him by the administrator of Palace."

Shango sat impassively. Lancaster glared.

"I'll take it under advisement, Mr. Brannagh," Barr said. "Ms. Lancaster, in your own words, tell us why you are requesting Mr. Golah's discharge."

"Because Golah beat Loren here," she said, pointing to Loren. If he were aware of his whereabouts, there was no hint of it on his face. "Look at poor Loren." She pointed to the side of his head with a finger, as if ready to pull a trigger and put him out of his misery. "He's gone down hill since Golah smashed his radio against the side of his head. There was no reason for hitting Loren." Lancaster had Barr's attention. "Loren was a week in the hospital. He would tell you himself what happened if his memory hadn't been damaged by the blow."

"Were the police called?" Barr said.

"Why no," Lancaster said. "You see how Loren is. He could never be a witness in criminal court. At first, we thought he fell in the bathroom. He did have considerable excrement on him. Our thoughts were to get him to hospital emergency, the head cut was bleeding so. It was only later that Loren told me Shango Golah did it."

"When did he tell you?" Barr said.

"When he returned to Palace." Lancaster thought the better of that answer. "No! He told me at the hospital. I remember now. Belle was there." A glance froze nurse Ricks to silence. "Every patient, even the Aides are afraid of that man," Lancaster said, pointing her trigger finger at Golah. It fired. "I did the only thing I could do under very dangerous circumstances. I gave Notice of discharge."

"If circumstances were so dangerous," Barr said, "why did you not immediately transfer Mr. Golah under Rule (8)?"

"I should have,"she said, "but who would take

251

him?"

"Oh," Barr said with no hint of impartiality. "Were there any residents or staff that actually witnessed the alleged incident?"

"An Aide did, but she quit out of fear of Golah. I've tried to locate her, but she lives near the Projects," Lancaster said, as if to excuse going there. "Residents are so afraid of him, none dare say anything against him."

"Why are you so sure Loren was hit by Mr. Golah?" Barr said.

"Golah's radio was on the floor, smashed, with blood on it. Here's the radio." She reached down beneath her chair and brought up a Ghetto Blaster, quite broken. She set it before Barr. "This is, was, Golah's radio. His name is on it. The blood on it is Loren's. Here's the laboratory's report confirming that." Lancaster smiled setting the report before Barr. "That's how we know for sure Golah hurt Loren. That's all I have to say." She glanced over to Unge.

"I'll mark the radio as Palace's exhibit one, and the laboratory report as Palace's exhibit two," Barr said. Mr. Brannagh?"

"We've haven't been told of the laboratory report, much less had an opportunity to check it out. It wasn't included in the chart," he said.

"Very well," Barr said. "What about the radio?"

"It was mine," Shango said. He smiled at Barr, a smile leaning toward a leer.

Mike had the frightening feeling Shango was caught up by the very pretty and prim hearing officer. That was all an ombudsman needed, his client hitting on the official judging the facts of the case. He scribbled a note and slipped it to his client, 'Lay off the goo-goo eyes!'

"Very well," Barr said, repeating the phrase, looking away. "It's your turn Mr. Brannagh."

"Thank you." He had an opening statement to

make to set the stage for the true facts, to contradict Lancaster's presentation. "Miss Barr, in the nursing homes I visit, incidents happen, residents are hurt, and many can't remember what happened or recall a thing about it. It may be these residents are in the twilight of a psychotropic, or their mental capabilities are so diminished recollection is beyond them, or they are in the throes of dementia or Alzheimer's. Whatever, they can't remember or recall. Loren, who sits with us today in body, in mind isn't here. Whether because of a psychotropic, dementia or Alzheimer's, I leave to the medical professionals. However, what if the facts of this incident are not those Ms. Lancaster told us? What if the facts indicate something as grievous as Loren here raping an Aide, and Shango, half his body frozen by a stroke, did the only thing he could do with one good arm in the defense of a third person?"

"That's a lie!" Lancaster said, exploding.

"A rape?" Barr said, her tone negative. Twitches ran a cross country race over her face. It wasn't pretty any longer. She looked at Shango. If there were a rape or sexual assault on an Aide by a resident, he was her suspect.

"There was," Mike said, "and because he defended a third party, there is no substantive basis for a discharge."

"That ombudsman is awful!" Lancaster said, standing up, pointing at him. "Other women administrators have trouble with his manner, too." She wanted him on trial too.

"His manner?" Barr said, confused.

"Miss Barr," Mike said firmly and without irritation, "whatever my manner, it's not a part of the facts in this Discharge hearing. However, where there is disagreement with administrators, female or male, my manner is to agree to disagree, nothing more, nothing less." He whispered a prayer to extricate himself from the sexual overtones in Lancaster's remark, that Barr not visualize him as negatively as she was his client.

"Please sit down, Ms. Lancaster, if you intend to stay in this room," Barr said. Lancaster sat down. "Proceed Mr. Brannagh."

"Nurse Ricks," he said gently. He hadn't an urge to get her back up. "I want to ask you a few questions about nursing staff on the day of this incident, do you understand?"

Lancaster was surprised. "Aren't you going to ask me questions?"

"Please, Ms. Lancaster," Barr said, taking control. "Wait until he does."

Ricks looked to Lancaster for permission to answer.

"Answer Mr. Brannagh's question, Nurse," Barr said overriding Lancaster's nod.

"I understand," Ricks said softly.

"You were working the day of the incident involving Loren?"

"Yes."

"You supervise RNs, LPNs, QMAs and CNAs, all employees who are included in the phrase 'nursing staff' who worked that day?"

"Yes."

"And management keeps personnel records on your nursing staff?"

"Personnel records are private," Lancaster said, interrupting.

She knew no Ombudsman had a right to her records, except a patient chart, and only then with the specific resident's consent. Discharge from a nursing home was no more than an informal hearing, not a court proceeding.

"Ms. Lancaster," Barr said curtly, "do not interrupt again."

Ricks said 'yes.'

"Nurse Ricks, you do have available for use a roster of all your nursing staff?"

"Yes."

"And you scheduled the nursing staff for the three shifts that day?"

"Yes."

"You have a listing of the nursing staff by each shift?"

"Yes."

"You have available the assignments of RNs, LPNs, QMAs and CNAs on each shift?"

"Yes."

"You keep this information nearby?"

"Yes." She was tired of questions that called for 'yes.' She'd get to the meat of his inquiries. "I know what you are getting at, Mr. Brannagh. You want the name of the Aide that Miss Lancaster said witnessed the incident. We wanted her here to tell what Golah did to Loren, but couldn't locate her after she left us."

"Didn't Ms. Lancaster say she quit?"

"Yes."

"And she worked on the nursing staff under your general supervision?"

"Yes." She squirmed going back to 'yes.'

"You know then who she was?"

"Yes."

"Her name?" he said, raising his voice to preclude a failure of memory.

"Fanny Brown." Ricks said sharply. She looked down that Lancaster's eyes not bully her.

"Thank you, Nurse Ricks." He looked to Barr. "If it's alright with you, Miss Barr, I'll call Shango Golah."

"Proceed."

"Shango, please tell the Hearing Officer what happened the day of the incident."

There was trepidation on the part of Mike as to what approach Shango would take. What language would he use? He already had visually undressed the hearing officer.

255

He detested Lancaster. Yet there was a noticeable change in him since Fanny Brown agreed to come to the hearing on his behalf. Even Aides and residents were waving to him on the way thought the nursing home, all now cousins, and Reverend Coppin Yard had come to visit.

"My roommate was Loren there, before they doped him," he said, pointing him out.

"He's not doped," Lancaster said, shouting.

"Please, Ms. Lancaster?" Barr said.

Unperturbed, he continued. "Loren was most times messing all over our toilet and bathroom when he stood up or sat, it made no difference. Before I could go to the toilet, I had to call housekeeping to clean the room, what with Loren's waste all over. It was morning, Loren's on the toilet and yelled out for the Aide who talked with a drawl, a pretty brown skin girl, to come on in there. She came on in. Loren called her into the bathroom and told her to clean him. She must have tried, because I hear Loren yell, 'you got my brand on your hand, pretty gal.' Loren pulled her out of the bathroom. He pulled her clothes out of the way and they fell onto his bed, his pants and underwear down and he pushed his, ah, thing in her, ah, private part. I said, 'get off man.' He didn't, so I hit him up side his head with my radio. He was knocked out. She got up more worried about Loren than herself. She pulled herself together and ran out, calling 'nurse.' They came back and put Loren in a wheel chair and took him away."

"What was that Aide's name?" Mike said.

"Nurse Ricks said her name was Fanny Brown. I never knew her name back then. Easy to recognize, though. She's very pretty, a brown skin girl, big smile, came from way down south the way she talked. Looked like a little girl in the face. Never saw her after that day."

"Miss Barr," Mike said, "I liked to pause a moment and call in another person."

"Is that person relevant to this hearing?"

"Quite relevant."

"Proceed."

He got up and walked over to the door, opening it. In the lounge were Jocko and Fanny. Mike's fingers called her into the room and directed her to a seat.

Shango rotated his wheelchair to follow her every move. He saw a woman with the purity of a child, one who hadn't a need to hurt anyone. It was her example that was his guiding light. She'd rushed from the rapist's bed to get Loren, not herself, medical help. She hadn't thought of her hurts, but his. A child at heart, she'd, no doubt, have forgiven her rapist.

"Nurse Ricks?" Mike said. "Is this the Aide, Fanny Brown?"

"Yes."

"She worked here as an Aide on the day of the incident?"

"Yes."

"She worked Loren's room the day of the incident?"

"Yes." Ricks looked mortified.

"Ms. Lancaster," Mike said, catching her by surprise, "is this the Aide, Fanny Brown, the young lady sitting next to Shango, the one you said quit that same day out of fear of Shango?"

"You're not going to push me around like you do her," Lancaster said, staring at Ricks.

"Please answer Ms. Lancaster," Barr said.

"To the best of my recollection," Lancaster said.

Mike wished he had eyes in the back of his head so he could see Dale Unge's face. "Shango, is this the Aide that was called into the bathroom by Loren?"

"It is. She looks just like I said. Pretty as can be."

Fanny smiled the innocent smile of a child.

Loren stirred. Looking at her, a hand went to his pants' fly. Opening the zipper, he began a massage within. He arose, moving toward Fanny.

257

Mike got up and stepped   in Loren's way.

Barr's eyes opened, taking in more than judicial notice of the rapid hand action, and said, "Nurse, please escort Loren out of this room and stay with him."

"I will," Ricks said, relief evident. She knew what to do with a disturbed resident, not an ombudsman meaner than an ambulance chaser, or a little girl of a lawyer pretending she was a judge. Ricks nudged Loren's hand from its imposition of tranquility. "Come with me, Loren." She virtually lifted him. Holding tightly to his elbow, she opened the door and led him out, heaving an audible sigh. She pushed the door closed. "Sit here," she said, directing his bottom to an easy chair. She paced. Not getting Shango discharged was the least of her trepidations. The lies she told for Lancaster topped her mental agenda. Was it perjury? Would Lancaster fire her for telling the Aide's name? Finding work at fifty-five, even for a DON, wasn't a path she wanted to again trod. What would happen to her?

Jocko did a double take at the big nurse with the old man. Was he the one who raped Fanny? Jocko was surprised he felt some sympathy for the ambulating mummy. A long life so disturbed wasn't life at all! It was existence. The old fart hadn't internal controls. He'd been embalmed, though living.

When the door closed, Barr said, "Proceed Mr. Brannagh."

"Miss Brown," he said, "for the record are you the Fanny Brown identified by Ms. Mary Lancaster, by the Director of Nursing Belle Ricks and by Mr. Shango Golah, that worked as a Certified Nursing Aide at Palace Nursing Home on August 31, a Monday?"

"Yes, I be her."

"What was your assignment that day?"

"I be working the old folks' rooms in Wing Four," she said, softly southern.

"You saw the elderly man that Nurse Ricks just

258

took out of the room. Was he in one of the rooms you worked that day?"

"Mr. Loren be Mr. Shango's roommate. Mr. Loren call me. He done poo-poo all down his legs, his back side. Said 'clean me.' He be taking down his clothes. I be washing him, then he be grabbing on me. He say, 'Fanny got poo-poo, Fanny got poo,' like little children play. He get to pulling me out of the bathroom to his bed. His boy thing sticking way out. He pull down my clothes, push me on the bed. I be trying to get him off me. He be putting a hand up on me, hurting me, getting on top of me, doing it." Her face reflected the terror. "Next thing I know, he fall off. I get up. Mr. Shango be there. Radio busted up good. Mr. Loren's head bleeding bad. I pull my clothes on, run, call the charge nurse. Come back with a wheelchair. Push Mr. Loren out the room. Nurse fix Mr. Loren's head. Ambulance done took him to the hospital."

"Did you go with him to the hospital?'

"No. Miss Mary call me to her office, say I play sex with Mr. Loren. Fired me. Said she call the Sheriff, I say a thing on it."

"That's a lie," Lancaster said, screaming at her.

"Ain't so, Miss Mary. You be knowing the right of it." There was steel in Fanny's manner, acquiescence submerged.

"Feel free to ask Miss Brown or Shango questions, Ms. Lancaster," Mike said.

"They are both liars," she said, turning her face away from Dale Unge.

"In that case," Mike said, "I have as my next witness Jocko Lee who was a witness to Fanny Brown's written statement made for the purpose of this hearing."

"Is it substantially the same as Miss Brown's testimony?" Barr said.

"Yes it is." He handed it to the hearing officer.

"I'll mark it as Resident's exhibit one," Barr said.

259

"Anything more, Mr. Brannagh?"

"No Ma'am, except a closing statement."

Before he said another word, the door flew open, perhaps from Loren's left hand, perhaps from the ramrod he held in his right. Whichever, his guided missile was programed for explosion against the surface of the sweet, little brown skin girl. It might have erupted there but for Shango blunting the trajectory with his wheelchair dexterously rolled into the path of the incoming rocket. Jocko recaptured the frenzied elder, removing him, returning him to Nurse Ricks.

Lancaster, rising to her feet, slumped. Unge was up on his feet to brace her. He guided her to his chair. Turning to the hearing officer, he said, "thank you, Miss Barr, for allowing me to be here. I have to leave now." He departed the proceeding as quickly as a city boy chased by a park goose.

"Well," Barr said, clearly astonished "What next?" She looked to Brannagh. "You have a closing statement?" It was said with regret.

"Loren gave it for me. Enough is enough, Miss Barr."

"Right!" Barr's expression indicated relief. She read the ex-parte warning; picked up her exhibits and departed. Scott, the court reporter, was right behind.

Lancaster stirred. She stood up, shook her head as if to rid it of pestilence, then rapidly moved out of the hearing room. Mike hurried after her, wondering if she were going to take a shot at Loren. She exited the building instead.

"She's gone crazy," Nurse Ricks said with the rasp of sandpaper on wood. "Well, I don't blame her, all you did to her in there, Mr. Brannagh. Come on Loren." She scooted him away.

"Have a nice day too, Belle," Shango called after her. "Fanny, this old man says thanks. You did me right."

"Did right for me, Mr. Shango. Right for right." She

took Jocko's arm. "Got to go. Going be lunch right soon over to Mr. Jocko's. I be working there." They left.

"Brannagh, man," Shango said, "you cut Lancaster's tits off, man. You ain't lost nothing. I tell you this. You ain't no worse with fancy words in there with that hearing officer than years ago in Juvenile Court with the Judge."

"What would you know about me at Juvenile Court?"

"I be, was, Joey Whistle."

"What?" Astonishment covered Mike's face like the flood the earth in Noah's time. The wheels of time hadn't erased the memory of the clash with Judge Vood of Juvenile Court over twelve year old Joey Whistle's being the one against whom a petition was filed in a sexual encounter with a sixteen year old street girl; or of Brannagh's fist fight in the Detention home protecting Juveniles, and Joey, from a youth called 'Schizo,' a sexual predator. "Joey Whistle of Juvenile Court?" He knelt next to the wheel chair and looked hard at the face of the claimant. "Joey Whistle? My Lord! There is a Joey behind those eyes. Why didn't you tell me? Why did you give me all that misery? You knew me all the time!" There was a mile wide smile. "Joey, it's good to see you again." He put his arm around him, pulling him close. "The good Lord moves in mysterious ways."

"Got to go, man," he said, embarrassed, pulling free, wiping eyes. He rolled away. "You come back. Always be here," he said, "unless Lancaster kick out my butt."

21

Refocused, Brannagh parked in Forget-me-not nursing home's northeast lot. A red brick sidewalk at the bottom of the lot ran from Market Road like a river tributary along the east side of the skilled nursing wing to a brighter red door into the three story wing. The facility looked like an overturned yellow chair, the red brick walk its seat pad. The red door opened out. He entered a small room, a one time resident room, its carpeting green and recently vacuumed. Walls were painted off-white. Ubiquitous paintings of country scenery were hung as if ordered to commit suicide. Recessed lighting mindful of a police interrogation room left no corner dark. Soft chairs, blue, white and green, lined the wall opposite a glass partition. Within it was a young woman working on a personal computer. A green telephone and a brown fax machine squatted like frogs on her small metal desk. There was another doorway out into a hall. An elevator door was across the hall. The blond, curly hair receptionist, 'Tiffany' as spelled on the name tag, was pretty as a Senior high school cheerleader. She wore a blue letter sweater with three white arm stripes and a smile as hypnotizing as Mona Lisa's. Tiffany looked but said nothing.

"I'm Mike Brannagh, the ombudsman," he said, "the advocate for residents. I've come to introduce myself to residents and the administrator."

"Mr. Melk's not upstairs in his office. I saw him get off the elevator. I think he's in the skilled wing," she said, "I'll page him."

"No need. I'll look for him." The sound of squeaky tennis shoes on tile flooring turned his head to the elevator.

A thin woman dodging the elevator's closing doors walked purposely into the reception room, and said, "Did I overhear you say you're the ombudsman?" There wasn't a spare ounce of flesh on the woman. Her minuscule femininity was in the grasp of tight denim jeans and shirt. Her nose hadn't the thickness of a razor bade. Exhumed?

"You did. I'm Mike Brannagh." He was pleased she knew what an ombudsman was.

"I'm social worker Mamie Sorr. I need to talk to you about a seventy-six year old resident. Please come out to the hall." He followed her. She said, "Waldo Clar's room is in intermediate two. He's frightening nursing staff, threatening them with beatings."

"A seventy-six year old? If he's up to inflicting a beating on a young staff member, why's he in a nursing home?"

"Age and illness don't always mean incapacity. Waldo is a big man who worked on buses up to the day he was sent to the hospital. His doctor directed him to our care."

"What's behind Waldo's threats to nursing staff?"

"It's because of his glasses. His eyes were giving him trouble so I arranged for a test. Since he's gotten them, he's all over me, yelling the glasses are no good, I'm no good, he's going to whack me a good one right after he whacks the nurses."

He thought Sorr was so thin whacking her would be whacking a fly swatter. "In what way aren't the glasses good?"

"I'm too scared to ask. You ask. His room is 124, the corner room on the first floor of this wing. The window of his room looks out on the street where Chickton Transit runs a bus every hour on the hour. He spends most of his day watching buses come and go. Few other interests," she said, pausing as if contemplating. "Maybe that's why he's so upset about his glasses; he can't see the buses well enough." Again she paused, but not to contemplate, to condemn. "It's Waldo's own fault. I got him an optometrist's eye exam, but he refused to use our optician to make his glasses. Went to an optician of his own. It's Waldo's own fault his glasses turned out wrong."

"If Waldo isn't an optometrist or an optician how can it be his fault the glasses turned out wrong? He neither prescribed the corrective lenses nor filled the prescription."

"Well!" she said, indignantly. "I don't see it that way."

"Whatever. Before I go to see if Waldo's home, I'll need to know if his per diem is being met by Medicaid, to know who is paying for the glasses. I'll also need the names, addresses and phone numbers of the optometrist and optician to work this out."

"Waldo's on Medicaid but the wrong glasses are his own fault," she said repeating her position. "I'll get you that information."

As Sorr departed, he was reminded that social workers catch a lot of grief from all sides, not least the administrator passing the buck. She'd worked up a reasonable approach, new glasses and resultant respect. Too bad the glasses backfired. Too bad Sorr took Waldo's complaint wrongly. Now she wanted to dump on Waldo that her boss Melk not dump on her.

Tiffany, in the reception room, smiled a smile brighter than the light bulbs planted in the ceiling. She waved as if a pre-school daughter welcoming home her hard working Dad, and beckoned him to reenter reception. "Mr. Brannagh. I overheard Mamie. Here's the names and addresses you want."

There were footsteps down the corridor. Tiffany returned to the computer at the appearance of a man square as a washing machine. He wore brown trousers and black hair, tugging at a red tie while unbuttoning the neck button of a long sleeve white shirt.

"Mike Brannagh?" he said, his pitch somewhere above a second tenor's. He received a positive nod. "Mamie told me you were here. I'm Mel Melk, administrator.

Pleased to meet you." Melk went instantly to the personal. "Call me Mel," he said, letting loose of his red tie to shake hands. Let me show you where Waldo rooms." He preceded the ombudsman through the door into the hall. "This way, last room on the right."

"This facility's layout," Mike said, "is mindful of a reform school."

"Close," Melk said. "Few know these modern rooms were once cells. It's quite a story. There was a time Market Road's red bricks resounded for eight decades with the weight of horse-drawn wagons heading to Chickton's Farmer's market across the road or to drop village idiots here at the County Poor Farm. Old timers called them that and this place 'Doomhill', because often after admission, and at County taxpayer expense, burials followed. The yellow brick three story dormitory for them had been extended westerly to house the insane when the farmer's market closed. To shelter the Depression's rising ranks of poor old folks, a yellow brick single story building went up to the north. It bisected the idiots and insane wings. In nineteen seventy-four, certain that massive sums of Federal and State tax dollars were readily available to private entrepreneurs for the underwriting of construction of nursing homes and long term care of the impoverished ill elderly, Old Home Inc., a closely held corporation, and our County Commissioners seized the moment. Old Home, the only bidder, bought the Poor Farm, its locks, bars and buildings. The Commissioners forthwith cut off County funding. A long term nursing home evolved. Old Home added a cement block modern wing parallel to 'Hatch', the old-timers' abbreviation for 'Booby Hatch.' The second and third floors of the 'Village,' no longer 'Idiots' Village' and Hatch were closed to residents and remodeled for Old Home's corporate offices. Hatch's and Village's first floors were remodeled for intermediate nursing care. Old Poor Folks wing was remodeled for skilled nursing care. At Old

Home's open house, owner Caleb Coll was proud to christen the magnificent nursing home Forget-Me-Not. He meant it for himself. It's applied to recollections of the County's Poor Farm's history. The sound of ambulance wheels on Market Road's red bricks was a chilling sound to the impoverished ill elderly. It meant a debilitating illness put them on the road to the old yellow brick home where, years before, town people placed the living dead. Back in those olden days, poor souls who were called feeble-minded were placed at the Poor Farm to live in a colony for feeble-minded. Later they were called idiots or imbeciles or morons. Then retarded. Now developmentally disabled. No need for cells today, but back when country folk feared the unknown and didn't understand anything about genetic defects, the blood of the feeble-minded or idiots or the retarded was dangerous blood. One generation of feeble-minded was enough, a Judge had said. It was sterilization or a cell. Rooster County put up cells to keep them from one another and the public."

"Wow!" Mike said. "A history of what we didn't know at the time, and still don't, except now there's a growing sense of humility on the part of us not yet fully debilitated."

Rooms, former cells, either side of the long hall with walls off-brown above a dark brown tile floor also had walls of light brown but the tiles' dark brown had been broken by streaks of yellow. Each one window room held two brown metal beds, hospital type, covered with army-blankets and brown spreads, two folding tan metal chairs and two tan metal dressers each with a turned-on TV encased in brown metal with a tan border. Curtains that looked like thick khaki ship's sails hung from brown rails fastened to a ceiling painted tan. The color of the rooms and hall left the impression residents were encased in a bowel about to squeeze out a dropping. Where a curtain was drawn around a bed it gave a pretense of privacy.

Privacy? Every room's door was open no matter within the state of the resident's clothing, on or off, or pulled up or down aging torsos. More than bare shoulders were in evidence.

Melk didn't seem to notice the backsides of the undressed. "The remodeling removed the bars from the windows. New doors replaced the iron doors. Every other cell was converted into two bathrooms with showers, so each of our rooms in the 100 unit has a toilet for two residents. Just like home. We also let residents pick their roommate. Here's Waldo's room."

Melk hurried away.

Had social worker sicced Melk on him? Was he being set-up. Being used didn't bother him. It was the nature of social work as he practiced it. Juvenile Delinquents used him to get into the military. Parolees used him for leads on shelter and work. Residents used him for approaches to their nursing home problems. Melk and Sorr were out to neutralize or expel Waldo, using the ombudsman as their tool. That was misuse! If he couldn't handle Waldo's anger, Melk would testify before a hearing officer his facility shouldn't be expected to put other residents in danger because of Waldo. Stopping at his door, Mike knocked.

"What?" said a man with the grunt of a wild boar.

He pushed the door ajar to talk through the opening. "Mr. Clar? I'm Mike Brannagh, the ombudsman. I hear you got stuck with a pair of lousy glasses."

"Come in if you dare, guy," he said, a boar with an attitude. Deeply sunk in a suffering easy chair, he filled red mechanic's coveralls with three hundred pounds of well marbled beef. Potato chip crumbs covered a football field of a belly. If crumbs on the floor around his boots were watered and potato chips had seeds, a bumper crop could feed the poor for a generation. A baseball cap covered a grass-less pitcher's mound. Eyes blacker than darkness were set off by frostbitten eyelashes. His assumed white beard was stained yellow as if deep fat fried. It added a decade to an attained seventy-six years.

Waldo reached for his glasses but knocked them off his bed's army-blanket onto the tiled floor. The plastic clicked on the hard surface. "Where they go?" he said in a roar. "Can't see much with them. Can't see anything without them." His head bent down to the floor but none of the rest of him. "I got stuck with these glasses. Sapling Sorr ain't no social sister at all. She won't do me right." He quit looking for the glasses.

If trees were the criteria of bodily measurement, sapling well described the dimensions of Sorr. Waldo was a giant redwood, Mike an oak. The oak stretched a branch and picked up the glasses. Lenses were as thick as telescopes. "I've your glasses, Mr. Clar. I'll put them in your hand." If he couldn't focus, placing the glasses in his hand was correct. Doing for a nursing home resident who could do for himself violated independence. Desired help was self help if feasible.

Waldo rested the telescopes on a Mount Rushmore nose. As if a dam had burst a river of tears flowed."Damn things hurt my head, guy."

"Let's do something about it. I'll get in touch with the optometrist and optician. They prescribed and filled the prescription. They're responsible for doing it right."

"So what? Sorr said they won't do it." Waldo took off the glasses to wipe his eyes with a red cloth like the ones he'd used to wipe oil off a bus' dip-stick.

"So we'll do it. A letter might bring about new glasses with the right prescription. We'll write they're responsible for whatever is wrong with your glasses, not you. If they don't fix them within a couple of days you'll ask the ombudsman to call in the State's Medicaid Fraud Unit, the Prosecutor's Adult Protective Services and a lawyer from Elder Law Center to investigate why the optometrist and optician took federal and state Medicaid dollars for services that resulted in a defective product."

"Hot damn guy! You're mean!" Waldo said, his face as red as his coveralls. Then his bellow modified to a bark. "You do it. I don't see good to write."

"Alright," he said accepting the truth of it, "and I'll mail you a copy of the 'ad terrorem' letter." Even if Waldo couldn't see it to read it.

"Terror them?"

"In a sense. 'Ad Terrorem' is a phrase from the Latin language. Loosely translated it means we let the optometrist and optician know there are   governmental agencies intended to protect elderly consumers."

"Will it work?"

"We'll find out soon enough. For sure I won't let them ignore the letter even if I need to make a personal visit with a worker from Adult Protective Services at my side."

"Can't make out your face, guy, but your voice got zip."

"My face is a very handsome face, my body all muscles," he said, the tease in his tone obvious. "Can hardly walk the street without women whistling." He had his attention. "Mr. Clar, do me a favor while I'm working on the letter. Maintain quiet dignity. When the optometrist and optician get the letter, one or both are sure to phone Melk or Sorr to find out what the hell is going on, but quiet dignity throws administrators and social workers for a loop. A smile instead of a cuss word completely befuddles them, because there's nothing but bad written in the Nurses Notes."

Waldo's eyes widened. "Quiet dignity you say, guy. Nothing bad in the nurses notes," he said as if meditating.

"I'll get the letter done and mailed very soon."

"Appreciate it, guy."

* * *

Back at his home office, his phone rang. "Hello."

"Mike, Millie here." She was breathless. "I overheard Cecil Jasper, Lobelia's administrator, talking to Hope Bedico today. I know she has no love lost on Alta Ridd or me, but imagine my surprise when the conversation centered on you. Jasper told her not to worry on you much longer, that the lawyer for Nursing Home Management had written a letter to the State Ombudsman."

"A lawyer? Well, I'm not the guy cutting the grass at the cemetery, working with hundreds of people under me. The hearing at Palace must have gone better than I'd thought. Fanny was a superb witness, but not as good as the resident Palace claimed was the victim. By the way, your boss, Dale Unge, was at the hearing. I suspect, because of Lancaster's poor show, he kicked his lawyer into overdrive. Thanks, Millie."

What now, he wondered? Nursing Home Management's CEO must not have taken well to the ombudsman. Now he's got his lawyer writing to State Ombudsman Donavan, he that certifies area ombudsmen. No certification, no area ombudsman for nursing home residents. If Donavan decertified him, Ziggie's inside investigation on counterfeits would be at an end.

22

Walking the three miles around the wetland as quickly as he could, Mike was ticked he didn't break forty-five minutes. Thinking about the lawyer working to get him canned must have slowed him. Just under sixteen minutes a mile had been his best. Fifteen seemed out of reach. He entered the house and dialed. "Good morning, Lizzy."

"You didn't phone yesterday. I should give you hell."

"Is there any place you've not been?"

She giggled. "One message. Call Lou Cooper." She gave him the number.

He dialed. "Lou Cooper, please."

"Hey Mr. Brannagh, this be Cooper."

"Nice to hear a friendly voice."

"You got troubles, man?"

"Hope not." He realized he sounded low-down. "What can I do for you, Coop?"

"Ain't for me, man. The job with them old shits going good, you know what I'm saying. Ain't no Project hoodlum messing with my old folks. As the dudes down to unemployment say, it's about my former employer. You ain't going to believe this, man, but Big-dough done called me on the phone up to my woman's place, say he ain't after my ass for quitting him. He be wanting to get hold of you, hearing as how I be working for Five Counties like you be doing. Makes me feel good, Big-dough calling me to get to you. I tells him I let you know what he want, so he tell me his old man be living in one of them homes way out in the country where white folks don't care for a colored dude in a Cadillac, you get my drift. Big-dough say they arrest his ass he drive on out where deputies don't do right by the black man. Want to talk to you, man. I get Big-dough's

271

private number, say you call. Okay?"

"Okay, Coop, and thanks. I appreciate your protection as much as the old folks in the Projects." Mike wrote the number down, then dialed. "Hello. This is Mike Brannagh calling for Benny Mack."

"Hey, man, Coop tell you what's going down with Big-dough?"

"Yea. That you want to visit your father, but worry cops might pull you over."

"Ain't no white cop in the sticks don't see a black man in a big car driving back roads ain't gonna' arrest his ass just for passing hogs and goats. Afraid a black man be coming after no good. You the one come to Calvin's to tell me Pop want me get Mama's bible. You gonna' get me out there next Tuesday man? Follow my drift?"

He did, not only because Big-dough's reasoning was accurate, but because his words were more a supplication than threat. "I do understand and I'll take you. Tell you what. You drive to Jocko's Place in Oldtown about eight and I'll meet you there. We'll take my pickup out to Larkspur, you visit, and afterwards I'll bring you back."

"Be about noon, man. Ain't getting up before the hens."

"OK." Mike felt gratified. There might be little done correctly in the eyes of Nursing Home Management, but he'd done right for old Projects' folks by Coop and Larkspur's Mack.

* * *

Violet Nursing Home was on Aquaville's southwest side, the home hidden on a back acre of a balding woods. A mile west was a roving sand dune deposited by a receding glacier around twelve thousand years ago. Too many more good winds and archeologists would have a dig at the nursing home. To the east, an asphalt parking lot was full of cars, except the distant side's *VISITORS PARKING*.

The '83 pickup found a suitable spot and stopped sighing. Colder days weren't its style. Mike walked the marked route through the parked vehicles. An asphalt path, two wheelchairs wide, led him to a wooden bridge over a drainage ditch that circled the rectangular home moat-like. No shark fins protruded from the green water, but sleepy tall brown reeds were as numerous as blood sucking mosquitoes. Four empty screened-in gazebos indicated cognizance of Fall's reality. Each gazebo appeared a prized soft and comfortable summer home.

Violet's architectural form was that of a very long ruler with camels' humps. A wheelchair might sprint the central hallway from east to west two hundred and forty feet where it would abruptly crash into the locked unit's security door. Double windows, twelve sets either side of the front entry, were two to a room, or twenty-four rooms. Kitchen and dining areas were in the back humps, therapy next to the kitchen. The Director of Nursing, as a sign indicated, was Annalee. She was in the room next door to dining. Seventy-two ill elderly lived three to a room in intermediate care. In the locked unit, twenty-four not-so-elderly lived two to a room and in their own worlds of psychopathology.

The office of Floyd Bluer was the second room to the southeast of the entry. The office next to the entry was marked *SECRETARY*. "I'm Mike Brannagh, ombudsman, here to introduce myself to the administrator and residents. Is Mr. Bluer in?"

The older woman working a keyboard had bony shoulders squaring a pink sweater buttoned tightly around her neck in apparent fear of sliding off monumental bosoms. Neatly stacked sheets of paper on the desk emphasized organization. She said nothing, but got up from her chair, stare foreboding, badge reading 'Azalia.' As if she didn't see the man asleep at his desk through the door that opened into the next office, she closed it before

273

returning to sit. "Mr Bluer isn't available. How may I help you?"

Amazement put a smile on. The taciturn, old, lame secretary knew he'd seen the phantom slumbering in the shadows. Did she sheltered him from residents' families, surveyors, vendors and, lastly on the chain of importance, ombudsmen?

"As long as you know I'm around, I'll go about visiting residents. Thank you."

If a protective tigress occupied the front cage and a hibernating bear was in Bluer's den, what was in the locked unit? Its double wide security door was painted grass green and made of tooled steel, no less a gage than that at the Francois County Jail. To open, the bar-handle had to be pushed within a second after entry of code numbers 9-3-4-5. He succeeded the third try. The great door opened into the quiet of a catacomb. Four ambulating apathetic people, hands on shoulders, were linked like sausages along the south wall. They slowly approached the entry where the lead lady, her long black dress as mournful as her pitted face, crossed the hall to the opposite wall. Her train of khaki clad men with disfigured features followed up the north side of the hall to the east end. Exercise for the mentally debilitated? Either side of the hall, room doors were open. Neatness prevailed within. Residents sat on chairs or were standing, none talking, none laying down on made beds. Older women in dresses were distorting already distorted images in their mirrors to scare whatever reflection was haunting frosted memories. Younger women in black slacks and tan blouses caressed mis-shaped vestiges of facial beauty. A tall young man in khaki flexed flabby biceps on crooked arms. An elderly fat gentleman wore an olive drab Ike Jacket. His attempt to expand his chest resulted in the puffing of his stomach.

The nurse station was inside a shatter proof glass room across from a lounge at the west end of the hall.

Visible were white uniforms of a nurse and two male Aides. They chatted   while sitting around a table the other side of a desk, apparently eating, oblivious to the ombudsman.

In the lounge, inoculated from their memories, seven warped residents sat on soft couches clustered around a large, softly sounding TV screen showing animated cartoons. The plight of a befuddled coyote entertained a few. The rest of the viewers, but one, were as expressionless as corn cobs. The sitting exception dressed in khaki pants and shirt folded and unfolded his lumpish body like a jack-knife, as if bowing from the waist to a TV goddess. Was the slap he delivered to his forehead each unfolding, atonement for bad thoughts?

A man came up off a chair. Bib overalls nearly swallowed the potbellied guy. With the voice of a newly castrated bull hunting his nutcracker and with teeth on hinges he faced up to Mike and said, "Heard this one? 'Know who created the horse, a cattleman's gunslinger asked a sod-buster?'"

Mike effected a happy but quizzical face at the man who looked as western as a cactus, what with six hairs like prickers sticking out of his bald head. Did Cactus want the punch line? Apparently not as he quickly repeated the gunslinger's question.

"'Who created the horse?' the gunslinger shouted at the scared sod buster. I must know who created the horse?' Scared as a barn mouse at a swooping owl, the sod buster cried out, 'It wasn't me!'" Cactus backed off a couple of inches, face pruning, eyes crossing. From the tip of a pointed chin to bluish lips, up his nose and across puffy cheeks a smile spread followed by a ringing laugh. He repeatedly slapped his right knee. "It wasn't me!" he said, shouting the sod buster's line. "That's good! It wasn't me," he repeated. His laugh went unabated several seconds until he sucked air like a vacuum cleaner did dust, then quit pounding the knee. "Make a good joke, I do."

Mike's smile enlarged though he feared his sweater would shrink absorbing a quart of spraying spit. "You do."

"Heard the joke on Rawhide," Cactus said. "Remember Rawhide on TV? I remember Frankie, can't recollect his last name, sang a song. I can't remember the words."

"I do." Mike sang them. Finishing, he felt a hand from behind encompassed his neck. There wasn't strength in the grasp. Nevertheless, an ounce of prevention was worth an avoidable neck bone fracture. He slowly turned to look at the assailant with the tender hold.

"Like your voice," said a visage with the pallor of limestone, his voice soft as a stuffed lamb's. Delivered of his appreciation he turned away to recapture a chair from a hissing woman.   Folding and unfolding, Jackknife's obeisance and repentance resumed.

"He say he like your voice," Cactus said, eyes showing as much astonishment as his sound. "Cliff ain't never talked, far as I know."

"Cliff? Good to know his name."

"Hey, man," said a male Aide, hollering from inside the glassed room. "How you get Phoby to talk? You his kin?"

"I'm the ombudsman. Phoby? Is that Cliff's last name?"

"No it's not," said a woman getting to her feet and coming forward. "I'm LaVada Morris, charge nurse. Phoby's a name Theo shouldn't use." LaVada turned her head half sideways. "Theo, I've I told you to stop calling Cliff by that name."

"Yes, Ma'am," Theo said. He sensed the big man with LaVada was somebody. "Don't mean nothing by it mister. Me and Phob..., you know, me and Cliff get on good."

"Why do, did you call him Phoby?"

"Oh man. I don't mean nothing by it," Theo said whining apologetically. "Ain't no fright Cliff don't pee his pants, him getting the scares. Hear tell Doc call it phoby. Cliff gets on good, man, you get my meaning, do what he got to do, opening and closing like a clothespin do."

"Can I be of help?" LaVada said, cutting off the ombudsman's access to Theo. She wanted him free of further scrutiny, so approached and whispered, "Whatever Theo's lacks of education, grammar or diagnostic skills, he has an intuitive rapport with the mentally ill. Perhaps they sense his concern. He does more good every work day than a year of the psychiatrist's infrequent visits and his most frequent prescription, psychotropics."

Mike registered 'psychotropics' in his mental notes.. "I understand," he said. "This is my first visit to Violet. I'm Mike Brannagh, ombudsman."

"I'm familiar with the program," she said. "Worked in Michigan. Glad to meet you, Mr. Brannagh." She seized the moment to lessen a bad impression. "This locked unit houses some of State Mental Health's mentally ill patients whose medical prognosis requires twenty-four hour nursing care. Our treatment programs are individualized and we have several group activities. The residents help out. They keep themselves and their rooms clean, with some staff assistance. We keep it restful. Particularly before meals. We take them to eat in the main dining room with the other residents. Staff have to eat here in the unit. You see, nursing staff helps serve the meal. After supper if the weather is bad, we join activities in the main lounge on intermediate care. If the weather permits we go outside."

She pointed out the side door to an eight foot tall wire fence around a twenty-five by twenty-five foot clay yard where dirt puffs were wiggling. Two brown picnic tables with attached benches shared the clay with a large boulder painted red, white and blue. Bird droppings seasoned the stone's blue circle.

"Time to eat, folks," LaVada said sweetly. "Theo, Howie, time to line up."

Murl the comedian, wasn't about being late. He hurried to his room's door, the fifth one from the entry, and stood at as much attention as he could muster. LaVada walked down the hall calling "time to eat." Theo and Howie, the other Aide, worked the rooms either side with professional gentleness encouraging residents to line up, telling of hot food on the plates, ice cream for desert. Long or short, thin or plump, male and female exited rooms obediently. Ambulatory residents lined up facing LaVada just as once Mike had lined up in grade school's corridor facing Sister Mary when she clanged her hand bell. The alpha and omega of aging, unformed or mis-formed minds and frames stood waiting!

Bodies were so mis-proportioned, Mike was lost in sadness. What birth or developmental catastrophes caused such physical malformations? Were they abandoned in youth because of it? Did deprived and worried minds add to the contortions of looks and   limbs? Was there no bottom to what illnesses did to the least of us?

The great tooled steel door open. There wasn't a move by a locked resident out of confinement though kitchen odors permeated and noses sniffed the source of the culinary fumes.

Theo said, "let's go."

Feet shifted   and shuffling began to the dining room. They entered with the gait of society's mentally wounded, a scene Mike hadn't before witnessed. It bothered him as did the stream of physically wounded soldiers from off Korea's main line of resistance. Sorrow flooded his soul over illnesses' destructiveness of minds, bodies or both.

Two score of intermediate care residents sat around dining tables, three here, two there, a table of four. They appeared unconcerned at the passing by of the deranged.

How long a time must expire before the physically ill, not mentally ill, get used to the disturbed from the locked unit? Or accustomed to their presence at meals? As beneficial as meals with the mentally stable might be for the unstable, was there an effect to the contrary?

* * *

On the way to Primrose nursing home, clouds of air-borne black lambs chased one another. A clouded sun floated in the sky, its light fitfully playing peek-a-boo with some of the black bottomed puffs that tickled its face. Below, on the four lane highway, truckers shattered sound barriers. They dueled to lead the convoy. No lead, the view never changed. The '83 pickup, uncomfortable just one mile an hour over the speed limit, quivered at each eighteen wheeler's passing. No where in the manufacturer's manual was there written a word on damages the result of rattling inflicted by diesel eating monsters. Mike felt worse than pineapple chunks mixing in a milk shake. Turning south, chancing township back roads, a lone deer watched him come on. A masticating buck at roadside was building fat for the rut. A tough time, the rut. For each doe, the buck fought other bucks. When successful, deer hunters intruded during the passion. A buck's life with hunters was like the '83's with truckers.

* * *

Primrose nursing home was a mile to the right off the state road. The main building was partially hidden by a woods of maples changing from summer clothing. Driving to the front parking lot, a yellow brick structure with numerous tall, lean windows and a entry that would be at home on the 'State Movie House' open itself to view. Flower gardens that engulfed the foundations of the intermediate and skilled wings were still quite pleasing to the eye. He parked and locked the pickup. No telling which of the frail ill elderly might break out and steal it.

Primrose housed a retirement community in its

279

seventy-five apartments, not inexpensive rentals, but with a highly pleased clientele, even at two thousand dollars monthly. To the west, a Medicaid certified hundred bed nursing home stretched out in three directions. It was full to the last bed. Belinda Fordice had indicated there was no vacancy and a waiting list because of the administration of Wayne Nyet, though his name translated from Russian as 'No.'

Buttons on the full bodied receptionist's brown sweater pulled button holes to elliptical patterns. A stack of wispy straw rested on top her head. Cheeks were a fire red and brown eyes peeked out of fat slits either side of a corn cob nose. The smile was as large as the entry door. She turned from her computer to the visitor. "May I help you?"

"Yes. I'm Mike Brannagh, Ombudsman, here to introduce myself to some residents and the administrator, if he's available."

Just a moment, please," she said, dialing her phone. "Mr. Nyet, the ombudsman is here." There were several seconds of silence while she listened and simultaneously studied the visitor. She hung up. "He'll be right out, sir."

The door behind the receptionist's glass cage flew open. An enormous frame six foot five inches from floor up and sixty inches of waist wall to wall filled every inch of the door jamb. Its face was that of a sickly elephant, eyes the size of woodpecker holes and as brown as the tree pecked apart. A monorail eyebrow ran from one ear to the other bridging gorges in between. Lips of a toadfish opened and a picket fence of teeth smiled.

He said, "So you're the ombudsman being dumped on? Welcome! Come in."

Dumped on? Probably all nursing home administrators in Five Counties' area, if not in the state, would have received phone calls from Palace's Lancaster even before Unge's Lawyer wrote to the State Ombudsman. The classic way of politicians, lawyers, and apparently nursing home administrators to undermine was a campaign against someone working in a bureaucracy. Nursing Home Management wasn't fooling around. They wanted Mike's butt, the submerging of the ombudsman's program to obscurity. Let their administrators run nursing homes without outside interference! But Nyet's welcome?

He stepped to the side of the receptionist's desk and open a door in the wood paneling. "This way." He waited for Mike to come to the door, to shake hands. "Pleased to meet you. Call me Wayne."

"And I'm Mike," he said, looking up. He followed the monument into his office.

Nyet's desk suited his circumference. He went around it, and sat on a chair more the width of a park bench, lavishly upholstered. Tall, thin windows let in considerable sunlight, if any beams should break through cloud cover. A lamp hung from the ceiling, its hundred and fifty watts making up what clouds didn't allow. Papers were neatly stacked across his desk top. Bookcases were full of the latest publications on gerontology and geriatrics.

"Have a seat," he said, his hand pointing to any one of three hard wood chairs. "Have a chocolate?" He lifted a full box to his guest. "Nursing staff tell me the boxes of chocolates appear more often than appointments I schedule."

"Thank you, but no."

"I'm cutting back," he said, plopping one, two, then a third piece into his mouth. "Out of shape since I quit coaching football. When the high school principal said I had to lose two hundred pounds or my coaching contract, I quit, lost the two hundred here at night working on maintenance. Got my license four years ago. Darned if the lost two hundred didn't rise up out of the sepulcher to re-inhabit me. Lost weight is ghostly, always around to haunt if you're not fasting. At table with my residents, the grandmothers, long removed from chiding their own offspring about obesity, cluck at me instead. I suffer it, claiming my balloons, whether denominated stomach, legs or arms, are the depositories of genetic glandular dysfunctionings."

"It is difficult to keep it off. I've not done too well," Mike said, thinking Nyet hadn't a mean bone framing his immense structure. Near the same height, putting on weight was a common affliction, Mike's less, considerably.

"So you're Mike Brannagh?" he said, studying him. " From what I heard, I pictured you as a used car salesman, wild mouth and flamboyant clothes. Not at all. You must have taken no crap from a certain hard boiled woman. A rooster hatched her head. She talked at the meeting like she castrated you."

"There was a meeting? About me?"

"There was a quarterly meeting of area administrators. You weren't on the agenda until a certain administrator brought you up. She and some others sure took unkindly to you, but several others welcomed your help with difficult residents. I'm not going to tell you which are which, but I heard negative things like 'he commented about poor care in other homes'; 'discussed an apparent problem in another facility'; 'makes inappropriate comments on the running of a home'; 'put the fix in with the Hearing Officer.' You get the drift. Your detractors said you walk in unannounced, and go where you want, the devil the privacy rights of residents."

A bit defensive, Brannagh said, "Look at me, Wayne. Invisible? Not only do I displace my share of oxygen but I introduce myself to the receptionist or first visible staff member upon arrival." He realized his temper was taking over. He cooled it. "I suppose, from the other side of the desk, an administrator sees someone not in his or her employ; someone with connections to the surveyors; someone in the home a couple of hours a month, not forty to fifty hours a week; someone who couldn't possible realized the degree of difficulty there is in caring for both the terminally and chronically ill three eight hour shifts a day, seven days a week; someone whose misinterpretations could cost them a job, a career. From where you sit or any administrator sits, I can understand their view point. Particularly, if the ombudsman verbalizes opinions of his own that differs with theirs." He paused to add emphasis. "Among the most difficult of all human relationships is agreeing to disagree. The fact that people differ doesn't mean one is all correct, the other is all wrong. There may well be shades of facts to which we can agree to disagree," he said, his voice now curious. "Why are you telling me about administrators?"

"Because," he said, "as an old offensive tackle, I hold to coming straight on, face to face. There are things that should not be said, so I don't say them. I informed my fellow administrators that I hadn't met you, but when I did, I'd make up my own mind, and if I saw fit, I'd update you on the opinions expressed, without of course identifying the speakers. It was violently disagreed I do so. In light of certain administrators denouncements of you, and, I heard, other actions, I didn't expect I'd have the opportunity."

"They have that much clout with the Governor and his appointees?"

"A certain lawyer has. He's retained as lobbyist for both an area chain and the State Association of Nursing Home Administrators."

Mike, a bit chagrined, hadn't an inclination to pursue the topic. How much time had he left before decertification? What about counterfeit psychotropics? At least he'd impressed Nyet. "Wayne, whether or not I'm around to come back to visit your facility, I appreciate your candor. I'll let you alone and go about the ombudsman's duties. Would you tell me who the council president is?"

"Gertrude Hicks in room 124. Used to live in a retirement unit." He wrote it down and handed him the sheet of paper. "Do you have to go?" There was a nod. "Okay, but please have a piece of candy?"

"Thank you, but no." He patted his stomach, leaving Nyet to his chocolates. The huge man was appreciated, the ombudsman wary, if not down right paranoid. If he took a single piece of candy would it be reported to the lawyer lobbyist as equivalent to a bribe? Intended to sweeten his disposition? Compromise him? Mike felt stupid for so thinking.

The layout of residents' rooms was different from most of the homes previously visited. Parallel hallways bisected a main hallway like so many slats running to a fence rail. Rooms backed on one another like tiers of cells in a penitentiary. Room wall colors were quiet with occasional splashes of flamboyant vividness. Well dressed women in wheelchairs lined the walls, carefully but silently appraising the man passing by. Conjecturing who he was to visit would take up a part of the day until the activities director called them for bingo. His mind wasn't on line with ladies in wheelchairs. He was thinking he could quit the ombudsman's job, but to what purpose? He knocked on the open door at room 124. "Mrs. Hicks?" A woman in a wheelchair ducked a can into a knitted bag hanging from an armrest. "Mrs. Hicks, I'm Mike Brannagh, ombudsman. May I come in?"

"Come in." She wiped her mouth with the sleeve of her brown dress, a gruesome old groundhog in a matching furry wig, but with quick eyes in a round head.

"I'm told you're the council president, Mrs. Hicks. I'm the new ombudsman." He handed her a brochure. "How are you?" he said, not only out of politeness, but because she was high on beer. The odor of fermented grain hung like a curtain in the two bed room.

"Fine, fine, fine" she said clearly, rapidly and high in pitch. A winter wren? "Sit in the chair, young fellow." Her skewed smile wasn't left on the barroom floor, but her slippery pronunciation of 's' and 'c' came off it. "Thought I been caught by Wayne." She reached into the knitted bag, pulled out an unopened can of beer. "This round's on me." She put it out for him. He declined. She opened it without a moment of hesitation and sipped, then leaned forward to talk in a confidential manner. "Out in the world I was alive, full of spice and ginger, into this and that. I was central, you know, the phone operator, for years over to Pontoon, a long distance operator ready to plug the caller into Washington D. C. Later I moved to D.C. to work for the government, then to Boston to work for a woolen mill. Married late. No children. Bob died ten years back. I returned to Pontoon, then had a ball with my bridge chums in Primrose retirement. Got too sick to stay, came here. My chums are afraid to come over and see me, think my skin troubles rub off. Won't. I drink to forget them. I must." Hers eyes moistened.

Drinking alcoholic beverages was rare inside a nursing home, rampant among the elderly on the outside. Isolation and loneliness in one's own home was as demoralizing as Hicks leaving behind her retirement home chums. The nearly physically well, ambulating elderly had considerable reluctance to be around the not-so-well elderly who used walkers or wheelchairs. Not seeing them was not being reminded what was ahead. They postponed the inevitable by ducking the obvious. Gertrude Hicks too.

"Go visit them," he said as if a challenge. "Show them the woman who plugged a U.S. Senator into Seattle, who bid seven Hearts and made it despite the defenders holding the Ace of Clubs. Bring your beer with you, throw a bridge party, show them how to do wheelies in a wheelchair." He was upbeat. "Spin a wheel on the tiles as you take off."

"That's reckless."

"Is it? As reckless as hiding out and drowning your spice and ginger in malt liquor? Go visit. You're on this side of Primrose because of its health care services, not to dilute spice and ginger. Go on over to the retirement area whenever you feel like it and do things. Bring your health care friends with you. Invite your retirement chums back."

Hicks was smiling. "Sure you haven't had more than a beer?"

"Just feel good being with you, like you will visiting next door. Go enjoy yourself over there," he said, getting up. He enjoyed the touch of cheerleading.

* * *

Life wasn't often easy on the long lived. The variations on the theme of disability were endless. In Ziggie's land of last life, an ombudsman saw bodies twisted, minds failing, spirits soaring or sinking. Perhaps the most surprising finding was 'dependency.' Nursing homes, theoretically, were to promote health and independence to the degree physically possible. That seemed not the case. It wasn't all the fault of the homes. Rather it was a combination of the Mrs. Hicks syndrome, the blues, and the home's doing for the residents to lessen the staffs' work load, wheelchairs rather than ambulation. Dependency was the precursor to lasting debility. He felt he'd visited a resident who might not remember it was the ombudsman who called. He needed to talk to another, one who might tell friends, and they theirs, that there was such a thing as an ombudsman to look into matters causing them personal anguish in a medical setting euphemistically called 'home.' There she was in the lounge, Whistler's mother with Mona Lisa's smile, a woman wearing a Halloween Jumper with spooks, pumpkins and witches applied to a black and white background. She sat wistfully in a wheelchair.

"You're sure anticipating the spooky eve," Mike said, several feet away.

Her revery was broken. She looked up. "Yes. I was thinking of the little children who used to come to my front door 'trick or treating.' How I enjoyed their little faces. I invited them and their parents to come on in and have warm cider. Such a nice memory."

"May I join you?" Her nod of approval quickly came. He pulled a wooden chair from a table over to her and sat down. "I'm Mike Brannagh, ombudsman, which means the residents' advocate. Here's a brochure that explains what an ombudsman does."

"I'm Eloise Renau." She turned her attention to the brochure, then read aloud its large print "'STRIVING FOR EXCELLENCE IN LONG-TERM CARE.' That's wonderful. You've come to the right nursing home. Wayne has brought about such changes since he took over. I was bedfast then, and didn't much care if I ever got up again. Wayne did. Not only did he see my nursing care and therapies were of the highest quality, but there's so much to do out of bed. He's bringing school children over this Friday after school for a party. He takes to the Mall as many of us as can go with a trained volunteer to take me to any store I wish to shop. It's like being mobile again. I love Wayne for it. It's so joyous in Primrose. I often think those who take an apartment in the retirement unit, do so with the idea to come here if health so dictates. Isn't old age interesting? We know so much in our heads, but can do so little about bodily difficulties."

"I don't know about doing so little," Mike said. "Seems to me age hasn't any adverse thing to do with communication, whether it's the written or spoken word on radio or TV. Why not contact the local radio and TV stations, go on and talk about how to care for the elderly. Lord knows you have ideas about that, whether the aged person is at home or in a nursing home. Maybe it will influence residents in other nursing homes to motivate their administrator and owners to do what Wayne has done at Primrose."

"Maybe," she said. "I'll go have a beer with

Gertrude and talk it over."

* * *

Mike stopped by Five Counties. "Hello Lizzy. Any messages?

"One from Ivy nursing home. A Dot Inge wants you to drop by. And somebody called from Blackthorn. I caught he was a resident, but not his name. I didn't understand him, or what he was trying to say. Something about a horn."

"A horn? I'll get to both homes soon."

"And, Mike, a letter from the State ombudsman."

He opened the envelope. A glance curdled eyeballs. A copy of the letter enclosed was written, not to Donavan, but Donavan's boss Carson Varter, the State Department of Social Services' Director. He was the Governor's direct appointee; and Donavan's boss. An enclosed note requested Brannagh respond to Donavan on Lawyer John Campton's letter to Varter.

"Hey, Mike," Ziggie called from down the hall. "Come in to visit a while."

Bringing Ziggie up to date on Nyet's information, and now the Attorney's letter, seemed wise. It was Ziggie who hired him and Five Counties that paid him, but it was Donavan who certified ombudsmen. Without certification, there was no authority to so act. Even Ziggie couldn't override that. Mike walked in and held out the letter. "This could be a big time worry for me as ombudsman, Ziggie. An Administrator warned me about it. A lawyer for Nursing Home Management, who's also a confidant of the Governor and a big time lobbyist for the nursing home industry, apparently wrote to Donavan's boss about me."

"Saying what?"

He read the letter to him.

288

Carson Varter, State Director
Department of Social Services

Dear Carson,

On behalf of our client, Nursing Home
Management, Inc., (hereinafter "Nursing HomeM") and
its affiliated Nursing Homes,   (hereinafter "Nursing
Homes") we would like to bring to your attention problems
we are having with a Long Term Care Ombudsman by the
name of Mike Brannagh,   (hereinafter "LTC Brannagh").

LTC Brannagh has subjected these Nursing Homes
to many instances of what they feel are inappropriate
conduct during visitations. A recent incident at Willow
illustrates such conduct: LTC Brannagh came in
unannounced, didn't tell the administrator he was there,
acted as if he were there to do a survey, spirited two
residents away from the administrator's office, thereafter
hiding from the administrator, and, after she located them,
heard him instructing a resident about how to renege on
her voluntary agreement to transfer rooms.

LTC Brannagh's other inappropriate verbalizations
or unannounced visitations in other Nursing Homes have
offended other Nursing HomeM's administrators, for
example: he said he knew most Nursing Homes were
for-profit, but more Aides on duty and less profit wouldn't
do corporate Good Will any harm.

He spoke disparagingly about poor care where a
survey hadn't. He entered Nursing Homes unannounced.
No one knew who he was. Residents have been frightened
by 'a man' they saw in the hall. He didn't listen to
administrators' point of views. He was ill informed about
residential care facilities and the chronically ill elderly.

It is this Attorney's opinion that LTC Brannagh's actions are clearly unauthorized by federal and state law, and LTC Brannagh's experience with criminals is ill suited to advocate for the aged. Because Nursing HomeM feels a solution to this problem can be worked out, Nursing HomeM and its affiliated Nursing Home administrators will be happy to meet with the State Director and discuss how to work out a better approach to the ill elderly under Nursing HomeM's care on the part of LTC Brannagh.

For the Firm,
John Campton

Mike hadn't any known problem with high blood pressure, but the face Ziggie saw was red as a rising sun. "Mike," he said, "don't answer, at least, until tomorrow. Cool off."

"Good advice."

23

He had slept well enough, but a walk over by the wetland was more refreshing. Showered and ready to go, he drove to Garland Nursing Home and into their parking lot not knowing Tom Cynge, administrator, was watching the junk of a pickup audaciously parade across its lot. Darned if it didn't park in the front lot the very morning the Bovine County Women's chorus was to arrive and entertain. Why didn't it go to the rear service entry? Whoever the driver, Cynge determined to cancel his company's contract. A tall burly old guy got out of the pickup wearing a shirt and tie under a wool sweater. He wasn't a workman. He fit the description of Brannagh. It shook Cynge, knowing the attorney's letter had been mailed. Follow up visits to Nursing Home Management's facilities like Lancaster's weren't unexpected, but nothing in Garland called for a follow up. Someone called in a complaint? Cynge put his newspaper in a desk drawer, reordered items on his desk, and crossed his office to open the door to the hall. Upon hearing the front door open he stepped out in time to bump into the ombudsman.

"Excuse me," Mike said, stopping on a dime, his arms holding off Cynge. "Nearly knocked you over." He let him go.

"It's alright," Cynge said, stepping back. "I'm okay. I should look both ways before I enter the hall." He saw no mole hill of a man, a whistle blower too often on turf where he wasn't wanted. If Lancaster couldn't handle him, Cynge worried he could. His hand trembled when he put it out to shake. "Tom Cynge, administrator."

"Mike Brannagh, ombudsman. My fault for not being more observant." He shook the hand of Cynge! Nearly as old and built like a top spinning on cement with a caterpillar of a mustache crawling a contemptuous upper lip under recessed eyes. He looked an upper-class Englishman.

"I heard you'd dropped in the other day," Cynge said, now worried something had gone wrong. "Sorry I was out. To what do we owe the honor of a return visit?"

"It's just that I ran into an old friend from years back when we both worked for Francois County. He worked for the prosecutor while I worked in the Jail. He speaks well of you."

"Who?" Cynge was pleased. He hadn't expected this.

"Marion Kap. Imagine my surprise after all these years to run into him, and Kap in such a bad way. I've no medical or nursing credentials to support my observation, but he doesn't speak too highly of his chances to survive much longer. The least I can do is to drop by and talk."

Though Mike might have upset Unge and Lancaster, nothing suggested to Cynge he was out to water log Garland's skipper. "That's nice," Cynge said, acting touched by the expressed care and concern. "Here's my card if you need to get hold of me. Come back whenever and as often as you wish. Marion will appreciate it."

"I will, thank you." He took his leave and walked the hall. "Kap, it's Brannagh," he said with exuberance. "May I come in?"

"Come in, Mike!"

"Good to see you. Where's your roommate?"

"Counter went to hear the ladies sing."

Looking at the frail body, Mike had second thoughts on asking for investigatory suggestions. Then again, who else was there? "There is something I need to talk about in confidence. It's about the prescription medicines you take. Do you get them from a pharmacy tied to Nursing Home Management?"

"No. From the Rock pharmacy. It's checked by a consulting pharmacist. Nurses account for each dose I get." His eyes squinted to better focus on his questioner. "You're after something?"

"I am. Since I came on as ombudsman, a source tells my boss there's replacement of FDA approved generic medicines with counterfeit generics in some nursing homes, maybe Nursing Home Management's. There! I said it. You're the second person I've asked about the origins of the drugs. Both of you tell me they come from independent pharmacies, his in Oldtown, yours in Rock. The only thing the two of you have in common is a Nursing Home Management operated facility."

"You don't think too highly of them?"

"I don't, but for reasons that have nothing to do with counterfeit medicines. I haven't a shred of evidence there's any validity to it!"

A slow shaking of the head gave a hint of Kap's professional curiosity. "And a source says someone is slipping counterfeit generics to us in nursing home? Back when I was working drugs, we'd sent samples over to the Oldtown Clinic for analysis to beef up our case. Never got over the bust I made of a kid peddling white stuff at the high school. Turned out to be baking powder. I was as dumb as the twirps that bought it as 'coke.' You need to get hold of a med and get it tested." There was a pause. 'Know what, Mike? I can get you a med. Since my illness seems to have no bottom even with the change in medicine, I'll get you one. You go out to your car to get something while I have the nurse bring me one of the newly prescribed tablets. I'll wrap it in a napkin for you. You take it. Run a test. Satisfy yourself. You're as likely to hit pay dirt as I was with baking soda."

"I'll go hear them sing."

Kap was all smiles handing over a napkin. Mike's wink expressed his appreciation and departed the room. The Chorus was singing 'God Bless America' as he walked out of the home across the crowded parking lot to his pickup.

* * *

Back home and reinvigorated, Mike placed the
medicine inside a glass bottle and the bottle in his
briefcase, then sat down before the computer to write
Waldo Clar's letters, the same format for the optician and
the ophthalmologist, with respective names and addresses.

'John's Optical Company
Chickton, Rooster County

> *Office of the Ombudsman*
> *Grass Lake, Bovine County*
> *Re: Waldo Clar,*
> *Resident of Forget-me-not*
> *Nursing Home*

Dear Sir,
At the request of Waldo Clar, I'm letting you know
that the present pair of glasses he received from your
service do not allow his eyes to focus; and cause him great
misery. Either the prescription or the preparation of the
glasses wasn't done properly; or both weren't done
properly. Mr. Clar expects that you will see to the remedy
of this in the immediate future.
As you may inquire as to what the Office of
Ombudsman is, you will find its basis in the Older
Americans Act and in the State's Legal Code. The hope of
an Ombudsman is to help residents solve their problems
without early recourse to Medicaid's Fraud Unit or to the
Prosecutor's Office and its Adult Protective Services.
Please feel free to write me at the ombudsman's
office or leave a message at 1-800-555-1212.
Yours Truly,
Mike Brannagh, Ombudsman cc: Waldo Clar

He addressed and put stamps on envelopes, folded
Waldo's letter and slipped it into an envelope to mail. Then

he reread the letter from the lawyer. A chill ran his spine like a bug up his pants' leg, yet he felt calm enough to respond to Campton's charges.

Charles Donavan
State Ombudsman

Grass Lake, Bovine County

Dear Mr. Donavan,
I visited Willow Nursing Home acting pursuant to my appointment to advocate for residents as set out under Federal and State Legal Rules.
I'd just entered the reception area where two of Willow's clerical staff and the president of the resident council were arguing vigorously. The council president wished to be allowed into the administrator's office to protest on behalf of a resident instructed to move from her room to another. The resident who had been so instructed, but hadn't consented to move, was also present. The council president was blocked from entering the administrator's office. I physically intervened to avoid angry contact between the aging president and the young woman blocking him, while introducing myself to all. The administrator wasn't present. The two residents and I adjourned to the room of the resident instructed to relocate. When Administrator Mallow appeared on her own invitation, rules on intra-facility transfers were reviewed with her, the resident and the council president. Subsequently, the resident declined to transfer from her room to another.
As for inappropriate verbalizations that have offended administrators in addition to Ms. Mallow, if at any moment during such conversations the offended administrator had brought it to my attention, (they didn't) I would have made an appropriate explanation and immediate apology, if warranted. It wasn't.

As for unannounced visitations, the law is clear no announcement is required, day or night. Yet, when I do appear, I introduce myself to a receptionist or, if there isn't one, to the first staff member I meet. No administrator has verbalized the contrary to me.

Mr. Campton, Esq., however, hasn't any hesitation to list a litany of my alleged sins and is quite prepared to have me attend his confessional that I might amend my ways. He sure knows how to get attention. He sent his letter on firm stationery directly to the State Director, with a copy to you, the State Ombudsman, but none to the allegedly offensive party.

Surely, Mr. Campton doesn't intend to undermine me with the State Official who appoints the State Ombudsman, who, in turn, certifies the Area ombudsman.

Surely, Mr. Campton doesn't intent to intimidate the office of the State Director and State Ombudsman.

Surely, Mr. Campton doesn't intent to limit the legal bounds of an Area ombudsman's work in nursing homes.

Surely, Mr. Campton doesn't intend to damage my reputation by the use of the phrase 'inappropriate behavior', a phrase loaded with impugning innuendo but devoid of substance in the manner of McCarthyism.

Surely, Mr. Campton intended no negative consequences befall me.

Whatever the intent of Mr. Campton on behalf of his client Willow Nursing Home and other unmentioned nursing homes, be assured this Area ombudsman, even if he dares to differ with an administrator, will always seek a healthy working relationship with nursing home staff, but the rights of residents first.

Yours truly,
Mike Brannagh, Ombudsman

He put it in an addressed envelope. Upon the arrival of his response at the State Ombudsman's office, him sending a copy to the State Director, there would follow an end to the Five Counties' ombudsman's certification. The State Ombudsman was appointed by the State Director who was appointed by the Governor. Law Firms contributed big dollars to political campaigns, lobbied with legislators and governors, had former partners sitting bottoms on Judicial benches. The wind of non-interference with Nursing Home Management's administrators blew hard. It wouldn't be the tree trunk or branches that fell, but a lonely little leaf out in a rural township.

Where would he find another job after quitting parole and losing this one so quickly? The years in corrections earned a modest retirement income, but where, until Medicare, would he get the money for ever escalating monthly medical insurance cost? He might survive if health stayed good. Where was a job out in the country? Puella Junior College paid more poorly than U. S. Corporations in third world countries. Maybe Jocko would hire him to wait on tables when football or basketball teams had home games. An hourly rate and tips, and BBQ! Not bad that.

24

"Good morning, Lizzy."

"Good morning, Mike. No messages."

He dialed Fordice. Three rings," Belinda, Mike. Do you know any of the chemists at Oldtown clinic, and will they keep a confidence?"

"I do, and she will."

"I'll explain why we need her at Church services."

"Right. Holiness. See you there."

* * *

Walking into Jocko's Place to meet Big-dough Benny Mack was soothing in contrast to Calvin's Place in Aquaville. Mike hadn't any trouble recognizing him. It wasn't his gold front tooth, but a hounds tooth suit cut to perfection. He was chewing on a BBQ sandwich, a glass of beer waiting its turn. His burning stare reemerged.

"Been waiting, man'

"You said noon. It's a quarter till. Time for a BBQ."

"Don't sit man. Need to go. Get me out there." He stood up.

Jocko took notice and walked over, a giant redwood next to a sapling. "Mike, my man, who's your friend?".

"Benny Mack from Aquaville. Benny, this is Jocko Lee. Owner."

"Welcome, Benny." Hands were shaken. "Any friend of Mike's is a friend of mine. Still hungry? On me."

Big-dough was taken back by the civility of the heap of muscles looking down slope. "Nice of you, man. Need to go." He motioned his head to that effect.

"Okay, Benny. Let's go," Mike led the little swell to the pickup.

Its sight got a grunt from Big-dough. "Shit, man. I got on my houndstooth. Ain't you got decent wheels, man? It be clean?"

"It is. I covered the floor hole with carpet. Can't do more than the speed limit. No cops."

They got in, the motor kicking over like a toddler kicking crib slats . It stuttered and backfired, to the ultimate distress of the finely fashioned passenger. He remained as silent as the broken radio the whole distance to Larkspur Nursing Home. They parked in front, got out.

"Man, you messing with me? Why you bring me back to Boys reform school?" Benny looked all about. "Man, we ain't down state, but how in hell they move the reform school here? Papa doing time in there?" He and his old man hadn't hit it off, but Papa didn't deserve finishing off a hard life in a place like Reform School. Papa had worked honest labor all his years. Larkspur was all he had to show for it? That wasn't right! Big-dough felt something he'd not before felt: shame. He entered the building through a double set of double glass doors. Old newspapers were stacked high on an empty desk off to his right.

The newspapers seemed to have life when something near them screamed."Connie!"

"What the shit!' Big-dough retorted, jumping a foot in contradiction to gravity, Mike at his side, not quite as high. Back on tile, they saw what appeared to be a Bag-lady riding a wheelchair, sprinting out and taking off down the corridor as if it were a race track, turning sharply to the right. Big-dough hadn't seen better driving since a Police chase. It wasn't five seconds later when a nurse who appeared to break away from a herd of sheep came toward them.

"Can I be of help?" Her eyes gave Big-dough a fishy look. No notice of Mike.

"I be here to see my Papa, Herman Mack."

"Herman? He's your Papa?" Said with doubt the visitor had a papa.

Big-dough felt the scorn of the white bitch. She had nothing on the Reform School's staff. Shit on them all. He could buy Larkspur from a week's cash with enough left over to buy the Reform school. To hell with them. "He be!" He pulled out a wad from his inside suit coat pocket and flipped through big numbered bills to impress the squab.

"You rob a bank?"

"Women lay it on me, girl." He put his right index finger to his lips and winked at the nurse, his brow making waves.

She had more sense, and held back, finally recognizing the ombudsman's silent presence. She pointed. "Go down this hall. The ombudsman will show you Herman's room." When the bag lady rolled back into the hallway and stared, Big-dough gave butt in top strut.

"Here's the room. I'll wait out here. Take your time, Benny."

Big-dough saw the back of Papa's head. He still had a lot of hair, white as wool. He spoke softly,"Papa, it be Benny."

"The old man stirred. "Who you say? Benny? You not in Jail?"

"Ain't never been in jail, Papa."

The broad face the son knew for its glaring stares, the hands huge as horse hoofs that shook the son's body, weren't more now than a Halloween skeleton's, but the eyes had fire.

"You did time!" He said, his sound curt, cutting.

"Juvenile time, Papa, not big time."

"They gonna catch you, Benny."

"Papa. I ain't here on that," he said, losing patience. "I here to get Mama's Bible like you told the white man."

"He done told you that?" A jibe.

"Don't shit on me, old man." Big-dough had enough. "That white fool put his ass on the line coming over to Calvin's just to tell Papa said come and get Mam's Bible. Shit! Could have waited till you passed."

"Wouldn't have missed you," Mack said, hissing

300

'missed'.

"Shit! I be going."

At that moment, nurse Connie came in pushing a medicine cart. "Time for your meds, Herman." She wore plastic gloves, counted out several pills, and asked her patient to open up. He did and plopped pills in, taking a paper cup to his lips. He swallowed. Her eyes followed the pills draining down his throat, those eyes turning on to Big-dough as if to size him up for a bout. A negative shake of her head dismissed him. Cart in front of her, she wheeled it away, passing the ombudsman leaning on a hallway wall.

"Like I be saying, old man, I be going."

Mack raised his fist, mostly knuckles with scarce flesh. "Going whop your ass first."

"Going what?" Big-dough was astonished the sickly old fart had enough energy to double his fist. "Never could catch me, Papa!"

"You was afast little dude." Herman looked at his son a moment and surprised himself by smiling. "Near as fast as Jesse Owens."

"Near as fast? Shit! Jesse see nothing but asshole and heels he run with me."

Mack, for a dying man, laughed fit as a healthy hyena. Big-dough chirped like a sparrow, triggering Herman to hilarity; he in turn igniting Big-dough to elation. Neither could explain which one first cradled the other or how Big-dough got the Bible, but neither was going to let loose of the other.

Back in the pickup, Big-dough held fast to Mama's Bible. He broke the silence. "What them pills the nurse be giving Papa."

"I don't know their names, but they would be FDA approved, most likely generics prescribed by his Doctor. As Herman's son, you could look into his chart to check."

"That nurse. She knows what she be giving him?"

"She follows Doctor's orders."

301

"How the nurse get them?"

"The Doctor prescribes, pharmacy fills, the medicines are delivered to the nursing home."

Silence.

At Jocko's parking lot, getting out of the pickup, Big-dough said as if he cared, "Papa and them old shits in that place look bad, man." Getting into his Cadillac, he drove off into the late afternoon

Mike watched the expensive car roll away. Thoughts of the prodical son filled his mind. The father forgave the son his wrongs, and gave him Mama's Bible. Better than the fatted calf any time.

* * *

Oldtowners living near or in the Projects rarely ventured out at night, daytime for that matter if winos and dope fiends were messing around. From the windows of the '83 pickup, he could see faces looking out of apartment windows wondering what was happening at Holiness. It's stained glass windows were brighter than liquor store neon signs. Spot lights lit the steps, the sidewalks, one highlighting the church's Celtic Cross, its lightning rod a brilliant knife cutting into the devil's darkness. The '83 passed a dozen men standing by the church's steps. Each man was brown as bark and big as the double oak doors of the church. They weren't angelic creatures. They were the Holiness' Defenders, Reverend Coppin Yard's safety first in their minds. Several more men in suits somber as the dimness lined all sides of the church's walls. A convoy of Vans and ambulances pulled up. Defenders opened van doors, lifting frail women and men like play dolls and helping Aides and a nurse push wheelchairs with occupants up the steps to the sanctuary.

Parking in a spot behind the church, a monumental man escorted Brannagh down back steps to the basement door. It was opened. The Defender within led him up a flight. A knock. Belinda Fordice opened the door to

302

Reverend Yard's office.

"Mike," she said, "come in and meet Jim Jackson."

"Hello Belinda, I was trained as an ombudsman by Jim. Good to see you."

"And you Mike. Darn if you don't look like a snowdrop in a coal pile," Jackson said from behind a desk, his ebony beard emphasizing flashing white teeth. "This is Adelle, steno-typist." Slight bows were made."Reverend Yard tells me your friend at Palace, Shango, has Aides who'll give affidavits. Have a seat, and let's get started."

Fordice opened the door to the sacristy.

Nurse Gloria of Palace's Alzheimer's Unit came in with Fanny Brown."Hello Mr. Brannagh," Glorio said, then left.

A twinge ran his nostrils right up to the eyelids. Nurse Gloria knew the hidden purpose behind the Prayer Service? He looked to Fordice.

She recognized the issue behind the baffled blue eyes, and said, "Gloria knows this isn't a healing meeting! This is her church, and mine. She brought two others who were Aides, fired for no fault and warned the police would be called. Reverend Yard is our Minister. Gloria and I are close friends, long before nursing school. We need her." Fordice sat down by Jackson.

Fanny Brown hadn't wanted to be the last to go inside Reverend Yard's office, but someone had to be. What pretty bluejay walls she saw, and smiling people dressed to the nines who sat on oak chairs. The prettiest lady had a funny machine set up. Fanny listened as Reverend Yard out in the sacristy led the congregation singing '*Leaning on the Everlasting Arm.'*

"I feel as if I know you, Fanny?" said Fordice. "I'm Belinda Fordice, a Nurse with State Health. This is Mr. Jackson, a lawyer. He's been asked by Reverend Yard to look into your termination as an Aide at Palace Nursing Home. The woman at the desk is Adelle. She's a steno-typist who works for Mr. Jackson and will write down everything you say to him, that is, if you agree?"

"Sure I do. My, my! A colored lawyer, a colored nurse, and a black gal what types!" she said, then turned to look a long while at Mike Brannagh who looked a tad whiter than a snow man. She looked again at the trio to her front. "Weren't but one colored lawyer back home when my Papa was fired from the city. Lawyer Washington couldn't do nothing about it, being politics was what they was. Hard food!"

"What do you mean, Fanny, hard food?" Jackson said.

"Papa ain't much account after he lose the city job and took to wine. Mama be going to clean white folks' houses, get some money, food what they don't eat. Took two eggs, shouldn't have, to bake Minnie's birthday cake. Got fired. That's hard food!" She looked carefully at the lawyer. "So I come up to Oldtown and get hired in at Palace. Doing right well caring on myself and sending money to Mama   before Loren done it to me and Ms. Lancaster fired me, saying I talk on it, she be calling the sheriff. But then come Miss Millie and Jocko. I work for Jocko. Send money to Mama again."

"I'm so sorry for the past, Fanny," Jackson said, moved. "Now I understand the meaning of 'hard food.' We've written it down," Jackson said. "Mary Lancaster and her bosses owe you the rights due all American citizens, those rights and privileges guaranteed by state and federal constitutions and statutory laws enacted to prevent discrimination in the employment of Americans in nursing homes for reasons of their race, color, religion or previous condition of servitude."

"My, my!" Fanny said. "Big words."

"And there's the record made by the Hearing Officer during Golah's hearing. It will have relevance, for sure," Mike said.

"Those big words, Miss Brown," Jackson said, "may apply to the situation of black Aides at Palace, because Palace is a state licensed facility, certified by federal tax dollars through Medicare and Medicaid. Palace's income is more than seventy-five percent from state and federal funds and State laws contain provisions pertaining to employment discrimination, and threats. Mary Lancaster in her capacity of Administrator is responsible for her Aides' employment and termination."

"Aides do what Miss Mary say do, you know, or hard food. Get my meaning?"

"I do, Jackson said. "May I draft an affidavit using those words?"

"What be affidavit?"

"A legal document that puts in writing your statement telling the truth about an event as seen by you, signed and sworn to before a Notary Public. Adelle will notarize it for you."

"Always tell the truth," Fanny said. "Be okay with me."

* * *

Prayer Services over, Palace's Aides and residents escorted home, Jackson and Adelle on the road to Capitol County, Reverend Yard was back behind his desk. Fordice sat to the side.

Mike said, "There's more I haven't yet told you, Reverend Yard." Tired brown eyes lifted. "About a nursing home resident who, some nineteen years back, ran a tourist program out of Oldtown called Elder Trippers. He arranged tours of retired couples to Mexico. It was a front to bring back Mexican prescription drugs to be sold across the counter of an inner-city Oldtown drugstore. It closed in 1976."

Reverend Yard, surprised, said, "What's it got to do with Palace's employment discrimination?"

"Perhaps little, but..."

Fordice interrupted and said, "What drugstore, Mike?"

"I wasn't told the name of the drugstore, just the druggist. I looked up his obituary. He was Maurice Grain, deceased on June 19, 1976, husband of Concetta Ramirez-Grain; father of the Javier Grain you well know, Reverend Yard. My source told me Javier sold his father's drugstore and closed Elder Trippers, apparently using the sale proceeds to finance Quality Care Inc., which owns ten buildings leased to Nursing Home Management, Palace among them. Javier might have some awareness of what's going on at Palace."

Reverend Yard saw envy's ugly head. It wasn't the first time a white man came forward in a ruse to wheedle his way into favor with a young, beautiful black woman: Millie. "You're stepping on my clerical confidences with your insinuations."

"I hope not. There are details I need to tell, Reverend. When I started the ombudsman's job, I was advised that FDA quality drugs were being sold on the street, their source allegedly from Nursing homes. I can confirm a drug I obtained from a dealer on the street tested FDA quality, but I can't confirm it came from a nursing home. Then the source had me review corporate papers of Nursing Home Management and its subsidiaries, and Javier Grain's Quality Care and its subsidiaries. Nursing Home Management's directors include a Jose Ramirez, surname of Javier's mother. She was a Mexican National. Normally that doesn't mean anything except the Elder Tripper told me it was her relations in Mexico who filled the prescriptions in Mexico in 1973 and 1974 for Elder Trippers. They were returned to Maurice Grain in Oldtown. The Elder Tripper said it wasn't Government approved medicines, but counterfeit generic medicines brought back in 1975 and 1976. Apart from what the Elder Tripper told me, new information from another source with no known connection to the Elder Tripper more than hints something along the lines of Elder Trippers is even now going on that replaces nursing home FDA generics with Mexican counterfeits. I can't confirm that."

"If there's an iota of truth it's horrible to conceive, but your evidence is thin." Reverend Yard's face, from horror to doubtful, rejected the data.

"You're correct. I don't know if I'll ever get it confirmed, nursing homes the source of street FDA drugs, counterfeit inside. I have obtained a psychotropic medicine from a resident in a nursing home. Here it is for testing, Belinda." He got up and handed her the bottle containing it.

She took it, getting up to leave. "I've good friends at Oldtown Clinic. We'll see."

"Yes," Reverend Yard said, "but what? Good night."

He watched the white man open the door for the black nurse. He heard the echo of their steps down the stairs; the back door closing. What allure had this white man that years back Shango Golah came to his Minister to protect this jailor? That Fanny Brown confided the secret of Palace's employment discrimination to Brannagh? That Nurses Gloria and Belinda put their professional positions in jeopardy supporting Brannagh in the face of their own Minister's reticence? That Jim Jackson drove upstate to gather evidence on employment discrimination? The Minister concluded he, himself, had done no less during the parole board kickbacks.

25

"Hello, Lizzy."

"Morning, Mike. There's one   messages. Lou Cooper wants you to call him."

He dialed. "Cooper, my man, what can I do for you?"

"Need to meet. Ain't worked out the place. Call you later?"

"I'll be out in nursing homes. Tell you what. I'll call you. When and where?" "Around noon. My woman's place."

"Okay." What was happening? Cooper sounded composed. Few addicts would dare trouble the ex-con, favoring unbroken limbs. Had Cooper taken and sold off some of the Projects folks' drugs he was hired to protect? A wrong thought. There had to be trust.

* * *

On a field where youth long ago played baseball, Daisy nursing home's staff and visitors now parked cars. Tooled steel screens on the upper two floors' windows of the square, three story school building reminded Mike of its pre-nursing home usage: a County Juvenile Reform School. Escapees had created considerable dismay among nearby voters. The County closed it; and, after public bidding, sold the school to entrepreneurs. It was remodeled for central offices, rooms, visiting, activities and dining. The two top floors were for storage.

He snuggled the '83 pickup into a rear row between two monstrous Recreational Vehicles. He entered a spacious waiting room. A bird cage large as three refrigerator boxes held birds of exotic feathers, a rainbow of pigments as if their Artist's imagination had burst free of all earthly restraints. It was unimaginable the tiny fluff flying about the cage descended from dinosaurs.

"May I help you?"

He turned to see the expected youthful receptionist tucked into a glass niche in the wall. This one had left youth on the front steps. She was old as Methuselah's great grandmother.

"Yes, thank you. I'm Mike Brannagh, ombudsman, visiting to introduce myself to residents. Feel free to tell the administrator I'm here."

"Hazel..., Mrs. Oldham is in the east wing. I'll page her."

"You don't need to page for my sake. Maybe I'll bump into her."

"I'll let her know you're here."

"OK. Could you tell me who is the resident council president?"

"Cally Chamin. She's changing. Used to be a lot of fun, but since the feeding tube, she won't leave her room. She can move about in her wheel chair. Nursing staff will take her to activities, to council, to view the birds, but no, Cally won't go. She's given up, poor dear, won't talk to her friends. Social worker been tying to cheer her up. Cally's in the East hall, it's to my right, your left, room 41, last room on the right."

"Thank you. May I leave a dozen ombudsman brochures on this counter for others?"

"Of course, but there's a display rack next to the bird cage. Every visitor goes over there."

"Good idea. I'll place them there."

Light fixtures inset in the ceiling illuminated East hall with a yellow glow mindful of a camp site fire. He walked down the long hallway indigenous to the homes already visited that separated sides of three bed resident rooms. Lining the walls, or in doorways, were little old ladies in wheelchairs. They were dressed in bathrobes over nightgowns. Slippers covered feet. He detected breathing but not a blink or response. All were sitting as still as

309

gargoyles crafted by stone masons. The unmistakably odor of urine emanated from room 24 where nursing Aides were changing bedding and, in privacy, showering the resident. The work of Aides had the glamor of water girls on a grade school soccer team. They were essential to the players' and the game's outcome, as were Aides to resident's, but unnoticed by the coaches and spectators.

It was dark within room 41. He knocked on the door. "Mrs. Chamin? I'm the ombudsman, the residents' advocate. I was told you were the council president. May I come in?"

"Yes," she said, her voice low as a seagull's flight over water.

He went in, eyes readjusting. Drawn curtains hadn't lost the fight against daylight. A woman was asleep in the first bed, another in the second. Deep within the innards, a lime face turned to the door, its eyes blinking. He approached. If her face had a body it wasn't initially visible. Up close, a fat form filled a dress mortician black. Its sweater, socks and shoes matched. She sat in a wheelchair. Bottles dangled from a pole. Tubes ran from the bottles into her parts.

Quietly, he said, "Mrs. Chamin? I'm Mike Brannagh, ombudsman, the residents' advocate. I didn't want to leave here without visiting the council president. May I sit."

"Do," she said. "I'm giving up being president."

He sat close to her to see her in the dark. She looked eighty plus. "Why?"

"Can't you see? I can't go anywhere without these bottles. Makes me look like an Air Force bomber being refueled, and my very own doctor ordered it." Her face was sorrowful.

"I haven't any medical knowledge, Mrs. Chamin, but he must have given you a reason."

"He says his tests tell him I better not try to swallow

310

food, even the mashed potatoes they feed us, or I'll throw up or choke." There was disenchantment in her tone. "I don't want to die with all these harpoons in me. I'm not a whale. Isn't there something I can do about it?"

"Ask for a second opinion."

"Already did that. He sides with my doctor."

What was he to say? Two doctors wanted her to not chance choking to death. Yet she wanted to take the risk. It was her life. He'd put a case to her. "Just curious, Mrs. Chamin, that you seem to be sticking with your doctor. You must have considerable respect for his wanting you alive, even if not for the result of his medical advice supported by another doctor?"

She gave him a double take. "Never looked at it that way. I guess I do respect him but I don't want these tubes in me. Can't I direct the nursing staff to remove them."

"It's the doctor who orders medical treatment. The nurses carry out his orders. They shouldn't remove them without his order."

"What can I do?" she said, sounding as if in agony. "I've lost liberty. Without liberty, there's little hope. Without hope, I'm useless. As caged a bird as those up front." The shine of unshed tears were in her eyes.

He was moved. Cally Chamin was an innocent who'd lost liberty to a swallowing illness. This contrasted to the criminally accused he knew who lost liberty to conviction of a felony. Innocent or guilty, there was a common bond, hope. She hoped to eat normally, felons hoped to be released among normals. Without hope, they felt useless. He had to give Cally Chamin some reason to hope for living, not dying.

"Liberty, Mrs. Chamin, isn't always physical independence. One's mind need not be incarcerated because the body is."

She gave him a surly look. It quickly turned motherly. "How do you know?"

"I really don't," he said, feeling somewhat embarrassed. He'd a similar battle when near deafness crept over him in Korea and with it the chance to get his big bodily target off the front line, but his independent mind kept him from bugging out on his combat buddies. Mental chagrin pushed his body back up the hill to his machine-gun squad. Yet, if he cited himself, he would be citing the worst of all sources. A meaningful example was needed. An idea! Hopefully Jocko Lee would cooperate. Would Chamin be repelled? "I do know someone whose body was incarcerated for years in prison, months in isolation, convicted for a crime he didn't commit. He knows how it feels to have liberty wrongfully taken, Mrs. Chamin. He was on the verge of hopelessness, but he determined not to let his mind become useless just because he was caged. He's out of prison now, a court declared innocent man, and he runs Oldtown's most successful BBQ. What I'm getting at is this. You and he can exchange notes on handling the loss of liberty."

"A convict?"

"A wrongfully convicted man. A black man. One who knows the consequences the loss of liberty had on him in his own neighborhood before prison, then in prison. He can tell you about the profound positive effects maintaining hope had on him."

"A black convict?"

"A blameless black man who lost liberty because white witnesses and white policemen couldn't tell one black man from another. His loss of liberty isn't much different from a blameless woman who has lost her's."

"I do seem to be in prison!" Her eyes told her mind was considering it. "Can you arrange his visit?" She was pleased he could.

* * *

There were pay phones up by the bird cage. "Cooper? Brannagh here. What's up?"

"Hey, man. Nine tomorrow morning. Over to Church of Holiness with Reverend Yard."

Cooper hung up. Succinct as hell. No use of Brannagh's name. Obviously avoiding letting Charlene, his woman, know who was on the other end of the line, though she'd heard Reverend Yard's name. Enough by itself to soothe a questioning woman. Mike remembered her fright when first he called. She feared Big-dough Benny was back in Cooper's life.

* * *

Chicory Nursing Home was built with wide windows and flower beds along side all exterior walls and in the court yard, the variations of ephemeral beauty succumbing to annual dormancy. The modernity of the home with interior insulated glass walls opened the court yard to window sitters year around. The beauty of the gardens when in bloom were in contradiction to its neighbor, a decrepit homestead. If there had been descendants interested in the old frame farm Gothic, now a residence for four legged critters of unpleasant fragrance, the family would never have sold the grandeur of a working farm's contented cow pasture to caretakers for the disconnected.

Chicory's main entry was the farthest door from the parking lot, beyond porches with bored wooden lounge chairs clustered against walls awaiting the breath of winter. If health forced him into nursing home residency, Mike determined to do his time in spring, summer and early fall out on a similar porch reading Irish History. For a certainty, he met the profile of a future resident: poor, minuscule real or personal property, no close family member, if any distant relative yet lived, was aware of his existence. He'd been educated, fought for his country, buried parents, siblings and wife when their time on earth expired, worked a life time, paid his way, his taxes, yet accumulated very little wealth to attract the interest of far-out-blood cousins,

313

most of whom, if not all, had a similar personal history. He'd be more likely to converse with distant cousins as residents in a nursing home than at family picnics. So many of the elderly lived isolated lives until admitted to congregate care, cloistered in effect, a shocking change!

Chicory's double doors kept out the wind. Inside the waiting area three grand-motherly women, dressed as if to go to a doctor's appointment, sat on couches, occasionally chatting. One, her moustache well smoked, sipped from a machine served paper cup of coffee. The three provided the ombudsman an opportunity to introduce himself.

"Ladies, may I give each of you a brochure about the ombudsman program?" He didn't wait for a reply. All three accepted. The lady with the moustache looked curiously at him. The other two looked at the brochure, one squinting so tightly her eyelids puckered more fully than lips. "The program is a part of the State's services to residents in nursing homes. I'm here to assist residents if any should feel things aren't going too well and the staff haven't been able to work it out just right."

"You're long winded," Moustache said.

"It takes a lot of wind to get all of that out."

"Going well for me," Moustache said. "We're waiting for the Van to come take us shopping. You want to come with us? You can carry our packages."

"Thank you, Ma'am, but no. Got to get around to tell others about the program."

Squinter looked up from the brochure. "You mean you can do something if things ain't right?" A nod. "See about Nicole Ely then. That husband of hers is beating on her. He's moved in with her, in the same room a month now. She's so sweet but he's mean as a trapped goose. Been beating on Nicole ever since."

"You don't know that for sure, Betty Lou," said the third lady. Her eyes looked all knowing. "You ain't never seen him give her a belt."

"Someone does, Dora. Isn't but Albert in her room the whole month. She wasn't bruised up before."

"There's truth to that," Moustache said. "You go on and work it out, young man. Don't seem Ellsworth can. He's younger than my grand babies, and he runs the nursing home." She turned her eyes to an elderly man opening the inside door at the entry. "Our driver. Gotta' go."

The three of them, as if in the same shoes, got up and exited. Moustache was personally escorted by the volunteer driver down the sidewalk to the parking lot. He opened the Van door and helped her up the step, then Betty Lou and Dora, closing the sliding door after Dora settled in. He went around, got in, and said 'buckle up.' He started the motor and drove away.

Who to see first, Ellsworth, the administrator, the batterer or battered? He chose Ellsworth. If the ladies were accurate about the Nicole Ely, the administrator should know. The administrator listing was checked. Obviously out of date. Chicory's was supposedly Lillian Korun.

"Good day, Ma'am," he said to the receptionist the other side of a horseshoe counter, "I'm Mike Brannagh, ombudsman."

"Yes, I know," she said, her pink sweater as fluffy as a powder puff, her facial features as pink but weathered from too much time on horseback. "I didn't mean to listen, but I overheard your conversation with the ladies. Ellsworth does know about it. I'll tell him you're here." She lifted her phone.

"Before you do, what's his last name?"

"Kraus. He's been here two months now. Everybody likes him." She dialed. "Ellsworth? The ombudsman is here to see you. Yes, I'll send him right in." She hung up. "Please go in, Mr. Brannagh."

"I heard there was a new ombudsman, Kraus said"

315

He was thin as the pole that held up a basketball backboard, a head of reddish-blond hair parted down the middle of his scalp. The face hadn't emerged from adolescent innocence. His smile, however, might disarm a librarian seeking an overdue fee.

"And a new administrator of Chicory," Mike said. "Whereas I'm long down the slope of senescence, you look barely this side of college."

"That's what my boss said when he first interviewed me. I assured him my college credits were earned, my work experience included four years nights in nursing homes, that my resume was legitimate. I am twenty-five, though everyone seems to doubt it."

"Everyone wishes they were twenty-five, and looked sixteen. It's envy."

"Have a seat, Mr. Brannagh. What can I do for you?" he said, coming around from his desk and sitting down next to him.

"Tell me about the Elys."

Had State Health heard? His boss? "Already you've heard of the Elys?" His tone carried hints of underlying fear. "Well, our nurses found some unexplained bruises on Nicole consistent with slaps. No one has heard or seen Albert hit her, even threaten her. As a matter of fact, since he's come in here he's been more of a caretaker to her than our Aides. Still, something is happening. He wants to stay in room 127 with her. I can't prove he's hit her, she's silent about it. I've reviewed both charts. Our social worker interviewed Nicole when she was admitted, then Albert when he was admitted. Nothing on domestic abuse. There's the daughter, Geneva. She lives out of state. Social worker's notes indicate she last visited when Albert was admitted. Still we called her. She said she's got her own troubles. If there were domestic problems we're not aware of them."

"Are the Elys long time residents of Door County?"

"Let me look in Albert's chart." Kraus opened it, flipped a page, reviewed it, and said, "Yes. They lived right here in Doorham. He worked for a beer distributor for thirty years."

"May I have his and her birth dates; their last address in Doorham, and where he last worked?"

"Yes, certainly." Kraus wrote them down. He handed over the sheet of paper.

"Have you a public phone?"

Kraus understood the need for confidence. He sat quietly through the meeting of nursing home administrators that poured molten lead on the manner of this ombudsman. Several hadn't taken kindly to him. Now that the man was flesh, there was doubt about his peers' motivation behind the copy of the lawyer's letter he'd been given.

"One of the public phones is in the far corner of the dining area. There are others in the various wings, if that one is busy."

"Thanks. Then I'll drop in and visit the Elys."

The dining area, festive with anticipatory Halloween spirits dangling on strings hung from ceiling tiles, had forty tables of four, the table nearest the public phone seating three smokers.

"Hello folks," he said. "Let me give you a brochure to read while I'm on the phone. It says I'm the ombudsman, the residents' advocate."

The old smoker in a prisoner's denim jacket and a gray beard stained from tobacco juice didn't seem to give a darn who it was, nor did his adoring prehistoric molls. The brochures gave them something to set coffee cups on.

No one was on the phone inside a booth designed for a single stick of spaghetti, so he sipped in his head, a shoulder and little else. The door wasn't about to close. He dropped in a quarter and dialed. "APS? Wendy Connor, please. Wendy? Mike Brannagh. I'm at Chicory in Doorham. There's a husband and wife in the same room.

317

The wife has been here over a year. Her husband came in last month. Since her husband moved in with her she's been seen with bruises that look like slaps, perhaps from a hand. Nurses have charted them. The wife won't say how she was bruised. He denies doing it. The administrator contacted their daughter in another state, but she wouldn't say anything about her parents. Maybe just afraid she'll be made responsible for them. Is it possible to look in the Prosecutor's and Police files to see if there is any history of domestic abuse, drunkenness?"

"It is," Conner said. "Give me some data." She wrote down the information: names, birth dates, last residential address, last place of employment. "Can I reach you at Chicory?"

"It's better I call you in about an hour. I'm going to see the Elys now. Thanks Wendy."

The smokers were still unconcerned as to who the big guy was. "I see you found a use for my brochure?"

The bearded guy gave a hard look out of eyes set in rust. A ring of smoke wheeled its way to the advocate's face. "Soaks up coffee, good."

"Glad of it. If your beard catches fire, slap it with the wet paper."

There was a moment's hesitation before the tough guy, a captive of infirm years, burst his dour lips with a smile. "Yea, slap it with the wet paper!" His ladies cut loose with smokey mirth.

Hilarity followed movement out of the dining room into wing one. Two residents occupied each room. The rooms were clean, the hall without the odor of urine. Walls were recently painted an off-white. Nursing staff were diligently entering rooms, talking with residents, charting. Seven wheelchairs lined a glass wall. Seven enthralled ladies, their dresses bright and clean, watched as a dust ghost danced a whirlwind ballet in the courtyard.

The door to the Elys' room was open. A bald

headed man wrapped tightly by a blue bathrobe sat in a wheelchair staring at a TV set. It wasn't playing.

"Mr. Ely? I'm Mike Brannagh, the residents' advocate, the guy that works for residents in nursing homes. I don't work for Chicory or any nursing home. May I come in?"

"You here about Niki's bruises?" he said, leaning forward in his wheelchair.

"Bruises?" He'd let Albert Ely tell the story. "May I sit down?"

"Go ahead," he said. "Nurse thinks I'm beating up on Niki. Nurse told the young kid up front Niki has slap bruises. They think it's me." He rocked back and forth. "I don't know why they think that. Niki never told it was me." He dropped his eyes.

Shading his meaning! Albert's sentence could be interpreted to mean Nicole was afraid to tell on him. Or, she had nothing to tell. "Never told it was you? What do you mean?"

"Don't mean I hit her and she never told." His face put on indignity.

"When was this slapping supposed to have happened?"

"Just since I came to Chicory. So Nurse told the young kid up front," he said, thumb pointed in that general direction.

"Since you've been here? When did Mrs. Ely come here?"

"A year back. Been married forty years to Niki." A smile replaced gloom.

"Don't hear that these days, Mr. Ely. Nowadays, husband sneezes, wife gets wet, they divorce."

"Niki and I had our fights, alright, but we stayed hitched." He leaned forward. "Couldn't hardly afford one wife," he said, smiling, if lip twisting could be counted.

"What work did you do?"

"Drove a beer truck making deliveries to taverns. Drank my share of draft, good customer relations."

"That was okay with the boss?"

"He poured down as much as me." He raised an imaginary bottle to his lips.

"No beer in here, though?"

"No beer, nothing in here! Niki just sits in her wheelchair after the Aides get her up. She don't talk much anymore. A man get's to thinking his wife gone a year forgets him." He sneered.

"When you were at home, and Niki in here, did you come visit her?"

"Once. Couldn't get no ride. Now I'm here and I ain't slapping her." He began rocking back and forth again.

"Some one is, Mr. Ely. If the nurses find out who, they'll call the cops. You see it's a crime, called battery, to hit someone. Even if a husband hits his wife, it's the crime of battery."

"Crime! They just think I'm slapping Niki." He claimed innocence but was uneasy.

Another inference! "Well, as you say, I suggest you protect yourself."

"What do you mean?" This was a turn he hadn't anticipated.

"I mean, remove yourself from the line of fire. Say you lived in another room from your wife and whoever it is hitting her does it again, you're in the clear. No more suspicion."

"Another room from Niki?"

"Yea. You said you lived apart for a year. Moving to another room may even make the slapper stop the hitting, knowing you can't be blamed anymore."

"You think so?" It sounded right. He'd get out of it!

"It's worth a try. Let's put it in writing for Ellsworth Kraus, the young guy up front, to get you another room." Mike ripped a piece of paper out of his notebook and wrote, saying aloud, 'I, Albert Ely, request a room transfer today, if possible.' Sign here, Mr. Ely." He did. Mike dated it. "For a while stay completely out of your wife's room unless nursing staff is in there. As long as you and Niki are visible to staff in the halls, at activities, in dining, no one can say it's you."

"Okay," he said, sitting straight up, relief running down his face. "I'll spend the day with Niki where we can be seen, not when she's alone in her room."

"Good. That ought to stop whoever it is doing her harm. He'll know you're not here to take the blame. I'll be back to see how it's going."

"I needed someone on my side," Ely said, even if it were a fool.

* * *

Kitchen staff were washing off dining room tables in preparation for the next meal. The three smokers weren't at table by the public phone. He stuck an arm and head inside and dialed APS. "Wendy Connor, please? Mike Brannagh calling."

"Mike," Connor said, "Albert Ely is a wife beater, two arrests, but after the deputies took him to Door County jail, she recanted. Albert has a couple of public intoxs, too. Need anything more?"

"No Wendy. I sure appreciate your help." He elected to keep those details in his own notes. The actual records might be had if necessary.

He turned the request for room change over to the administrator.

26

Cooper opened the door to let Brannagh into Reverend Yard's office."Got to be moving on, Mr. Brannagh."

"What? I thought you wanted me with you to meet with Reverend Yard?"

"Got three old ladies to walk to the Clinic." He closed the door keeping Mike within.

"You may wonder what's going on, Mr. Brannagh," Reverend Yard said. "It's what a man of your Catholic faith would call the seal of the confessional. When one of my congregation wants to talk to me in confidence, it's just that, confidential." The movement of eyes indicated his guest understood. "Please have a seat." He watched as Brannagh sat, hoping the tone used would sound considerably sweeter than the other night's after the mention of Elder Trippers, the Grains, father and son, and counterfeit generic medicines from Mexico. "Information has reached my ears that in addition to crack and other street drugs, FDA approved drugs called uppers and downers are also being peddled to addicts, and," he noted Brannagh seemed aware of it, " the source of the FDA approved drugs is a connection to nursing homes."

Too quickly Mike came to a conclusion. "Grain?"

Reverend Yard shook his head. "You're jumping to conclusions. Grain's Pharmacopeia Wholesalers sells FDA drugs only to drugstores and has to account for its inventory. No, I'm told the source is connected in some way to nursing homes, but not via the rental of buildings."

Mike's lips puckered, his face wrinkled as he said, "Connected to nursing homes? A Director of Nursing? A charge nurse? A pharmacist? MD? Those are four connections to nursing homes with access to FDA drugs. "Belinda told me psychotropics were often prescribed for

Alzheimer and dementia residents. Taken from them? Replaced? When? How?"

"I wasn't told when or how, only that recently somebody has had a great deal of awakening knowing FDA drugs sold on the street were connected to nursing homes. Seems this somebody had a soul cleansing experience over the horrid effect of bad medicines on old folks and wants you, Mr. Brannagh, to know what that somebody knows. There's more to come. As it does, we'll need to meet and confer."

"Okay with me, Reverend Yard," he said getting to his feet, "but Belinda should be here too." There wasn't disagreement.

As he exited the office, Mike saw the tall oak doors at the front of the church close on the tall Cooper. Who told him of the connection? Obviously the somebody who had a soul cleansing experience thinking bad medicines may be given the elderly. Big-dough Benny? Mike was exultant! It had to be Benny! There was a cleansed soul in the son of Larkspur's Herman Mack.

* * *

Mike handled elation as gently as the pickup rode the smooth highway to Basketham. Its main thoroughfare revealed a dozen of two or three story turn of the century buildings, all vacant but four business with few customers. The town's largest business, the place of last resort for females downsized elsewhere and needing an hourly wage, thought minimum with no benefits, was the nursing home. He parked across the street. His notes indicated Blackthorn held one hundred and twenty beds; that a phone call came in to Lizzy at Five Counties complaining about a 'horn', complainant unknown; that the local hospital called in an incident report alleging Alice Mowan was left on the toilet, tried to get up, fell and broke her hip. If attention to Mowan was matched by the attention maintenance gave the littered yard, Blackthorn was a forlorn operation. Its front door

323

window had more greasy fingerprints than a greasy spoon's hamburger skillet. Opening the door, wet heat hit him like a washrag. Sounds of screamers ruffled watery air. Four women in wheelchairs in the vestibule didn't seem to mind the shrieks or humidity. Colorful dresses were more inclined for summer than fall. Sweaters and stretch socks were contradictions.

"Ladies," Mike said, returning the smile of the woman wearing a red and white sweater, "I have something to give each of you." He handed each a brochure. "When you read it, you'll find out the ombudsman is a part of the State's program to assist residents in nursing homes." He was going over like an umpire calling the winning run out at the plate. The red and white sweater lady's smile hadn't deviated a centimeter. None of their expressions had changed from the rigid inflexibility first noticed. Were they drugged out of awareness? He'd move on to more receptive residents.

Two doors in an alcove to the left of the hall bore signs, the one to the right 'Amber Hilt, Office Manager', the other 'Russell Voig, Administrator.' Both were out of their offices.

The dining room was on the left, an activity room on the right. Popcorn was popping in Activities, its buttery odor wafting throughout the facility. On either side of a long hall, pale pink walls were bedecked with posters of the three candidates for Governor. One flashed a wide smile, another a nose magnified twice the size of real life, the third a grimace. Blackthorn was readying residents to vote absentee.

"Smells great," he said to the back of a black hair man, his red sweatshirt advertising 'Road Kill Charley's, Basketham.'

Road Kill turned around, long hair and displacement of considerable space in harmony with a full bearded face broad as the Mississippi's five hundred year

324

flood plain.

"Ain't opened yet."

"I'm not yet a resident. I'm the ombudsman."

"The what?" His tone was a verbal sneer.

"I'm a part of a State program to see to residents' rights in nursing home. The position is called ombudsman, an advocate for residents."

"Don't know nothing about that," he said, looking beyond Mike to the door. "Fifty cents a bag, Walter," he said to the man.

"You raised the price of 'horn' again?" Walter said, his pitch high; his words trembling.

He stood at the door beneath a railroad engineer's cap twice the size needed to encompass his white head. His brown ill fitting windbreaker was zippered to his thin neck; his gray work pants baggy, probably even back when purchased a half-century ago, but ox-blood boots were polished.

"Why are you charging for popcorn? Mike said."

"How else do I fund Activities?"

"You fund it through the per diem payments to the nursing home. I imagine Blackthorn gets about ninety bucks a day to meet Walter's needs. He pays in all his social security but thirty bucks a month, slightly less than a buck a day for his own personal needs. Fifty cents for popcorn is nearly half a day's allowance. I don't see any movie screen around here but you're charging movie house prices for something that should be free in the first place, or no more than costs."

"I charge what Russ tells me to charge."

"Yea, I see. Just following orders." He turned to Walter when a stylishly dressed young man appeared in the door way. His regimental tie was slightly askew, his belt buckle off center and the creases in his pin stripe blue suit trousers were tousled. Walter exited quickly when the young man entered the Activities room.

"Anything the matter here, Steve?"

"Nothing Russ, but this guy here is bitching on the popcorn price."

Mike noted Walter's precipitous departure after Voig's appearance. Why was that? It called for a look-see. First, the 'horn' issue.

"I am questioning the price, but of the wrong guy. Are you administrator Voig?"

"Yea, Russ Voig," he said, smiling and coming forth to shake hands. "I take it you're related to Walter."

Voig played dumb. The old balding guy in the big wool sweater, blue dress shirt and tie, khaki pants, brown shoes and carrying a school notebook had to be the ombudsman he'd heard about at the administrators' meeting. What was he doing here? Had Walter got in touch?

"I'm not related to Walter. I've never met him, but if needed, I'll be his advocate. I'm the ombudsman, Mike Brannagh.."

"Ombudsman! Glad to have you, Mike. What's this about the price of popcorn?"

"Why is Blackthorn charging for popcorn? Giving it out free shouldn't cost you much more than pocket change."

"Ten cents a bag isn't so much," Voig said. "That's our cost."

Rather than confront the activities guy about the difference between his price and Voig's, Mike opened his notebook to a blank page. He took out his pen, a tactic he adopted from police interrogations, the interrogator repeating out loud the suspect's words, but with a twist or two calculated to bring psychological pressure to bear on the subject to elicit denials pregnant with negatives or outright admissions. He wrote, speaking the words as he did so, "Administrator Russ Voig says pop corn is ten cents a bag." He looked up. "What size bag?" A folded paper bag about eight inches high was presented. "Russ Voig indicates Activities is to use a bag about eight inches tall, which when opened is about three inches wide. Total costs of bag full of freshly popped popcorn is ten cents." He looked up from his notebook. "Russ," he said in the same friendly tone Voig had used, would you mind posting in Activities and on all bulletin boards a bag this exact size with ten cents written on it in large block letters?" There was a nod indicating he wouldn't mind. "Good. That clears up any misunderstanding I might have had with the activities director." A ten cent bag was placed between notebook pages.

"Can I show you around the facility?" Voig said.

"No need, but seeing that you have a spare moment, I'd like to talk to you about an incident." A quick look was given. "In private."

Voig cared little for privacy, and said in anticipation, "Alice's falling? Sure. She's still in the hospital. I've checked into the incident. Seems she asked the Aide to help her to the toilet, then asked the Aide to go fetch clean underwear. While the Aide was gone, Alice got up and fell. That's all there is to it. Sorry for Alice. The poor Aide was so upset, she quit."

"I'd appreciate a copy of your written report with the name and address of the Aide."

"Are you going to look into it?" He was a bit disturbed.

"Along with APS and State Health. Routine. I'll pick it up now, if you don't mind."

"No, not now." He was flustered. "I need to finish it. I'll mail it to you."

"Okay. Here's a brochure with my mailing address. I'll go about introducing myself to a few residents at random including the council president."

"That's Colene Kee. She's in the 200 wing, the wing to the left."

Mike veered to the right wing to look at the state of the place. The building was old, worn, in need of repairs and fresh paint. It wasn't difficult to believe the cut in the price of a bag of popcorn from fifty cents to ten might close Activities, if not throw the home into bankruptcy. Residents looked impoverished. The only thing bright was clothing. Sweaters, dresses, shirts and shoes had an Easter egg glow.

There was mystery in the elderly. Few common symptoms, but as many medical themes in residents as there were in symphonic music. Age played games with the five senses: poor vision, hard of hearing, arthritic hands, taste buds flattened, bodily gasses escaping. Diminished sensual awareness played vigorously with minds.

A knock on the door. "Mrs. Kee? I'm Mike Brannagh, the new ombudsman. Russ Voig told me you're the president of the resident council. Have you a few minutes? "

"Yes," she said, opening the door. She was behind a walker. "Come in and sit down. Excuse my house coat." She was a chunky woman with a big smile on a face with chipmunk cheeks. She moved her walker a few feet to the left, turned, a few more feet, another turn, and a few more feet and the pivot was completed. She lifted the aluminum walker gently a foot ahead, stepped with the right, another foot, a left step, again and again until she reached her lounge chair. She made another slow pivot and sat down. "You're the ombudsman?"

"Yes Ma'am." He grabbed a chair from the next bedside, moving it to the foot of Kee's bed and sat." He handed her a brochure.

She glanced through it. "I heard about this from the nurses who work with the State, the ones who write up report cards. I hear Blackthorn didn't pass. Is State going to close Blackthorn? I've been here so long, I don't want to move."

"The State report is supposed to be kept out in the

open up front, Mrs. Kee, for you and visitors to read."

"State was here last week," she said.

"Last week? Then it's probably too soon for the new survey report to be available to the public. Usually State Health sends the survey findings to the nursing home for a response before it's made available to the rest of us. I haven't heard of the State closing any homes, though there are some States that do. Missouri did." Particularly those as nostril penetrating as Blackthorn's environmental odors were. His eyes were smarting.

"Seems we should know what State's going to say before Russ twists it up," Kee said.

"It's all politics, isn't it? Did you see all those political posters in the hall?" She didn't wait for a response. "That's why we need a better independent candidate than Mr. Tyrone. One like my own boy, Adam. He doesn't curse, doesn't smoke, doesn't drink, no time for dirty stories like the workers down to the factory. Adam asks the Lord's blessings before meals, reads the Bible on his breaks. He's a God fearing man but his Union Steward called him immature. Adam will never be in politics. I hope we're not closed. I don't want to move."

He found it amazing how well human beings adapted, even to Blackthorn's decaying environment. What choices had the very ill and poor? If Mrs. Kee had seen upscale nursing homes, would she want to be in Blackthorn? She never had the opportunity. Medicaid paid no more per resident to well run homes. That was the rub. Medicaid paid the per diem no matter the quality of care. State Health might issue deficiencies, but not diminish the per diem.

He used the pay phone to call Lizzy for messages. "Just one to call Belinda Fordice, but there's a letter here for you."

"Please open it and let me know what's in it."

There was several seconds of silence. "The Hearing

329

Officer's findings of fact and conclusions of law favor Shango Golah of Palace and Quinta Ray of Coralroot.

"That's good news," he said, hanging up. But prevailing for residents against Nursing Home Management's Mary Lancaster and Zelda Hann was going to expedite it's lawyer's lobbying the State's elected and appointed officials.

He dialed Belinda. She sounded harried. "Can you meet me at Reverend Yard's about ten tomorrow morning? He's onto something and wants you and me there."

"Sure, Belinda. By the way, any test results back?"

"Not yet. Favors take time."

"I have another favor to ask. Will you sent one of your team to follow up an incident at Blackthorn?" He told of Alice Mowan, helped to the toilet, left and forgotten, who fell and fractured a hip when an Aide left to fetch underwear, an Aide that then quit. Additionaly, the facility's   physical plant is in deep stress."

"Yes, Blackthorn is in bad shape. Our last survey listed several health endangering findings. I doubt, even after a follow up, the Governor's Chief of Staff will let State Health close it. I envision another operating company coming in and a moratorium being granted just like last time. Ring around the rosy. Can't let the well being of the State's elderly infirm override election contributions."

27

From the back roads to Oldtown's Holiness Church at fifty-five miles an hour, the '83 pickup was up to it, took an hour to drive. A glance out the truck window at the church took note the child moll armed robber was on the second step up to the oak doors of Holiness. Mike would have to run the gauntlet. Parking out front he slipped out the pickup's door to face up to the twelve year old in blue jeans, white sneakers and the black nylon jacket she wore at the attempted robbery.

The spark in her eyes told she remembered her putative victim. "You be 'big guy' out back," she said. "Why you come to Holiness so much?"

He'd not expected a civil question. He'd be as friendly as Santa. "Reverend Yard's the man, that's why! Glad to see you come as often. Saw you here one time wearing a real pretty red dress." It merely gilded the flower of her youth.

"It was Millie's," she said.

He was caught by surprise. "Millie's? The woman who was with the man back then? That Millie?"

"Yea. She come to the Projects looking for me. My best friend now. She fit me in the pretty red dress. We be coming to church services. Hope I grow up pretty like Millie, or Fanny. She ain't no ugly, no ways.   Fanny do right by my little sisters and mama, bring mama food, like Millie do. Waiting on Big Sister now. Going fit me up with another pretty dress."

God bless Millie and Fanny turning a Projects' armed robber of a twelve year old girl and her kid sisters from the street. Mentors! Every child needed a mentor. "Tell Millie Mike said 'hi.'"

The church's oak door opened just as he reached for the brass handle. An elongated man was to the dark side.

He came out.

"Cooper!" Beyond a doubt he was Reverend Yard's source.

"Got me the spirit, Mr. Brannagh!" He stepped on down the stairs, said 'hello' to the pretty child, moved onto the sidewalk around to the side of the church and out of view.

"You know Cooper?" the young girl said.

"I do. He and I are friends. So, too, are Millie, Fanny and I, friends."

"I be Talika." .

"My pleasure, Talika." Friendship, a twist of lemon!

This time he had to pull the brass handle to open the door and enter the church. He walked the aisle to the sacristy and knocked on the office door. Responding to the invitation, he opened it, entered and closed it, sitting down in an oak chair. Reverend Yard was seated behind his desk. On it were a few   tablets and pills. There was another knock on the door. Mike got up and opened it, stepping back for Belinda to come in. Salutations were exchanged.

"Belinda, before you sit down, come look at these drugs," Reverend Yard said.

Mike joined her at the desk. She spent several minutes looking the pills over.

"Am I seeing counterfeit or FDA approved?" She said.

"Can't you tell?" Reverend Yard continued, "My confidential source told me they are from the drugs sold on the street, real FDA approved uppers or downers. You'll have to have them tested to be certain."

"No doubt," she said. "I told Mike last night the results weren't back on the med he gave me for testing. It may well take longer to test these."

"Can't testing be expedited?" Reverend Yard said.

"My lady at Oldtown Clinic is testing as a favor," she said.

"Please, the both of you have a seat," Reverend Yard said, pointing to the oak chairs, and waiting until they did so. "There's more to tell. Yesterday, Belinda, I informed Mike a confidential source indicated there was a connection between nursing homes and the FDA drugs sold on the street." He appreciated Belinda's expression of irritation and non-interruption. "The source brought these street drugs to back it up. There's more. Information made available to me indicates the connection between nursing homes and street FDA drugs is a licensed pharmacist. The name of the pharmacist is," a pause, "Victorio Pulvis."

"I don't know the name, Pulvis, Mike said. "I haven't met Victorio, although his name has come up with residents I've talked to, one in Palace, another at Garland. Your source says he's behind the FDA drugs that get to a street dealer?"

Belinda's hands went to her face. She looked up at the ceiling, and said, "I know Vic Pulvis. He's consulting pharmacist to Nursing Home Management's facilities."

"What's that mean?" said Reverend Yard.

Hands coming off her face, and folded on her lap, she said, "He owns and operates his own company, Prescription Consulting, focusing on geriatric pharmacy. His company is an independent contractor with Nursing Home Management. His work with patients is to help avoid unwanted consequences of the drug use process, for instance drug misuse and adverse drug reaction or interaction. Geriatric pharmacy got its start in 1965 with passage of Medicare and Medicaid. Since 1974, a Federal rule requires pharmacist become involved in monitoring nursing home patient's drug regimens, at least on a monthly basis. Vic looks to correct a home's system. For instance, setting up a system of dose and identification checking that formerly relied entirely on eye inspection. So many drug packages look alike and drug names sound alike the potential for drug error is high. The whole system of prescribing, transcribing, dispensing and administration of drugs invites errors."

"Then he could be the source?" Reverend Yard said.

Mike left unsaid Big-dough Benny knew the source, told Cooper, who told Reverend Yard. Though Benny put out the name of Victorio Pulvis, he would stay clear of the Pulvis's connection. No fear of Pulvis, but fear of whom?

"I don't see how, Reverend Yard," Fordice said. "He doesn't dispense drugs."

"If," he said, "Mike's Elder Tripper says he brought to Oldtown Mexican counterfeit drugs in 1975, a year after the Federal Rule required a monthly monitoring of patients drug regimens, couldn't there now be an exchange of drugs, Mexican for FDA, by the very consulting pharmacist involved in avoiding unwanted drug consequences?"

The acuity of the observation shocked Belinda.

Mike wasn't as stunned. "Heaven help the residents."

Belinda recovered. With sincerity, she said, "It just can't be so, Reverend Yard. The mortality and morbidity rates of residents in Nursing Home Management care aren't significantly difference than others in care else where in the state."

"Let's hope your right, Belinda," Reverend Yard said. "If you're not, what can we do to uncover it?"

"I'll ask my contact at Oldtown Clinic to expedite the analysis of the drug Mike obtained, and those on your desk. What if the tests prove they're all FDA psychotropics, even Mike's?"

"Then," said Mike, "the Elder Tripper and Reverend Yard's source are wrong about replacement. Supplying the street dealer with FDA isn't our focus. What the residents are getting, is. As of now, we have but one drug from inside. So we go about our work, Belinda. Nursing Home Management after me for bothering them over the quality of care; State Health after you for honest surveys." He grimaced. "Just in case the test of my drug does lean counterfeit, we'll need data on Pulvis. Can you look up his pharmacist background?"

Unsaid was Mike's urge to check out Victorio Pulvis. Was he connected in any way to pharmacist Guido Nozlo who smuggled FDA drugs into the jail back in 1973, Mike's time as jail director? Modus Operandi was similar.

28

All seasons had pluses when one walked around the wetland. Behind the last farm house, October revealed soy bean fields naked and yellow after the harvest. Tall gray-brown corn shocks, their gold dangling as if baiting combines to return, whispered in flighty winds. As cut corn's moisture was high, the low whine of a distant dryer was unabated. Pumpkins were orange and full in their patches. A gust of winter roughed a splendid maple causing it to exercise via a rain of reddening leaves. Mike came in from his walk and nestled into his chair reading the morning paper. Political stories were beating sports hands down. Tyrone, the state's third party candidate for governor reopened his quest satisfied his campaign operatives hadn't misappropriated funds, all the while claiming the other candidates had failed to address their own fiscal messes. They had written him off with only seven percent of registered voters. At that, the polls weren't overwhelming for Governor Study, the incumbent. He remained around thirty-eight percent while his challenger, Attorney General Puts, was at forty-six percent.

Politics! Like rewriting State Health Survey's of Nursing Home Managements' facilities and Fergus Orr playing politics with Puella's President for a Honorary degree for Mary Held.

* * *

Inside Grass Lake nursing home, a preacher's voice resounded boisterously with sulphuric damnation, hopefully on sinners outside the walls. A sniff of incense floated in the air. Mike followed the sweet odor, knocked, and opened the door: "Hello!"

"Come in." On the window ledge an incense ciborium was smoke-signaling. Orr was at his desk, white hair and whiter face highlighted by a military appearance.

He could have come off war's front line wearing combat boots and a camouflaged shirt.

"Why the incense?"

"Before I answer, let me tell you I'm making progress on Mary Held's Honorary Degree. Puella's President Lucia Dorth is interested. She senses a winner. As for the incense you inquired about, I burn it to retaliate against the pious blusterer up front. One must prepare defenses to ward off attacks from the devil's devoted preacher who calls himself religious."

"You rate him highly."

"His church is a ramshackle barn in Big Pond, a community of thirty trailers on a pig puddle. I always doubted the Reverend, as he calls himself, worked for heavenly good and that's why Nurse Lotta stays away. Reverend Feat lusts after her, which riles up her paramour Victorio Pulvis. He's the home's consulting pharmacist. A handsome man. Reminds me of myself decades back, powerful backside, broad shoulders, full body, the vein not varicose."

"Even that vein can get varicose?" Mike laughed to mask the surprise of hearing Orr so easily addressing Pulvis and his attributes. "By the way, Professor, I looked up the obituary of Maurice Grain. The son that closed Elder Trippers is named Javier. He owns this very building. Coincidental?"

"Yes, quite," he said with noticeable indecision. A chill hit his temple. He rubbed his brow. "Excuse me. I'm very tired." He spun his wheelchair and rolled to the bed.

The suddenness of the exhaustion was so startling that Mike not only helped him into bed   but left the room and fetched the charge nurse. On the way home, he puzzled over the old man's foundering. The mention of the Grains? Javier? Did both father and son deal in Mexican counterfeit drugs? If Orr told of Maurice, why remain silent about Javier? Had Orr something to fear from Javier whose

337

Quality Care Inc., owned the building? Orr was in a private room, usually far more costly. Was there more to confess?

* * *

Returning to his home office, he edited his letter.

State Representative Tommy Tube
House of Representatives
Statehouse

Blanche Kessner
Larkspur Nursing Home

Dear Representative,
Thank you for inquiring into the fiscal impact increasing the Personal Needs Allowance (PNA) might have on the State's Budget. I've made many inquires to support my findings.
At first glance, the State Budget Officer's statement that the annual fiscal impact of a twenty dollar a month increase for eligible Medicaid residents to be a total of $13,676,160 (State Funds = $5,387,747) is mind boggling.
At second glance, the Budget Officer didn't mention that the Federal Medicaid Rule already mandated the PNA be not less than $30 a month. The Budget Officer failed to mention that the Social Security Administration indexes social security benefits annually, as well as forgetting to mention the State Budget Officer does not do the same, that is, index the PNA annually for us residents, or ever, for that matter.
For example, if the average social security monthly check is $400, ($4,800 annually) and a cost of living increase of 2.6% is granted, it would equal $125.00 new dollars for each of the 56, 986 eligible nursing homes residents in nursing homes, or $7,123,250 new dollars coming to the State from the Social Security Administration for nursing home residents. None of those annual increases

338

have ever been given to residents.

Please change the rule to cause the State Budget Officer to annually index the PNA in the same percentage granted by the Social Security Administration.

Over the last several years while the consumer price index has increased about 33% and the Social Security Administration has annually indexed residents benefits, all of which was kept by the State, the PNA has remained unchanged. In effect, the buying power of the personal needs allowance has been reduced by one-third.

Residents need to buy many things for themselves, like shoes and clothing. If we can get a ride to a Mall, the ever increasing commercial prices make us wait and wait and wait to build up our cash to pay, as we haven't credit any longer. So we hunt for bargains at the second hand stores. We pretend not to look like 'Second Hand Rose', but penny-pinching is the last companion of old folks in nursing homes.

Faithfully Yours,
Blanche Kessner, Resident.

* * *

Daisy Nursing Home's charge nurse hesitated to allow entrance to the huge black man, even when, Mike Brannagh, the old white man with him identified himself as the ombudsman. They were to see council president Cally Chamin? So what if he said he had made prior arrangements with the administrator, she wasn't in. Suggesting a check be made with Mrs. Chamin, the charge nurse was surprised the visit was confirmed. Well, she told them, there was another woman, the roommate, who had to be considered. An Aide was ordered to roll her bed, roommate in it, to the next room pending the visit. "You can go visit Cally now," she said, misgivings in her tone thick as cream on milk.

Mike knocked on Cally Chamin's door. "I'll wait

339

out here."

"Is it Jocko Lee?" she said softly.

"Yes Ma'am, it is." He affected the sound of an obedient field hand. What was this old woman to him? Why was he doing this? Visiting an old cripple white woman just because Mike asked? Talk to her about confinement in prison isolation? This nursing home wasn't a prison and she wasn't locked up. He wished he had a mind of his own.

"Come in Mr. Lee."

He went in. A fat woman whose dress and shoes suited grave side fashions was sitting in a wheelchair. Tubes from bottles hanging on a pole ran into her like she was a rocket refueling.

"Ma'am," he said, eye-balling the tubes, "Mike say you doing hard time here."

"Hard time?"

"Stuck in one cell."

"Were you stuck in one cell in prison?" she said, not waiting for him to answer. "I don't see too good. Come over here and sit on the end of the bed."

He did and said, "Yes Ma'am, I was stuck in one cell. I was stuck in the hole like to never see daylight, and all the time ain't done no crime."

"Were you mean in prison? Is that why you were kept in one cell?"

"I reckon I was mean, Ma'am. You see, some white woman said it was me done the crime, but she didn't know a black's man nose from his ear." He strained to keep his language clean, but didn't care to inflect the King's English. She would just think he was putting on airs. "I got extra time for contempt of court yelling I ain't done nothing, but no one but Mike, the man who sent me on you, cared. He said do good time, that he going to get at the truth, but I don't pay him no mind. When them convicts mess on me, ain't no way they eat meat after. Got me the

340

punishment hole. For a month it ain't bad, no screws, that's what convicts call guards, Ma'am. Then every day, twenty-three hours in the same cell, one hour in another cell to exercise, all the time not another inmate to jibe, no radio, TV, no books, no magazines, no nothing but flushing water in the sewer pipes and steam cracking in the heating pipes. My mind got to thinking days were nights, nights were days. I got to counting cracks in the floor and walls, and catching cock-roaches and spiders that snuck out. Raced them. Had to be quick, or them bugs got back to the cracks. I was going nuts, Ma'am. Ain't never realized before I sunk to the dark of deep max isolation, the delight in the sound of a human's voice, even a hostile's voice, or the beautiful colors in the sky, the smell of clean air."

"Oh my goodness," she said. "How did you ever get out?"

"Mike done it for me, Ma'am. Convinced me he was on to the woman what mistaken me. I was near out of my tree, if you follow my drift. I had to do something or crawl up a wall crack with a spider. Mike got the warden to let me work out with weights. Got to throwing them weights around like they was pebbles. Built me up real good. Warden, he sees my doing it, and wants the Governor to know the prison's turning around scum like me, so I get to compete in weight lifting. Done won, sure enough."

"That's wonderful," she said. "Did the warden let you go home?"

"No Ma'am. Didn't even let me out of the hole."

"How did you get out?"

"Mike Brannagh, Ma'am. The woman that identified me, didn't. Got me a new trial. Won it and was acquitted."

"That's wonderful."

"More wonderful was a human's voice, seeing the sky, smelling fresh air."

"Oh yes," she said excitedly. "Will you call the

nurse for me?"

"What's the matter, Ma'am, I tire you?"

"No, not at all. The nurse will help me get out of this room back to where I can hear human voices, see the sky, smell fresh air."Thank you for coming to see me, Mr. Jocko. Illness may limit my body, but you've freed my mind."

* * *

Mike had a Shango Golah to tell he needed not leave Palace, at least at the whim of Mary Lancaster. The nursing home's circle was alive with music and doddering codgers dancing to exhaustion psychologically, fingers and toes physically. Smiles were as plentiful as mosquitoes over a warm swamp. Even Aides were upbeat.

A knock on the door turned the wool capped head, then his wheelchair around. "Shango, my good man. Good news! The Hearing Officer says you won. You beat Lancaster."

"Hot shit, man! She needed taking down. People around here going appreciate that big butt tailing the bitch been kicked good and hard. Tell you, man, winning over Lancaster be big. Big like that robber telling you about the Jail Grand Jury."

"What?" Mike was as shock as when Fergus Orr used Victorio Pulvis' name.

* * *

In 1973 the Grand Jury had cut into Mike's stability. It had obtained secret information that someone, believed to be on his jail staff, was smuggling prescription drugs to inmates and hustling inmates' families for the tab. County Commissioners ordered lie detector tests. Mike had argued no evidence existed to support the supposition that it was jail staff, and that lie detector tests weren't any more accurate than the reading of palms. He argued taking one wasn't a condition of continued employment. Hell of an argument, but persuasive value nil. Still, he refused the order. A subpoena issued for his appearance before the Grand Jury. In front of the Chamber's tall oak door, his heart in his throat, his social work career at an apparent end, he'd worried if he were sentenced to do contempt time in his own jail, the loss of his group medical insurance would expire, and wife Jane was very sick.

The tall oak door of the Chamber opened and the Francois County Prosecutor appeared. Inside, around a table big enough to seat a corporate board of directors, sat citizens sworn to hear the evidence, a shield between the Prosecutor and individual constitutional rights. Mike was told to remain outside. Hours later, as if a County Court House elevator had vomited, the corridor was flooded with detectives collaring an ex-jail inmate, escorting him into the Chamber. Upon the hour, more detectives and another ex-jail inmate entered, the first group exiting like a changing of the Guard. Another hour and the second cluster of Detectives exited, followed by the Prosecutor and Grand Jurors. All passed Mike, trousers stuck to the bench. No words were spoken. Grand Jurors and Prosecutor entered waiting elevators. Mike watched the elevator arrow indicator descend to ground floor. The hum of motors stopped, power off. He'd felt like a cowboy who lost his horse the long walk down the stairwell to cross the empty court house parking lot to drive home. He hadn't heard a night noise until the threat came from an inner-city voice hidden beside a trash dumpster 'put them up, man. Don't turn.' He gave thought to wishing the armed robber deadly aim, but was told if he'd read the Inner-city News he'd know the Grand Jury had changed targets. A copy of the paper was tossed to his feet. The sound of running feet followed. Mike hadn't turned in time to identify the form disappearing into the night. Lifting the paper he saw a front page story that alleged the jail's prescription-drug smuggler was a local druggist who claimed the drugs in his briefcase were prescriptions for jail patients ordered by the jail's medical director. Mike and staff were in the clear.

* * *

"What do you know about that night, Shango?"

Mike had been taken back by reference to it. He'd never spoken of the incident. Brow wrinkled, he sat down. "What's going on? First you knock me for a loop telling me you're Joey Whistle, the boy I had in Juvenile Court. Now you know something about that guy that night outside the jail?"

"Time you know, man. Joey had done become Shango. My construction crew was working the Prosecutor's suite of offices during the Court House remodeling when you was getting your bell rung by newspapers and TV. Took guts not to order staff to take lie detector tests. I figured you no drug smuggler. One of them investigators was working the case in the prosecutor's offices, an ex-cop I got to know. He couldn't figure you for it. Bothered him you was being chopped up. We was in the right place at the right time. He suggested Shango work after hours on the remodeling, you get my drift?"

"Marion Kap?"

"You on it, man. Kap set it up and Shango ran a mission like back in 'Nam. I owed you. You were the man who put your throat in front of Schizo's knife. Photographing them documents was easier than running a night ambush. They brought out the truth you claimed. Sure enough, the Prosecutor's boys suspected the druggist while their boss leaked on you, man. So, Shango took the photos to Reverend Yard. Inner-city News done wrote it up. The rest you know, man."

344

29

"Hello, Lizzy."

"No messages, Mike."

"Is Ziggie in?"

"Mr Zigmont is in. I'll transfer you."

"Hello Ziggie, Mike here. How long before, if not already done, that Lawyer meets with Donavan's boss, and I'm decertified?"

"Not yet," he said. "Keep in touch."

* * *

Mike viewed a series of four parallel buildings bisected by a connecting hall. A misdemeanor workhouse? Had Amaranth's nursing home staff effected the entry strategy of a workhouse, visitors through Wing Two, and subject to frisking? "Good afternoon, Sylvia." He said as her name plate indicated.

The young woman in a black ribbon sweater jumper was furiously pounding on computer keys, its screen lighting a face paler than a Halloween ghoul's. She wouldn't be quite that bad looking if her pepper and salt hair wasn't drawn into a bun round as a wasp nest. She turned brown eyes big as the bun to the voice at her ear. "Yes?" Her tone intimated an interruption of a letter to the editor.

"I'm the ombudsman, Mike Brannagh." He handed her a brochure. "I'm here to meet some residents, the council president, to introduce myself to the administrator if she's in?"

"Vivian is in her office. The door's open. Walk right in." Sylvia returned to her computer.

So much for chit chat. He ambled twenty feet further into the wing to a door, its glass lettered 'Vivian Edir, Administrator.' If the pretty youth with a narrow face and corn blond hair behind a huge black desk was Vivian

Edir, she was a poster child for high school honor students engrossed in a computer spread sheet. He knocked. Eyes bigger and browner than Sylvia's looked up from her papers.

"I'm Mike Brannagh, ombudsman, stopping by to introduce myself. Are you Miss Edir?"

"Yes. Come in," she said in an alto voice that didn't matched her youthful looks. Her smile was that of a scholar receiving a Doctorate of Philosophy. Standing up to greet him, her slim figure was well out of puberty and into a black side-tie pantsuit over a long sleeve kelly green blouse. "I'm Vivian." She came around the desk and shook hands. "Please have a seat."

She sat in an upholstered chair next over from Mike's. So, she reflected, this disheveled elder was the scourge of Nursing Home Management's administrators! Impossible! There was nothing to fear from such a scruff.

"I'm as new as you, Mr. Brannagh. I understand we both started our nursing home careers in September."

"It's Mike. Career? I'm long over the career hill, but I did start as ombudsman then. I'm trying to get around as quickly as I can to all the homes in the Five County Area to let some residents and administrators know there's a new guy working as the residents' advocate."

"What's your background, Mr. Brannagh?"

She was interviewing him? "Bigger than my foreground." He smiled so not to intimidate.

She wasn't intimidated, but tickled. "I'm sorry," she said, the radiance of her face concurring, "that was a bit bold of me."

He relented. "I'm thirty-seven years a social worker prior to this position, all of it with criminal offenders. I was in that work so long, I could name the annual top ten criminals in Francois County. Talking to residents, advocating for the elderly, has been a catharsis."

"What have you to purge?"

Eyebrows rising like a morning sun, he said, "Years of politicians, judges and police officers taking credit when crime decreased, blaming corrections when it increased. It was hot air, but steam can burn. Advocacy for the elderly, I thought, might singe me less."

"Mallow of Willow?" She got right to the point.

Edir was a tough little being. "Who knows?" At the moment, he didn't. Time would tell if the State Ombudsman applied a soothing cream to the butt or a blow torch.

"I'm glad," she said, "I told Mallow, as I hadn't met you, I wasn't about to decide. Now, I won't decide her way," she said with the smile of one who'd won the race, "though I admit we administrators aren't unlike judges and politicians. We don't thrive on State Health and ombudsmen waltzing in at any hour to challenge the way we do things."

He returned the smile. The young lady was impressive. There was hope for the nursing home industry with administrators in the pipeline as capable as she appeared. "I best get about challenging. I'd like to meet Mr. and Mrs. Malt."

"Oh yes!" Edir said. "About his personal preferences. The Malts have agreed to see a marriage counselor. Casimir gave up wearing his wife's underwear, he's buying his own. For the moment Janet is satisfied."

"I'll leave them alone."

Many of Wing Four's residents, covered by multi-colored bathrobes or sweat-suits, were out of their rooms sitting in wheelchairs, or geri-chairs, gathered about the nurse station like an audience at a theater in-the-round. A nurse, apparently oblivious to the din, sat within the station alternatively observing residents and charting in records. Five Aides worked in the circle of residents, offering water, pulling up blankets, buttoning bathrobes, wiping drool, putting tissues to running noses, feeding a few as if infants. There was concern and order to the Aides' nursing care, but the babbling, crying, laughing and moaning of residents blending with the resounding of a TV program challenged the concept of human dignity. He could but stand and gaze like a curious deer. It was a sight hard to assimilate by visual and auditory senses. Dignity! So little of it allowed the residual human spirits of the very ill in the throes of dementia. Care in this unit wasn't individual but collective! Too few nursing staff for the chronically ill besieged by physical calamities and mental aberrations. Individualized, not group, nursing care was the objective of Federal and State Rules. Owners and operators of a skilled wing were paid a higher per diem, but hired too few nursing staff to treat human beings in the sense of living at 'home.' They were a living in a 'group' home, treated as a group. To pyramid profit? Why else? If State Parole could individualize treatment for criminals, why couldn't State Health stop circular care collectives?

A tall, elderly man wandered in, circling the group like an Indian a wagon train. His gray hair wore a brush-cut, the rest of him a khaki shirt and pants, brown socks and shoes. The white tee-shirt across his throat emphasized an all teeth smile. He looked fit enough to conduct close order drill. There was hesitation when he came upon the ombudsman.

"How you doing?" Mike said.

The drill instructor's smile faded into a cavern, lips drawing closed like gates in a castle's wall. There wasn't a friendly gleam in eyes not long ago bright as Christmas tree bulbs. Words spoken weren't comprehensible. The right side of his face was drawn up, crushed as if it were fabricated of card board.

The nurse at the station noticed. She came over. "Are you related to Lucas?"

"I'm the ombudsman, Mike Brannagh. Lucas, apparently, isn't smitten with me."

"Probably thinks you're one of his mechanics goofing off," she said. "He's suffered a stroke. Just last July he was on the job hours a day in his garage. He wouldn't stay home after the hospital. There have been subsequent strokes. Now he's here." She spoke with empathy. "I can usually understand him, but not when he's upset. We worry he'll hurt someone. A better place would be in a dementia unit, which we do not have." She took Lucas' hand. "Come along, Lucas. Time to eat." He relaxed and went with her.

Mike would have liked to talk to Edir about collective care, but she'd left the facility.

* * *

"Checking in, Lizzy."

"There's a letter for you from Blackthorn nursing home."

"What's it say?"

She opened it. "It's an incident report on an Alice Mowan who fell in the bathroom and fractured her hip. It says the Aide had gone to fetch underwear, but hadn't been recalled in time to assist the resident off the toilet."

"What's the Aide's name?"

"I can't find it."

"Thanks." So, administrator Voig excused his staff. It was Mowan's own impatience that caused her accident. Was it accidental his report omitted the Aide's name and address? Knowing the law's limitation on an ombudsman's authority, his inquiry couldn't proceed. He dialed. "Belinda, Mike here. Blackthorn's incident report on the Mowan fracture had no Aide's name. Were you able to come up with anything?"

"Gerri Knit was there. Mowan was forgotten, got up, fell, and broke her hip and the Aide quit, not because she got busy with other residents and forgot Mowan, but because she was threatened by a male employee fearful State Health would come down with another level 'A'

349

deficiency and close the home. Gerri will come down with a level 'A,' but the State Health Director won't close it."

"What will it take? Blackthorn is run down and substandard."

"More incidents like Mowan's publicized with resultant public non-usage of Blackthorn. Politics may not allow closures, but public distaste and non-use will ultimately make that facility commercially unviable. Profit is what it's all about, Mike."

"I can understand profit, but in clothing, cars and so on. People can decline to buy or use things. That creates competition, reasonableness, price wars. But not in an industry accepting admissions of people whose health is so debilitated and resources exhausted that government has to underwrite their care. That leaves the last chance for human dignity in the hands of bottom liners. Profit shouldn't make an Aide so busy she can't wait a few minutes to help a frail elderly woman. Profit on human frailty is a crime!"

"It should be," she said. "As to crime, I may know something today on the items up for testing. Tonight after work. Reverend Yard's. Alright?"

* * *

Celandine Nursing Home's five additions left it with the appearance picadors worked overtime in the ring to anger the bull to more aggressively fight a matador. The expansive white brick frontage of the facility was daunting with no less than four porches and entry doors. Which one wasn't locked? He parked the '83, hopped out, tried a door, got it wrong. The east door was locked but not without a greeting. *'Hi there friend! This door is locked to the outside for the safety of our residents. Please enter two doors down -->.'* The next door down burst forth with similar verbiage, closing with the phrase, *'Please enter one door down -->.'* At last, the main entry. *'Welcome to Celandine. Enter here.*

"Are you being helped?" Said a gentle looking guy.

"I'm the ombudsman, Mike Brannagh." He handed

350

over a brochure. "I'm here to introduce myself to residents, the council president. Would you let the administrator know."

"Of course I'll tell Miss Mow," gentle guy said with considerable unexpected snideness. He took his time to carefully scrutinize the brochure. "Might I see some State identification?"

"Yea, sure," he said to the undoubted author of the quaint signs on the four entries. He pulled out his wallet, and from it a laminated Ombudsman Card, which was handed over.

"My, my," dandy said." He handed the card back quickly, as if his fingers were being defiled from placement residue. "Why do you carry the card in your back pocket?"

"Just in case someone wants to kiss it," Mike figured he'd found an applicant.

"Well!" dandy said indignantly, "I'll let Miss Mow know you're here."

"Thanks. I'll be visiting residents." He wished he hadn't succumbed to matching snideness. Judging by Nursing Home Management's lawyer's letter, Mike hadn't admiration with some administrators. Why alienate the lesser ranks? Receptionist's were often aware of happenings within the walls. The ombudsman's words must be rewritten if he were to last long enough to finish the case of replacing FDA generic medicines.

He walked Celandine's wings. Generally, the rooms were clean but many residents hadn't straightened bed covers after a nap. Exposed sheets and pillow cases weren't discolored,   changed but weekly. Clothing was hung in the closet; each bed with a nearby chair. Dresser drawers were closed. Personal items on top of the dressers appeared dusted. Most residents weren't in their rooms. A few were afoot, or with walkers, or in wheelchairs going to the dining room. Was it that late? There was a woman in 117 looking at an old face in a new mirror. The card in the slot by the

351

door jam read, 'Mrs. Eva Masten.' She was dressed casually in a peach tunic and striped slim knit skirt, the sweater a light yellow.

"Are you home to a visitor?" Mike said after knocking on the open door. It was a room like all others, but with one bed. "I'd like to introduce myself, Mrs. Masten."

"Are you from the pharmacy?"

"No, Ma'am. I'm the ombudsman." He held a brochure out.

She turned from her mirror to study the huge man blacking out hallway light. "Tamra thinks I'm suffering from 'leprosy of time.' A nursing home is a terrible haven." Her wrath remained on simmer.

"What's 'leprosy of time', Mrs. Masten?"

"Read French literature. It means one's mind is giving away to aging. I'm ninety-two and living in sepulchral solemnity for a year now. Alice, the Director of nursing, forgot to order my prescriptions, so Faith, the charge nurse, called for an emergency order from Grupps.' I pay the regular discounted price at Sandsun Drugs, but Grupps is closer to Celandine than Sandsun. They charged nearly half more for the same medicines because I'm private pay. That isn't fair."

"No it isn't," he said. "Would you like me to look into it for you?"

"I can handle my own affairs, young man."

* * *

Holiness kept its electric bill low. A single light up front showed the way to the minister's office. Mike knocked, opened the door to a 'Come in' and saw the sitting twosome. He closed the door. The desk lamp lighted the faces of Reverend Yard and Belinda Fordice, each as sable as basaltic rock. There wasn't a cheerful line among the many crossing serious faces.

Mike knew why, "I take it Kap's psychotropic

352

tested counterfeit, street stuff   FDA."

"You take it right," Belinda said. "I would never have believed it. So? What do we do now. Go to the police?"

Mike sat down "What did the test of Kap's med show?"

Belinda looked at him, and said with sorrow, "its active ingredients deviated from the chemical formula. My friend at Oldtown Clinic said it was a counterfeit, and couldn't do what the studies proved to the FDA it should do. If there are other such psychotropics out there, adverse reactions can be expected, the seriousness of which depends upon the degree of deviation from the chemical formula."

"I would never have believed anyone was so low," Reverend Yard said. "I think the Oldtown Police should be called in."

"Well, Reverend," Mike said, "the Oldtown police might give us a polite listen because Kap was one of their cops, but he's in Bovine County. Kap's psychotropic comes from Bovine County. We don't know if there are any like it in Francois County. All we know for sure is the drugs you had Belinda test are FDA approved, and someone is selling them without a prescription to street hop heads, not to nursing home folks."

Reverend Yard pouted, and said, "You're saying we have no where to go with what we have on hand."

"For the moment. We need much more before we can contact the cops, or State Police, or the FBI. We need to know if counterfeit drugs are being given to residents in other nursing homes. If we bring the police in now, counterfeit will evaporate, as will the perpetrator."

"How do we find out if there are counterfeit in other homes?" Reverend Yard said.

"I have an idea." Mike looked at Belinda. "If you had a nurse on the inside of a Nursing Home Management facility, she might make copies of three or four residents' medical charts, the part that lists psychotropic prescriptions. We get them filled with FDA and back to the nurse. She works the switch, returning to us the stuff monitored by the consulting pharmacist. If tests prove they're counterfeit, we've evidence."

"I know how we can do it," Belinda said. "Gloria Fantry, my friend! She's the charge nurse in Palace's Alzheimer's Unit. I'll ask her to do it. I'll get the pyschotropic prescriptions filled through Oldtown Clinic and back to Gloria to switch. She'll retrieve the medicines the consulting pharmacist has monitored. Back I go to the Clinic. Then what if there are more counterfeit, Mike?"

"Then we meet again and work out what to do, where to go with what we have."

"Yes," she said rather dreamily, "work out what to do. By the way, Mike, State Health's vital statistics recorded the day of death of pharmacist Guido Nozlo as August 8, 1982."

30

After bedding down, Mike worried too a long time over nurse Gloria of Palace encountering trouble when she switched existing medicines in her unit. If caught, even suspected, she'd get fired and the Police called. If the one allegedly perpetrating switching medicines got wind of it, he'd back off. All would be lost. Yet, it had to be done.

* * *

Periwinkle nursing home was located on top of a well landscaped hill. The '83 pickup took unkindly to the climb but pulled its weight and that of its driver into a well marked parking lot. Unlike the for-profits, non for-profit Periwinkle's lot hadn't any assigned spaces for bigwigs. On that basis alone, the ombudsman felt good about the status of visitors. He parked a distance from the main entrance to allow others to park closer. Wasn't a hundred foot walk a ten calorie burn?

The gardens around the rectangular building were asleep, but not the evergreens. He entered the main doorways through the usual set of glassed double doors. Two rather elderly ladies were conversing down the way and dressed as if to go on an outing. The administrator's office was to the right, the reception desk, left. In response to vibrations from footsteps, as if a reclusive spider, a big boned pale skinned woman came out of the office behind the reception desk. Her brown skirt and jacket over a lighter brown blouse were clothes plain as her looks, until she smiled. Then the sun rose and blue seas glimmered. A dowdy transformed to dandy.

"May I be of help?" she said from behind the counter.

"Yes, thank you. I'm Mike Brannagh, ombudsman." He handed her a brochure.

"How nice," she said. "I'm the administrator, Pearl

Jumper."

"Nice to meet you, Ms. Jumper. Do you often work reception?" He presented her with a smile of his own, but in contrast to hers, a pale moon.

"Our business office is behind me. Near the close of the month all of us gather around the computer to see if we made ends meet. I was closest to the reception desk, so I greeted you. Just a moment, please." She turned to the business office. "Susie, I'll be in my office for a while." She turned again to him. "Please, lets talk in my office."

Her small office was as clean as a hospital's operating room. A desk, chair, an easy chair, a couch, two end tables, a coffee table and a book case occupied the space.

"Please have a seat."

"Thank you," he said, sitting down on the couch. She sat on the easy chair. "Judging from the gardens and the landscaping, I take it ends are being met."

"That's the work of our volunteer landscapers," she said. "Our residents are blessed with trained volunteers. You'll see many all over the building. They come at all times during the day and evenings. A few stay after midnight; some come as early as five in the morning. All our volunteers are certified nursing Aides. A few were nurses before retirement. They've been retrained as qualified medical assistants. All passed State tests."

"Very impressive." He wondered if she were cutting back on full time paid nursing staff with so many volunteers? "They supplement nursing staffs?"

"No," she said, sensing what he was after. "We exceed State staffing minimums on all shifts, that's why we agonize at the end of each month, but there's always been enough money to meet our payroll and other requirements. Our volunteers simply add to our residents quality of care and life. That's their mission. Periwinkle is sponsored by a not-for-profit organization called 'Run to Help.' The poetry of Ann Taylor says it best: *'Who ran to help me when I fell, And would some pretty story tell, Or kiss the place to make it well? My Mother.'*"

"I'm sorry to say I never heard of 'Run to Help.'"

"Our residents have and that's all that is necessary. Periwinkle is Run to Help's only endeavor. Our volunteers are all members. They are daughters, sons, who attend to mothers and the few fathers who live long enough to need Periwinkle. Its origin sprung from the need of this generation to care with dignity for their elderly parents. The founders weren't satisfied with the usual nursing homes, so they gathered together to raise funds. They built Periwinkle and partially fund its nursing care. Our residents pay as much as their circumstances allow. We are licensed by the State, but not certified by Medicare or Medicaid. We do, however, adhere to federal and state rules. Come, I'll show you around!"

"You don't have to," he said. "I know you're busy on the budget. If you could tell me who the council president is, I'll drop in and introduce myself."

She understood. "Gwendolyn Robn is our council president. She's most likely in the activities room. That's down the hall, right turn." Her hand outlined the directions. "Gwendolyn loves puzzles, spends hours working on them."

A tour of Periwinkle's halls found nursing staff in whites, female volunteers in pink or red or green dresses in residents' rooms tending to the bedfast, pushing the elderly in wheelchairs, walking residents, assisting those unable to raise drinking cups. The rooms were as spotlessly clean as Jumper's office. There were no detectible bodily odors. It struck him that many of the volunteers were as brown skinned as many of the residents. He prayed 'mea culpa' for thinking 'Run to Help' was organized to avoid mixing the races. Discrimination, whether of volunteers or residents, wasn't a plank in the platform of this not-for-profit entity. He stopped at the Activities room. Walls of half glass allowed revelation of a Bingo wheel, a caller of numbers, and four seated clusters of laughing residents covering the numbers called.

In the midst of this gaiety, but to the back of the room, seated within a 'U' shaped table and surrounded by hundreds of sharply cut pieces of a gigantic puzzle was a lone woman. Her face, pale as flour was lined with blood streaks. She looked motherly in her yellow dress, one who, when young was never bored with her babies, or now old, with her puzzle pieces. Her mind had her fingers working results. She had to be Gwendolyn Robn. He entered the room, nodded to the bingo players, but walked over to the concentrating puzzle worker.

"Mrs. Robn, I'm Mike Brannagh, ombudsman." He set a brochure down. She didn't look at it, or him. "Ms. Jumper told me you were the council president."

She looked up, shook her head disapprovingly, and said with a whistling sound, "Pull up a chair and take a load off."

He grabbed a chair and pulled it over to the table, sitting to her right side. When she looked again, there was a piano keyboard where teeth should have been. It explained the whistle in her toots. He slid the brochure into view.

She saw a boyish face reddened by the outside weather. "I need some help." Her eyes were suddenly hung with canopies. "I thought I had lots of money in my checking account at the Third National to pay the monthly bill here. My daughter tells me I don't seem to have as much as I thought. Can you help me?"

Several thoughts ran sprints through his mind. Family misappropriation? Poor bookkeeping? Nothing, other than a sex offense, was as inflammatory as looking into an unrelated oldster's checking account. His answer called for discretion.

"I can contact your daughter and we can all go talk

to your banker."

"Not Joyelle. Her husband, Pete, died in an car accident. He had been a help in keeping my financial records. I miss him. Joyelle is a lovely woman, but she failed high school."

His surmise of family misappropriation was beginning to take on substance. "Then I suggest you and me go together to see your banker."

"No," she said. She raised her eyes to his, when suddenly, as if the discussion were a collectible, she put it away in the attic of her mind. "This puzzle is impossible." She got up from her chair and left the Activities room.

His sorrowful eyes followed her departure. What happened? Had he miscalculated her alertness and she didn't have a financial problem? Or she did have financial problems and had second thoughts after refusing to involve Joyelle? He couldn't discuss it with the administrator. Confidential. Should he go to the bank? Would anyone there see him as an advocate, or a con-man? What bank was it? The Third National. If there were suspicion of abuse of an elder, financial in this case, why not call APS" He found a pay phone. "Wendy," he said, "there's a resident in Periwinkle whose caretaker may be mishandling funds." He gave the resident's name and bank. Wendy suggested he follow up her call to the bank. He left Periwinkle to its nursing staff and legion of volunteers and drove the '83 to Third National branch in Currus City's Central shopping center. Parking out front, he entered.

Vice President Eleanor Plic occupied a desk."Ma'am," Mike said, "have you a moment?"

She looked him over. Was he the one APS phoned about? The old fellow looked orderly. "Please have a seat," she said. "What can I do for you."

He showed his State identification card. "I'm Mike Brannagh, an ombudsman for the elderly in nursing homes. It's part of the State's program to assure residents' rights in such homes. I asked APS' Wendy Conner to call you. I'm here to follow up because a resident in Periwinkle hinted something was wrong with her checking account at this bank. I don't know more than that because she faded out on me. So I called APS to have them call you. If there's no violation of any banking regulation or right to privacy, all we need to know is that there's money enough in Gwendolyn Rohn's checking account to pay her costs at the beginning of next month?"

"So you know Wendy of APS?" Plic said, smiling.

His eyes brightened. "I do know Wendy Connor."

"Just a minute, please," she said, turning to her monitor. She used a computer mouse to open a program, her eyes studying several lines on the screen. She closed the program and turned and said, "Mrs. Rohn has more than enough money in her interest bearing checking account to meet her financial obligations at Periwinkle, and," she added," there's no apparent misuse of funds. We're aware of her account."

"That's all I needed to know," he said. "Again, thank you."

* * *

At the library, the August 8, 1982 newspaper obituary indicated Guido Nozlo's survivors included a married sister, Agnes Pulvis, and nephew Victorio Pulvis. He was the licensed consulting pharmacist involved with Nursing Home Management. His mother, Agnes, was a sister of Guido Nozlo. Old Guido, the pharmacist who ran drugs into the jail in 1973. Mike couldn't stop from thinking the nephew picked up his uncle's scam, but on a larger scale with old folks in stages of dementia.

* * *

Going to Holiness, there was no mandate to bring food. Yet, transporting a half dozen of Jocko's BBQ sandwiches with fries, hot sauce, paper plates and plastic knives, forks and cups and bottles of soda pop would go a long way to satiate Belinda's, Reverend Yard's and his own hunger at the end of a day of anticipation. Had Nurse Gloria agreed? She'd spoken her mind the day of the first visit to Palace. She was at the Prayer Service for Palace's residents when Fanny Brown and Aides were interviewed.

Juggling food, Mike exited the pickup and hustled up the front steps and into Holiness Church. He guided on the pulpit light to the office. A knock. He entered at the 'come in' and held up the bag of goods. Its savory aroma preceding him. Belinda and Reverend Yard smiled. Another woman then spread newspaper over the desk. She turned.

"Nurse Gloria!" Mike said. "Good to see you again."

No matter the importance of the meeting, Jocko's BBQ took precedence. They talked of October's changing weather, local crime, child neglect, school failures, as if fearful any conversation about large scale usage of counterfeit drugs among the elderly would prove true. Satiated, minds turned to the meeting's purpose.

Gloria presented copies of randomly selected prescription orders that included psychotropics. "I copied these from charts of residents in my Alzheimer's unit. We currently dispense these medicines. Dr. Terry Box is our medical director. He and other MDs prescribe. A central and some local pharmacies fill and deliver the prescriptions. Vic Pulvis is our consulting pharmacist. He continually reviews the prescriptions of residents dependent on drug therapy, hopefully to prevent, or at least to decrease frequency of drug related problems. I and my nurses administer them. When Belinda told me about this, I gagged. I hope there's not an ounce of truth to it! I need to know!"

"As do we all, Gloria," Mike said. "We know one med, not from Palace, checked out counterfeit. If FDA drugs are delivered to the nursing homes, have you any guess, if an exchange, counterfeit for FDA, were made, who might do it and where?"

"I don't. I work only in the Alzheimer's Unit." She gave it more thought. "I don't believe it would be Dr. Box. His eyesight is poor. True, he tends to write psychotropics but he knows his medicines. The Director of Nursing could, but she doesn't often handle drugs in my unit. We have meds on hand per resident to dispense as directed. If those meds in my unit were exchanged, it would have to be before we get them on the floor to dispense. Vic Pulvis is the middle man. He keeps the inventory. The deliveries go to his work area in the basement, and from there up to the units."

"What hours does Pulvis work?" Mike asked.

"I don't know his hours. I'm told he comes in quite often. The few times I've seen him is on break in the basement's staff lounge. Even then he's often out of sight." Her eyebrows semaphored. "There's gossip more than one of the nurses or Aides on break join handsome Vic in the basement's can goods storage pantry. They, for sure, aren't stacking cans of beans."

"Thank you, Gloria," Belinda said with a touch of exasperation. "I've picked out those prescriptions of these residents. I'll get certain FDA meds for you to exchange for Pulvis' meds on the unit. Get the Pulvis meds back to me. I'll have them tested. It may all be for naught if the active ingredients test true."

"That is the prayer of your minister," Reverend Yard said. "There's already enough wrong, like wrongful termination or employment discrimination in Palace."

"About that, Reverend Yard," Mike said. "If Jackson moves against Palace's administration before we know just what kind of meds are being administered, whoever's doing the replacing may be warned. We're working on a criminal matter if the tests prove counterfeit. What I'm suggesting is for you to call Jackson, not telling him about testing the meds, but asking him to hold off until we all meet here again."

Reverend Yard's look was irresolute. He said, "Indignities, inflicted a lifetime on our elderly and those who help them, must not continue."

"Reverend Yard," Belinda said, tenacity in her tone, "our people, you, Gloria and I know how to contend with psychic indignities. We've done it a lifetime. We'll suffer physic indignities to the grave. But we, the three of us, have not had to undergo the possible physical affronts being inflicted on the most vulnerable and non-communicative nursing home patients, those caught in the pangs of dementia. Until we know their meds are safe, Jackson must wait."

Reverend Yard was quiet. His hands joined as if to pray. He said, "As it was Brother Brannagh who brought the infliction of psychic indignities to our attention, and the possibility of physical outrages, it is wise one not take precedence over the other. I'll call Jackson in the morning."

Mike said. "By the way Belinda, would you please check out the Victorio Pulvis we're talking about, his credentials, etc. See if his parents are listed, and if his mother is named Agnes. I looked up Guido Nozlo's obituary. Surviving him was a sister, an Agnes Pulvis and nephew Victorio Pulvis."

"If he is Guido's nephew, so what?" Reverend Yard inquired.

"If the meds test counterfeit, and we know Purvis is the middleman between MDs and RNs, we can surmise where he learned his craft. It not proof, but it is more than coincidental."

31

He dialed   Lizzy. "Good morning."

"When you visit Cornflower," she said "a Joyce Sols wants you to come see her. And Jocko Lee called. There's an art exhibit at 10:00 AM this coming Sunday."

Fanny Brown must be exhibiting. Paintings that is. His mind refocused on the investigation, now in the hands of Nurses Belinda and Gloria. There was nothing he could do until the medicines were exchanged, tested, and the results proved or disproved the counterfeit theory. What if the test confirmed Kaps' counterfeit wasn't happenstance. If it were Pulvis, where did he keep counterfeits? Did he get counterfeits in town? From Mexico? Mexico! The Elder Tripper! Another confession from the Elder Tripper? A revisit was in order.

* * *

The sign on roadside   read Riperidge. Ripe-ridge? What had turned ripe on the ridge that gave the town its appellation? Thyme Nursing Home, a fifty bed facility, had to be Riperidge's leading business after the Unified School District. The nursing home was 'U' shaped, constructed of cement block with a slanted gravel and tar roof, from which raindrops rolled to a center yard. Air conditioners were snuggled within canvas blankets. They jutted from the wall below each room's single window. The left wing was built when President Kennedy replaced Ike in the White House. A right wing was added when President Nixon took over from Johnson. Entry was in the bottom of the 'U.' The double door opened into a wide hall. Patriotic stuffed sofas, red and white to the left, blue on the right lined the hall, couch corners holding somnolent ladies swaddled in sweaters. A soda pop machine, large and red as Santa Claus, beamed a neon smile for twenty-five cent pop!

Suspicious eyes of a geri-chair sentry, a woman

wrapped in a green robe and white slippers, followed the entry of the stranger.

"How are you, Ma'am?" Mike said. No reply.

"Mazzie don't talk at all," a voice from a red sweater on the white couch said. Her head came up out of the sweater like an elevator from the basement. She once had beauty, but a blond wig and sunflower skin offset its remnants. Wrinkles ran her face like threads in a quilt. She got up, her length a size sufficient to look up to a door knob. "I ain't of a mind to nap, rather talk, but no one's awake. So I'll talk to you, big guy. Who you be?" He told her his name and purpose. "Let's get some coffee," she said. The diminutive woman lead the ombudsman into a dining area twenty by thirty with a kitchen to the north, a visitors' lounge south. There were fifteen tables, most having but one chair. Wheel chairs would fill the other places. The tiny person boosted herself onto a chair. She looked as if two New York telephone books were needed for her eyes to clear the table top. She didn't ask for elevation on high, so none was offered. Her guest fetched a chair and sat. The smell of a roast beef or the culinary secretions created by a round cook in whites tantalized olfactory senses. She, spider-like, left her web to refill the coffee pot.

"I'll get us some, Ma'am."

"It's Tullulah. Call me Tullulah."

"And I'm Mike." The glass coffee pot rested on a plastic tray set on a stainless steel table. He filled two Styrofoam cups with the warm liquid. "Here you are, Ma'am. Hot."

"Tullulah!"

"Tullulah it is, but I have a tendency to use last names. And yours is?"

"Tullulah!" she said, her voice the sound of a breaking violin string, mouth a peculiar form of a resonant box. "It's been Tullulah so long I can't remember the rest.

365

I'm eighty-eight. Ain't I of age to forget?"

"Tullulah it is." He didn't pursue her claim to forgetfulness. "I'm the Ombudsman, the guy that goes to nursing homes to visit residents, to assist them in getting their rights."

"I thought I was going to do the talking!" Red pepper was sprinkled in her inflection.

Before she said another word, a tall man wearing an old fashion pilot's leather cap which captured his head, ears and chin came up to the table. He was ninety, maybe a hundred, genteelly haughty, sprightly and with a face tanned to sand. Clothes were those of a bi-wing pilot right out of the cast of the movie 'Wings.'

"How do you do, sir!" Mike said.

"I was a barnstormer. Captain Jerry's my name. Got to fly." Arms out, lips puckered, a flicking tongue propelled him up the home's right wing.

"Jerry's a bit touched," Tullulah said, "but nice." She returned her brown eyes to Brannagh. "You say you work for resident's rights? Never had any one talk with me on rights."

"Well you have them in here. Set out in law and summarized in this brochure. The right to be treated respectfully by the nursing home's staff."

Interrupting, she said, "the staff are good people. I love it here," her smile agreeing, "if you can love living in other than your own house. Over to Currus City at Lobelia where I stayed a while, all I can say is bless the Aides and housekeepers that didn't call off sick of a day. The cook there knew how to mash everything but the potatoes, and the bookkeeper came to my room like a pool hall swamper on pay day when the mail brought my social security check."

"Call offs? Did nursing staff call off often?"

"Often? Like they were avoiding swimming pools of polio," she said, looking him in the eye and seeing interest. "I ain't at Lobelia now, but if I were I'd worry telling my troubles to any one that couldn't fire steadies. Life at Lobelia was miserable enough with call offs. Didn't need the steadies thinking I'm aggravation."

"Aggravation?"

"You complain out loud, you're aggravating. The steadies are already doing the work of the call offs. Didn't want to get the steadies thinking I'm aggravation. Ticks them off. Won't answer calls, forget baths, won't get you out of bed until it damn well suits them."

"And that's not so here at Thyme?"

"Not at Thyme. Only has fifty beds. When I came back to my senses and knew the suffering of Lobelia's ways, I begged my son to set me free. If he hadn't dumped me so fast when I got sickly, and me not knowing a skunk from a sparrow, I'd never gone to Lobelia. But it had a social worker I could count on. She told me in secret she heard good things about Thyme. I revoked my son as POA faster than the five minutes the lawyer's secretary took to run it off their computer and charge $200 and went to Thyme like a bear to honey. Aides here, whether I'm aggravating or not, help me to the toilet, do my hair, don't lose clothes. Plenty of Aides on second, third and weekend shifts. And Sam Code, he runs the place. I'd marry him the minute his wife gave him a divorce!" Her smile shoved ears backwards. "There's Sam now! Come here, Sam." A buck tooth sparkled a little less than eyes at Tullulah's call. "I love you Sam." She meant it. "Sam, this here is Mike."

Sam was somewhat emotional, judging by the way he clasped his hands over hers. Perhaps unwontedly emotional, for tears came to his eyes as he gazed upon the aged lady. A big broad-faced man who looked the former farm boy, he totted heavy jowls and a hanging lock of black hair blown upward with hisses of hot breath from pursed lips. Sam reluctantly released Tullulah's to shake the hand of the visitor up on his feet.

"It's Mike Brannagh, ombudsman. Sorry I missed you when I came in but Tullulah and I got caught up real quickly in conversation."

"She's a talker. Aren't you Tullulah? And a wonderful lady." He painted her with another smile's flash. "I'm about to drive residents in the Van to the antique mall. Aren't you going Tullulah? This is the last load."

"Going faster than Captain Jerry's propeller," she said, "but I worry I'll get lost among the antiques." Her ears slid again. "Hope some sheik bargains for me."

Sam's head bobbed. "Its wonderful women like Tullulah who keep me from changing singles to doubles though it means dollars. I haven't the heart to go back on my word. I think on it most mornings, but I gave my word and I'll live by it. Nice meeting you, Mike. I got antiques to haul." He moved on.

Captain Jerry was flying but the few residents not gone to the mall were asleep.

* * *

The drive to Cedar Nursing Home gave time to reflect on Aides' call offs. If they were screened for the profession and paid a living wage, would absence decrease? With full nursing staff on duty each Aide should have fewer residents to attend. It was a financial proposition with quality of care implications.

Coughed clouds of diesel fumes from a convoy of hurrying eighteen wheelers masked Bookville's town center from sight. Caught within the convoy, Mike drove right past the tired buildings and houses on Main Street out into the countryside before he realized he'd blinked and missed the town. He turned around on a weedy tarmac of a long abandoned Gas Station and 'TAUR', the remnants of 'RES-TAUR-ANT.'

A building's sign advertised 'Antiques' and fought a fight against abandoning its two story walkup. Renovation of nearby brother and sister buildings hadn't

368

been undertaken. Would it ever? Might the onset of home and small business computers and world wide instant communication allow a number of free thinking pioneers to relocate and use small towns to market their production, like pioneers of the past did to market their produce?

Cedar was on the south side, between 'B' and 'C' Streets. Fourth was the last block south of Main. 'A' to 'D' Streets ran East to West. The north marsh floated a dilapidated house boat. If there were a heavy rain, former Main Street proprietors might have complained of business interference when the boat floated in, house and all.

Red and White Cedars with rather dense, wide-based pyramidal crowns on thirty to forty feet high trees formed a fort-like enclosure around two, joined at the umbilical, rectangular one story red brick buildings. Remnants of mums of many colors decorated the home either side of the entry door. Gardens ran all sides of the buildings. No residents were outside in the brisk wind. Paved paths for wheelchairs and walkers around gardens and picnic tables gave evidence grassy yards were favorite places to while away the warm days under the shade of tall cedars.

Two women were at the reception desk. The sitting one, in a burgundy knit cardigan, flashed a big smile in spite of braces on her adolescent teeth. A brass plate on her desk revealed 'Larissa.' Standing to her side was a woman engrossed in the document on a computer screen.

"May I help you?" Black hair and green eyes contrasted with paler lips.

Mike gave name, title, and handed her a brochure. "I'm here to introduce myself to the administrator and some residents."

The lady at the computer straightened up. Tall, slim, attractive and in her early thirties with brunette hair down to her shoulder blades, she was in a gray cable mock T-neck sweater, plum wool wrap skirt and shoes black high tops.

"I'm Brooke Parks," she said, "Administrator. So you're Mr. Brannagh?"

Inflection revealed more than disillusion. From the tone he'd be the reincarnation of General Sherman before Atlanta. "I'm sorry. It's the best my genetic inheritance allowed."

She blushed. "Please excuse my crassness. We're out of the loop here in the country. It's been a long time since an ombudsman called in person."

He hadn't a doubt an alert system existed among homes that rivaled Lobbyists' electronic connections to State Representatives and Senators. "Well, here this one is."

"Please let me introduce you to our council president." She led him down the corridor of the west building. "The lay out of Cedar is parallel buildings. We house residents in double occupancy rooms in the west building."

The rooms were glistening, beds made, dresser drawers closed, closets with clothes hung neatly. Equipment in the rooms, beds, chairs, looked in working order. Glances into bathrooms revealed cleanliness. Housekeeping was doing a decent job. No one was in bed.

Parks stopped at the connecting hallway and said, "After you visit with Alonia, she's the council president, you'll want to visit the east building. The kitchen, dining, activities area, resident and staff lounges, social workers's offices and maintenance all have space there. Most of the time our residents are there. We have an excellent Activities Director. She keeps things busy. Alonia's room is the third from the last. Here we are." She knocked. "May I come in?" Responding to the invitation, Parks motioned Mike to follow, "Mrs. Alonia Predieu, this is Mike Brannagh, ombudsman. He's come to visit you."

A dresser was heaped high with rag dolls from ages

past. Dolls hung from hooks climbing the wall behind the head of the bed. She sat upright on the bed's spread working rags into arms, legs, torsos. Guillotined heads with crying eyes crowded a sewing basket. Gray hair sprouted in an oasis on Predieu's head. An egg of a face was lined with a dozen minor paths that ran from her high forehead to converge at an outcropping chin.

Alonia fastened green eyes on a man as big as a washing machine. A doll buyer? She wasn't going to let him slicker her out of her dolls like that drummer did years back before Rufus divorced her. Rufus hadn't believed the door-to-door salesman in the bright red and white plaid coat and a wide blue stripe on black pants only paid for dolls.

"Nice to meet you, Ma'am. May I sit down?" Noticing Parks wasn't departing, he said, "May we sit down?" Normally he'd have excused any staff present when meeting with a resident, but this resident's eyes hadn't much of a sign of cognitive occupation. Did Predieu nod? He pulled two chairs over to the side of the bed. He and Parks sat down.

"Are you here to buy my dolls?"

"They are beautiful, Mrs. Predieu, but I'm not in the doll buying business. I'm the advocate for residents, the guy who works for residents if one or more feel things aren't going too well while here in Cedar."

"What did you say your name was?"

"Mike Brannagh." He handed her a brochure with his name printed on it.

She took it and straightaway tucked it under her mattress. After sizing up his features, she said, "I'll make a rag doll that looks like you, if I can find enough rags."

Parks efforts to get up succumbed to the counter force of chortles. The third time she succeeded, but hands hurried to re-fasten her wrap around shirt. "Thank you for your time, Alonia. Let me show you the other building,

Mike." She accompanied him up the residence hall to the passageway connecting to the parallel building.

He said, "I take it Mrs. Predieu is not only hard of hearing, but deeply down a fork of the road to dementia?"

"Yes, poor dear, but her general health is fair for her eighty-four years. Alonia's very popular. She gives rag dolls on birthdays. Our residents love her. They voted overwhelmingly to reelect her president." It came to her the ombudsman was intimating she shouldn't have an incompetent as council president. She knew that, but dared not tell she'd rigged the election for council Vice-President. Predieu's apparent life-estate in the office of presidency meant she'd not make any demands to improve services. Parks needed a strong council if she were to neutralize Corporate's back stage smothering. So she'd convinced Ivan Todelli to run for Vice President. Where Todelli was there was heat. Out of heat came friction. Friction led to fire, fire to light. He was her mole, the presenter of her objectives to the council. He wrote the minutes and saw to it they were printed for all residents and family council to read. He mailed the minutes to State Health and the key Operating Company stockholders. This awareness kept the nursing home running well.

"We have a very alert vice president," she said. "Ivan Todelli. You'll find him over in the residents' smoking lounge. I'd introduce you, but there's a matter I must tend to."

"Thank you for you time." He watched her go down the hall at least thirty feet before he turned and walked into the passageway. A glass roof gave the area the ambience of a crystal palace. It was wide enough for four wheelchairs side to side. It had to be. Gatherings of silent ladies sat in their wheelchairs, backs of five against one wall, the backs of four across from them against the opposite.. Advanced years freed them to loosen a stomach full of boiling vitriol, especially if residing in a nursing home and sitting in a wheelchair along some wall painted off-white. He walked to the other building. The kitchen and dining areas were to the north. No residents there. A corridor ran the length of the southern side. Doors opened off of it. He walked the corridor looking into different rooms, all painted off-white. Tile floors were clean. Residents were neatly dressed in sweats, or trousers and shirts; dresses or pants and blouses. They were cutting clippings out of newspapers, playing checkers, listening to music or a recorded book, reading a magazine, talking. TV sets were off. Aides, one working in a room, wore two-pleat white pants with white tunics that fell below their waists. They looked sharp. In the last room on the right, the resident's lounge, six women sat on chairs around a kitchen table smocking and sipping coffee. Their mouths replicated the belching chimneys' of Great Lakes' steel plants.

A wheelchair held the remnants of a man dragging on a cigar. He hadn't any legs, not just to the knees, but clear up to his buttocks. He sat in the wheelchair as if a half statue placed in a niche. What there wasn't in his lower extremities, there was in arms and hands with fingers thicker than Elm tree branches. A chest tugged at the buttons of his shirt. The face was manly, the head's abundant hair white as pasteurized milk. A smile was life giving. The scars on cheeks and chin hinted his past knew violence. Todelli? A legitimate counterweight to poor old Predieu? Legs were mere modes of transportation. The rest of his externals seemed up to the task of getting him around. Had he a working mind?

"Mr. Todelli? Mrs. Parks told me you were here in the lounge. I'm the ombudsman." He looked down at him. It was uncomfortable. "Let me get a chair." He pulled it over and sat down. "I'm Mike Brannagh. I'm new, so I'm introducing myself to Presidents and Vice-Presidents of the councils."

"How did you know I was Todelli?"

Sensitive? Mike was careful. "Mrs. Parks said look in the residents' lounge for a handsome man surrounded by beautiful women."

"Brooke got that right," said a chubby lady in a green sweat suit that advertised beer. The other five women nodded confirmation.

"Thank you, Veronica," Todelli said to the chubby one. "Veronica writes short stories. Been published a lot."

"Only in my church's magazine," Veronica said.

"Must have a hundred thousand Methodists read it, Veronica."

Her face glowed more brightly than the fire on her cigarette.

"Rebecca can dance a mean Charleston," Todelli said looking at a slim, tiny woman in a black pants suit. The edge of her former facial beauty had worn smooth, "She was a great dancer back in elementary school days. Turned my head, she did, but 'Razor Sam,' her dad, was well known to discourage callers by placing his straight edge near certain parts of the male anatomy."

"Weren't them the days, Ivan. Papa would have let you take me to the picture show had you come to my front door and took my little brothers too. I loved movies. Remember when talkies first came?"

"I remember 'You were meant for me', he said, singing the lyric. "You were meant for me way back in 1928, Rebecca, but I had to wait sixty years."

A woman whose breasts separated her sweater as if it were two vests, each clutching a shoulder, let loose in a ringing voice, "'Gimme me a little kiss, will ya, huh.' My beau use to coo that ditty to me on the front porch."

"You can still belt out a song, Regina," a blond wigged woman in a clay silk shirt said. "By the way, what ever happened to front porches?"

"Don't know for sure, Nettie, but during the war, I didn't want to be sitting out there with Mom when the telegram came."

Nettie's eyes enlarged. "Twice on my brothers," Nettie said, eyes misting. "Two Gold Stars."

"You never said, Nettie," Regina said. "I'm so sorry. Forgive me?"

"You're forgiven."

"You must miss them so, Nettie."

"I do, Rebecca. I can remember little boys acting big going off to first grade, riding bikes to the baseball field, their first dates. Their pride in uniform. Billy was in the Army. Ted joined the Marines. Billy's buried in Normandy. Ted disappeared in a cave on Iwo Jima." Netti looked to Todelli. "Is it wrong for me to only remember my brothers on this earth, Ivan?"

"Not at all, Netti," he said, "not at all. We're all of this earth. We remember our lives on earth while we long for heavenly happiness. There are many mansions in heaven. Billy and Ted will have prepared a room for their sister."

"Yes," she said, "they and my Arnold. He and my brothers may be working on it this very minute. Arnold knows my favorite color is ivory." She looked up and said, "Billy, Ted, don't let Arnold forget to paint the walls ivory!"

"Sure to hear you," Todelli said.

"Did you lose your legs in the war, Ivan?"

The questioner was a pretty woman with dyed blond hair sitting apart some five feet from the end of the kitchen table shared by her elders. She wore a medium denim skirt with a French-Terry jacket over a white blouse and looked the age of a an experienced check-out cashier. She was the newest addition to, and youngest by twenty years, of Cedar's smokers' club. Her life's most memorable experiences since ninth grade revolved around a nicotine stick, never mind that cancer was spreading within her more rapidly than dandelions infested her yard grass.

Puffing on a cigarette wasn't the bad habit she'd throw overboard to survive. She gave up alcohol, cursing, chasing around, playing loose and fast with employers' sick and vacation days and amended her ways by returning to church, but giving up one of hundreds of daily drags on firmly packed tobacco wasn't within the reach of her will. Too ill for home, she chose Cedar for its smoker. She wanted to belong to the group, age or no.

"Not to the war, Amanda. To diabetes. Don't believe serving in Army Ordinance caused my diabetes, but the Army took five years of my life. You been in the service, young man?" Todelli said, looking over to Brannagh.

He wished the conversation wasn't redirected to him. He'd been privy to snatches of the past and wanted more. Young? Amanda was younger than he. Youthfulness was relative.

"It's Mike, Mr. Todelli. I served with the Army Infantry in Korea."

"What happened to your predecessor?"

"I don't know. I only know he retired. Was he of assistance?"

"When ever I left a phone message for him, he returned it. He visited once. Residents here speak up at the council meetings. These ladies make a lot of suggestions. Mrs. Parks is good about carrying most of them out, right away. We print the minutes for all to read. Even mail them to the family council's members and to others we consider important."

"That's the way it should be, Mr. Todelli," Mike said. "If a resident ever needs my help, just have them call." He passed out brochures. "When I return, you'll know me."

"Return?" Todelli said.

"Yea. I hope to come by regularly, needed or not, so you and other residents of Cedar get to know me, maybe ask me to do something." There was a nodding of heads but restraint on verbal expressions. "Mr. Todelli. I'm writing my address on this brochure in hope you'll include me on the mailing list."

"I'll put your name and address into next meeting's minutes." He was pleased. He thought there might be real use for the ombudsman. Some of the members of the smokers club were getting nervous about introducing topics at council meetings, topics the VP suggested. He cursed the need for secrecy to help Parks get adequate nursing staff from Corporate in a nursing home where both an administrator, Aides and nurses were strongly inclined in that direction. But Parks was in a pickle with her back office because the Press reprinted a story from the residents' minutes that told the reason behind night shift call offs was a pay differential two-thirds less than other nursing homes paid their Aides. Corporate felt some insider had given the council payroll information that was confidential. It responded by ignoring the pressure of residents' families. It took a reprinting the story in Oldtown's Letters to the Editor before Corporate acted. It came up with a simple cure for most call offs: the miraculous healing power of an adequate wage.

Todelli had impressed Mike as a man who knew what he was about, mailing out minutes of council meetings. It was a written record not the making of the nursing home's management. What an excellent idea! It should spread to all nursing homes.

* * *

His pickup took Mike by a lake side acre of manicured grass with a house to match. Clipped hedges on the grounds were soldiers on parade. White-washed trunks of maples stood tall as sailors at attention up from the shore's licking waters. The two story house of Dale Unge, CEO of Nursing Home Management, Inc, was three rooms wide and two deep with doubled black shutters on each window. Brickwork was a facade of running bond with white limestone lintels capping the windows. Local carpenters had told the interior of the house was grained woodwork with a marble mantlepiece in the front parlor. Windows opened a view the length of the lake for the permanent occupant.

Thoughts turned to Dale Unge's attending physician Dr. Terry Box, MD of Oldtown. Gloria Fantry RN, of Palace's Alzheimer's unit had said   Doctor Box knew his medicines, thought eyesight was poor. If so, how did Box read the small print of 'Action of Drugs': their therapeutic effects, side effects, drug to drug interactions, drug to food interactions, precautions like the drug manufacturer's warnings of conditions under which the drug should be prescribed, of disorders the drug was designed to relieve, of precautionary measures that should be observed, of warnings of dangers in the drug's use? Did Doctor Box's poor eyesight cause too much reliance on consulting pharmacist Victorio Pulvis' reviews? If so, and if Pulvis weren't virtuous, it put him in an ideal position to remove FDA quality drugs in exchange for counterfeit psychotropics. If? That was the rub.

Mike wanted to keep close ties to Nursing Home resident Fergus Orr if   more details were forthcoming on Mexican counterfeits. Inside, four ladies in kindergarten colored clothes played cards while talking at the top of their lungs over the blasting TV. One in a wheel-chair lowered her cards, her cheeks rosy as her smile. She lifted thick glasses to her eyes, glasses that had dangled from a golden chain around her neck to look.

"I'm the ombudsman." He handed her a brochure."

She viewed it. "Bath lady quit a week back," she said.

He noted downcast eyes in two of the other ladies at the table, another's eyeballs hopping like bunnies in her sockets. What was going on? "I'll look into it for you." The possibility she was putting him on, misusing him, played a score in his mind. She exuded no detectible bodily odors. Her clothing was clean, so too her wheelchair. The other ladies hadn't an untidy look or smelled, nor did the living unit or its rooms. Sensory awareness didn't support her assertions. He identified himself to the charge nurse. A perusal of the bath sheet revealed no resident bathed less than twice weekly, up to minimum standards. Why the misinformation? No answer.

He knocked on Orr's open door He was in the wheelchair at his desk; a closed book on it. In white pants, a shirt under a snowball sweater, and white shoes, if not for pits where eyes kindled on a pale face beneath ashen hair, he was the epitome of an ice cream vendor.

"I'll take chocolate, Professor."

Orr ignored the sarcasm. "When I retired," he said, "I couldn't afford a place on the lake, nothing but the devastated rooms of Mena's rundown rooming house moldering in the shadow of the collapsed co-op." He gave his listener a high chin reminiscent of FDR. "My visibility as a gimpy, old coot of a retired professor who lived too close to the walkway along the lake from Puella Junior College brought in the County Health Department's potato shaped nurse supervisor, Tessie Spug. She was a former student of mine just as deaf and dumb during her years at Puella as when she visited me at Mena's. She wrongfully concluded I might die from my own neglect and threatened me with guardianship proceedings. Rather than be brought before the court, I elected to live my demented last years here."

How to get him onto the Elder Trippers? "I noted you said, on retirement, income was so meager you lived in a hovel before coming to the nursing home." An affirming nod, hoped for, was received. "Who pays for your single room?"

Orr blinked. "A slip up and you noted it. I admire

your acuteness of mind, Brannagh."

"Is it a fringe benefit for your contributions to Elder Trippers?"

"I wondered if you noticed my tension at the mention of Javier Grain. As you did, I'd like you to hear my full confession. If there's a trial, I'm too old to do time," he paused to make light of it, "perhaps not to hang." A pair of chunky glasses, removed from his shirt pocket, were put on. He coughed consumptively and hacked, spitting into a handkerchief returned to his rear pocket. His lips parted and a tiny smile escaped. "Javier Grain owns this building. He comes by from time to time when major repairs are suggested. I was rolling down the hall to dinner when our eyes met. He remembered me from Elder Trippers. We had quite a discussion, a result of which was a private room. I told you I removed myself from Elder Trippers when counterfeit replaced Mexican medicines. I told you Javier, Maurice Grain's son, closed Elder Trippers. I didn't tell you the Elder Trippers were replaced by   migrant farm workers. Elder Trippers on tour with me, they didn't know it, bought a ninety day supply of medicines from Mexican Pharmacies, the prescriptions written by local Doctors and filled by Maurice's Mexican relatives. I know Javier was active with migrants into 1977, a year after he closed Elder Trippers. You know the rest. I moved to Grass Lake, taught at Puella for ten years, retired, had a stroke and here I am, this private room a fringe benefit, as you say, compliments of Javier!"

Back in the pickup and heading home, Mike's restless mind wandered from nursing homes to harvest season's crop fields full of little bent men and women side by side with children. All labored under a hot sun harvesting tomatoes and cucumbers. Full crates were counted by a fat, greasy crew chief. Did Javier use migrant workers to import counterfeit? Or Crew chiefs? If one or the other, how did they smuggle drugs?

* * *

Mike entered Garland, it's visitors no less bored than residents being visited. Had no one a story to tell, retell? A joke? 'How about the one where the Director of Nursing overspent on her credit card and was arrested for impersonating an administrator.'

Mike knocked. "Kap?" No invitation. The door was nudged opened. "Kap?" The curtain was drawn around his bed. They wouldn't leave him if he'd died? Would they?

"The cock crows three times," he said. He sounded weak as a worm.

"No denial though," Mike said. "May I come in?"

"Yea." Blacken eyes on a face strained of color looked windows in a white house. Kap said, "Counter passed away. I miss him. What you know, Mike?"

"I know your antidepressant was counterfeit."

"Wouldn't you know it? Who?" Red streaks, like sun beams, lighted his eyes.

"Maybe a Nozlo relative, a nephew," he said, "the home's consulting pharmacist, but I haven't the evidence to confirm it. We're testing other stuff from another facility he works. Should have results soon. We know genuine FDA uppers and downers are getting to the street. A source connects them to Victorio Pulvis."

"You'll bust it open, Mike."

"You gave me the med, aimed me right, Kap."

"Good to know, bad stuff or not. Pulvis will never know from me. Can rest easier now." Eyes closing, breathing so soft, Mike anguished if he should call the nurse. If death were imminent, Kap had in mind a good thought. His eyes closed. Breathing slowed. Mike left the room to fetch the nurse. They returned to hear Kap's last breath, a soft satisfied sigh.

32

Oldtown might have been a pretty residential city a century back, but the more than nine decades of this one hadn't done it any favors. Zoning was a law only recently discovered by the protegees of business financiers in the prosperous subdivisions and strip malls of the money lenders. In the city, after five decades of industrial might had crowded residences into interstices between manufacturers, residential areas fell captive to laundromats, taverns, alley garages and small shops. Most factories were as abandoned as dinosaur bones. The destruction of human habitation on curb sides was phenomenal. Block after block, houses were rubble, or ashes, or boarded with plywood. Vacant lots separated the few livable homes still standing.

In the inner-city there was such outrage over living conditions, lack of stores and services, the enraged destroyed the houses of absentee landlords, looted their own neighbors, robbed local stores that did open to serve the neighborhood. There were more inner-city men in prisons than in colleges. More died annually from gun shot wounds inflicted by other young men than died from all other illnesses combined. Living in an inner-city was as dangerous physically as living in no man's land between warring armies. Socially, it was as devastating. The percentage of unwed-mothers was nearly sixty percent of all inner-city women. Child support was basically non-existent, jobs were scarce, there was little money for bus fare or day care. A cure? Inner-cities would have to be closed down, residents relocated to mixed race areas to even start an effort to alleviate the psychological ravaging. There had to be stable pepper and salt neighborhoods, but so far that was the case only until the last salt flake left.

Mike looked at the high rise building poking its

upper floors into a smoke ring smog. Long ago he used to go in and out of the Projects. Now it was a multilevel dungeon filled with trapped old folks, single mothers' with children and preying juvenile delinquents. Big Al's University, 'Albertus Magnus', that was, was a few miles to the north.

"Mike!" Jocko said, his shout turning heads. "My table, man"

Millie and Fanny Brown came over. There was delicate fagoting at the neck line and cuffs of Fanny's black tunic; a drawstring about her silk creamy sarwal pants. Flat gold slippers covered her feet. She wore Millie's finery, no less an enhancement on Fanny. Millie really didn't need a French Blue silk-washed pinwale cotton corduroy dress, black wool tights and high-heeled ankle boots to appear beautifully proportioned. Jocko, too, was as elegantly attired, a tan vest over a solid and striped cotton shirt opened at the neck and blue poplin pants. It was the day of Fanny Brown's Art exhibit!

"Fanny's being discovered all over the place," Jocko said with exuberance. "Newspaper reporter, a couple of professors from the university, students; all of them want to buy her paintings. She's so g-o-o-o-oood! Come on. Look for yourself."

Fanny's pen and pencil sketches hung on the restaurant's walls as if in the Louvre. Field hands lived again on eight by eleven inch paper. Children totted bags of water. Mules were stubborn. Cotton pickers sweated under a sun as hot on paper as in the sky. An old woman sat in her rocker on a cabin's porch.

Mike said, "what she's looking for while screening her eyes against the sun?"

"Be looking for me," Fanny said, her eyes misting, "my Momma. Her cabin."

"You miss her," he said, a social worker's consoling.

"That be right. Be sending Momma money. Saving up. Momma won't come up here. Can't go back till I gets up cash to buy her place for her."

"Sell me a drawing. This one with the children."

"No! They my kin! Can't sell my kin."

"Then sketch me. You can sell me."

Fanny giggled. Coming from a cranium mindful of an innocent child's whose brown eyes were as bright as sunset.

"That's it Fanny!" Jocko said with a touch of jubilation. "Sell portraits. You can charge a fair price and save up enough to buy momma's place a whole lot sooner. We'll do a deal, Fanny. You draw portraits. I'll advertise. I'll get more business. We both make money."

"I'fen you don't mind, Mr. Jocko?" She sketched Mike.

Adjourning to Jocko's office phone, Mike dialed Fordice to invite her to Jocko's.

"I can't make it Mike, but remember we meet tomorrow morning with Reverend Yard."

"I'll be there."

"Purchase made, he thought of Fanny's skills all the way home.

* * *

Before Holiness, there was time to drop by Five Counties to check for messages. Why not talk up Lizzy? She was quite comely. Just a few feet from her, Ziggie stayed conversation. "Mike, please come in my office a minute. They took seats. Ziggie handed over an envelope.

Mike opened it and took out its single sheet of paper. "It's a list of companies: Bookkeepers Inc., Mallard Inc., Coos Inc., Stowe Inc., Esbon Inc. I never heard of them."

"My source has, but he only sent this."

"If they are registered corporations in the state, they'll be on file. May I use your phone to call Jim

Jackson?" A nod of approval. Jackson agreed to check out the information.

* * *

A lone candle's dancing light had replaced the dim light of last visit to Holiness. A knock brought Reverend Yard's invitation to enter. Within, he sat behind his desk, Belinda and Gloria on oak chairs. "Take a seat Mike. Belinda has filled the prescriptions. She has the FDA medicines with her. Gloria will exchange these known FDA prescriptions for the others."

Belinda said somewhat apologetically, "I couldn't get it done since our last meeting. My Oldtown Clinic connection wasn't available. However, I was able to confirm through sources that pharmacist Victorio Pulvis is, as you suspected, the nephew of deceased pharmacist Guido Nozlo, your Jail drug smuggler."

Mike nodded his thanks. "If the nephew is like his uncle, it runs in their genes."

Gloria said, "It shouldn't present a problem to make the exchange. I'll do it in my office before I give out the meds. We've selected six meds from six patients. The meds that cleared Pulvis' review will be isolated by patient packet and go into tissue kept on my person. I'll bring them to Belinda. She'll take it from there."

Reverend Yard said, "There's no check on employees' belongings when they leave?

"No. But meds are counted before and after administering to patients, Reverend Yard. I'll be sure to have another nurse with me when the counts are taken. There will be no discrepancy. Not even Pulvis will know. He doesn't come on the floor. He does his work in the pharmacy in the lower level, basement in effect. Which reminds me. I went out of my way today to take lunch off the floor, downstairs. I saw Puvlis leave the pharmacy and go into the food storage pantry two times without a woman, but if he took something in, or brought something out, I

385

failed to see it."

Mike asked, "why would a pharmacist have to go a food storage pantry? Is there a bathroom in there?"

"For maintenance and kitchen staff," said Gloria.

"I'll check out the sanitarian's report," Belinda said. "For your info, Mike, let me tell again about prescription drugs distribution systems. Javier Grain's Pharmacopeia Wholesalers buys FDA drugs from licensed manufacturers and in turn sells to drugstores. Medical Directors and other Doctors prescribed ethical drugs for residents. Their prescriptions are filled by licensed pharmacists out of a central facility or drugstores' stock with only FDA approved brands and generic medicines. They deliver directly to a specific nursing homes. As consulting pharmacist for each Nursing Home Management facility, Pulvis checks out all deliveries, checking for drug interactions, side effects, individualization of doses, equivalency of different brands of the same drug, and for adverse drug reactions. All proper before the drug is sent to the floor nurse to be administered to specific patients."

"Proper!" Mike said. "For sure, Pulvis has access to residents' prescription files and their FDA drugs. Reverend Yard's source said it was Pulvis selling FDA uppers and downers to dealers. We know the street drugs given Reverend Yard tested FDA quality. We don't know if Pulvis is getting his FDA uppers and downers from drugs delivered to the nursing homes. We don't yet know, except for one resident in another county, if the psychotropics screened by Pulvis and being administered residents are counterfeit. We know Pulvis is the consulting pharmacist where one counterfeit med was uncovered."

Gloria jumped in. "If a dealer say its Pulvis selling uppers and downers, I wonder if he carries them out in his brief case when he arrives or leaves Palace."

Reverend Yard stirred. His handsome facial features twisted in righteousness, he thundered. "How long do you expect me to sit still before a stop is put to this barbaric assault on the sick elderly, Mr. Brannagh? You seem to be excusing Pulvis!"

Mike maintained composure. "Not so! You told me you got into the Parole Board scam to see to the indictments of white board members, not black parole officers. You know how that turned out. If the testing of Gloria's meds indicates six other psychotropics are counterfeit, it's an atomic bomb if we disclose it too soon. The whole world plus the police will come down on Palace, yet no one will know where the counterfeits came from, or how, when and by whom they were exchanged. The police don't have a tendency to focus on white licensed pharmacists. Like the white Parole Board members, if it's Pulvis, he and those in the system that bring in the counterfeits may escape."

Belinda intervened. "Reverend, we need to know with certainty if Gloria's meds are counterfeit. Then we make the final decision."

His cheeks puffed, air exhaled with a swo-o-sh. "If you say so, Belinda."

Jackson was ticked off Brannagh's call wasn't to give clearance to proceed with the tort notice. Dropping a hint Elder Law Center wasn't a branch of the Secretary of State's corporate records division, he would, however, do a favor for the man who uncovered Palace's wrongful terminations. Jackson's irritation, however, turned to lava when Mike said he'd call back for the results. Pressure wasn't to Jackson's taste.

* * *

Driving to the next call,. Mike's mind kept ruminating over Reverend Yard acting through Inner-city News before Belinda received the test results. Who could blame the Holy man? Mike worried the whole distance the '83 took took to drive the Reverton highway, then west on a wide asphalt road. Ranch style family homes lined the

387

south side, Bellflower nursing home the other. He pulled over to that side of the spacious parking lot and parked next to a fancy foreign car. Which door in the front of various wings was the main entry? He looked for signs. Most signs read "PRIVATE ENTRANCE.' One with print small enough for a loan agreement read 'Nursing Home Entry.' An arrow tiny as Cupid's pointed to the door. His Directory indicated Medicare and Medicaid certified thirty intermediate and ten skilled care beds in wing one. Wings two, three, four, six and seven were not certified beds, but suites privately leased. Residents enjoyed a common lounge, dining room, activities area, kitchen and laundry in wing five, not to mention an eighteen hole putting green out the back door. It wasn't used when flagpoles froze in their holes and looked like harpoons in Moby Dick.

The usual set of double doors were unlocked to the public. He entered what appeared to be a utility tunnel. The ten feet from the entry was blessed by whatever sun escaped a cloak of nimbostratus clouds. The first resident door on the left was open. It was lighted as brightly as a presidential podium. It had two beds, the women in them immobilized by bed covers, heads tossed back, thin faces expressionless, mouths wide open. He preferred to think they were asleep. Down the rest of the long hall overhead lights could guide an airplane to landing. A nurse station was strategically placed mid-hall. A youthful looking woman wearing a white dress and nurse's cap leaned over the counter.

A scrawny cut of horsehide came up behind the nurse, removed his false teeth and chomped in her face while his other hand pulled out a dangling participle. Her leap reversed all records in national backward broad jump contests. Scrawny's flight away to his room was slower than a three legged mule. Mike envisioned another informal hearing with the ombudsman as the administrator's chief witness. He elected to knock on the next open door and let the nurse go about running Scrawny down.

He waited until the young nurse was back behind the desk.'Terri Habib RN' was on her name tag. Scrawny was nowhere to be seen.

"I'm Mike Brannagh, ombudsman." He handed her a brochure. "I would have come to the nurse station on entry to let you know I was here, but when I looked you were moving away."

Habib's eyes dropped from him to his brochure. "An advocate for residents," she said somewhat snidely. "It's I that needs an advocate."

"I don't handle marriage proposals to movie stars."

She smiled. "Do you advocate for sex offenders?"

"Well," he said, a facetious grin crawling on his face, "Do you mean you?"

"Are you always this obtuse?" she said, but still with a smile on her face.

"Hey!" he said pretending indignity. "Learned it in the Army."

"Well, Ombudsman, turn it in at the quartermaster's. I need you to do something about Bobbie Abreh."

He was tempted to say something obtuse, but bypassed the opportunity, instead, acting seriously, said, "I take it he's a resident?"

"A particularly disgusting resident. He clacks his teeth in one hand and exposes himself with the other. He exposed himself to me a moment ago. It's not part of his health problems, it's misbehavior. He's an old homeless inebriate, forced to be sober in here."

"You shouldn't have to put up with it. I'll talk to him. May I talk about your incident."

"I don't mind. Bobbie's in room 107. Vern should have discharged him long ago."

"I'll go see him now." His guidebook listed the administrator's name as Vern Nuh. Why hadn't he already

389

sought involuntary transfer of Bobbie Abreh? The ombudsman wouldn't inquire. Advocacy for residents meant keeping the burden of persuading the Hearing officer on the administrator of the home. In other words, force the administrator to do his job proving the preponderance of evidence supported the involuntary transfer. Perhaps this Bobbie Abreh was an exception to shifting the burden of persuasion. A nursing home was usually a female environment, staff and residents, all of whom deserved to be free of sexual affronts from a pathologically disturbed male, no matter if elderly.

Mike knocked on the open door of room 107. "Mr. Abreh, I'm the ombudsman, an advocate for residents. May I come in?"

A skinny snake of a body dressed in dark clothes wiggled on the covers of the bed next to the window. He raised a dried fig of a face off a pillow, long strands of yellowish hair dangling from the back of the head like so many noodles. In a voice long used when roused from a deep drunk by police, he said, "What you want?" There was confusion in the man's eyes.

Mike had seen many like him in jail, their thinking processes pickled, combative, though no bigger than a nat, feisty as a mosquito. Though they usually had the moisture pounded out in fights, they weren't easily confronted physically, but if the illusion of an ambush were planted, natural paranoia sharply curtailed pseudo aggression.

"To talk to you," he said entering the room, pulling a chair over next to him. "I'm the guy who visits residents in nursing homes and works for residents rights. There are about thirty-nine other residents in Bellflower, more than thirty-two of them women. So are ninety percent of the employees women. It's the wrong place for a man who flashes his weeny."

"Who told you that," he said with the indignation of one the world's better bluffers.

"I saw you clop your teeth in one hand, your spaghetti in the other. You shoved it, meat balls and all, at Nurse Habib. That's a crime, you know."

"What Judge is going to put me back in the can," the often incarcerated ex-inmate said.

Mike switched to the ambush tact. "Remember those Black Muslims in the jail tanks, how their religion forbid them from eating pork?" There was a remembering nod. "And they weren't fundamentalist like the Arabs over in the Mideast. Now there's fundamentalism."

"What's that?"

"An eye for an eye, tooth for a tooth. They believe if a hand offends, cut it off."

"What's that to me?"

"Habib is an Arab name. Nurse Habib is married to an Arab, a fundamentalist. Soon as she gets home tonight, I imagine she'll tell hubby about the pickle you snapped out of your pants. An eye for an eye, a pickle for a pickle!" The little man pushed up to a sitting position. "That's right, Abreh. He's going to show up when you least expect it, maybe tonight, tomorrow, soon, and circumcise you right up to your stomach. You'll have to squat to pee. More likely it'll drain like a leaky oil pan. Don't know if it's too late to do anything about it."

"Keep him out of here!"

"Hell man, his wife works here. He has a right to come in to get her after work."

"Not get me."

"You expect just because Nurse Habib is a woman, or the others you flashed are women, that none of them have men willing and eager to slice your cucumber? You pulled it out. Take your punishment like a man. I mean as long as your remain a man."

"Oh, man. I got to get out of here and back to the homeless center."

"Can't hide there, either."

"What I do?" he said, sitting up.

"I don't know for sure. Maybe too late," he said, shaking his head in despair, then, as if a brain storm poured, "try to convince Nurse Habib you won't do it any more to her or any woman. Maybe she'll not mention it to the Arab. Worth a shot."

"Yeah, yeah!" He hopped up, cross the room and disappeared.

Mike moved to the doorway and watched the scrawny twirp squeal and grunt while talking emotionally to Habib. What was he saying? At least there wasn't a willy waving. He returned and said, "She ain't going to say nothing."

"Don't chance it again or the Arab is sure to hear. See you next time," he said, accepting a nod of submission. He approached the nurse station.

"What's this about my husband? Bobbie says he's all done pulling it out. What did you say to him?"

"Nothing really. But as for your husband, from time to time, remind Bobbie your husband is a fundamentalist Arab."

"He's from Lebanon, and a Catholic."

"You and he know it, now I do. Bobbie needs to hear he's a fundamentalist Arab."

"And you're the residents' advocate?" Her smile was ear high, her tone facetious.

"I am, for one and for all." His tone wasn't facetious.

* * *

Mike's phone call was put through to Jackson. "Jim, my man, find anything about those corporations?"

"Yea, I did." His sound over the telephone conveyed boredom. "They're all located in Oldtown. The corporate purpose of each is clear enough. Coos is a meat locker. Mallard handles institutional can goods. Bookkeepers do bookkeeping. Esbon is into janitorial services, and Stowe does maintenance. They are all closely held with stock restricted. One thing though, but it shouldn't have surprised me in this day of minority businesses, but it did; seems those companies' Directors are mostly Hispanic. At least, the directors have Hispanic surnames: Fernandez, Hernando, Castillo, Garcia, Mendez, Gonzalez, Lopez, Velasquez and Santana. I had no idea the Hispanic community in Oldtown had these many companies and for so long. According to their annual reports, all of them got into business during the later years of the seventies. That's a long time for small businesses to survive and remain independent. Most fail within a few years. The successful ones usually merge or are bought by bigger companies."

"Each must have good management."

"Probably. Except for Bookkeepers Inc., the annual reports show but one President for all of the other companies since each was incorporated, a Ramirez-Grano. Why are you interested in these companies? Do you know something about them or their directors I should know? For instance, any ties to Palace?"

"I don't know if any of those companies have ties to Palace, Jim. I personally don't know any of the directors by name. I've heard the name 'Ramirez', but not Ramirez-Grano. A Concetta Ramirez was the mother of Javier Grain. He owns the building called Palace, as well as other buildings which Nursing Home Management leases to operate nursing homes."

"Javier?" Jim's cough resounded over the wire. There followed an explosion of insight expressed in very loud words. "That's the first name of Ramirez-Grano. I barely passed high school Spanish, but I remember 'grano' translated 'grain.' What's going on Brannagh? First you tell me of employment discrimination and get me up to Oldtown to take affidavits at Reverend Yard's office, then call me to hold off acting until another meeting with

393

Reverend Yard, which, as of yet, I've not been informed, and now ask me to check out certain corporate records? You know something I should know about Javier?" Before there was time to answer, Jackson's second-sight intuition took hold. "If Javier Grain, the owner of ten buildings, is Ramirez-Grano, that may explain why nothing was done about Palace's employment discrimination. Now I know! He not only controls nursing home buildings but the Hispanic companies. None have a separate mind or existence of their own apart from him. Do I sniff complete domination and control intended to commit inequitable consequences proximately causing injury to nursing home residents, unjust loss to the tax payers?"

"Good Lord, Jim! You're running a legal football across a ghostly goal line in an empty Judicial stadium. You nor I have the vaguest idea those companies deal with Nursing Home Management. Hold off your field goal attempt. Give me a few days to look around."

He needed that long for Belinda to have the tests run. If that issue failed, and nothing came of the Hispanic companies, Jim had the employment discrimination ball to take up.

"I'm a litigator, Brannagh. My clients want and need relief. Call that meeting right soon."

* * *

Jocko's office was available, so too his phone book. The entrepreneur allowed the ombudsman the use of his desk and chair. Jocko sat across from him. Mike opened the Yellow pages to 'Accountant Services.' "Here it is. Bookkeepers Inc. It's in the Lindo Building, downtown Oldtown. Let's see." He turned to 'Meats-Wholesale,' then the pages to Coos Meat Locker. "Coos is in the industrial park in North Oldtown, on Progress Avenue." He wrote the address down in his note book. From 'Food Products' he turned the pages to find Mallard. "Well, Mallard's also in North Oldtown on Progress." He continued down the index, then turned the pages. "Esbon and Stowe share the same building address as Coos and Mallard." He turned to the white pages looking for Quality Care, Inc. It's address was numbered next to Bookkeepers in the Lindo building. Pharmacopeia Wholesalers was next door to Coos, Mallard, Stowe and Esbon.

"Why you interested in Coos and Mallard, Mike? Because Grain runs them?"

"You know that? How?"

"Every businessman in the inner-city knows. It's common knowledge he located his drug outfit and the other companies out in North Oldtown just to keep away from the inner-city. Seems like only Hispanics work for him."

"You do business with any of them, Jocko?"

"Naw. I get my meats from Heifer, Inc. Grain's companies do janitorial and maintenance work at Lobelia, where Millie works. Service and maintain all the buildings he owns. Coos and Mallard sell the nursing homes meat and can goods."

"You know for sure?"

"I keep up with business at the Chamber meetings. You ask 'for sure'?" He questioned the questioner. "Grain's businesses never been of interest to me until Millie came into my life. Sometimes she mentions his doings. When it comes to big business, I can't compete."

* * *

It wasn't a long drive to North Oldtown's industrial park. A slow drive down Progress Avenue gave time to view shingles on signboards advertising the presences of housed businesses. Pharmacopeia Wholesalers was alone in an alabaster building, modern as a new appliance. The sign next down the road, the one in front of a warthog of a common brick building, a squished cow dropping in contrast to Pharmacopeia, revealed the offices of Coos, Mallard, Esbon and Stowe. So did the Hispanic truck driver driving his rig away from Mallard's ramp. Mike followed the truck to Palace, parking across the street at curbside. He watched the driver oversee two men roll dollies into the truck, load boxed canned goods, then roll the dollies down the ramp into the basement entry of the nursing home and inside where they were apparently unloaded. Out of the kindness of his heart, likely in violation of Union Rules, the driver carried inside the last box. If there were something wrong, Mike failed to see it.

On the way home, he wondered if Jackson's suspicion of some kind of fraud had any validity. There was some basis to think so because Grain used the name 'Ramirez-Grano' in the corporate papers. But if businessmen in the inner-city knew Grain was the owner-operator, what was the deception? The only apparent reason that came to mind for using a different name was pertinent to billings, Quality Care in the name of Grain; Coos, Mallard, Esbon and Stowe in the name of Rodriguez-Grano. Perhaps he was overpricing? Perhaps not! Perhaps he was just one hell of a good businessman owning buildings leased to an operating company, and to protect assets, maintained and kept them clean. As for selling meats and canned goods, Nursing Home Management would have to put out specifications and ask for bids, all subject to competition; and to Medicaid scrutiny from time to time. Grain's companies could well have been the lowest and best bidder. Why not? Someone had to be! If Bookkeepers had a different President than Grain, had it also an independence? Mike decided not to call Jackson back, to hold off until the meeting with Reverend Yard on the results of the medicine tests.

* * *

From home, Brannagh dialed Belinda, updating her on contents of the envelope Ziggie had received from his source. Both wondered who was Ziggie's source. No clue. The call to Jackson was covered as was the surprising finding revealed by Jackson and Jocko that Grain was not only president of Quality Care and Pharmacopeia Wholesalers, but as Rodriguez-Grano was president of four companies that did the businesses of supplying meat, canned goods, janitorial and maintenance services to Nursing Home Management's operations. Mike pointed out, though the board of directors of the vast majority of America's big businesses were the exclusive province of Anglo-Saxons, the boards of the foregoing were following a different road: Hispanics, as in the Elder Tripper.

Belinda soaked it all in "I've Gloria's meds from Palace in testing. Now I'll ask my   contact in Medicaid for cost reports and analysis of expenditures for leases, meats, canned goods, janitorial and maintenance services contracted for and through Nursing Home Management for its ten nursing homes."

33

"Hello, Lizzy."

"Good morning. Just a moment, please." Lizzy waited for a social worker to leave the file cabinet and return to her cubicle. "Sorry for the delay, Mike   Mint nursing home council president Mel Hers called and said there's been a change in administrators. The new one is Mary Lancaster" She paused.. "By the way, Mr Donavan, the State Ombudsman is in town Mr. Zigmont told me. That's it!"

Donavan here? To decertify? Or inquire? "Is Ziggie in?"

"No. He's with Mr. Donavan." .

Well, time to move things along, Belinda and Jackson needed to know about Lancaster. "Hello, Belinda. Mike here. Nursing Home Management has pulled Lancaster out of Palace!" There was a noise of surprise. "She's at Mint. I think we should unleash Jim Jackson."

With a testy touch hinting there was no rush, she said, "I won't get the test results; or the Medicaid financial data for a day or so."

He answered with delicacy. "Unge, of Nursing Home Management, obviously took notice of Fanny Brown's testimony at Shango's hearing, that she was threatened and wrongly fired. Moving Lancaster may be an effort to avoid litigation. Let's add to his worries. A Jackson press conference might focus Nursing Home Management's attention if it's held today in Oldtown, Reverend Yard at his side."

"A reasonable diversion," she said.

On the phone again, he told Jackson of the change of administrators, and the need for a news conference right away.

Jackson agreed. He would involve Reverend Yard.

The pickup's radio's music banged ears as loudly as the muffler. The noise mercifully gave way to the news. The reporter was forthright. 'Here's a News release. Lawyer Jim Jackson, who's in charge of Capitol County's Elder Law Center has indicated he is mailing a notice to Palace nursing home that alleges employment wrong-doing by the facility's administrator. Palace is in Oldtown. It's alleged there is a pattern of employment discrimination against black Aides working at Palace. Lawyer Jackson will detail the allegations at a press conference today at 2:00 PM at Church of Holiness where the Reverend Coppin Yard is Minister.'

Going about the business of the ombudsman, but for the chill wind and frost on the lawn chairs folded open on Poppy House's front porch, Mike envisioned sitting there sooner than he would want on a summer evening watching Yuppies across the street restore the area. What better rest had a man than to watch others work. A neighborhood psychedelic eyesore among gentrified Queen Ann houses, Poppy's second and third story bedrooms were filled from the ranks of debilitated men burned out on drugs and alcohol, and conflicted women tired of doping up for breakfast, boozing for supper and suffering nights of bruises and multi-rapes from male acquaintances. Admission to Poppy was conditional upon a guest's prior acceptance of treatment from Pathia Psychologica Center. At the Center, drug abusers were carefully assessed by psychiatric teams. As psychotropic drugs reflected differences in individuals with regard to effects, side effects and potential interactions with other drugs, the response to prescribed psychotropic drugs were observed objectively by the Center's trained and experienced professionals. Ongoing improvement prepared an individual for the freedom of the place. Behavioral modification,

399

environmental manipulation, supportive psychotherapy, group therapy and other related techniques, refined from the protocol of long ago Treatment Alternatives to Street Crimes programs, were used to diminish the need for drugs.

A sign on the door read 'Enter, Bell Out Of Order.' There were nine panes of leaded glass and a door handle of brass with a trigger like mechanism. He pulled the trigger and pushed open a door heavy as a bank vault. The vestibule was eight by eight, stairs on the left running up to the second floor, a hall way on the right back to a kitchen. To his far left was a dining room, to the far right a large living room the length of the house. Furnishings were cast offs from the fifties. Where was everybody? There was a noise from the kitchen. Back in the corner of what once had held a wood burning stove stood a white uniformed woman filling a cup with coffee.

"Ma'am, I'm Mike Brannagh, ombudsman," he said, and watched the   middle aged woman's head spin to see him, black hair whip lashing, her face, the color of a golden delicious apple, looking a suspect for a criminal offense. He'd put her at ease. "I'm here to introduce myself to a few residents."

She sighed. "I'm Alberta. Ain't none of them around. They be in group sessions at the Center. They'll eat over there. Won't be back until later."

"How many are in residency?"

"Twenty-five of the strangest folks the good Lord ever put on this earth, ten women and fifteen men," she said, "but I love working here because they are on good behavior and look out for the rules, that is unless someone falls weak and slips on dope."

"Does that happen often?"

"Lord no! Maybe once a month. That's a long time for some of them to stay straight."

"How do you handle it when that happens?"

"I can call the Center for a male Aide."

"What if someone comes after you?"

"Never happened in the eight years I've worked here. Sure there was one who copped feels, but he's been good since then. None of the ladies are complaining."

"I must say I admire you, Alberta. Not many folks willing to work alone with twenty-five struggling ex-addicts."

"We just get along. Maybe because I saw so many in high school go down to dope. I had parents who loved me and the Lord and taught me right."

"Loved by stable parents, the difference for staying or getting on the right path."

He left the kitchen and started up the oak stairs. The five bedrooms on the second floor had windows, the interior of the spaces reasonably clean, beds made, the drawers of three dressers closed. A large closet was color coded, blue, green and orange. Two of the three beds in each of the rooms were in use, the third with mattress rolled. Two bathrooms with shower stalls and tubs were at the top of the landing.

He climbed the stairs to the third floor. Windowed rooms circled interior bathrooms and showers. The living accommodations were smaller than those on two, surplus Army bunk beds in each of the eight rooms, the beds made with GI blankets. The expected foot locker at the base of the beds was missing in favor of a two tone dresser and closet to match. A gentleman resident had access to either the yellow or green side of the dresser and closet, his roommate the other. Which had access to the stuff stuck in the space under the lower bunk wasn't up to decoding by color. Not much individual defensible space in the bedrooms of the third floor.

* * *

Jackson's anticipated revelations perked the ombudsman to look for a place to get cups of elevated caffeine coffee. He'd need the shots of psychic energy if

Belinda's tests proved the exchanged medicines from Palace's Alzheimer's Unit were counterfeit. If not, there still was the issue of employment discrimination and Grain's, or Ramirez-Grano's, corporations dealings with Nursing Home Management's operations. There also remained Ziggie's purpose in hiring a whistle blower was to have him blow that damned whistle one more time. But Donavan?

Mike's mind whirled. It was taking a while to estimate the consequence Jackson's news conference might have on Ziggie's, Belinda's and his investigation into alleged counterfeit drugs. Ahead was 'Eats', the road side sign sporadically advertised. He pulled the '83 into the vintage 1950 greasy spoon's gravel parking lot. He exited and entered the café to ride a stool at the counter. The waitress slid down her side like a baggage car too full. An enormous pink dress covered a 747's hanger. A white apron's ivory glow was lost long ago.

"What you have, guy?"

"Coffee and a donut, please. I hear the radio. How about getting the Oldtown station?"

"Cold outside!" she said, pouring a cup of coffee. "It's them sun spots. Ozone layer's gone crazy and them sun spots ain't doing right at all. Coldest October ever!" She sauntered to a plastic cake cover, lifted it and removed a donut on a plate and as slowly returned to serve her only customer. "It's the cold what's cut into our business, Leonard's and mine. Can't hardly make ends meet." She turned to the pass-through and said, bellowing, "Leonard! Turn the radio to the Oldtown station." She slow marched to a rocker, oozed her posterior in, and settled back. "Don't see your rig, guy."

"I drive a pickup."

"You're a big man. What work you do?"

"I visit old folks in nursing homes."

"You do, sure enough? Been one the news talking

on about racial stuff. You'd think East side folks working to help old folks be free of that crap. Enough's enough!"

The donut was hard as a golf cart tire. Nothing to do but dunk it in the coffee. Even then the donut's malleability was limited. The coffee itself had to have been drained from the golf cart's two cycle engine.

Jackson was erudite on the violation of the legal rights of Aides versus Palace Nursing Home, Administrator Mary Lancaster, Nursing Home Management, Inc. and its CEO Dale Unge. Reverend Yard was profound on human dignity. Neither spoke a word that hinted at the involvement of Five Counties' ombudsman, or State Health's Belinda Fordice or Palace's Alzheimer Unit's charge nurse, Gloria Fantry.

"Good of Minister Yard to put a stop to it, don't you think?" the waitress said. "That's the good of that old preacher man. He don't let nobody walk over his people."

* * *

Reverend Yard, signaling for silence as all gathered in Church of Holiness, led his   investigators to the office, closing the door after them. He sat on his chair behind the desk. Belinda, Gloria and Mike sat clustered around him. A lone desk lamp cut a sliver through the darkness.

The Minister leaned forward, face freeing a whisper: "Jim Jackson's in his car, waiting for my message. What do you have, Belinda, in the matter of the drugs."

"We have six counterfeit psychotropics, Reverend Yard," she said chillingly.

"Lord!" Mike said, not in spiritual exultation but in despondency.

"Gloria's eyes misted. She sobbed. "I've been dispensing them. Forgive me, Lord!"

"Your's is not the hand of evil, Gloria," Reverend Yard said. 'May the Lord punish those who would contaminate the minds and bodies of the ill elderly poor with silent slow poisons. The police should know."

403

"Know what?" Mike said. "Know that we now have seven counterfeit meds. True, that's enough to take to the prosecutor or to court for a search warrant, maybe an arrest, but a search of Palace would also be a revelation to the big shots behind the counterfeits, whomever. They'd never be caught. We don't know how the counterfeits got to Palace or Garland. We believe it's Pulvis who does the switching because an informant told us he's the street source of FDA uppers and downers. But where does Pulvis get the counterfeit to exchange for the FDA? My Elder Tripper told me back in his day, Mexican migrant Crew Chiefs brought the stuff into the State." A pause. "That's it!" It was an excited utterance. "Give me a chance to revive my Elder Tripper's memory of any remaining details. I'll be with him again soon. If he hasn't anything, then we should go to the police."

Belinda broke in. "I'm convinced Pulvis, while he's in his basement office at Palace, goes into the pantry. Maybe that's where he keeps the counterfeits? I got the sanitarian's last report. Palace didn't have a supply of stable foods to meet emergency needs, just enough for a two day supply for normal needs. There were also seven critical and thirteen noncritical violations of the food safety code. Lancaster's response indicated all deficiencies were corrected, but the sanitarian hasn't made a follow up."

"Grasping at straws, Belinda?" Reverend Yard said.

"So am I," Mike said. "The other day I followed a delivery truck from a company whose Board of Directors are Hispanic, and whose driver was Hispanic. He delivered boxes of can goods unloaded at Palace."

"Yet," Reverend Yard said with dubiousness, "you propose we again wait until you talk to your Elder Tripper?" A nod affirmed it. Reverend Yard looked to the others. "Do you all agree?" More affirming nods. "Alright. And, as of yet, but not much longer, we keep the matter of the counterfeits to ourselves." There was unanimity. "I'll send for Jackson and restrict our conversation to employment discrimination."

"And to the corporations with the Hispanic directors," Mike said.

"Yes," said Belinda. "I've gotten financial data from Medicaid on that."

It was but a moment before the jet bearded lawyer was in the office. He felt the change of administrators would resolve, with reasonable immediacy, the difficulty Aides had endured, and new job losses, but ultimately, only a trial would bring about resolutions for those wrongly terminated.

Handed Belinda's Medicaid financial data pertinent to Nursing Home Management's suppliers, Jackson ventured an opinion the company had paid high dollar for canned goods, stable foods, meats, cleaning supplies, janitorial and maintenance services. He'd fully research the issue. It wasn't incidental to his mind Javier, whether known as Grain or Ramirez-Grano, controlled those companies, including Quality Care that did business with Unge's operating company. Jackson opined Grain and Unge had set it up to skim cash from every aspect of the business. "It's simple to skim, Reverend Yard," Jackson said. "It isn't rape, it's a long and steady fondling. None of Grain's companies have a separate mind or existence of their own. Javier Grain, alias Ramirez-Grano has complete domination and control intended to commit inequitable consequences, perhaps even fraud. His complete control over buildings, their leases, canned goods and so on, proximately causes injury to nursing home residents, and unjust loss to the tax payers."

Meeting over, Mike used Reverend Yard's phone to call Five Counties for messages.

Lizzy whispered "There was a clash of tempers between Mr Zigmont and Mr Donavan. I didn't know Mr Zigmont had a temper. Was I ever wrong. He and Mr

405

Donavan roared at one another like lion kings for a half hour. Donavan was furious over something the secretaries couldn't make out. Nor do the caseworkers know what it was all about. All they made out was a word here or there, like 'end it.'"

Mike guessed Donavan was telling Ziggie about the State Director's reaction to the Nursing Home Management's lawyer's letter. A smile crept over his face. He never imagined a lawyer would write a letter to the State Ombudsman's boss to terminate the area ombudsman for upsetting Ida Mallow of Willow. They sure wanted to forever rid the nursing home industry of a meddlesome advocate. It was enjoyable in contrast to past throat twisters. All they could do was decertify him, though at the wrong point in time. All those years he spent in college, combat, corrections, counseling and court, an infantryman turned penologist, he'd survived, never worried he would succumb to the pressures of the powerful when ordered to transfer to Juvenile Detention or be fired; when the Grand Jury's fool for a foreman and punk for a prosecutor worked to stash him in jail; when the wheels of High Justice oiled with contributors dollars turned grave during the Parole Board kickback probe. Now, given the possibility of uncovering the perpetrators damaging old folks in care, his nerves were tightly strung worrying Donavan would take him out of the ball game in the ninth inning.

Belinda would come on in relief.

* * *

Enthralled with the flames in the fire place, ensconced in a red easy chair, Fergus Orr looked the modern day casual professor in a long sleeve green and blue plaid sport shirt over a white turtle neck. Tan corduroy trousers enhanced the effect. The sound of the door opening turned his attention.

Mike saw enter a middle aged lady with a very pretty face, cheeks like the features of Venus de Milo, a brunette, about five foot seven. Her well formed figure was in a multi-colored Scottish wool plaid blazer, with a three button notched lapel. Blue jeans and boots were stylish.

"Ah Brannagh! This is Doctor Lucia Dorth."

"Doctor," he said getting up, "my pleasure."

"Mr. Brannagh." She extended her hand to shake his. "Please," she said, "have a seat." They sat down in easy chairs, the flames of the fire jumping and leaping like little kids skipping rope. "Professor Orr told me of Mary Held, the wonders she has done for nursing home patients. My mother was in a nursing home in another state. As long as I visited her two or three times a week the quality of her life was adequate. When the Trustees of Puella brought me in as President, I couldn't leave her to periodic visits. So I found a place at Garland in Rock, and within a month regretted it. The man who runs that place is insensitive, to compliment him. I took Mother out. Her last year of life with me and my family in our house atoned for my sin of commission." There was a head shake of regret. "But self educated mechanical engineer Mary Held intrigues me. I'll personally visit her to ask her to honor our graduates as our mid-term commencement speaker. If she accepts, Puella Junior College will be pleased to grant her an Honorary degree." The smile given Brannagh and Fergus was radiant. "Mary Held typifies the type of women Puella wants to enroll and educate. Thank you, Mr. Brannagh, and you, Professor, for bringing her to our attention." She excused herself.

Mike stood out of respect. "Thank you, Doctor." The door closed. He turned to shake Fergus' hand. "You did it, Professor. You'll not only get Mary a degree, if she elects to be honored, but a fellow resident at Iris everlasting happiness. He wanted a degree more for Mary than his own good health." He moved over and sat next to Orr. "I would prefer the penitent in your chair, Professor, to completely unfold his entire roll of fate. Your confessor wants you to free your soul forever of Maurice Grain's Elder Trippers and Javier Grain's importing Mexican counterfeit drugs via Crew Chiefs of Migrant field workers." He looked Fergus straight in the eye. "Just how did Crew Chiefs smuggle prescription drugs in reasonably large quantities without some law enforcement officer, some where, happening upon the abundance?"

Fergus didn't hesitate to answer. "They did it in large food cans labeled chili style beans, refried beans, tamales and so on. Normal Mexican fare. Migrant crew chiefs brought them up here with other can goods labeled peas, corn, carrots, pear halves, whatever."

"Institutional size cans?"

"That's right."

"Oh my! I saw them doing it the other day and I hadn't the vaguest awareness. Professor, I don't have the power to loose sins on earth. I told you that. I do have the power to tell you, but for you, I'd be following Mexicans driving trucks until my pickup's wheels rotted. You've pointed the way to redeeming the health of numerous ill people. The good Lord above knows it. He'll forgive you."

34

Down the street from Holiness, when the tall oak doors opened and Reverend Yard stood on the steps to chat with members of his exiting congregation, Brannagh climbed down from the pickup, crossed the street, went up the steps against the flow, nodded to the Minister and entered the church where Belinda and Gloria were deep in conversation. A nod to them was met with surprised looks. Folks watched as the stranger walked the aisle to the sacristy and entered the office. Belinda was caused to fend off a man moving forward for a pummeling of the milky faced intruder.

"Mike," she said coming into the office, "you missed services and a sermon fit for an apostle. Why are you here?"

"I've got the missing link." He was all smiles

Reverend Yard wasn't. He stood in the door, Gloria at his side. He said, "the way you paraded the steps and aisle some of us thought you were the missing link." They all entered the room. The door was shut. "What missing link have you?"

He took a chair, the others the oak chairs around him. "My Elder Tripper finished his confession. He told me, back in 1976 and '77, counterfeit psychotropics were brought in for Javier Grain by migrant worker crew chiefs. They used large institutional size food cans with labels like chili beans or refried beans. Mexican food stuff. They mixed them in along with other boxes of can goods like corn, peaches, whatever. The goods were, and still are delivered to Mallard Company. If it worked back in the Elder Tripper's time, its working now. The delivery I watched of canned goods from Mallard Company to Palace was just such a delivery. Workers unloaded all the boxes but one. The truck driver, I'd call him a crew chief, from

Mallard Company carried that one in. I was too far away to read any label, but the attention the driver gave that one box supports my missing link theory. He carried the one with counterfeit psychotropics."

"Is that it?" Reverend Yard said.

"It ties into everything we know, Reverend Yard," Belinda said as if in ecstasy. "It explains why Pulvis goes back into the food storage area, sometimes without a woman. It explains how he gets counterfeit to replace FDA, and removes the FDA to sell to street dealers."

Gloria got into the swing. "His brief case explains how he moves the counterfeit from the Palace pharmacy to other homes to make   replacements! He has access to every chart."

Reverend Yard's eyes glowed. "You're convinced?" The ladies nodded. "What, then do we do about it if, as Mike says, we shouldn't call the police?"

Belinda took charge. "He's right. Not yet. I'll line up two sanitarians, and conduct an early morning surprise food storage pantry follow-up survey. We'll check every box, listen for strange noises, open suspects. If a single one of the canned goods has pills or foreign objects, that, in and of itself, is an obvious violation of Health rules. I'd be authorized to act, right then and there. We'll carry them out."

Reverend Yard had a contra look. "If it is Pulvis, and he's present, it could be very dangerous, Belinda." He paused before continuing. "I've a thought. There is an excellent detective on the Oldtown force who would act at my request. I think it wise Detective Eric Dee go with you."

Mike interrupted,   "the presence of a detective without a search warrant would afford a criminal lawyer grounds for a motion to suppress evidence. The big shots would beat the rap."

Reverend Yard looked aggrieved. "Revelation of

and stopping the wrong-doing should be enough! It must be stopped."

"I agree, so I'll be there, too. An ombudsman meets with residents. So Shango and I, by happenstance, will be in the lounge sipping coffee. We'll watch for Pulvis."

"That will work," Belinda said. "With my sanitarians, we'll conduct the follow-up inspection without the detective."

* * *

Mike stopped Belinda on the church steps. "Belinda, make ready the rest of your survey team to react. I know you're going to find the cans with counterfeit at Palace, and when the clinic confirms it is counterfeit, call Reverend Yard. He'll kick the detective into high gear to protect you and the clinic and to seek search warrants. Remind the Reverend, not just of Palace, but of all Nursing Home Management's facilities. The News of counterfeit drugs in nursing homes will spread like lady bugs on garden vegetables..Everything will break open."

She nodded. There wasn't an ounce of fear in her.

* * *

Mike, sipping machine coffee, felt out of the line of fire where, several feet away, Belinda and staff were searching for counterfeit medicines in food cans. He felt guilty because she, with legal authority to inspect every inch of a nursing home, its food, medicines and all therein, but not he, was the one undergoing danger. She was a courageous woman. The extent of an ombudsman's authority was defending residents' rights, counseling consenting elderly, alerting State Health and/or Adult Protective Services. The Lord knew he was good at whistle blowing. Still, decertification was just around the corner.

Shango, a very pretty Aide pushing his wheelchair from the elevator, waived to Mike. "Thank you, Vessie. Join us?"

"You so nice, Mr. Shango." She looked around, as

if looking for someone. "Not right now." She appeared disappointed.

"Big Mike!" Shango exclaimed. "Coffee early morning in Palace? What's up?"

"You read me, Shango. You and I will drink the stuff that trickles out of the coffee machine until our bladders pout, waiting for a State Health Nurse and her two staff to walk out of that storage area with a food box."

"She that hungry she steal Palace food?"

A smile. "Not exactly. Checking contents. We'll keep eyes open for Pulvis. If he shows, we keep him here."

"Should have told me when Vessie was here. Aide what brought me, tight with Vic. When she's on break about nine, they check out storage."

"Plenty of time."

State Health's Fordice and staff were unobstructed exiting Palace Nursing Home, most likely because the new administrator didn't want an interview. Mike, knowing he wasn't a part of clinical analysis, or police efforts pushed by Reverend Yard, said goodbye to Shango who called Vessie when Pulvis finally showed up.

* * *

Off the road, Mike pulled into Corydalis Nursing Home. A building with forty beds that hadn't displaced any valuable land zoned agricultural at the time it was built. Over the years its location turned prime as Basketham's highly priced suburban housing grew out to the facility's two acres. Upwardly mobile home owners' sense of aesthetics were often unsettled at the sight of the nursing home's visitors, not suburban sorts, who held picnics on the grounds or parked in front of private homes. More than once locals hinted to administrator Marjorie Ollen she might improve neighborhood relations if visitations were conducted within, not without. Ollen hadn't a need in her educated mind or middle class up bringing to run contrary to local mores, but Corydalis, long before her birth, had admitted residents whose relatives never walked the greens of country clubs.

With a three hundred thousand dollar brick colonial house with trimmed hedges and chemically treated lawn as a backdrop, Mike parked his pickup. The house's front door flew open and a man in a pin striped suit and a head of hair a Comic Book hero would envy, moved with the agility of a forty something long distance runner. Curious, Mike got out of the truck and waited. Pin Stripe arrived with a flurry, walking around the conveyance like an inspector from the State's Motor Vehicle Department. Dissatisfied, he faced it's driver with more than a touch of superiority, "Deliveries to the rear of Corydalis, fellow."

A bit surprised, but undismayed, Mike said, "If I were delivering something, I wouldn't carry it from here." He used his jail voice, a low tone used to let inmates know he wasn't about to be bullied.

Pin Stripe doubted. "You're not a delivery man with a truck like that?"

"It delivers me from 'A' to 'Z.'"

"May I ask what you do?"

"What's required," Mike said, starting to enjoy himself. "What's this all about?"

"Visitors to Corydalis park all over the place except there," he said, pointing to the small parking lot. "It's a nuisance."

"Some where in the Law it says if Corydalis were here first, and you moved to what you call a nuisance, tough luck."

"Are you a lawyer?" Irritation was high.

"I imagine you are?" was said with equivalent disparagement.

"I'm a Certified Public Accountant," he said as if God's anointed, "and we in this neighborhood are not going to stand around while our streets are defiled by the likes of this truck and others that park on the street instead of over

413

there."

"Really! So you're an example of today's American the old wounded and ill soldiers in care of Corydalis fought for? They should have surrendered to Hitler and Tojo or to Chairman Mao. None of that dynamic trio would have tolerated my truck, or the folks of sickly veterans, to park just anywhere and defile this pristine neighborhood. Do as you will, Mr. CPA. Perhaps, the Court will see it your way and restrict the likes of us from visiting old soldiers. We'll know when the Court rules against wheelchair veterans, won't we?"

A snort was heard when CPA wheeled about and left. That cut off further chit chat and left nothing to do but visit the elderly. Corydalis' front door was locked! Were there wanderers within the home eager to cross the street? The door bell pushed, it jangled. A very young, very thin but tall woman dressed as if to date the CPA answered.

"Come in. I'm Marjorie Ollen, administrator. I noticed Chauncy Snodly talked to you"

"Nothing of consequence. I'm Mike Brannagh, ombudsman. Pleased to meet you."

"The ombudsman? Oh yes! Please, come into my office." She lead the way to a glass enclosed office a bee line fifteen feet from the front door. "Have a seat." She sat on her desk chair. "Did Mr. Snodly think you were a delivery-man?"

"He did. I take it he's a pain in the, ah, neck."

"He is. I don't know what to do about him."

"Have you any World War Two or Korean War veterans in residence?"

"One from the world war," she said, "but two of our ladies were Waves."

"Then do this, if you will. Raise and lower the flag every day out front. As often as you can in good weather, make it a ceremony with residents that can go outside. From time to time, invite veterans from the VFW and

414

American Legion to conduct a few ceremonies; or get a high school ROTC to come over, sponsor a American Legion baseball team and have the kids visit wearing uniforms. Make Corydalis a beehive of patriotic veterans, American flag flying and your well dressed Vietnam draft free Yuppie neighbor may slink quietly into his atomic-proof underground shelter."

"By flying the flag?"

"It's not the wisest thing in the world to defile the American flag or those who raise and lower it. I fed Snodly war stories about the wounded and ill veterans Corydalis cares for. Make patriotism visible and he may come around to toleration, avoidance at best."

"I'll try it. Now, are you here on a complaint?"

"No complaint. I'm here to introduce myself to some residents, to you. I'll follow up all complaints as rapidly as I can, of course, but otherwise I'll just drop in to chat."

"That's welcomed," she said, hastening to add, "my family has run this nursing home for four decades now, and the ombudsman's program is only a few year old, but you're the first to visit, complaints or not. You'll bring complaints to me."

"A resident would need give me consent to address her specific problem directly to you. A resident may want to handle it herself, or ask the council to handle it, or the ombudsman, or State Health."

"State Health!" she said, her face darkening. "they're been on the news." She turned the TV on. A local news reporter spoke: *"For reasons yet unknown to our reporter on the scene, although it is certain there is no fire, Police have been called to Palace Nursing Home and have closed all entrances to the public. Stay tuned for further developments. We return you to scheduled programming."*

Ollen turned to another channel. Camera's were at the scene, the gilded facade of Palace gleaming as a background. A pretty young woman dressed for a society ball reported, *"This is reporter Tanya Culpa. Several of Palace's staff members have told me this all started after a State Health nurse carried out a box of food cans. At first, staff members thought when Detective Eric Dee showed up, he came to arrest the nurse for stealing food. Detective Dee is well known to many in this neighborhood. Now, the staff doesn't know what to think, because after Detective Dee arrived, three more State Health nurses and several policemen showed up. We do know Detective Dee and the nurse with the food box have left the scene. We don't yet know the exact reason why Detective Dee, the nurses, or the police, are here at Palace, but we have been assured by a nurse there is no epidemic, or contagious disease running rampant. All Palace residents are safe, the nurse said, and care of residents is continuing. Families with loved ones in Palace are asked to direct their inquiries to the Director of Nursing. More news when it breaks. We return you to the scheduled program."*

Ollen's look was of wonderment. "There's also something going on right here in Moose County involving State Health and the Sheriff. Cecil Jasper, he's the administrator at Lobelia, called and told me the Moose County Sheriff came into Lobelia and Willow a short while ago with search warrants. A deputy and two State Health surveyors, both nurses, seized all the medicines in both homes. Cecil said the nurses were on the phone to residents' doctors about replacing each such prescriptions." Her eyes caught Mike's. "If the medicines got mixed up in the two homes, that's awful. I pray it never happens here. We're so much smaller we can run with a greater focus on the individual than do the chains."

"If you're right, too bad for the elderly in large nursing home chains."

"Oh my, I didn't mean to imply that," she said. "Work with the elderly isn't easy no matter how well

416

staffed. So many residents are too run down to fend for themselves. They despair over their afflictions."

"Let's hope good care can lessen despair," he said, getting up to leave.

"Just a minute, Mr Brannagh. It's time for the news." She turned on the TV.

A handsome male face was talking. *'We just received a report that Sheriff's Deputies in Rooster, Moose and Door Counties, along with State Health Nurses have entered several other nursing homes in the listening area. The report indicates the deputies are there to minimize interference with the nurses who were sent in to follow up previous surveys. A survey is done to determine if a nursing home is meeting state standards, and follow-ups are done to assure compliance. I've been told follow-ups aren't that unusual. However, the presence of police is. Earlier, our reporter at the scene of Palace nursing home in Oldtown told our listening audience Palace had State Health nurses doing a follow-up survey, and not long after a nurse removed a box of food cans, the police swooped in. Now, State Health nurses and police are swooping into other nursing homes in Francois and Bovine Counties in addition to the counties of Door, Roster and Moose. The nursing homes entered are all operated by Nursing Home Management, Inc. We are unable to get a statement from Dale Unge, CEO of the operating company. However, State Health Nurses at all homes have indicated all residents in those homes are safe and care is continuing. Family members are instructed to phone the Director of Nursing at any of those homes to inquire into the well-being of their relative in care.*

In summary, State Health Nurses, police and/or sheriff's deputies have entered nursing homes operated by a company named Nursing Home Management. Oldtown's Palace was the first entered by State Health on a follow-up survey. Just why Palace and the other nursing homes have

417

been entered by police has not yet been revealed. Stayed tuned for developments as they occur.'

Mike beat her to the question. "What's going on, Ms. Ollen? Lobelia and Willow had deputies enter with a search warrant? What were they searching for?"

"I don't know."

"Search warrants?" he said. "Keep the flag raising in mind."

He left Ollen's office, the TV News still ringing within his cortex, but going about ombudsman business, there were residents to visit. Stopping at the first open resident door in a small brightly lit room sat a woman in a lounge chair. She was smartly dressed, salt and gold styled hair, face pink as a Tunic flower, a stone colored shirt highlighted by a blanket vest with burgundy and tan-loden stripes. A long full blue skirt fell like a curtain from knees to ankles. He knocked. "I'm Mike Brannagh, Ombudsman."

"Well, just don't stand there, Mike, come in and have a seat. I'm Verajean Tempe."

He sat on the edge of Tempe's bed to better see her.

"In Corydalis," she said, "what else is there to do but read the works of the Great Poets? Watch TV? Their program plots are so contrived, even I hadn't found myself in situations comparable." She smiled and winked.

His eyebrows raised rows of fleshly plowed brow. "I sure you don't expect me to inquire into the non comparable situations in which you were found?" Of course she did. Hadn't most of the ill elderly he'd met in nursing homes want to talk about their past. They'd seen America and the world change from horse pulled buggies to Sky labs. Hadn't he looked forward to hearing their mythic tales?

She laughed. "You wouldn't expect to hear racy stories from an old lady, would you?"

"No," he said with a touch of sincerity.

"Well then, I'll omit the racy parts. I was an Executive Secretary, a woman with it all, not just typing and shorthand skills, organizational abilities and a take charge mentality, but a beautiful face with a body that turned heads at Board Meetings and in the Executive Suites. I was proposition often and received many presents of clothing and jewelry to get my affections, Mae West would have worn out hanging them in the closet or changing rings."

"You said you would omit the racy stuff," he said with gentle persuasion.

"My, you are squeamish. Well, suffice it to say if I'd held out for diamonds, like Marilyn, I wouldn't be in Corydalis today."

"Why are you in nursing care?"

"Neurosyphilis," she said without a hint of embarrassment. "I'll never know which of my men was the donor. My last husband hadn't that disease, nor, apparently the Divorce Court Judge. My settlement was minuscule and future employment bleak. I ran out of money but not illnesses. Well then, lets change the subject and talk about Corydalis' saucy young Miss Marjorie Ollen?"

"The administrator?" he said, perplexed. Ollen was young, but saucy? What was with Tempe? Syphilis messed up her neurological system? Was there a phase of the disease that stimulated the sex drive, or was this mere recollection? "I work only for residents' rights, Mrs. Tempe."

"Well," Tempe said, "she's very attractive to old men."

"She seemed able to handle herself with this old man," he said. "Most of us old men remember how it was, but that's the extent, literally."

"That's cleverly said," she said, gushing, her smile blooming. "Well, so much for finding a gossip. '*A naked thinking heart, that makes no show, Is to a woman, but a* kind of ghost. '"

"Sorry Mrs. Tempe," he said, "for the no show."

"Well, another stanza from Donne, *'Death be not proud, though some have called thee*

Mighty and dreadful, for, thou art not so, For, those, whom thou think'st, thou dost overthrow,

Die not, poor death.' Not a night in the nursing home comes that I don't pray that death be my dawn charioteer. *'Swear by thy self that at my death, thy Sun shall shine as it shines now, and heretofore; And having done that, thou hast done, I have no more.'* Thank you for you visit."

* * *

Curiosity walked the lobes of the brain like an old man exercising at the Mall. Down the road was a cafe. Brannagh got out to buy a copy of the Inner-city News.

REVEREND COPPIN YARD UNCOVERS DRUG SCAM IN OLD FOLKS HOME

State Health Nurse Belinda Fordice, worried medicines being administered to Palace's old people suffering from dementia and Alzheimer's disease were doing harm, took the advice of her Minister, Reverend Coppin Yard, and asked Oldtown Clinic to test some of those medicines. The tests proved the drugs were counterfeit. Nurse Fordice, Supervisor of a State Health Survey team, then followed up by conducting a surprise follow-up survey. She found a box of food cans, the cans which were supposed to be completely filled with food, also held drugs. Realizing the drugs in the cans shouldn't have been there under any legal circumstance, Nurse Fordice carried the cans to Oldtown Clinic. Tests proved those drugs were counterfeit. Inside the food cans the drugs were in bottles labeled just like those from a legal drugstore. Shocked, Nurse Fordice called Reverend Yard who called Detective Dee to protect the courageous nurse. Then Dee and the nurse went to court which responded with a search warrant. Oldtown police came in to protect the old folks, though Palace's nurses and Aides aren't under any suspicion. However, janitorial, maintenance and food vendor companies' employees were barred.

State Attorney General Andre Puts responded to Reverend Coppin Yard's plea to protect the old people in nine other nursing homes. General Puts, acting along with Dectective Dee's search warrant sent lawyers to courts which also responded with search warrants, then directed the Sheriffs of Bovine, Moose, Door and Rooster Counties to get involved. It's an election year after all, and all the Sheriffs cooperated and arrived with search warrants at all Nursing Home Management facilities in their counties. All suspected medicines in those homes were seized but quickly replaced by local licensed drug stores. The seized prescription drugs are also under going testing.

State Health Director Homer Newbern, responding to Reverend Coppin Yard's plea to protect the oldsters in all five counties, sent in State Health Nurses from other survey teams to take charge of the medicines already in the homes. The Nurses are in touch with patients' families and doctors. All removed suspected prescriptions will be refilled from local licensed pharmacies which will deliver safe medicines directly to State Health Nurses.

As Reverend Coppin Yard said, "There is a stop to the monstrousness of those inflicting a silent tyranny on the minds and bodies of our dependent ill elderly."

The enervated ombudsman was troubled. A silent tyranny had been stopped, but what of the monsters? Not a word in the Inner City News, TV or radio about Pulvis, Grain or Unge. Reverend Yard must have told Detective Dee the box of canned goods containing psychotropics came, not from Javier Grain's Pharmacopeia Wholesalers with its FDA approved quality drugs, but from Javier Rodriguez-Grano's Mallard Company, the descendant of the Elder Trippers! Had Dee a search warrant for Mallard?

The corporate setup was not only complicated, but ingenious. Reverend Yard, to protect his confidences, wouldn't tell Dee that Cooper or Big-dough Benny had fingered Pulvis as the peddler of FDA uppers and downers. But Dee would have heard Gloria's story of Pulvis's brief case. Had Dee a search warrant for Pulvis while the police were in Palace? Would Dee determine Pulvis and Grain were partners on the psychotropics? Was Unge a part of counterfeit drugs? Would Lawyer Jackson uncover fraudulent dollars paid by Unge to Grain for rent, meats, foods and services?

An October wind gave a forewarning of the severe winter ahead. He stepped out lively, mind still on Dee's investigation but not one more thought came forth about the monsters behind the counterfeit drugs. Instead it was Donavan's decertification of Five Counties' ombudsman that haunted him. Was it because Donavan who answered to the State Director wouldn't know, or want to know of the area ombudsman's involvement in Reverend Yard's revelations? Pride went before a fall.

Time for coffee and a donut. He went into the café. It's TV was on. *'Attorney General Andre Puts, working with prosecutors in Francois, Rooster, Bovine, Door and Moose Counties, has obtained court orders taking over the operations of nursing homes operated by Nursing Home Management. General Puts stated it was in the best interest of the dependent elderly in residence that he and the local prosecutors took legal action to remove Nursing Home Management and its administrators from day to day operations. They have been replaced by qualified State Health administrators. Nurse Belinda Fordice has been appointed coordinator of central operations. Stay tuned for further developments.'*

The volume was turned up. *'Attorney General Puts announced his staff has launched an investigation into the Medicaid payments made to Nursing Home*

422

Management Inc., which leases buildings from Quality Care Inc., Also under investigation are payments to suppliers Coos, Mallard, Esbon and Stowe Companies of Oldtown. All of those companies and Quality Care are owned and operated by Javier Grain. Large sums of State and federal dollars are involved in payments to those companies.

One of Nursing Home Management's leased homes, Palace, already has to answer to an investigation into employment discrimination. All of Nursing Home Management's nursing homes administrations have been taken over by State Health.

Allegations residents were being administered counterfeit drugs has shaken the nursing home industry to its foundations.'

Mike silently counted, one, two, three outs in the inning. They're going to get Grain, Pulvis and Unge where it hurts because Herman Mack of Larkspur wanted to see his son and Fergus Orr wanted to make a confession. The Lord works in mysterious ways. Without them Mike felt he would be chasing employment discrimination allegations, not counterfeit psychotropics until Donavan, instructed by political bigwigs, decertified Five Counties' ombudsman. When was that word coming down?

* * *

Ziggie might have the answer. Without stopping for a donut, Mike went down the sixteen stairs to enter Five Counties.

"Brannagh!"

.Whose was that voice? It had a tinge of familiarity. He turned to see the State ombudsman, gangly Charles Donavan.

"Charley!" he said as congenially as possible, considering the prospect.

"You must be very upset about the news concerning Nursing Home Management?"

"For sure," he said, attempting to re-inflate a spirit deflated by Donavan's presence. "Thank goodness for Reverend Coppin Yard."

"I've never know a Minister," Donavan said, "any where in the State to become so involved in nursing homes. I wonder who got him into it?"

Mike knew, but kept quiet: Chester Zigmont, Fergus Orr, Belinda Fordice, Gloria Fantry, Marion Kap, Lou Cooper, Big-dough Benny Mack, Shango Golah and Fanny Brown did. He answered, "the news reports said it was State Health nurse Belinda Fordice and her team of surveyors."

"For sure," Donavan said, "because of them, the consulting pharmacist, Victorio Pulvis has been taken into custody. Sources indicate he's cooperating."

"That's great," Mike said. If Pulvis were operatic, the cast of Javier Grain's Crew Chief Cartel would be brought on stage.

"Homer Newbern, Director of State Health," Donavan said, "has a direct pipeline to Governor Study. He, and his campaign headquarters, were staggered by the extent of counterfeit psychotropics, but thrilled Newbern's State Health staff uncovered it. Meanwhile, the Governor's opposition, if there are good things to say about this affliction of contaminated drugs, has Attorney General Puts' all out effort to get to the bottom of the drug switching before the election. Who ever is elected in November has promised his first budget would sharply increase the number of State Health surveyors. How I wish we Ombudsmen were included. With an increased budget, I could have one ombudsmen for two thousand residents, and cut in half the counties served."

If only the current ombudsman were to be numbered among them. What would he do with his time, if there were only two thousand residents, and two or three fewer counties to visit? What would be the reaction of administrators? Few were presently pleased about him trying to visit two and a half times that many residents.

"There's a matter we need to discuss," Donavan said. "There's a room with chairs available over there, come on. We need privacy." He entered and sat down, motioning Brannagh to sit. An envelope was pulled from inside Donavan's suit coat. A piece of paper was removed. The letterhead was that of the State Mental Health Department, addressee, the State Ombudsman. "The contents of the letter," he said, "is a personal note from Director Wind to me. He excoriates Five Counties' ombudsman because a resident at Honeysuckle Nursing Home, Plet Band, wrote Mental Health asking for a meeting to discuss the dumping of their aggressively mentally-ill patients on Honeysuckle's elderly and defenseless residents. Band wrote of abuse and injuries that fights have inflicted on elderly residents and nursing staff alike. He sent copies of his letter to every important politician and advocacy group in the state. Governor Story and Attorney General Puts are on the mailing list too. Band will get his meeting soon with Mental Health because the election is just down the road. Mental Health's Wind doesn't want the Attorney General, or the Governor, seeing him sitting on his credentials. By the way, about that letter sent to State Director of Social Services Carson Varder by John Campton, the lawyer representing Willow nursing home's Ida Mallow and Nursing Home Management, Varder's and my response was mailed yesterday to administrator Mallow, Lawyer Campton and CEO Dale Unge." Donavan smiled. "None of us could compose a better reply than you had. So Varder dictated and I wrote a note on your response saying your letter fully represented the position of the State Director's office and the State Ombudsman's office."

From a shirt pocket, Donavan removed a folded piece of paper. Unfolding it, he said, "It's   your letter. I enjoyed your alliterations, but most of all, the closing paragraph: *'Whatever the intent of Mr. Campton on behalf of his client Willow Nursing Home and its affiliates, be assured this Area ombudsman, even if he dares to differ with an administrator, will always seek a healthy working relationship with nursing home staff, but the rights of residents first.'* The rights of residents first. That's our mission. It will continue to be your mission." He got up and handed Brannagh the letter.

Ziggie entered. "Congratulations, Mike. I look forward to your months ahead advocating for those in the land of last life."

Mike shook his head negatively. "from those residents I've met, they don't feel they've gone into that land. Rather they went into nursing homes to live; to get professional care. Unfortunately, too often professional care is secondary to owners' profit taking."

"Good point, Mike," Ziggie said. "And by the way, Charley, here, is a social worker. Before becoming the State's Ombudsman, he worked for State Mental Health to rehabilitate drug abusers. Some of his former, now sober, clients remembered him."

Donavan stood up and said, "They have. I'm Ziggie's source!"

END

www.ingramcontent.com/pod-product-compliance
Lightning Source LLC
Chambersburg PA
CBHW071146250626
47159CB00001B/5